Joss Stirling owes her existence to Scotland Yard. In the early 60s, her father, a hotshot detective in the Metropolitan Police, met her mother, a 19-year-old girl from East London. Love over the criminal records led to marriage and children. Unlike the police detectives you see on TV, Joss is pleased to report that they are still happily married (to each other).

Joss was born on the borders of East London and Essex and grew up in the area. Leaving Essex behind for Cambridge, she went on to have careers in British diplomacy and as a policy adviser on conflict and arms at Oxfam. Somewhere along the way she also gained a doctorate in English Literature from Oxford University. More recently she has written for children and young adults, winning national awards in both categories. She has published over fifty novels that have been translated into many languages. She lives in Oxford.

Also by Joss Stirling

Don't Trust Me

The Silence

JOSS STIRLING

KILLER READS

A division of HarperCollins*Publishers*
www.harpercollins.co.uk

Killer Reads an imprint of
HarperCollinsPublishers
1 London Bridge Street
London SE1 9GF

www.harpercollins.co.uk

A Paperback Original 2019

First published in Great Britain in ebook format by Killer Reads 2019

A catalogue record for this book is
available from the British Library

ISBN: 978-0-00-835821-1

This novel is entirely a work of fiction.

This novel is entirely a work of fiction.
The names, characters and incidents portrayed in it are
the work of the author's imagination. Any resemblance to
actual persons, living or dead, events or localities is
entirely coincidental.

Typeset in Minion by Palimpsest Book Production Ltd, Falkirk, Stirlingshire

Printed and bound in Great Britain.

For Richard Blackford

Prologue

Jonah, Present Day

Jonah never thought he had it in him to kill a woman, but he was wrong. She was lying at his feet.

He had to make the call. Grabbing the receiver on the old landline phone, he dialled in the number. It took so long for the dial to turn back. 9 *click-click-click*, 9 *click-click-click*, 9 *click-click-click*.

'Which service do you require?'

'Ambulance – police – both.' Her scream still drilled in his ear even though she was silent. He'd only thought to shut her up. 'I think I've hurt someone.'

There was a microscopic pause before training kicked in. 'Address, please?'

His mind went blank. Despite living here for two years, he couldn't remember the postcode. 'Gallant House. Blackheath. Off the Hare and Billet Road. Postcode? Can't think ...' He scrabbled among the papers on the console table, shaking petals from the arrangement of lilacs, until he found a letter and was able to read it off.

'And your name?'

He was in so much trouble. 'Jonah Brigson. But don't waste time! I need someone here right now!'

'I've already dispatched an ambulance, Jonah. Please try to stay calm. I'm going to ask you about the casualty. Are they breathing?'

'I don't know – can't see from here.' She was lying on the cold tiles, a little on her side, one arm across her stomach, the other out as if reaching for something.

'Can you keep on the line and check at the same time?'

'Yes.' The landlady's reluctance to update anything in the house resulted in the phone base and vase of lilacs crashing to the floor as Jonah dragged the attached receiver with him. Water chased him over the tiles. He touched the slim throat his fingers had squeezed.

'Are you still with me, Jonah?'

'Yes.'

'Are they breathing?'

'I don't think so. I don't know.'

'Do you know CPR?'

'Yes.' Stupid, so stupid! He'd done this enough times. He should've realised what to do.

'What's the patient's name?'

'I'm putting the phone down on the ground.' Jonah gently rearranged her on to her back so he could tip her chin slightly into the required position. This felt so wrong – he the one to have hurt her now the one who would try to save her.

The voice on the line babbled away but Jonah ignored it. He began to breathe for her.

Part 1 – The Fair

Fil de voco – 'thread of voice', very quiet, *pianissimo*

Chapter 1

She couldn't stand it any longer. Jenny staggered back, hand over mouth as bile rose. Someone had thrown up in the bathroom and not cleaned after themselves. Not for the first time. But today some joker had dropped a rubber duck in the middle of it. Really, she shouldn't have to face this; no one should.

Jenny slammed the door on the mess and ran down to the small toilet on the ground floor, which was fitted at an awkward angle under the stairs. Thankfully, it was vacant, as none of the house's other inhabitants were up yet after last night's party.

A party that had included all but her. That hurt. When had she become Jenny-No-Mates? Jenny rested her aching head in her hands. She'd let this happen, hadn't she? When her last relationship broke down, she'd let her ex carry off their friends into his new Jenny-free circle. Shannon, Tilly, Gina – when had they last messaged her – or for that matter, she contacted them? Maybe their loyalty had always been to him? It was stating the obvious to say that he was much easier-going. Any communication with her was so bloody frustrating – she could hardly blame them. But she'd have to try harder, find people who would understand

5

her need to withdraw into herself at times and not take it personally, but be there for her when she felt like mixing. Did people like that exist in London? And how did you find them?

Jenny flushed the loo and washed her hands in the tiny basin, splashing the floor as everyone did. She air-dried her fingers, having noticed that the towel was a scrunched-up biohazard. She'd been working last night but her housemates probably wouldn't have invited her anyway. The party had still been going strong when she returned from her late shift. She'd been majorly pissed off to find people grazing on each other on the stairs, cans sprouting like cylindrical mushrooms on every ledge, raucous mating calls in the lounge – all signs of the weird party wildlife of the urban jungle. She had to chuck two rutting lovers off her futon and secure the sliding door with the flimsy lock. Then she had to rip the sheets off the bed, put on clean ones, and set the room to rights, frantic that her safe space had been violated. Only then had she been able to go to bed.

To sleep? That was a joke. With the noise she hadn't managed that till three, barricaded inside her room.

She steeled herself to face the carnage that would be the kitchen. Some letting company was running a campaign on the Underground about the annoyance of passive-aggressive notes from aggrieved flatmates, suggesting all you need do was find a new place to stop the nagging. As if it were that easy to move. In her case, she didn't know how far she'd have to go to get through to her flatmates. She'd need at least a passive-aggressive billboard to get the attention of the people that shared the same space with her. Three Billboards Outside Ebbisham Drive. She could see them clearly: black words on red on the approach from the Underground. *Clean Up! Do Not Leave Your Sick For Others To Find! Put Out Your Rubbish!* They probably wouldn't notice. The place was beyond saving. The landlord kept packing in more tenants, subdividing rooms with flimsy partitions. Her garden view window now had a plasterboard wall down the middle, leaving her just half to look out on the wheelie bins and broken paving slabs. No one complained as it was that or have the rent increased. Yet the more people moved in, the greater the pressure on Jenny, like the person crushed at the front against a barrier as the crowd surged behind her. Hard now to remember that it had started out so well as a flat share – just three of them, Harry, Luke and Jenny, friends from the orchestra; but the centre of gravity had shifted as Harry and Luke brought in more people to satisfy the landlord's rampant greed. Now there were six, five men and her, and personal responsibility for the house had become so diluted it no longer had any meaning.

Jenny would no longer count herself a friend of Harry, or Luke for that matter.

I'm going to find a new place today. It's that or throw myself in the Thames. And that's not a joke.

So what was the damage? She opened the kitchen door. It was worse than she feared. She couldn't eat breakfast in there.

'Morning, sunshine,' said Harry, coming out of the front room, his good mood an insult. Adjusting waistband elastic, he shuffled past in the music notation boxers that she'd given him that first Christmas in a Secret Santa.

She gave him now a single finger. He was usually the one to invite the guests to his famous impromptu parties and there were probably several left with him on the couch in various states of undress. He was proud of being adventurous in his love-making. Horn players had to live up to the jokes, he claimed.

'Now, now, Jenny. No need to be jealous.' He folded his six-foot plus frame into the too-small toilet and locked the door. At least she'd got in there first before he stank the place out.

This is making me into a horrid person, thought Jenny, turning her back on the kitchen. She couldn't cope with that. I used to be happy, fun-loving, now I'm cast as the household Grinch. She plodded upstairs.

Hearing more retching from the main bathroom, the urge to

escape reached boiling point. She grabbed a set of clean clothes, toiletries and her violin from her room. Life in the flat had devolved to the stage where she didn't dare leave her instrument, fearing someone would throw up on it or use it as a cricket bat in one of their 'hilarious' drunken games. It was worth more than a year's rent in London. Slinging her bag over her shoulder, the instrument case over the other, she hurried out of the house, and headed by bus for the sanctuary of the Brixton Recreation Centre.

Avoiding the pool and its battalion of early morning lengths swimmers, Jenny took a long time under the shower, soaping her body clean of the grim her house left on her. She fantasised about living somewhere completely under her control; one of those Japanese pod bedrooms would do for her, clean lines and minimal furniture. The best thing about the pod would be that she'd be alone when she chose. Completely Robinson Crusoe before Man Friday showed up alone. No need to communicate with a soul. No Harry. Just her and her music.

Her slippery fingers wandered to her throat, gentling over the scars left by surgery. A ghost of a touch still lingered; fingers squeezing, squeezing ... White streaks lightninged across her lids. She dropped her hand, braced herself against the shower stall, and breathed through her nose. Not this. Concentrate on the here and now. Find something to focus on.

The ache in her neck was back. She didn't want to think about the pain but it was better than the panic. She'd better get out of the shower and deal with it. Yes, that was good. Pain was like the conductor's baton bringing scattered thoughts to attention.

Wrapping a soft white towel around her chest, tucked under her arms, she padded to the sinks. Filling a plastic bottle at the tap, she downed a couple of Tramadol in a gulp. It was a strong painkiller. Give it a few minutes and the relief would kick in with a little flip of pleasure; she'd feel near human again.

Tension easing, Harry struck up in her brain – her subconscious playing dress up. Other people her age liked Saturday-night parties. Why did she get in such a bloody twist about them? Mess was just mess. There were worse things in life as she well knew.

It was hard to explain to him, though, the sheer distress it caused her to find that her safe space was not safe, that Harry and her other flatmates thought it fine to let friends shag on her duvet, that they didn't listen to her. She was screaming for help and they had their fingers in their ears.

I can't take it any longer.

Then stop moaning and do something about it. Sometimes even subconscious Harry had good advice.

On time for her shift at the Royal Festival Hall café, Jenny set about cleaning tables with gusto. *Con Forza*. The seating spread far out into the acre of square-pillar-and-glass atrium and played host to a constantly shifting population of tourists and concertgoers. These faces were always different yet somehow the same, like the river in that saying about never stepping in the same one twice. School parties – the violins. Elderly couples from the home counties – the violas. Korean girls with kitten headbands or backpacks – the piccolos. American ladies with clarion tones – had to be the brass section. Each fell into their part on her imagined stave, weaving their different notes together. She was able to work quite alone for long stretches of time, absorbed in the logistics of carrying trays and discarded cups. She let music flow through her like her blood-stream. If she hadn't had her violin to sustain her, she knew she wouldn't have survived; it was the only thing that brought pure joy to her life. She craved it more than any lover or drug. For nothing less would she put up with crap pay and ridiculous hours. As she tidied, she let the exuberant strings part of Vivaldi's 'Autumn' run through her mind. Yes, she knew that the piece had become a cliché, ruined by lifts and hold music, but it was still the best workout for a violinist's fingers. Harry and his boxer shorts, the bathroom, the rubbish-strewn kitchen, all were blown away.

She was so absorbed in her mind-music that she didn't see

the lady who was getting up from a table behind her. Jenny collided, spilling the dregs from a teacup over them both. She stared at the lady's stained white coat in silent horror.

'Well, really! What's wrong with you?' trumpeted the customer. 'You could at least have the decency to apologise!'

Frustration mounted inside Jenny. How to explain? God, she hated herself sometimes. She held out a cloth.

'I'm not using that thing. This is a wool-cashmere mix!' The woman blotted the stain with a clean tissue.

Her manager and good friend, Louis Palin, appeared at her elbow with his admirable ninja skill of sneaking up on her. Not bad for a heavyset guy the far side of forty. 'Is something the matter, madam?'

'Look what she did to my coat!'

'I see – please accept our apologies. Here's my card if you wish to contact me further about this.'

The woman grabbed her coat and the card. 'It's probably ruined.'

'I sincerely hope not, madam.'

With a sniff, she exited.

'Why the fuck is she leaving a priceless coat on the back of her chair in a canteen?' marvelled Louis. 'Stupid cow.'

Jenny rested her head on his shoulder and he patted her back.

'Forget it, Jen. Women like that won't be bothered to follow through with a claim – it takes too much time and she probably has six in her wardrobe. Sweetie, can you do a double shift today?'

Jenny nodded, eager to oblige her rescuer.

'What do you think about doing a stint on the counter?' asked Louis.

Jenny gave him an 'are you sure?' look. Not being able to speak due to the scarring on her larynx made customer-facing roles a tortuous challenge. Most musicians made ends meet as teachers but her disability meant that wasn't an option for her. She was lucky they knew her here and looked after her.

'We'll give it a go, all right? See how you get on.' Louis helped her clear the table. 'It can't be as bad as that woman and there'll be others on hand if you can't manage. It's just that I'm really short-staffed for the pre-concert rush.'

All right for him to speak, thought Jenny, then realised the irony. See what I did there? She told subconscious Harry. I do still have a sense of humour. Just about.

'How are you fixed for tomorrow?'

Jenny got out an iPad that she used for people who didn't know sign language. It had revolutionised the speed of her messaging with its predictive spelling and she felt it was another instrument for her as her practised fingers flew. If she felt like it, she could even get it to talk for her, though she avoided using that function as she didn't like any of the voices. None of them sounded like she did in her head. *Rehearsal tomorrow at 11.*

'After that?'

Can do five hours. That would leave one hour's break before the concert. Living on breadline wages meant she had to take all the shifts she could when the orchestra was in London just to make the rent.

Which reminded her. She cleared the screen, her signal for a new subject. *Do you know anyone who has a spare room? I'm going crazy.*

She had told Louis something of her struggles with her current living arrangement. 'That bad, hey?'

She nodded vigorously.

'Funnily enough, I do know someone who's just moved out of a place. I thought of you when he mentioned it, but it's on Blackheath.'

Her hopes flew skyward and wheeled like doves. She waved her hand asking for more information.

'Blackheath's on the hill above Greenwich. I realise most the people you know are mostly central and south-west London, so I thought it would probably be too lonely for you?'

11

Your friend moved out? Why? She didn't want to step into another nightmare flatmates scenario as the other person fled.

'He's finally seen sense and moved in with his boyfriend – which would be me.' Louis gave her a wink. Louis had been wooing ex-serviceman turned singer-songwriter Kris for months now, using Jenny as his agony aunt through the ups and downs.

Kris had given up his old place? It must be love. Jenny tapped her right palm on her left in the sign for happy. Even Louis could understand that.

'Thanks, Jenny.' But he didn't look as ecstatic as Jenny expected, his tone a little downbeat. 'It's getting something good out of a bad situation, I suppose.'

She circled her fist over her heart, the sign for 'sorry'.

'You know Kris. He's been struggling silently with his pain management but has finally had to acknowledge that he needs more help, and I volunteered. Anyway, before moving in with me, he lived with this eccentric old bird in her house just off the Hare and Billet Road. Did he ever tell you about it?'

She didn't know Kris as well as Louis so couldn't honestly remember him mentioning it. She wavered her hand in a 'not sure' gesture.

'He didn't talk about it much as, you know, grown up guy living with old lady …? Sounds a little weird. Anyway, it's an amazing place.' Louis took the tray from Jenny and threaded it on the rack for dirty dishes. 'She takes in young disadvantaged people involved in the Arts at very low rents – peppercorn ones. Kris got to know her thanks to his GP and has managed to save up quite a bit from his army pension.'

Jenny raised her brows and drew a pound sign with a question mark.

'Because she doesn't need the money herself. Wouldn't that be nice, eh?' Louis started pushing the trolley of dirty trays towards the kitchen. 'Kris says she was once a dancer so she understands how hard it's to survive doing the kind of jobs we do.'

Jenny could only agree. She was lucky if she made twenty-five thousand a year even with two jobs, and that still went nowhere in London once student loan, rent and transport were paid.

'The story goes that she crashed out with an injury just before she hit the big time.' Jenny nipped ahead to hold open the swing door. 'Thanks, Jen. But then her Prince Charming came along and she married money, moved into the husband's family home, and stayed happily wed for years.' They left the trolley with the washer-uppers. 'Then her husband had the bad fortune to up and die on her from some long-term condition he developed. That left a great gap in her life. Kris says she amuses herself by taking in her waifs and strays – him the wounded soldier turned musician qualified in spades.'

Jenny was totally ready to be a waif or a stray if it meant escaping her shared house.

How do I contact her?

'It's by word of mouth only. Personal recommendations. She doesn't advertise. I'll get Kris to put in a good word for you. Come to think of it, I'm sure you'll love Mrs Whittingham's house. It's stylish, like you.' He was teasing. There was nothing the least stylish about her.

She nudged him playfully. *Address?*

'Didn't I say? Gallant House.'

13

Chapter 2

The House that Jack Built – Chapter One – Conception

Captain Frederick Jack dreamed of me – a house of his own – while he sailed the Caribbean in 1780. He was just a captain then. He'd done nothing of note, merely ferried cotton, pineapples and black ivory for a living. His days of fame as an admiral of the fleet were to come later when the little French upstart shook the thrones of Europe.

So, when I was conceived, my Captain Jack was distinguished only by the fact that he had the good fortune to marry a woman from the merchant class. With her money he could order my measurements from architects, adjust and fashion me completely to his taste. When he returned from his voyage, Jack gave his wife a perfunctory kiss, looked in on the infants bawling in the nursery at Deptford, then hurried along the Thames to climb the hill that led to my cradle. The builders were waiting to cut the first trench, spades poised. Jack bounded across the heath, waved his pocket handkerchief as his Blue Peter, and they set off, digging deep in the soil.

Chapter 3

Jonah, Present Day

'So Jonah, we have a call here logged to the emergency services at 23.53. The caller identifies himself as you. Is that correct?'

Jonah sipped his water. 'Yes. I made the call.'

The senior of the two police officers in the interrogation room flicked through the transcript of the brief conversation. Seen across the table like this, it looked like a script. 'You said that you feared you'd hurt someone. Is that also correct?' The inspector wouldn't have been cast though in this role if this were a drama; he looked too scruffy and had several piercing holes in each ear. A director would've put him on the other side of the table with Jonah. 'You requested the police as well as an ambulance. Please answer for the record.'

'Yes.'

'And can you tell us what you meant by that?'

'I don't know.' The events were an ugly mess, like dropping a plate of spaghetti Bolognese and trying to retrieve the pasta strand by strand. Why was he even thinking of food? Jonah hadn't slept since they arrested him. How many hours ago? God knows. He ran his hand over his face. This place was scarily familiar. He'd sat in numerous sets exactly like this one recently but none had the same smell as the real thing, the smell of sweat and some cheap industrial floor cleaner. TV sets weren't around long enough to get the odour infused into the walls.

'Jonah? Can you answer the question please?'

'Sorry: what did you ask?'

'I asked in what way you hurt her?'

He had a sudden jolt of realisation. These people would know. He wouldn't be left speculating as he had been in the police cell. 'Is she OK?'

The officers exchanged a look, debating between them if this was something that was better kept from him or not.

'Please. She's a …' what was she exactly? '… she's a friend.'

The scruffy man, Detective Inspector something, nodded to his female sergeant. Jonah had already forgotten their names. Nothing was sticking in his brain, wiped clean of everything but her scream.

'Her respiration was compromised,' replied the sergeant, a fresh-faced woman with sandy hair tucked back behind her ears, 'she's still in a coma, still critical, and we've no word yet as to whether she'll survive.'

He'd heard the ambulance men discussing it. They hadn't realised at that time that he was the chief suspect and instead they'd been impressed to meet the actor who played them on TV. They'd talked to him like he was one of them for real. They told him as if he already knew: interrupted breathing leads to oxygen deficiency which in turn could result in brain damage. He probably had known that, but he just hadn't been thinking, only reacting.

'Will you let me know the minute she wakes up?' he asked.

'There's no certainty she will. We're still trying to establish exactly what took place. This might turn into a murder enquiry. Are you prepared for that?'

16

He bit his ragged nail. 'I still want to know.'

'Why, Jonah? Are you afraid what she might remember?' The inspector leant forward, body language intended to dominate.

Wishing his brain would stop note-taking on movement as if he were studying for a future role, Jonah shook his head. What he'd meant was that he wished to apologise for losing it with her, but he didn't want to make anything that sounded like an admission of guilt. His frantic words on the emergency call were bad enough without adding that. 'I just want to know that she's OK.'

'I wouldn't wait until she can tell her side of the story, if I were you,' said the inspector. 'Tell us the truth now, hiding nothing, and your cooperation will be taken into account when the CPS comes to consider your case.'

He hadn't really expected to walk out of here without some charges, not with his record, but he was hoping they would let him go on bail. 'It's complicated. I'm not exactly sure what happened.' Jonah scratched at the spiderweb tattoo on his knuckles. He wondered if he should call a lawyer now. The last one that had been appointed for him by the courts had been a disaster so he'd not gone there yet, but from the seriousness of their expressions, he should reconsider the wisdom of talking to them alone.

'Then start at the beginning. Tell us what your relationship with her was like.'

'I wouldn't say we had a relationship.' He gave it the double meaning that the inspector hadn't, mainly to stall while he considered the lawyer question some more.

'Help us to see what went on in Gallant House, Jonah. At the moment, I have to say, things aren't looking that good for you. We've got your call, there'll be forensics, so dodging these questions is not going to help.'

'I'm not sure anything is going to help.' Jonah said this under his breath.

'Sorry, I didn't catch that.'

He gave the inspector a bleak smile. 'Nothing. I'm just really tired. Not thinking straight. Gallant House? That all goes back to Bridget.'

Chapter 4

Bridget Whittingham was exactly as Kris had described when he
rang Jenny to say that he'd fixed up the interview. Tall, thin, with
fine-boned neck, wrists and ankles, Bridget moved like the dancer
she had once been, her arm unconsciously leading her as she
swept from room to room. Her auburn hair – Jenny assumed
this was dyed – twisted into a soft peak on top of her head like
a Mr Whippy cone. Not that Bridget looked the sort to buy that
kind from street vans with blaring tunes. Jenny imagined Bridget's
ice cream came from hushed artisan shops that made flavours
that included elderflowers or Madagascan vanilla pods.

'And this is the drawing room.' Bridget opened the door onto
a high-ceilinged chamber. The walls were covered in an astounding
plum flock wallpaper patterned with stylised peonies tumbling
from urns. It was only saved from being overpowering by the white
panelling that reached waist height. Chairs and sofas with well-
turned wooden arms competed for attention in dusky pink
upholstery like Victorian children come down from the nursery
for their daily parental inspection. Family portraits hung in heavy
gold frames; those pictured looked either faintly amused or terribly

19

bored to be gazing down on a room that appeared not to have changed for a century. It was like walking into Schmann's Symphony No. 1, thought Jenny. She'd played it recently with its nineteenth century lush inner tensions somehow resolving into harmony.

'It's still as Admiral Jack intended – the first owner. I redid it on my marriage to freshen it up and I have to say it's held its colours quite well. North-facing – I suppose that accounts for it.' Bridget's tone was very BBC Radio Three, gently refined and pitched low for a woman, fit for commentating on the Proms. She would've been shocked by Jenny's Estuary English if they'd met before Jenny lost her voice.

Jenny didn't know if she should be appalled or impressed by the room. She was certain she would be too afraid to use it in case she damaged one of the vases on the side tables. Where were the ropes and reverential guide steering a party past a glimpse of historical old England?

'Of course, we don't use this much – just high days and holidays.' Bridget adjusted a blind. With a tilt of her head catching the light just so, Jenny was suddenly aware of the skull beneath the skin, the high cheeks, eye sockets. She disliked these moments when her brain went x-ray on her. Bones, we're just a collection of fragile bones. 'We prefer to gather in the snug,' continued Bridget.

Jenny shook off the disturbing vision. She was quickly learning that posh people had a different language. Drawing room, she'd met before in nineteenth century literature but snug was a new one. She decided to wait to see what it meant rather than show ignorance.

Bridget took her towards the back of the house through a generous hallway tiled in geometric patterns and into a room half the size of the first. This one looked out on the garden; south-facing French windows were partly shaded by a vine that clambered over the wrought iron balcony. New leaves were just unfurling.

'That's a Black Hamburg vine, sister plant to the famous one at Hampton Court, or so my husband claimed.' Bridget opened a window to let in the sound of birdsong. 'How anyone would know is beyond me as I've not found anything about it in the family archive but it does bear some passable black grapes in good years.' Seeing Jenny approach, she added swiftly. 'Don't go out on the balcony, please, dear: I can't swear to the soundness of the structure. The wretched thing is listed but far too expensive to repair. I'm afraid I'll just have to let it moulder elegantly until it rusts entirely to nothing.' Her gesture indicated the intricate wrought iron structure that ran across the back of the house. 'It's debatable if it's the vine keeping it up or the other way around.'

Jenny smiled politely as if she understood the headaches in keeping a listed house going. Bridget was quite something, like a dinosaur left over from an earlier age found unexpectedly still roaming the earth.

'You see that it's much more comfortable in here compared to the drawing room.' Bridget patted the top of the old television set. It looked like an antique rather than something capable of streaming Netflix. 'The sofas I admit are a bit lumpy but I hate to throw anything out.'

The grey couches with winged armrests did indeed look like warty Indian elephants reclining on sisal matting. Bridget had attempted to liven them up with ruby red scatter cushions but they still looked a little sad, their best circus days over. The walls too had once been white but now had faded to a buttercream colour.

'There's nothing that you need worry about harming in here,' said Bridget. 'You can put your feet up on the sofa and no one will tell you off. That's why it's called the snug: it's the place you come to feel comfortable. Now let's go into the kitchen. I'll make us some tea and you can tell me about yourself.' She led the way past a console table with its black Bakelite telephone. It looked like it was expecting to receive a call from an earl or a duke, certainly not some telephone marketer sitting in Swansea or Bangalore. Jenny had to hope Bridget bent enough to the modern world to have a mobile as she didn't do calls, only messages.

Bridget put a kettle on the hot plate of the Aga. The kitchen was surprisingly rustic for London: a long dresser displaying willow pattern china and lace-edged creamwear plates; scrubbed oak table; blue and white Delft tiles. Jenny had been awed by the drawing room, not sure about the snug, but the kitchen was a case of love at first sight. She could be very happy here, its neatness keeping the chaos of life at bay. She waved to the room and gave Bridget a broad smile.

'I know what you mean, dear: this is the heart of the house. Now, tell me about yourself. Kris said you're a violinist with the London Philharmonic, is that right? And he also said you don't talk?'

Jenny nodded to both questions.

'Is that can't or won't?'

People rarely asked her that. Jenny pointed to her throat. There was a white scar across her larynx that should answer for her.

'What, no sound at all?'

Jenny shook her head. Long ago, when she was recovering, they'd tried to make her talk. All that had come out were ugly grunts and Jenny had freaked out; she'd felt like her voice had been eaten by a monster. She'd felt safer with silence.

'You poor dear. An accident, was it?'

Jenny shook her head.

'Illness then. I'm sorry. Does it still pain you?'

Jenny nodded. She let Bridget keep her assumption that illness had taken her voice; it was easier than the full explanation. That particular horror was better left locked away, her ugly Jack-in-the-box.

'How terrible for you. You're getting good treatment, I hope?'

Jenny nodded.

22

'So how do we communicate?'

She got out her iPad. *Who else lives here?*

'Oh, what a clever little device. At the moment, just myself and Jonah. He's been with me about a year. He's a darling. Making his way as an actor. Recently he's joined one of those hospital soaps. Tells me he's spends all his days rocketing around London in an ambulance, talking urgently into the radio. He's got the lingo down pat.'

He sounded normal enough but she would reserve judgement until she met him. She'd thought Harry would make a good flatmate, hadn't she? *Any plans to take in more people?* She didn't want a repeat of her current situation.

'Not at the moment. Not that there isn't room; I just think three makes a good number, don't you?'

Jenny smiled. *Perfect.*

'I'll show you your bedroom.'

You don't want references or a deposit?

'Oh no. Kris's recommendation is good enough for me. If you'd be so kind as to arrange for monthly payments into my account – I'll give you the details when you leave – that's best for me. Then we can forget the sordid detail of the rent and just pretend we all live together like a family.'

Jenny was beginning to think Bridget was too naive for this world. *I'll do that as soon as I leave here. I promise.* With the minimal rent being charged, she'd be stupid not to.

'No need to promise. You've the kind of face I know I can trust. There are very few house rules – nothing that'll bother you, I'm sure; just ones to make sure we all get along well together, like tidying up after yourself. Are you originally from England? You don't mind me asking, do you? Not very politically correct, I've been told. It's just that if you had an accent I wouldn't know, would I?'

It was tricky writing while mounting the stairs. Jenny paused to tap out her answer. *I'm from Harlow.* You couldn't get more

23

prosaic than that Essex new town. *But my dad's from Lagos. He's an academic. Currently at Princeton teaching literature.* That was Dr Jerome Lapido: always somewhere else. At Jenny's age of twenty-nine, it shouldn't matter, but she still hadn't let the abandonment go.

'And your mother?'

Music teacher for the county music service. Her mum, Diana Groves had given her life to making Essex girls and boys just that little bit more musical. Driven by missionary fervour to convert her pupils to the same love for music as she had, she worked tirelessly. Jenny had thought it a thankless task until her mum explained that her reward was when she saw their eyes light up with joy when they discovered their own skill in playing a masterpiece or even just a nursery rhyme. With this as her motivation, Diana had more success with her students than one might think from the generally low cultural reputation of the county in the media. Jenny often met past pupils in her line of work who credited her mother with inspiring them as players and helping with the more practical task of getting them into music school. Harry had been one of Diana's protégés, coming for tuition in music theory when he needed the extra help.

'So that's where you get it from!' Bridget had the pleased expression of someone finding the missing puzzle piece. Was it a sign of a snobbish assumption that a girl from Essex wouldn't be in classical music without some extraordinary explanation? That was too common for Jenny to waste time feeling offended. *TOWIE* had a lot to answer for. She'd be more offended if it were because she was mixed race – a fact that still surprised some old timers who didn't recognize that society had changed. She chose to counter it by keeping on turning up in the second desk of violins. At the beginning of her career, with all that she had been battling, each rehearsal, every concert, had been an act of courage and defiance, but it had got a little easier as time passed. The music made it worth it and one day no one would question her right to be there.

24

'You must tell your mother that she's welcome to visit you at any time. And your father, of course. As you'll see there's plenty of room in yours.' Bridget guided Jenny into a pretty front bedroom on the first floor, explaining the top floor was just attics. 'You have a bathroom through there all to yourself.'

With a swoop of joy like a lark ascending, Jenny saw heaven before her. It was a huge house with only three people and she wouldn't have to share even so much as a bath mat!

'The mattress is new. Do you like the four-poster? I know it's a little twee but Kris was always amused by it. I thought it might do for a daughter one day but sadly we weren't blessed with one.'

It was perhaps a little early for Bridget to be telling her this kind of personal information but Jenny was used to the strange effect her silence had on people. They felt obliged to fill the gap and ended up divulging more than they planned. Sometimes that was very awkward, almost a burden as she shouldered the secrets of others; at other times, like now, she didn't mind. They would be living together after all. Bridget was right: it was a bedroom fit for the missing daughter. The wooden bed had thin finial posts that held up a light square frame. Over this were draped net curtains, rather like a wedding veil. A sprig of lilac lay on the pillow. It was the kind of bed Jenny had dreamed of owning as a child but would never have fitted in her bedroom in Harlow.

It's like a fairy tale.

Bridget laughed, a tinkling sound partly smothered by the hand she placed over her mouth. 'Isn't it? I'm afraid I have romantic tastes. Now what's that lilac doing there?' She moved it to join the others in a glass vase on the dressing table. 'You should see my own room. I've gone the full satin curtain route in there. My husband thought I was insane. It was the late eighties, you know, and we were all terribly modern then, shoulder pads, permed hair, God forgive us. I was out of step with the times by about a hundred years, according to my husband. Do I take it you approve?'

Jenny poked her head into the bathroom with its clawfoot bath and black and white tiles, vanity unit and large mirror. She'd miss a shower but she was hardly going to complain about that when she had it all to herself. She mimed applause.

'I'm pleased you like it. Yes, you'll do very well here, I think. When would you like to move in?'

Jenny tapped her watch, indicating now.

'Then come as soon as you can, dear. We look forward to having you.'

There was one drawback: it was around ten minutes on foot from Gallant House to the station down roads bordering the heath but Jenny decided not to care. The long dark walk in winter and fear of attackers lurking in bushes was a problem for another day. Sitting on the train heading home, she was still reeling. A beautiful house in mature gardens, an ancient vine, an overgrown tennis court, even a mulberry tree: she would be living in a Grade A daydream. She'd even possibly – maybe – be able to carry on as a professional musician and have only one job. It felt too good to be true.

Then she remembered the single jarring note: the sprig of lilac. If Bridget hadn't put it on her pillow, that left the absent Jonah as culprit. That didn't seem an appropriate gesture when they'd never met.

She didn't want her perfect house spoiled. She was leaping to conclusions. There had to be a cleaner to keep a house that size in such good order; she might put flowers on a pillow to welcome a newcomer without it being odd, mightn't she?

Chapter 5

Harry rapped on the flimsy folding door, making it rattle on its sliders. 'Jenny?'

She looked up from her suitcase and signed 'What?'.

'I just wanted to apologise for Saturday.' He was holding one arm awkwardly behind his back.

Her answer was a shrug. Her flatmates had tried to clear up; someone had tackled the bathroom and they had filled the wheelie bin to overflowing. Two days later the house had moved from unspeakable to merely foul.

'I realised how it must've seemed to you. It wasn't planned. We didn't leave you out on purpose.'

Really? She could've bought the unplanned part but all it would've taken was a text for her to feel included. But what did that matter? She was moving to paradise.

'I heard that you're leaving. You don't have to do that. We had a house meeting ...'

Without her?

'... And we agreed we've been pigs. We don't even have the excuse of being students anymore. We've drawn up a rota.' Like she hadn't suggested that a million times. 'So, please, don't go. This is from us.' He presented her with a bunch of mixed flowers

27

which looked like they'd been culled from the derelict garden and a local park. The forget-me-nots were already wilting.

She took them. What else could she do without being a complete cow? She laid them on the windowsill and got out her iPad.

'A new room at lower rent? Are you sure?' Harry read more of her typed explanation. 'Do you even know the woman? There has to be a catch surely? Are you going to be doing the cleaning or something else for her? Walking her dog?'

She shook her head.

Harry fiddled with the tie of her dressing gown which hung by the door. He was always restless. Even after they'd made love, when both should've been feeling mellow, he used to play with her hair, twisting it into braids or bunches. He couldn't stop touching things. She missed people touching her. 'I worry about you – that you might be taken advantage of.'

Or maybe I finally got a break.

'I hope so. I'm still sorry. You wouldn't have been looking if it weren't for how we behaved.'

She shrugged. A lot of her reactions to Harry could be summed up in that gesture. It meant everything from 'don't care' to 'life's shitty that way'. He could pick his meaning.

Harry sat uninvited on the edge of her futon. The last time he'd perched there she'd believed that they'd still been a couple. He'd then told her that it was over, that he liked her but not enough for the long haul, like she was an around-the-world flight he chose not to board. Did he even remember that? She should've moved out at that point but he'd persuaded her they could be adults and share the same space without recriminations. Jenny had caved, scared of the unknown and taking her problems to a house of people who didn't know her. It was important to her to feel safe. Plus she'd just signed up for another six-month lease. That was coming to an end now so she could leave without penalties.

'I used to find your silence restful, did you know that? I probably mentioned it once or twice.' He fluttered the pages of a novel she was reading, losing her place. The more she looked at the thirty-something Harry, the closer the resemblance was to a petulant schoolboy. How had she missed that? He was waiting for a response.

Shrug.

'Later I got frustrated with you not doing anything about it. That was the real reason I ended it. I should've said.'

So it was her fault, was it? What a surprise. He'd learned to read basic signing but that hadn't stopped him nagging her. He wanted her to use an electronic voice so she could converse like an ordinary person. She still resented his insinuation that a disability stopped her being normal. Besides, she had a voice, a beautiful voice, that came from the four strings and bow of her violin. If he would only listen, she was more eloquent than most.

'If you used a voice, you could tell me what's really going on with you. You're always so bloody enigmatic. It doesn't have to be robotic – not like that crap one on your tablet that makes you sound like a sat nav. I looked into it. You can get a better app than the one you use – one where you can pick accents, tone, everything, to suit you.'

He'd looked into it? Jenny supposed that was a sign that Harry still cared at some level, but his rejection had hurt. He may've hidden his real reason but it wouldn't have changed the verdict. The words that she was 'not enough' had haunted her. She wasn't enough for him or any man to stay with her, not even her dad.

Thank Dr Jerome Lapido for that particular neurosis, she thought with grim self-knowledge.

'Jenny? You'll keep in touch, won't you?'

'Why?' she signed.

'I do care, you know. We've been friends for nearly ten years.' And went out for three of those. 'You're just a lot for a selfish guy like me to handle. Complicated. Not just the voice thing but the nightmares and such from … you know?'

Of course, she knew: it was her life that nearly ended at fourteen. She regretted she'd eventually told him the details but she'd had to as he needed to know to avoid some of her panic attack triggers. At least he appeared to have kept his word and not told the others. It would've been much worse to be looked on with horrified pity.

She almost typed her wish for him to have an empty, uncomplicated future of meaningless, no-strings sexual partners, but thought better of it. It would show she still carried a grudge from their break-up. *You've got my number* she wrote instead. *We'll see each other at work.*

'Yeah.' He seemed reassured by that. 'And good luck. Do you need any help with your stuff?'

She shook her head.

'OK then. And sorry.' He got up and gave her a quick kiss on the cheek. He still smelt good, the bastard. 'Look after yourself, Jen.'

Jenny splashed out on a taxi to transport her stuff from Ebbisham Drive to Blackheath. To avoid the taxi driver striking up a conversation, she thumbed through her old messages. As friends and family knew not to call, there was plenty of these. It was hard to keep up with her mother's continual one-sided chat. She'd turned texting into a Virginia Woolf stream of consciousness and Jenny would often find her phone had fifty or so unread message if she neglected it for a few hours. Scrolling down she came across one from a number her phone didn't recognise. She could see the beginning of the message. *Well done. You kept your promise.*

What was that about? What promise? Was it a marketing technique? On any other day she would've ignored it, but she had time. Opening it, she read the rest of the message.

Well done. You kept your promise. I enjoyed our time together when you were 14. Want to relive the experience?

Her heart thumped against her ribcage with the first flutter of terror. So sick. She had thought these had stopped. Initially after the attack, she attracted messages from all sorts of weirdos. Her mum and the police shielded her from most, but occasionally she'd see one, or they'd find an innocuous cover and get through. They had ranged from suggestive messages, like this one where someone was pretending to be her attacker, to the seriously disturbing glitter and cutout words in cards or letters that seemed a celebration of the crime. She'd learned that there was a whole subculture of people who followed violent attacks. Her counsellor had tried to explain the pathology but even she, the professional, had struggled. As Jenny got older and seen more of life, she felt she had got to grips with some of it. People had fantasies, horrible, shocking ones, and projected them onto victims who hadn't asked for any of this to happen to them. These sick people either liked tormenting victims or wished to be one themselves – the second seemed even worse. In Harlow, Jenny had even attracted a few so-called friends who only hung out with her because they found a vicarious thrill in being associated with her. Unsurprisingly, her trust in the goodness of people had taken a severe battering.

What to do? In the years after the incident, Jenny had had a number to forward the messages for the police to examine but she guessed that was long since defunct when the case went cold and got shuffled into the pile of unsolved. Her mum would still have a record of a current contact if one existed.

Her thumb hovered over the message, weighing up whether to upset her mother with this.

Oh fuck it. She wasn't going down that rabbit hole again. She was so tired of being terrified. The past was the past. She was on her way to making a new start and wasn't going to drag this into Gallant House with her. Sick caller, goodbye. She blocked the number and hit delete.

The taxi driver, unaware of the turmoil Jenny was experiencing on the back seat, couldn't refrain from whistling appreciatively as they drew up outside Gallant House.

'Lovely place.'

Still shivering, she nodded. With its tawny bricks, white sash windows, privet hedge and black railings it was the house equivalent of a person dressed up for a night on the town.

'You live here?'

She smiled a 'yes'.

'A nanny, are you?'

She nodded. Sometimes it was just easier to agree. Her life was a confection spun of such little white lies to avoid having to admit she couldn't speak.

'Best of luck with that. In my experience, kids from houses like this can be spoilt little monsters. You'll have your work cut out for you.' He helped her pile her belongings just inside the gate. She gave him as generous tip as she could afford which probably wasn't as much as he'd hoped. 'Bye, love.'

She turned away as the taxi headed off across the heath to scout for fares by the exit from Greenwich Park. Taking her violin and computer bag to the front door, Jenny pulled on the bell. It literally was a bell: she'd seen it hanging in the hallway; the bell was connected to a metal rod which ran to a white knob outside, all pleasantly direct and mechanical. It took a while for Bridget to answer, long enough for Jenny to start slightly panicking that maybe she had been dreaming the offer of a room.

'Jenny! From Kris's message, I wasn't expecting you for another hour. Come in, come in!' Bridget stood by the door as Jenny ferried her belongings in from the road. 'Do you want me to get someone to help? I'm afraid with my back I daren't risk it.'

Jenny shook her head. There wasn't much.

'Just leave it in the hall for now and come and meet my guests. I didn't tell you about my Tuesday gatherings, did I?' Jenny shook her head, wondering what excuse she could conjure to avoid being dragged before a crowd of strangers. It was always so humiliating for her and frustrating for them. 'You're welcome to bring friends. It's such a lovely evening, we're in the garden. Keep your jacket on. There's a definite nip in the air.' She didn't wait for an answer but assumed Jenny was following her down the stairs to the basement, out of the dark passageway and into the brightness of the garden.

Run upstairs, or follow? There wasn't really a choice, was there?

Bridget's guests were having drinks under the huge lilac tree that dominated the upper lawn nearest the house. It was a patchy, twisted thing, dead branches mingled with those bearing blossom, attesting to its great age. The flowers were white, their scent quite overwhelming. Dark butterfly shadows fluttered to rest on hair and shoulders of those below every time the lilac tossed its branches in the evening breeze. Jenny blinked, trying to clear her sight of the sun-dazzle on cut-glass tumblers.

'Pimms? Or is it too early in the year for you?' asked Bridget, going to the table.

Jenny gave a thumbs up. Doing this with a cushion of alcohol was preferable.

Bridget handed her a tumbler filled with pale red liquid and floating fruit and mint leaves. 'I'm glad you're like me and never think it's too early for Pimms. Now Jonah here swears he won't touch the stuff. He says he's strictly teetotal. Jonah, this is our new house guest, Jenny.'

One of the three men at the table got up and came to her. He wasn't how Jenny had imagined. In fact, she assumed the other youngish man was Jonah, as he looked more the part. As an aspiring actor, she'd predicted her housemate would have the classic good-looking Brit appearance, the floppy hair of Sam Claflin, the smouldering gaze of a Kit Harington. Instead he was crewcut, and decidedly edgy in appearance, skin in poor condition, blue eyes flicking from her to Bridget in a sure sign of nerves.

Crudely drawn tattoos webbed the backs of his hands. He had two bolts tattooed either side on his neck.

'Hi, Jenny. Mrs Whittingham warned us that you didn't talk.' His voice was much the most attractive things about him: a little bit London, but deep and resonant. It was a surprise coming from his strung-out frame, a bit like George Ezra's bass-baritone emerging from such a lean person.

She smiled – her equivalent of 'hello'.

'And these are our friends,' said Bridget, turning to the rest of the group. 'Rose, meet Jenny. Rose has known me for ages, haven't you, dear?'

The thirty-something woman laughed. She was small, and had an elfin haircut framing a heart-shaped face; Jenny got the impression of someone packed with energy. 'If you call ten years ages, Bridget. I was one of Bridget's tenants once upon a time, Jenny, when I thought I might make it as an actress. That's until life disillusioned me. I went into psychology instead.'

'And this is Jonah's friend, William Riley.'

A bearded man, hipster to the core, whom she'd wrongly guessed was an actor, got up and offered his hand. 'Call me Billy. I'm not supposed to be here you know. I just came to check up on Jonah and got inveigled into drinks.'

Jenny shook his hand.

'And last but by no means least is darling Norman.' Bridget placed her hand lightly on the shoulder of a rotund man with a balding pate. He was dressed in a tweed suit with a mustard yellow waistcoat straining across his middle. 'Norman's our neighbour and local historian. He also manages to fit in being our GP. A man of many talents.'

'Bridget, you are a terrible flatterer! I'm no historian – I merely dabble. Bridget is compiling a history of this house and I'm helping her with some of the context. She's got into the bad habit of overstating my qualifications.' His exuberant white eyebrows arched over dark eyes.

34

'Give Jenny one of your cards, Norman, so she knows where to register with a practice.' Bridget patted the seat of a spare garden chair. 'Now sit down, dear. No one is going to grill you so you can relax and enjoy this lovely evening. I do believe it's the first time I've been able to have my drinks outside this year.' Bridget deftly turned the conversation to Jonah's latest role. Jenny noticed how everyone present took what seemed like familial pride in his achievements: Rose was beaming like she was his big sister at prize giving; Billy regarded him like an approving brother as Jonah described his latest episode attending an accident in a prison; Norman guffawed like everyone's favourite uncle at Jonah's navigation mistake that saw the ambulance turn into a real A&E bay, rather than the fake one the crew had constructed; and Bridget presided over the let's-love-Jonah Fest with a matri-archal poise. No one made clumsy attempts to include Jenny or make her communicate. Her fear that she would be humiliated subsided.

Would she be here long enough to have this sense of family pride extended to her? Jenny wondered. Her mother was her main cheerleader but Jenny no longer lived at home to have her minor triumphs praised on a daily basis. It might be nice to be included.

There was a lull in the conversation as Bridget went in to fetch some nibbles to go with more drinks.

Jonah rubbed his hands. 'Thank God she's setting out the grub. I'm starving. Bridget's Tuesday nibbles are spectacular, much better than a bag of crisps or bowl of peanuts. You're a violinist?'

Jenny nodded. She couldn't keep her participation limited to nods and shakes of the head. They'd given her enough time to feel the ice was broken. *How long have you been acting?* she wrote.

'Not long. A year maybe. I'm in drama school but they let me have time off when I get a job.' She wondered how old he was as he looked at least her age, rather mature for drama school. 'It's what we're all there for after all. I have Dr Wade to thank for that: she helped me get in and find an agent.'

Rose waved that away. 'It was your own talent that did it, Jonah. I'm pleased you've graduated to ambulance driver and got away from all those gang member roles.'

Jonah rubbed at his spiderweb on one knuckle. His hands looked raw, like he suffered from eczema. 'Yeah, but my character has a drug problem and I'm stealing from the hospital pharmacy. I'm not sure I'm going to survive beyond the season finale.'

That explained the edgy look. Perhaps he was a young guy who just had the misfortune to look older, like those men who go bald prematurely? He had all his hair but his face wasn't the smooth one of the newly hatched student. Lines bisected the top of his nose and dug in round his mouth.

'You might,' said Billy in a bolstering tone. 'And eight weeks of steady work looks good on the CV. More jobs will come your way, I'm sure.'

'It does look good, but my tutors tell me I have a problem.' Jonah cracked his knuckles, not noticing the number of winces around the table. 'If I change my looks, I don't get these parts; and if I get these parts, I can't change my looks. They think I might get boxed in.'

Jenny was pleased to hear that the 'just got out of prison' vibe he projected was for show. She wouldn't like to be sharing a house with someone who might be a threat to her.

'Maybe you should just look the way you want to look and leave the rest to hair and makeup?' Thus spoke the psychologist.

Jonah scratched at his close-shaved head. 'Maybe I'll risk it. I'd like to grow this a little longer. People don't sit next to me on public transport.'

'Keep it, m'boy. You don't want people sitting next to you. Each of them is a disease vector.' The GP rattled the ice in his gin and tonic. 'Can't wait to retire and get away from the lot of you!' But he said it with a smile to soften the words.

A bell rang inside – not the front door but another one with a higher tone.

Jonah leaped up. 'That's my summons.' He dashed inside.

'Very Pavlovian of Bridget,' said Norman. 'She always gets her houseguests very well trained by the time she's finished. That boy was the epitome of rudeness when he first moved in and now look at him.'

'She shames us all into manners,' agreed Rose. 'Not that she's going to have any trouble with this one, I can tell.' She smiled warmly at Jenny. 'You've fallen on your feet here. When I couldn't get a breakthrough as an actor, it was Bridget who gently nudged me from dead-end jobs towards doing something with my psychology degree. I think I've learned some of my best tricks with patients from her.'

Jenny drew a question mark in the air.

'Things like how to put them at ease when they come into my office for the first time, how to draw the best from them. Jonah's a case in point: a more lost young man I'd never met and now look at him.' She stopped. 'Sorry, that was very unprofessional. Forget I said that.'

'It's tempting to talk shop. We get it, Rose,' said Billy. 'I have to remember not to take my work home with me.'

What do you do? asked Jenny.

'I work for the probation service. I find it very rewarding, especially on a day like today.' He toasted her with his Pimms.

Jenny couldn't quite see the connection but replied with a raised glass as expected.

Bridget and Jonah returned with trays of food – little asparagus quiches, salmon blinis, Parma ham wrapped around mozzarella balls, and tiny chocolate brownies. Jenny could now understand why these gatherings were so popular. Everything tasted as good as it looked.

'Tell me, Bridget, that you got these at Waitrose,' said Rose after eating her fill. 'You make me feel so inadequate.'

Bridget collected in the empty side plates. 'You know I like cooking. Anyway, these are simple to make. I could show you.'

'I might take you up on that, but not tonight. I've got some work to do. Goodnight everyone. Billy, can I give you a lift to the station?'

'Thanks, Rose.' After a quick round of farewells, they left together.

'And I must be off too. Got the grandson of an old friend coming to stay till he can find his own place. Better move some of my books off the spare bed.' Norman hefted himself to his feet. 'Here's a card, Jenny. Don't forget to register. You don't have to sign on my list as they're putting me out to grass soon. I've plenty of youngsters as my partners, including a female colleague or two.' He winked and then waved farewell to the others. He headed home, not through the house but through a gate in the wall that opened into his garden.

'I found Norman using the downstairs bathroom this morning. Red faces all round,' said Jonah when the GP had gone.

'His boiler's out. I told him to come and go. We keep an eye on each other's house,' said Bridget. 'We don't stand on ceremony.'

'I was just warning Jenny. I found it difficult to meet his gaze tonight after the eyeful I got this morning. He appears to think a towel enough covering to walk between his house and yours, and I'm afraid to say it doesn't quite hide everything it should.'

Jenny made a note to be careful when venturing downstairs in the morning in case she met the streaker doctor.

Bridget stacked the empty tumblers on the drinks tray. 'Don't tease, Jonah. Norman is a perfectly respectable man; he just has a boiler problem.'

'He has a buttock problem,' muttered Jonah.

'I didn't think the young were so prudish. Jenny, what do you think?'

There was nothing Jenny could write down that wouldn't sound completely wrong.

'Mrs Whittingham, what do you expect her to say? That she's fine with nudity?'

They picked up the trays and carried them towards the house. 'We're all human.'

'But not everyone wants to be reminded of that in the shape of a dotty seventy-year-old man. You have to protect my delicate sensibilities, Mrs Whittingham.'

'You – sensitive!' Continuing to bicker good-naturedly, they went into the house, Jenny trailing after them. This house was proving even more interesting than she thought.

Chapter 6

Jonah, Present Day

They'd had a break during which Jonah had decided to keep lawyers out of it for the moment. He knew how to talk without saying anything.

'Tell us how you feel about the women you shared the house with.'

Jonah was struck by the inspector's use of past tense. 'I'm not going back there?' The sergeant was looking at him as if he disappointed her, like there was something obvious he was missing.

'Do you think that would be appropriate under these circumstances?' said the inspector.

Had he lost the right to walk those corridors, rooms and gardens of Gallant House just because he'd lost his temper the once?

But you hurt her, Jonah, said a snide inner voice.

He could no longer remember clearly what he'd done, just that he'd been driven to it. Not his fault.

So for that, he'd been kicked out of paradise. An overwhelming feeling of relief swept through him.

Chapter 7

Jenny, One Year Ago

Jenny hauled her bags and boxes up to her room one by one. There was no sign of Jonah when she would've welcomed the help. Maybe he only carried things in exchange for food? She didn't even know which room he was in to knock on the door. Never mind: she was used to doing things alone. Hadn't she decided she preferred it that way?

Belongings safely ferried, she stood for a moment to take stock of her new kingdom. It was clean and neat – just as she liked, no, *needed* it to be. The light was fading but the view out front was unsullied by streetlights. A bold orange tinge flushed the horizon, indicating the busy heart of London just over the hill, but here it could almost still be the eighteenth century when the house was built. That's if you ignored the cars and the planes winking by, lining up with the Thames to land at Heathrow.

Pulling her duvet out of a box, she went to the bed to strip off the white lace counterpane. A bouquet of orange Californian poppies lay on the pillow. Petals fell off as she lifted it. Someone should tell the cleaner that poppies made terrible cut flowers. All she was left with was confetti and unattractive stubby heads on hairy stalks. She placed them in the bin, reminding herself to get rid of them before the next visit by the cleaner so as not to offend her.

Odd though. Bridget hadn't mentioned anything about a cleaner in her briefing on house rules. Jenny didn't expect one but she should make it a priority to ask. She liked to know if someone was coming into her space so she could prepare.

It didn't take long to unpack. Her books went neatly onto a shelf by the fireplace, Maya Angelou, Chimamanda Ngozi Adiche, Jane Austen and Vikram Seth all snuggled together. Growing up, she'd craved culture of all sorts – theatre, literature, but mostly music. She'd been teased for it as a child as other kids didn't get it; now she found there were far more of her tribe out there than she expected, people like Louis. That was the best thing about adulthood: not having to apologise for your taste. Next was her mini speaker and docking station. She thumbed on Stravinsky's *Petrushka* on her phone as she had to play that piece the following day. Shaking out her clothes, which were heavy on the black skirts and shirts, light on anything pastel, she hung them in the white wardrobe. That amused her: it was shaped like the one that danced in the *The Beauty and the Beast* film. She waltzed a few steps with one of her long dresses and laughed, before putting it away. Underwear hid itself in the top drawer of the dresser – it didn't look fine enough for this place. Perhaps she'd buy herself some silky lingerie with her savings? Could she even consider dating again? Harry's rejection had scared her off men for months. She'd foolishly thought he was the one, her childhood sweetheart. Her mum had warned her not to fall for her own fantasies about the relationship. Nikki Groves had done that with Jenny's father and ended up a single mum in Harlow.

Mum would love it here.

And now the bathroom. Jenny swept into it in manner gently mocking of Bridget's prima ballerina style. She emptied her toiletries into the vanity unit, leaving out on the ledge her favourite

42

perfume, a tub of moisturiser and her seven-day pill dispenser. The plastic compartmented box looked ugly compared to everything else. She'd have to see if she could find an antique one on one of the junkeroo stalls in Greenwich market. She ran the tap. With a few groans and splutters it eventually ran warm, then scorching hot. Nothing wrong with Bridget's boiler. She added some cold and washed her face thoroughly, removing all trace of makeup. She was going to be happy here, she could just tell.

Dabbing her face dry, she went back into her bedroom, clicked off the music and took her violin out of its case to tune it. A little thrill ran through her. Though she held the instrument for hours each day, she still got that shiver of anticipation, like the wonder of first love, when she knew what they were about to do together. An ocean of classical music gently lapped before her mind's eye: everything from the storms of Beethoven to the silences of Arvo Pärt. The violin brought it all within her reach. They would have to wait though because she really needed to practice for tomorrow. Would that disturb anyone? It was bound to annoy Bridget and Jonah if they were having an early night. The snug? Was that far enough away from the bedrooms? Taking her music and folding stand in one hand, the violin and bow in the other, she went downstairs and set up the score for the concert. Her fingering for the opening scene still wasn't right. She loved the Russian folk tunes that weaved in and out of the composition but she hadn't quite captured the spirit of them. Violin loose at her side, she closed her eyes for moment and breathed to ease the tension in her back muscles. She tried to summon up her impressions of Tsarist Russia: bright peasant clothes, long winters, furs, puppet shows, dancing bears, sleigh rides. Ready now, she set the violin in its notch under her chin, ignoring the familiar twinge of pain, and launched into the first song. Yes! That felt good. The high ceiling flattered the sound of her violin solo. It was so much better practising here than in her old house. Reaching the end without a mistake, she held the last note.

Applause shocked her. Spinning round, she saw that she wasn't alone as she had assumed. Jonah was on the balcony, cigarette in hand. If she could speak, she would've shouted at him for creeping up on her.

'I don't know what that was but it sounded great,' he said easily, taking another puff. 'Don't mind me. I sneak out here as Mrs Whittingham doesn't allow smoking in the house.'

The last five minutes that had felt so perfect were now tarnished by the knowledge she'd had an eavesdropper. She had thought she was sailing on her classical ocean alone and Jonah's appearances was as shocking as a U-boat surfacing next to her. She put the violin down and gathered up her music.

'Don't stop.' Jonah stubbed out the cigarette, pinched the end and slipped it in his pocket. 'I guess I should've announced myself but, you see, I'm not supposed to be out here.' He gestured to the rusting balcony. 'Mrs Whittingham is always full of warnings of dire disaster but I figure that the vine will hold me if the ironwork doesn't.'

Jenny told herself to slow down, not to flee as instinct was telling her. He had been here first and that it was her negligence to check that meant she'd been overheard.

'Are you all unpacked?'

She nodded.

'Got time for another tune?' He pointed to the violin. 'I've never been to a classical concert. Don't you want to expand my horizons? People keep telling me they do.'

She shrugged.

He laughed and clapped a hand to his chest. 'Jenny, you wound me. You're saying you don't fucking care one way or another? You're right. No need to care about me. I was just curious. I'll go.'

She held up a hand. She might as well try to make a friend of him if they were to live together – it would be safer that way. And it was hard for her to imagine a life that hadn't included concerts. Going without classical music was akin to missing out on a sense.

Jonah perched back on the rail of the balcony, surely testing its strengths to the limit. He saw her aghast look.

'Chill, Jenny. What's life if not just another day cheating death?'

He had a point. Since her fourteenth birthday, she'd shared that philosophy. Everyone lived on borrowed time. So, what to play him? She needed a piece where the violin part was complete in itself, something in the easy listening category, and that she happened to know by heart. She settled for John Williams' theme for *Schindler's List*. If Jonah could listen to that and not weep then he had a heart of stone. Setting bow to strings, she yearned her way through the music, putting into it all the senseless pain of the tragedy it described, rising on to the balls of her feet as she did when caught up in a theme. She'd heard the piece during a televised Prom when she was a teenager and it had set her on the path to her current job, that ambition surviving even her own personal tragedy. God, she loved this: it felt like the top of her head opened and she was floating. There was nothing more powerful in life than this, not even pain, not even violence, not even love.

Jonah was still, with the pent-up tension of a predator crouching, ash drifting unregarded from cigarette tip.

The silence went unbroken when she finished, strings still resonating with the last sweet high note.

'Fuck me, what was that?' Despite his crudity, his voice was reverential. 'It was amazing. Can I stream it?'

She nodded and jotted down the name of the piece.

'John Williams. Is he the same as the *Star Wars* guy?'

She drew a tick.

'Amazing – I know something about music. I've surprised myself. Can we talk without this?' Jonah tapped the iPad.

She made the gestures for 'Do you know sign language?'.

He followed her hands like he was studying her. 'Is that sign language?'

45

Duh, yes. She nodded.

'Teach me.' He patted the spot on the rail next to him. 'Come on, it's nice out here. Trust me, it's not given way yet and won't tonight.'

Jenny was wryly aware that the dynamics of the playground were in operation. He was daring her, seeing if she was on his side or Bridget-the-rule-maker's. She'd hated that when she'd been a schoolgirl; she wasn't much fonder of it now. Putting down the violin – she wasn't risking that – she stepped out onto the balcony. It creaked a little which made her gasp.

'Steady now.' Jonah caught her sleeve before she could retreat. 'It's just adjusting.'

There were no more creaks so she perched next to him, her back supported by the thick stem of the vine. She'd already planned to grab that if the balcony gave way. Jonah didn't appear to need such reassurance. He sat with nothing but a drop behind him.

She held up her index finger. First sign. She ran through the basics: yes, no, please, thank you, 'how are you?', 'what do you want?'. He mastered them quickly.

'We're studying movement at drama school,' he said, which might explain his aptitude. 'I should ask them to include this. Give me something, I dunno, emotional? Can you swear in sign language?'

Of course. She gave him a few of the mild ones.

'That's "wanker"? Right, I'm using that tomorrow. There are a few of the other students who really deserve that.'

She made another sign.

'What's that?'

She typed the translation. *Be careful. You never know who understands.*

'It's OK. They expect that kind of language – and worse – from me. So how did you lose your voice? Bridget said it was an illness. Was it cancer?'

46

He certainly tackled things head on. She shook her head and made the universal sign for 'goodbye'.

'You're going? OK, sorry for being so nosey. Thanks for the song. The cast and crew are going to think I've gone all uptown when they hear that playing in my dressing room.'

Jenny contemplated trying to explain to him how music wasn't the preserve of the posh but decided she wasn't up to challenging the commonly held view tonight. She made a final sign combination.

'What's that.' Jonah watched her lips. 'Sweet dreams?'

She nodded.

'Never had any of those, but thanks, Jenny. Goodnight.'

Chapter 8

The House that Jack Built – Chapter Two – Foundations

The turf peeled away revealing the black soil beneath. In the first spadeful – not that anyone noticed – was a scrap of ribbon let fall by a careless maid who once attended the fair on this very spot. She should never have trusted the promises of her sailor. Next came a penny from Sir Thomas Wyatt's pocket. He dropped it when he pulled out gold coins to bribe his flagging supporters as his rebellion against Mary Tudor faltered. Further digging turned over the blood, sweat and tears of yet more thwarted revolutionaries: Lord Audley, the Yorkists, Jack Cade, Wat Tyler and Jack Straw. Over the centuries, so many came to dream their impossible dreams on Blackheath's open space, lost in blue sky thinking that the capital was theirs for the taking. They believed that this was the day when society would change for the better. They were, as axe and sword went on to prove, mistaken.

The spades dug down to more primitive times. The cutting edge severed in two a discarded leather sole from a Dane's boot. That bloody-handed man abandoned it, a casualty of the long march from Canterbury where they'd done away with the archbishop.

Go deeper yet, I begged from the rolled paper in which I gestated, tucked under the architect's arm. I need my foundations to reach further back if I am to stand steady.

One digger unearthed a fragment of a stone age tool. The pick was fashioned from antlers by a practical man squatting in his round house on a cold winter's evening. Chucking it aside, not caring what it was, the labourers carried on until they passed through the thin level of human habitation and reached down to that of the terrible lizards.

Chapter 9

Jenny

Nights were never easy.

Jenny lay in bed, telling herself that she was in her perfect bedroom, in a perfect house, safe from intruders.

But sleep still evaded her, whisking around the corner just when she thought she'd caught up. It was probably the unfamiliarity of her surroundings. Each house had its own time signature of beats and clicks; this one was no different. She could hear the pipes settling, the wash of water as someone used a distant tap. Overhead, though, footsteps paced. One-two-three, one-two-three. It had the pulse of the waltz, relentless and driving. She imagined silken skirts swirling as ladies leant back in the arms of dark-suited men, throats extended, vulnerable. She shuddered. Was Bridget's bedroom up there? Or Jonah's. She thought not. Her landlady had said it was only attics. Maybe it wasn't coming from up there but just sounded like it did?

Jenny put the pillow over her head trying to muffle the steps but it didn't work. Her brain was now worrying over the unexplained. She was still that child who lay rigid with terror, scared of the monsters under the bed – because she knew – oh, she knew – they were real.

Just go out into the corridor and find out which room it's coming from.

Frustrated by herself, she threw off the duvet and slipped into her mules. This is the bit in horror movies where you scream at the ditsy female character to go back into the room, she thought with dark humour.

But this isn't a horror flick. I'm in a feel-good girl-gets-a-break movie, she decided firmly. Anyway, I'm not going into the attics, just listening from the corridor.

She opened her door. A table lamp supplied a little low lighting. Bridget had said she left it on so that houseguests could find their way around in the dark. She didn't want anyone taking a headlong dive down the stairs.

Jonah appeared at the far end of the corridor, heading for the bathroom in a towelling dressing gown. His room evidently didn't have the same luxury of an en suite.

'Are you all right, Jenny? Need something?'

She pointed upwards.

'What?'

She beckoned him closer. Couldn't he hear it? Actually, she couldn't hear it out here either. He approached looking a little confused.

'What's the matter?'

She pulled him into her room.

'Hey!'

Shaking her head at his protest that she was ravishing him, she pointed upwards.

Nothing. The steps had stopped.

That was awkward.

She dashed for her iPad. *Waltz on the ceiling.*

'A waltz?'

Steps in a three-four pattern.

51

'A three-four pattern?'

Give me strength! She shoved her fingers through her mass of black hair. She'd let it loose for bed and knew it must look like a wild halo around her head and shoulders. *Time signature. 1 - 2 - 3.* She mimicked the movement.

'Jenny, I can't hear anything.' No wonder he was looking at her like she was crazy.

She bit her lip and signed 'sorry', a closed hand circling at her chest.

Jonah repeated the sign back. 'That's "sorry", isn't it?'

She nodded.

'It's OK. You probably just heard a bird. They nest up there. It freaks me out sometimes when I hear them scratching on the tiles. Can't shake the idea that they're rats.'

But birds don't waltz, neither do rats for that matter.

Ghost?

He read her message and had the gall to laugh. 'Probably. The ghost of Admiral Jack come to haunt us.' He made a spectral arm flapping gesture to show he wasn't taking her seriously. 'He was a nasty piece of work according to Bridget's history. You should ask her. It would be like him to do something so spiteful.'

OK, so Jonah was the wrong person to ask. In fact, she couldn't blame him as it had been her to drag him in here.

She signed 'thanks' and 'goodnight'.

'You really OK? Don't want someone to give you a cuddle? I'm volunteering in case you're wondering.' He put his hand up.

She shook her head vigorously. Maybe on another occasion she'd be unnerved by his suggestion, but right now she was only conscious of her own embarrassment.

He grinned with boyish charm. 'Can't blame a guy for trying. Goodnight.'

He closed the door as he left.

Jenny thumped her forehead. How embarrassing had that been? She thought she'd managed quite well on her introduction to her new home but she'd spoiled it all by sending Jonah totally mixed signals. He'd either think she was cracked or that she made a habit of pouncing on men in corridors dressed only in night shorts and a Tee. She looked down. She didn't even have a bra on so she'd have been bouncing all over the place.

Kicking off her mules, she got back into bed. The house was silent now, pipes settled, footsteps ceased. Bloody brilliant. Her phone told her it was eleven-thirty. She switched it to night mode and pulled the duvet up to her chin.

At two in the morning, the steps started again. One-two-three. One-two-three.

This time she didn't go and look.

Chapter 10

Yawning, Jenny entered the kitchen carrying her small box of food supplies. Daylight made the ghostly waltz less frightening. In fact, she'd rationalised it away completely. That was what she'd learned to do with her fears – tidy them away, paper them over. She was prepared to accept Jonah's explanation that there were birds up there. Perhaps they'd been doing something perfectly normal, mating or fighting over territory maybe, and her brain had turned it into a pattern?

'Good morning, Jenny. I see you're an early riser?' Bridget was sitting at the oak table, papers spread around her, pen in hand.

Not by choice. Jenny tapped her watch, indicating she had a shift starting at nine.

'Sleep well?'

How to reply to that? She nodded.

'Good. I never slept well the first night in a strange house. You must be built of sterner stuff than me.'

Jenny pulled a packet of muesli out of her box.

'I should've told you last night: you're welcome to keep your groceries in the pantry. I'll clear a shelf for you. In fact, I'd appreciate it if you did as I don't like food elsewhere. Old houses attract mice. So many voids under floorboards and wainscots for them to explore.'

Jenny didn't think she'd heard anyone actually use the word 'wainscot' before. It was rather lovely. She gave Bridget an 'OK' sign.

Taking her bowl to the place opposite Bridget, Jenny gestured to the papers.

'What are these? Ah, this is my history of the house. I can be a terrible bore on the subject as my friends will tell you.'

Jenny pressed a hand to her chest and shook her head.

'You won't be bored?' Bridget laughed. 'You say that now but give it a few weeks. I swear Jonah dives into the shrubbery when he sees me coming at him with a new chapter. I suppose it isn't really his thing.' Her eyes lit up as they rested on Jenny. 'Maybe you'd appreciate my book?'

Jenny put out a hand. No harm in pleasing Bridget and she did have a genuine interest in the house, not least the fact Jonah had dropped into their late-night conversation about Admiral Jack being a rascal.

'I'll give you a sample then, see how you get on.' Bridget rifled through the papers. 'Might as well start at the beginning.' She handed Jenny the opening chapters.

Jenny glanced at the first lines and looked up at Bridget.

'I know: unconventional, isn't it? I've tried to approach it like a novelist rather than historian. I've styled it an autobiography of the house. I've given so much of my own life to it that I felt I knew the old girl so well. She seems to speak to me like this.'

Jenny re-read the opening. Actually, it was a good idea, and felt very fresh, once you got past the oddness. She wouldn't be surprised if Bridget did get it published one day. She could imagine a whole load of spin-offs as historians told their story from the point of view of the objects rather than the people. What would it have been like to be Beethoven's piano, for example? Or Nelson's flagship? Hitler's bunker?

'You can keep that. I have it all on computer.'

Jenny raised her brows.

'I'm not totally technology adverse, dear. I just restrict myself to purchasing the very minimum I need to be part of modern life.'

Jenny held up her phone.

'I have one but it's not one of those smart ones everyone seems to have these days. Mine makes telephone calls.'

Jenny typed: *can we text?*

'I suppose that would be useful. I'll give you the number. I can't swear I'll remember to check it. If you need me urgently, get someone to telephone for you. When you're in the house and can't find me, leave a note on the hall table.'

Jenny gave her a thumbs up.

Bridget gave a pained smile. 'I can't say I like that gesture – so reminiscent of the Colosseum and a verdict of life or death. Odd how it's become ubiquitous, used on everything from cat videos to world changing announcements. But don't listen to me: I'm stuck in the past.'

Making a show of tucking her hand behind her back, Jenny smiled her agreement. She wasn't a fan either of the thumbs up, or any of the grading systems that had proliferated online. Everyone now was a critic and could destroy, mock and troll a person without even knowing them, as she found out to her cost as a few years ago when she'd first started playing for the orchestra. A mute black female violinist attracted the crazies. It was enough to make you give up on humanity. She gathered up the papers and slipped them in her bag with her music. Getting up, she tapped her watch.

'You have to run? I'll see you later maybe. Actually, dear, it would make life easier if you put your comings and goings on my calendar so I don't have to keep asking.'

Jenny noted down her shifts for the next two days in last few slots left to April and the upcoming Glyndebourne season, when she expected to be away. Jenny then washed her bowl, drank a quick glass of water, did the same for the tumbler, then dried both. She put them in the cupboard.

'I like a tidy person,' said Bridget, settling reading glasses on her nose.

That reminded Jenny. *When do the cleaners come?'*

Bridget frowned over the top of her spectacles. 'I do have a company in to clean the windows and polish the floors once a month but I'm afraid we keep it tidy ourselves, dear. I hope that won't be a problem?'

Jenny shook her head. Bridget sounded a little offended. *Didn't expect it*, she added on the iPad.

Hurrying to the station, aware she was running behind for her shift, Jenny tried to make sense this new piece of household information. It had to be Jonah leaving the flowers then. Or maybe Bridget was getting forgetful? From the impression Jenny had got of both, Bridget was far more likely to be the one bringing cut flowers into the house.

Anyway, it was only flowers.

Chapter 11

The House that Jack Built – Chapter 3 – Birth

'You've dug deep enough,' Captain Jack told his men. 'Now you can start to build her.'

And they obeyed, birthing me from course of brick and seam of mortar, eyelets of windows, ear flaps of doors. Seasons changed as my skeleton rose from the heath. The next spring, my head they tiled with slate brought from Wales on the slow-running arteries of canals once the ice had broken. Finally, the churned earth was turfed and gardens planted and I stood proud: a gentleman's residence.

Gallant House.

But I know those earlier people are with me still, the cave dwellers, Vikings, failed rebels and heedless maids. They lie in the soil with my foundations, whispering their secrets to the black heath.

Chapter 12

An oddly disturbing tale – not at all what she expected. Jenny put the manuscript away as her train drew in to Waterloo East. She wasn't sure what to make of Bridget's origin story for the house. Her landlady gave it the voice of a needy mistress rather than a family home. After all these years living there, unable to keep up repairs to expensive features like the balcony, did Bridget feel the house absorbed attention in that way? Was she even a little resentful of it even while she was loved it?

Jenny joined the commuters funnelling through the ticket barriers, her violin buying her a little extra room in the crowd like a pregnant woman's bump or old man's stick. That was welcome as she hated people breathing down her neck.

The history of the heath sounded fascinating, she thought, even if told obliquely. But did it have to be told in macabre images of burials and unearthing? It wasn't a reassuring thought for the already problematic night-time to dwell of the numerous sad ends that had been met on the spot. Bridget had made the foundations sound like catacombs. All old houses had seen deaths – of course they had – but Jenny thought that it was better sometimes not to know.

Louis waited for her in the café, eager to hear how her introduction to Gallant House had gone. Jenny was pleased to see that he was joined by Kris, who had chosen his favourite seat overlooking the river. A big man with sandy hair, jug handle ears and a flushed face, Kris appeared the least likely person to have the soul of a poet. That just went to show prejudging was a waste of time and energy; people were rarely what they seemed on the surface. She gave both a wave and dived into the staff room to stow her violin in her locker and put on her uniform.

When she returned, her manager beckoned her over. 'I've got you tea. We're quiet at the moment so, come on, tell us all about it.'

With a smile, she sat next to Kris. He kissed her cheek. 'What do you think of the inimitable Bridget?' His voice was a deep bass rumble, the kettledrum in the Festival Hall orchestra of visitors. 'Has she got you curtseying yet?'

Not quite yet. Maybe that's day two?

'And have you met my guy, Jonah?'

What was it about the man that everyone wanted to adopt him as theirs? She nodded.

'And?'

Jenny debated withholding the information about dragging Jonah into her bedroom but decided that an embarrassment shared was an embarrassment halved.

'You didn't?' Louis chuckled, after reading her confession. 'You don't let the grass grow, girl!'

'I bet poor Jonah felt all his birthdays and Christmases had come at once.' Kris patted her hand in consolation. 'A classy lady like you enticing him into her boudoir. Want me to have a word with him?'

She'd prefer just to forget it. *If he mentions how a nymphomaniac has moved in then yes. So what about the house?*

'The isle is full of noises,' said Kris. 'Sounds, and sweet airs that give delight and not hurts.'

The Tempest? She'd seen that at the Barbican.

'Correct.'

So I should just ignore the waltzing?

'Put it like this, I lived there three years and heard odd things all the time. I considered for a while that there was a mad woman in the attic ...'

'How very Jane Eyre,' murmured Louis.

'... But when I looked I just found bird nests and a broken window.'

Jenny felt a surge of relief. Her imagination had begun to people the mysterious attics with all kinds of horrors. It was just an attic floor.

'I decided after that not to worry. It never progressed – no ghostly apparitions, no clanking chains, just noises. Old houses have quirks.'

It was reassuring that she wasn't the only one to hear things. *Did you read Bridget's history?*

Kris rolled his eyes to the ceiling. 'Don't say she's trapped you into reading that already? Damn, that's fast work. She's been beavering away on that for a decade. I think it's become something of an obsession. I told her to get out more, volunteer as a reader at the local primary school, or join a gardening club, but she is attached to that place like a limpet to a rock. She says the best day in her life was the day she was able to do her shopping online.'

She never leaves?

'Not that I recall. Maybe she did at the beginning but by the time I left, I can't remember her going as far as the corner shop. She even gets Norman to make home visits when she needs a doctor. You've met Norman? He's always there on Tuesdays.'

She nodded.

'Don't sign on with him. I started out on his list but quickly caught on that he's no longer what he once was. They've shuffled him into a figurehead role and his retirement is imminent.'

Recommendations?

'Dr Chakrabarti if she's got space.'

How are you now?

'Aw, sweetie, thanks for asking. I'm much better, due to the tender loving care I've been receiving. If you'd met me a month ago, I wouldn't've been able to come out like this. I was getting as housebound as Bridget.'

'So she's an agoraphobic?' asked Louis. 'You never said, Kris.'

'I wouldn't describe her like that exactly as she loves her garden. Is there a word for someone who doesn't want to venture into the outside world?'

Scared, thought Jenny, feeling kinship with her landlady. That had been her for a year between fourteen and fifteen. The violin was the thing that had dragged her out of seclusion as it was the only way she could get to play with others. Her mother had always said it was a blessing she hadn't taken up with a solo instrument like the piano or she would never have emerged.

'I'm not sure I'd even call her a recluse as she loves having people round. I'd say she was an original. So, Jenny, what's on your agenda today?'

She told them about the performance of *Petrushka* that afternoon for invited schools. Thank goodness she wasn't involved in the children's workshop beforehand. No one escaped those raucous sessions without a headache.

Kris laughed. 'No, I've never thought of you as a particularly child-friendly person.'

Jenny was oddly hurt by this, it was like being told that animals didn't like you, suggesting some inherent flaw. *I like little ones.* The ones that did not require her to speak.

'I stand corrected. What's the story of that piece? Forgive my ignorance but the only ballets I have any idea about are *The Nutcracker* and *Swan Lake*. I saw those as a kid.'

'You went to see *Humanhood* with Hazel at Saddler's Wells last week,' said Louis.

'Doesn't mean I had the first idea what their performance was all about. I just went to admire the dancers.'

'See what I have to contend with?' said Louis in a stage whisper. 'He ogles Rudí Cole and then comes back home to me.'

Cole?

'The most gorgeous dancer God made.'

'But he probably doesn't give as good back rubs as you,' said Kris consolingly.

'He probably does.'

They both gave sad sighs in unison. These guys were such a good duo.

'OK, enough, *Petrushka*. What's it about?' asked Kris.

Jenny's fingers danced over the keys as they read over her shoulder. *Weird Russian story. Starts at a fair – usual street scene – then a puppeteer arrives with three marionettes – Petrushka, who's this kind of the fool figure in Russian stories, the ballerina, and the Moor.*

'The Moor?'

Totally not PC these days, but this was made up around 1910 in Russia. The dance suggests a love triangle between the three. Petrushka loves the ballerina, the ballerina fancies the Moor, and the Moor prefers his coconut tree.

'I see what you mean about not very PC. What do they do with it these days for schools?'

Jenny shrugged. Her business was the music not the visuals. *And then it gets wacky.*

'Only then?'

The next act is inside Petrushka's box – very surreal. The one after that is in the Moor's room where, after worshipping his coconut, he gets it on with the ballerina, breaking Peeping-Tom Petrushka's heart.

'And children watch this?'

That last part's implied. I'm more worried by the messages they get from the coconut bit. Last act the Moor chases Petrushka back to the fair and kills him for interrupting. The crowd is about to turn on the Moor but the puppeteer points out Petrushka is just a doll. He carries the slain mannikin back to the puppet wagon. Jenny was enjoying herself. She had always liked this bizarre story with its shifting perspectives.

'Is that the end?'

In a poorer ballet it would be, but no! She grinned, fingers hovering.

'Stop teasing us. Tell us how it finishes.'

The puppeteer is now alone and the stars are out. The spirit of Petrushka rises from the doll for a final defiant gesture. You are left wondering what is real and what is not? Was Petrushka to be considered a doll or human? And then, it's all a show anyway so what do we believe? Everyone was acting roles.

'Very Russian,' said Louis. 'Anguished and melancholy. I blame vodka and long winters.'

It's beautiful. There's a fantastic chord in the middle that's known as the Petrushka chord. Two major triads clash – it's really bold.

'I guess we aren't talking Chinese gangs?' said Kris.

She elbowed him. *C major and F# major.*

'I forget when I look at my hardest worker cleaning the tables that she had all this culture at her fingertips,' said Louis.

'And when she looks at her boss, she probably forgets that she's looking at one of London's top Jazz vocalists,' said Kris.

We are all overlooked treasures.

'If we weren't on duty that would be the cue for the group hug.' Louis stacked their empties on a tray and got up. 'Unfortunately, us overlooked treasures have overlooked customers to serve.' A small queue of early birds had gathered by the till with only Frieda to serve them.

Kris put his hand on Jenny's arm before she followed. 'I hope you like the house, Jenny, but I think it's a bit of an acquired taste. If you have any problems with Bridget or Jonah, let me know, OK? I can talk to them for you.'

She patted his cheek in thanks and blew him a kiss.

'I can't help worrying about you!' he called as she moved away to her cleaning station.

All the guys in her life seemed to feel that way. She'd prefer someone just to love her but that didn't appear to be on the horizon. A selfish schoolboy ex and two gay pals: not promising prospects. She really should make the effort to get back on the dating circuit. Now she had a nice place to bring someone home to without Harry looming in the corridor, maybe she would.

Chapter 13

Bridget, One Year Ago

Today I'll go beyond the front gate.

Duster in hand, Bridget stood at the window of Jenny's bedroom gazing down the path to the untrodden green beyond. This room had the best view of Blackheath; hers looked out on the garden, to the lilac tree and the shrubbery, a closed, safe prospect. She came in here at least once a day to challenge herself.

I'll put on my coat, make sure I have my keys in my handbag, and I will go for a walk in Greenwich Park. Simple. Nothing to fear in that. I remember the park well and it won't have changed too much, not that little red brick museum on the hilltop with the absurd ball on the roof. I'll watch the tourists straddling the line marking Greenwich Mean Time, holding sticks up to take selfies. Ridiculous, funny people. They'll make me laugh. Yes, that's what I'll do.

Admiral Jack had built the house here because it sat on the exact same longitude as the observatory. Bridget imagined the line running through her front door, through this room, and out through the lilac tree, hopping over the fence and continuing beyond. It was like Mercury, messenger of the gods, circling the

66

globe so fast you only saw the grass bending in his wake. It linked her to all those foreign countries that lay on the same line on the map: France, Spain, Algeria, Burkina Faso. Who lived in Burkina Faso? It sounded as made up as Timbuktu, which was also a real place apparently, in Mali, another country on the Prime Meridian. Ghana, Togo, the long stretch of the Atlantic and finally Antarctica. Bridget closed her eyes, summoning up the eerie vastness of the southernmost continent. Her husband's great-uncle had died with Scott somewhere out there. His family were full of people who went on adventures and never came back. The empire was casual about its sons. The Jack dynasty never learnt the lesson that it was safer to stay at home.

She idly wiped a fingerprint off the pane. Her new tenant must have tried to open it but the lower sash was broken. Only the upper one slid on its ropes. Bridget pulled it down a little to let some fresh air into the room. Jenny used a strong perfume; Bridget could still smell it even though her lodger had left several hours ago. Jenny favoured that fake strawberry scent that was in so many of the cheaper deodorants. Bridget found it unpleasant but she could hardly ask the girl to change something so personal.

Bridget emptied the bin into the plastic bag she carried. What were dead poppies doing in there? She should remember to mention to Jenny that there was a compost heap behind the gardener's shed and not to use the waste basket for recyclables. She hadn't yet made up her mind about her new lodger. Change was not easy, not for Bridget. Kris had filled the house with his booming bass and his immoderate laughter. She'd like the military forthrightness he brought to every situation, the precision with which he'd made his bed and folded his towels. He played his new songs to her, flattered her outrageously, and managed to head off any arguments with some novel distraction techniques learned from his army days. Her favourite was when he had prevented her bickering with Norman about who was suffering from the worst aches and pains by throwing his prosthetic at them both. As a dramatic gesture it had been priceless. She and Norman had been properly shamed into not mentioning health matters on a Tuesday again. In fact, it had been solemnly entered into the list of house rules right at the bottom. Number twenty-four: thou shalt not moan about thy health in company.

As for Jenny, she was best described as Kris's opposite. Her silence made others fill the gap.

We all end up talking too much around her, Bridget mused. She went into the bathroom to clean the mirror over the sink. And that can be dangerous.

When did I get to be so old? She turned away from the dark-eyed, hollow-cheeked woman who rose from the depths of the mirror-pool.

I'll soon deal with you, my pretty. She sprayed blue glass cleaner onto the surface, blurring her reflection. Like Dorothy in Oz making her foe melt. Switching to a J Cloth, she briskly polished the mirror and didn't meet her own gaze again.

The jury in Gallant House was still deliberating their verdict on Jenny. The vine liked her but the lilac tree wasn't sure. The birds in the attic resented her music and the mice in the pantry approved her choice of breakfast cereal. And as for Bridget ... It was like the space between dropping a stone into the old well in the kitchen courtyard and hearing it hit the water many feet below. Many had come and gone over the decades since Paul died. It would be interesting to find out if Jenny was one of the ones who stayed the course.

Taking her bucket of cleaning supplies, Bridget walked downstairs to prepare herself a light lunch as a reward for her housework. She paused in the hallway by the front door.

Today, I'll open it and walk right out and keep going, she promised herself. She touched the coat hanging on the peg, her best one, not the old one she used in the garden. It was getting a little dusty on the shoulders. That wouldn't do. She took it down and shook it. She should send it to the dry cleaners. Feeling in the pocket, she found a bent railway ticket. She checked the date. 8 January 2002. Definitely time it went to the cleaners. She wouldn't be able to go out, would she, not until it came back?

Relieved, she went into the kitchen, made herself a salad, and set about revisions on her latest chapter. She'd reached the part where she entered the narrative, the young bride of the much older Paul Whittingham. He had been the son of the first owner of the house not to bear the Jack surname. His mother had been the eldest of a string of daughters, and wrenched the place from being owned by Jacks to settling disgruntled under a new dynasty, that of the undistinguished Whittinghams. It hadn't lasted long, had it? She wondered if she should contact one of those ancestry websites and have a family tree drawn up. That way she could leave the house to some lucky Jack who was unaware he stood to inherit. The house would like that; she would feel happier back in familiar territory.

But what if the Jack the tree turned up were American, or, God forbid, Australian? She would have to take that into account, of course, when it came to choosing, vet the individual thoroughly. Better the house was left to charity than that. Her own relatives – all distant cousins – would fume when they found out what she had done only at the reading of the will. It would be like a scene from Dickens. Such a shame she by definition would be unable to attend.

I'll specify that my will is read in the drawing room, she decided. If there is an afterlife of the sort that allows me to come, then I'll make sure I'm present. I'll swing from the chandelier with the ghosts of past Jacks. That is something to look forward to in all the grim prospect of death. A last hurrah.

She looked down at her chapter.

Chapter 14

The House that Jack Built – Chapter Thirty – My Old Age

At first, I wasn't keen on Paul Whittingham. He never appreciated me in his youth, bringing his long-haired friends home to smoke spliffs in the snug and tell his mother that the smell came from the joss sticks. Employment sobered him. The hair was cut, a suit donned, and the city beckoned. He followed his father into Lloyd's shipping. How his ancestor the admiral would've scoffed to see his flesh and blood sitting at a computer screen analysing the risks of going through the Suez or around the Horn. Go out there and see for yourself, he would've bawled in his voice that carried over the storm. But Paul was made for comfort. Not for him was life on the High Seas; he was born for riding a desk and drinking down the pub with his friends. They all grew soft, rounded faces and bellies, hair retreating, courage shrivelling. The irony is that the Eighties made these men out to be heroes. Insurance, as he told the woman he was wooing, is much more interesting than it seems.

He was lying to her, of course. All the men who brought their wives here have lied to them one way or another. All have had mistresses. Sometimes that mistress was a woman, more rarely a man, on occasion the sea. Best of all was when their first love was me.

I dismissed this new wife of Paul's at the beginning, thinking she was too flighty for the flabby insurance broker. A dancer, he told his mother proudly. A prima ballerina. Or had been. Bridget Taylor had risen through the ranks of the Royal Ballet but, before she could take on any of the leading roles, she was diagnosed with rheumatoid arthritis. She rejected the temptation of pushing herself beyond her body's limits, resigned from the ballet and took to temping – quite a come down for one who had dreamed of her name in lights. And then Paul fished her from the typing pool. Needing a respectable date for the company Christmas dinner at the Savoy, his eye fell on the elegant secretary in her neat French suits. As the date turned into a relationship, he found he wanted to lose a few pounds, take up some active hobbies, even attend the opera with her if she so wished. They never went to the ballet. She didn't ask and he never suggested. He learnt tactfulness in his middle years.

His mother was delighted her lacklustre son had polished himself up. She handed over the house and moved to Bournemouth where her sister lived. A Jack returning to the sea – none of us were surprised.

Paul went on one knee to propose under the lilac tree while it rained down bridal confetti. He offered his bride his love, his considerable income, a share in his pension, and a house. It was me that decided the lady in his favour. She liked him well enough, but her first love had been dancing and that had died on her. Rather than be a widow for the rest of her life, she settled for the pleasant prospect I offered.

They hoped for children to fill the empty rooms, but Paul was never the most virile of men. His wife languished, wondering what was wrong with her. It was only after his accident that she discovered what she was missing.

71

Chapter 15

Bridget put a line through that last paragraph. It was all true: Paul in another age would've realised that he was gay, or at least more suited to celibacy. Instead he'd taken the route most thought inevitable in those days: a heterosexual marriage. That didn't mean she wanted that private failing laid open to all those who read her account so they could dissect and dismember. The house had witnessed it, as well as their mutual relief when they no longer had to pretend they enjoyed the marital bed after Paul had retired from active service. It was his sporting hobby that brought about that state of affairs. Tennis. Not a collision on court or anything of that nature, but a tumble from the balcony of the tennis club when he'd drank too much champagne – a more middle-class fate could not be imagined, he had always joked. She didn't want readers to get the wrong idea about Paul. He could be huge fun and was blessed with an acerbic sense of humour about himself. They'd liked each other quite fiercely. The way he dealt with his injury was the truly heroic period of his life. They may even have grown to love each other a little.

His injury had also set her free. With his tacit consent, she had looked elsewhere for sex. As long as there were no consequences, she was free to choose. The house had witnessed her embarkation on what was to be a series of affairs. It had been with their first tenant, an Italian naval officer who lodged with them for a glorious six months, that she'd discovered the sensuous woman hidden inside her. If only she could've still danced professionally, she was sure she would now have produced incandescent performances as the many lovers in the prima ballerina's repertoire. She hadn't known enough when she was twenty-one, even though she had thought she knew it all, in the way the young have to think they are the first to discover love. Silvano he'd been called, which sounded romantic even before he started whispering sweet demands in his husky Italian. They'd had their trysts up in the attics on a daybed she'd stored up there, safe from interruption as Paul kept to the ground floor. She'd even danced again, just a little, as her lover lay back on the cushions and watched. *Brava!* he'd said. *Brava!*

Everyone should have one lover like that Italian in their life, she thought. One Silvano.

'Mrs Whittingham! I'm just off!' called Jonah.

'I'm in the kitchen!' Her tenant was a very different kind of man to Silvano but equally interesting in his own way: a talented actor if she was any judge.

He stuck his head round the door. 'I'll be late – night shoot.'

'I'll leave the chain off the front door for you.'

'Thanks. Hard at work I see?'

'I don't suppose you want to read it, do you?' She was only teasing. Jonah hadn't proved to be a sympathetic audience for her work so she didn't pursue him any longer. She'd given up with Kris too, and Rose all that time ago, and the forgotten ones in between. Perhaps Jenny would be the right reader? Her bookshelf was promising.

'I'm afraid I won't have time. I've got to learn my lines.'

'You dodged that bullet very nicely, Jonah. Well done.'

He returned her smile with a brief one of his own. She'd been helping him have an easier time at college and on set by teaching him some of the tact than he'd missed out on in his unorthodox education.

'What do you think of Jenny?' she asked, curious what he'd made of this rival in the house.

'She's lovely and odd all at the same time.'

'Lovely and odd. Hmm, yes, I suppose that's accurate. She should fit in then. You find her attractive?'

He shrugged, clearly not wanting to answer that. 'She played me a tune on that fiddle of hers that put a knife right in the gut – it was amazing.'

'I thought I could hear music when I went to bed.'

'We were in the snug. Did we disturb you?'

She knew full well he'd gone out on the balcony again but unless she actually saw him on it, she didn't feel it her place to reprimand him. It meant he didn't fog up the snug with his little roll up cigarettes. She had an acute sense of smell and stale tobacco numbered amongst her least favourite odours.

'I enjoyed it. I might have a problem if she decides to practise in the middle of the night but as an evening serenade it was very pleasant.'

Jonah rubbed the back of his neck making the tattooed bolts twitch. Did he know that the Frankenstein creature in the book didn't have those; that it was the clumsy interpretation of film? The original had been stitched, not bolted, together. 'I spoke to her later too. We had what you'd call an embarrassing encounter. She thought she heard a ghost.' He gave her a straight look.

'Most people hear odd things here. I've always rather hoped there is a ghost but I've never seen one. Have you?'

He dropped his gaze and laughed; a short bark, not a belly laugh, of real humour. Poor Jonah: so sad under everything. All she could do though was offer him her affection to make up. 'I'm too unimaginative for a ghost to waste its time on me. Anyway, I told her not to worry.'

'Good. I hope she'd not naturally highly strung. I had another of those once.'

'Another what?'

'Highly strung tenant. Gillian her name was. She couldn't settle here, thought people were interfering with her things, told terrible lies about me. I had to get rid of her in the end.'

'You kicked her out of Gallant House?'

'I'm afraid I did.'

'Well, it's your house, your rules. I reckon Jenny will be fine, though, once she's got used to it.'

'I hope so. It's so good to have music here again. Kris leaves big shoes to fill.'

Jonah glanced up at the clock. 'Right, really must go. Don't work too hard now, Mrs Whittingham.'

She pointed to her cheek and, after a slight hesitation, he bent down to give her a perfunctory kiss. He didn't like doing that but she wanted him to see her as family. Everyone who lived under her roof had to understand that. He also never stopped calling her Mrs Whittingham even though she had invited him to address her as Bridget numerous times. Jonah was stubborn that way, a core of steel she didn't think she would bend. He quit the kitchen in a hurry and the next thing Bridget heard was the front door slam. She hadn't managed to break him of that habit either.

I could follow him, she thought. Trail him to the station, then to the set, and watch them film the next episode. Perhaps I could be an extra, sit in the waiting room with a bloodied handkerchief to my temple, or leg in plaster?

She got up, went to the kitchen door and put her hand on the knob.

What am I thinking? She snatched her hand back as if the handle burned her. People don't do that, they don't go haring after their lodgers to thrust themselves into their work. I'm turning into a crazy old woman with stupid urges. She sat down again at the table, gathered her papers and patted them into order. Maybe she would revise Chapter One again. That was her favourite. Yes, that would be best.

Part 2 – The Fool's Room

Fuoco – fire; *con fuoco*, in a fiery manner

Chapter 16

'I've been reading your file, Jonah, and it says that you've had anger management issues for years, ever since you were young, in fact. The first serious incident came when you were nine. Is that right?'

The way the inspector said it made it sound so tidy. Anger management. Turn left in the brain past accounts and record keeping. Jonah shrugged. 'Can I smoke?'

'Not allowed anymore,' said the female detective. 'Public building.'

'Yeah, and we can't have the boys and girls in blue dying of lung cancer thanks to all these chain-smoking criminals.' He twiddled his thumbs instead on his lap, so hopefully they wouldn't see his nervous gesture.

'So you view yourself as a criminal?' The inspector swooped in on his use of the English language.

'Reformed. But not yet kicked the habit of Mr Benson and Mr Hedges. Sorry, I can't remember your names.'

'DI Khan and DS Foley,' said Ms Foley.

'Like in foley artist? The guys who do the backing sound for films?'

'Sorry, not following.'

'Sergeant, we're getting off the point.' The inspector looked at his watch. They'd been at this for hours and they were all a little punch drunk with tiredness. Khan looked scruffier than ever. Maybe he did undercover work? No, too senior. He was just a mess. Let's just end this, thought Jonah.

'Of course, sir,' said the sergeant.

Jonah waited until she looked back at him. 'Next time you go to a film, stay for the credits. You'll see foley artists somewhere in the sound section. Cool job.' He sounded calm enough but inside he was crawling with unease. Strung-out. Desperate. Serious tobacco withdrawal.

'Jonah,' said the inspector sternly, 'you were telling us about your anger management issues.'

'Were we?' He gazed up at a cracked ceiling tile. Christ, he wanted to punch something. He could feel it building ... building ... He had to get out.

'Issues arising, it says here, from an abusive upbringing.'

'No!' Jonah slammed his forehead on the edge of the table. Blood streamed from a cut. 'Don't ...'

'Jonah!'

'Talk ...'

'Stop – you'll hurt ...'

'About ...'

'Call for a medic.'

'That.' With the last hit he slumped on the table, head buried in his arms. He wanted out.

Chapter 17

Jonah, One year Ago

Jonah turned a corner out of sight of the house, put his head down, hands on knees, and breathed through his nose. He wasn't going to throw up, he promised himself. Bridget had only asked for a kiss on the cheek, nothing more.

One ... and two ... and three. His school counsellor would be proud of him.

OK, mate, under control now? He could almost hear Mark's soothing tones, counting him down from his full-blown panic mode. Yeah, I'm OK. Just one of my tripwires: being kissed by an older woman, smelling that ladylike perfume, brushing up against the soft pillowy skin. Shit. Don't think about it.

Jonah forced himself to stand up and saw that his sudden stop in the middle of the pavement had persuaded a mother with a pushchair to cross the road. She was watching him with that suspicion he was so used to seeing, tugging her toddler close to her skirts, a hen gathering in her chicks. He tried to defuse her panic by smiling at them, but that only made it worse. Don't look at the nasty man, darling. She was practically running for the shops, toddler trailing, his packet of crisps scattering. Jonah could hear his wailing protests.

What the hell am I doing here? A year on and he still wasn't used to it. He looked up at the multimillionaire homes, the waxed-to-a-shine German cars parked on paved driveways, the manicured gardens. No wonder she ran. She probably thinks I'm housebreaking. Shows how much she knows. These houses would be a difficult target – alarmed and sensored up to the hilt, probably staff coming and going unpredictably, almost certainly big dogs. A bite on the arse was no joking matter, as Jonah knew from experience. A different grade of housebreaker went for this kind. If you wanted to make a quick quid, you went for the easy marks, the laptop left briefly unattended in a café, the house full of students where they'd each have a couple of grand of electrical goods, the neighbourhoods where no one bothered to watch for strangers as they didn't even know what the people downstairs looked like. You could jimmy a back door or window, grab whatever your contacts on the black market would fence, and be gone before anyone knew you'd been there. The police hardly bothered to investigate that kind of crime.

Jonah began to feel more at ease, more anonymous by the time he got to the train. There were a few people like him on the London Bridge service: scruffy, hungry-looking men, all watching each other to see where the trouble would start. Not with me, mate, he thought, keeping his eyes down on the free newspaper. The passengers would probably be gobsmacked to find out that the dangerous-looking guy with the tats was actually heading for afternoon classes in the Royal Academy of Dramatic Arts Gower Street studios. How fucking posh was that? He wanted to laugh at the preposterous sound of it: him at RADA! But laughing suddenly was another thing that didn't go down well in public.

His class would be immediately followed by his call at six for the night shoot: hair, makeup and wardrobe in a trailer parked in the backstreets of Hackney. Yeah, filming was so glamorous. He only had one line – 'Don't worry, love, we'll find out', spoken to some road traffic accident victim as they stretchered her into the ambulance – so he didn't need much time to prepare despite what he'd said to Bridget. It wasn't exactly Shakespeare this hospital soap, but the money was good.

The train rounded a curve and the Shard slid into view, the icy heart of the city. If he knew that more work like the soap was in the pipeline then he'd be in a financial position to move to somewhere more central where his presence would go unnoticed. The ugly truth was that he was stuck for now because his credit history was crap and his past unlikely to make him anyone's first choice of tenant. Gallant House was his best of bad options. To stay all he had to do was curb his language and fall in with Bridget's pretence they were a family.

Jonah wondered what the new tenant made of him. Kris had treated him like a younger brother, the wet-behind-the-ears squaddie in Bridget's brigade, Kris the NCO. Nothing Jonah said or did shocked him as he'd seen worse. Jenny's silence was interesting, by contrast, a challenge even. She wasn't really quiet though, was she? Her instrument was a means of expression, and so was her body language. At college, they were taught to think about what a character said with all of his or her faculties, not just speech. It was a useful training. For so much of his life others had told him what he thought or felt. Now he was able to return the favour and read that Billy fancied Rose even though he was supposedly in a steady cohabiting relationship; that Norman was intensely lonely, regretted most of his life choices and probably gay; that Bridget ... well Bridget was something else entirely, a kind of elegant disaster confined by her own neuroses to that house. He sometimes thought she was like a whirlpool, dragging what she needed to her.

But what about Jenny? What did she need? When she'd pulled him into her room the night before, he'd hoped for a second that it was an invitation to tumble on the bed. She was an appealing armful: masses of soft black hair, caramel skin, and as many curves as her violin. Out of his league though unless his luck changed. He was used to well brought up girls choosing him as their one walk on the wild side, quick shags at parties or in their bedsits. He'd long ago decided that he could be insulted or appreciate the benefits. Guess which door he'd chosen? It didn't make him popular with the guys on his course, unless they also hankered after a bit of rough. He'd been known to oblige if he was interested enough. Sex didn't mean that much to him. Means to an end.

He'd been wrong about Jenny though, as he should've anticipated from her hesitancy in the snug. Sex hadn't been on her agenda. She was just spooked, like a kid scared of things that went bump in the night. It was the first time that he could remember ever being the one to show another person that there weren't monsters under the bed, that noises were just the meaningless sounds of an old house.

And anyway, there was only one monster in the house – a tame one – and she'd been holding his hand.

Jonah slid in at the back of the movement class. He was coming to the view that it may have been a mistake to enroll on the full time BA Hons course as he was very behind with his assignments, not up to the mark academically, and the other students were complaining about him not pulling his weight in group projects. The little shits took everything so seriously. As if perfect scores were going to get them cast. If he made a second season of the hospital drama, he'd jack it in.

How much of the moaning was envy that he had an acting job, and how much it was genuine, he couldn't tell. He had little in common with the nice kids who joined this course at eighteen and nineteen, fresh from nice schools and nice families. He was ten years older and a lifetime apart from them. Only coming across an idealistic admissions tutor who wanted to bring a wider cross section of society into the Academy had gained him his place. Yet he also knew, and so did his classmates, that his very difference was what made him more employable. He could act and he wasn't identikit youth. Look at their head shots and you could swap many of them for the other with no one noticing. His ugly mugshot looked like he was posing for a police photographer at three a.m. – and it got him cast. He'd even heard one TV producer saying to the director of a film how refreshing it was that Jonah's looks hadn't been just for show but turned out to be genuine. He was gaining a reputation as a kind of mascot to any project that needed grit or a hard edge. His name, according to his agent, Carol, had been mentioned to the top casting directors. These sheltered people in the industry deferred to him as an expert. Jonah, what kind of weapons would gang members carry? Where would they get their drugs? How would they fight? It was fucking weird to be treated as someone special. He could take them to a part of town where he was the norm, not the exception; but they probably wouldn't last long there.

'Today, class,' began Maurice, the movement instructor, strutting like the boss screw in front of the prisoners, 'we're going to build on our mask work that we were exploring last week. You'll remember the clip of *Medea* I showed you?'

Fuck, yes. If he'd remembered what was on the schedule, he would've cut class. Jonah felt in his pocket, wondering if he could dip out for a quick smoke.

'We're going to act out the central event – Medea's slaughter of her children – not with words but movement.' Maurice sounded so reasonable, full of nothing-can-shock-a-real-actor bullshit, convinced by his own conviction that they had to plumb the depths and scale the heights. 'The incident happens offstage so it's up to the chorus to express the horror with our bodies. We react to the screams. Here, I'll play you a clip of the soundtrack we'll be using.'

Cries of 'no, Mummy, no!' and childish screams rent the air. Voices ripped the room apart into tattered lumps like flesh. Fuck, the sound engineer was good. In his mind's eye, Jonah could see great gashes on the walls and ceiling as blood seeped, darkness encroached. He slumped against the skirting and leaned his head back. One … and two … and three.

Maurice switched off the recording. 'Remember, this is the only murder of children in Greek drama to happen in cold blood rather than through temporary madness, and with the perpetrator – the mother – going unpunished at the end. It is meant to shock in every way, so nothing is too much here.'

Everyone but Jonah seemed to relish the idea of reacting to infanticide. Fucking pathetic. Anger was better than panic. Arseholes. He watched them cynically from the side as they limbered and stretched. A couple laughed nervously as they held up Greek masks to their face. It was at times like this that he felt a million miles away from them.

'Jonah, are you going to join us?' Maurice offered him a mask.

He shook his head. If he stretched out an arm, they'd see his hand wasn't steady.

'You need to complete the course to gain the credit – and that means joining in.'

Jonah could feel the rage building at the patronising tone. The tutor was the king turd of these little shits.

Maurice was now watching him warily, instincts picking up that an explosion was close. 'Jonah, would you like to … er … take a breather?'

And let them all prance away while he threw up outside? Fuck that. 'This is about child murder, right?' Jonah snatched the mask from Maurice's hand. The chatter subsided. The neat little party tricks some were trying out to gesture to horror faltered. 'That fucking crazy mother slits the throats of her kids to spite their fucking father? You want us to react to it?' He stalked into the middle of the room. 'Here's what I fucking think about Medea.' He stomped on the mask. 'Her kids are dead and she waltzes off Scott free. The chorus should fucking well have ripped her to shreds.'

One of the girls in the class made a move as if she were going to argue, but Maurice motioned her back. Now was not the moment for a feminist intervention.

'No excuses. No "he had it coming". No one should do that to a child.' Jonah kicked the mask away. 'No one.' He was shaking. He recognised the adrenaline. It would take just one wrong word, one snide comment, and he'd probably end up in jail for GBH.

'You're right, Jonah,' said Maurice, finding the right words to avoid a fist in the face. 'We forget that this should also be about the children's right to life because the play focuses so much on Medea's anger. I don't think any movement training would come up with a more eloquent reaction than yours so I'm going to leave it there. Put the masks away please. I'm going to anticipate next week's lecture on Jacques Lecoq and mime techniques instead. Everyone, take five. Jonah, a quick word please.'

'I'm going out to smoker's corner.'

'Then I'm coming with you.'

Jonah went out, expecting a reprimand. To prepare, he shoved his anger back in the cage where he kept it, driving it in with mental whips and prods. The smoking zone, huddled in a dank alley at the side of the building, was deserted. He went through his calming routine, getting out his cigarette papers, pealing one off, pinching just the right amount of tobacco, squeezing, teasing it out, rolling, sealing … As he brought it to his lips, Maurice offered him a light.

'All right now?'

Of course the fucking turd of a movement tutor could read his body language. Jonah drew smoke into his lungs, held it, then exhaled over their heads. Maurice was calmly smoking his own factory-made brand.

'Yeah.'

'I'm sorry. I should have included a warning at the beginning of the class that we were dealing with difficult subject matter.'

'I'm not a fucking snowflake.'

Maurice smiled wistfully. 'No, you're not. But your reaction reminded me just what I was dealing with. Others in the class may be carrying their own baggage and hide it better. It was good you did what you did – cathartic for us all.'

'I broke a prop.'

'Forget it. I won't mention it to the bursar if you don't.' They stood smoking in companionable silence for a minute or two. 'How's the job going?'

'Good. Got some interesting shoots coming up.' He felt steadied, calmer thinking of the job that validated him in this world of aspiring actors. OK, OK: he'd overreacted and Maurice was taking it well. Maybe the movement tutor wasn't so bad?

'Great. We're all envious. Look, er, Jonah, I have something I want to ask you.' As suddenly as they had risen, Jonah's spirits sank to the red zone of his internal petrol gauge. He knew what was coming. Maurice stubbed out his cigarette on the edge of the receptacle for fag ends. 'I like to relax at the weekend with a different kind of roll up, you know what I'm saying? But my normal supplier's gone away for a while.'

Doing time probably, thought Jonah bleakly.

'I don't move in that kind of world normally.' Maurice laughed softly at the idea. 'So I wondered if you knew anyone?'

Because as far as Maurice was concerned, Jonah was and always would be part of the drug culture, the hotline for these nice refined people to the Colombian cartels and their London middle men. This wasn't the only request he'd got at RADA but it was the first from a tutor.

Jonah considered a number of replies. A threat to report the approach? Blackmail: silence in exchange for a good grade and stellar references in future? Laughter? Outrage? The first two he dismissed as being against his nature; the second two required more energy than he could muster right now.

He dropped his cigarette and ground it out under his shoe.

'No, I don't. I've been sober for four-hundred and eighty-six days. Ask me again and I'll punch you.'

Leaving Maurice gaping, Jonah strode away. Walking backwards a few steps, he flicked the BSL sign for 'wanker'. Fuck mime anyway.

Chapter 18

Jonah, Two Years Earlier

'So Jonah, how're things?'

His probation officer leafed through a file. Buried under an unmanageable caseload, Mr 'Call-me-Billy' Riley probably hadn't had time to read through it in advance of his eleven o'clock. The manila cover only had one handwritten note on it: the date of Jonah's release from Belmarsh some six weeks ago. The rest would all be on the computer. Jonah didn't know why they still bothered with paper.

'Good, thanks, Mr Riley.' Jonah hunched over, hiding the spiderweb tattoo on his fingers. The blue plastic chair rocked where it had come adrift from the screws on one side. He rebalanced his weight before it came apart entirely.

'Call me Billy.'

Like hell he would. Mr Riley was system and Jonah didn't want that masked by false friendliness.

'Any work come in, Jonah?'

'Yeah, maybe. I got a call back for a part.'

Mr Riley looked up, a smile of surprise crinkling his cheeks. He had been a sceptic when Jonah mentioned that he'd been taken on by an agent. 'You did? That's great!'

'It's just a small part – drug addict in alley.'

Mr Riley's pleasure dimmed a little. Well shit: what did Call-me-Billy expect? That Jonah would go straight from prison to landing a part as the RSC's Hamlet? 'And you're pleased?'

'Hell yeah. My agent says it's a good role. He's got three lines – gives a vital clue to the police.'

'Is it for anything I might watch?'

'I dunno.' Jonah scratched at a graze on his palm, caught himself, and stopped before it bled on his smartest jeans. 'They said it's one of those police procedurals with a quirky detective.'

'I like those. I'll definitely watch you when it comes out.'

'I might not get it.' If his life ran true to form, he'd be rejected.

'I understand, but well done anyway. I'm pleased for you.' Mr Riley found the page he wanted in the file and popped the nib on his ballpoint pen. 'So what's the quirk?'

'What?'

'Of the detective: jumper fetish, Asperger's, tortured past, opera lover?'

Jonah shrugged. He hadn't watched that kind of programme inside, or even before that. 'Don't know yet. I only read my scene.' And when he'd read it, he'd been thinking how it was too fucking polite for life as he knew it on the street; but he guessed the TV people had to think about audience and watershed and shit.

'Best of luck then. OK, here we are. Your psychologist is very pleased with your progress.' Mr Riley put a little tick in the margin.

The tightness Jonah habitually felt in his chest loosened a little at this rare praise. It was like he'd been given permission to breathe.

'I get the impression Dr Wade likes you.' Mr Riley grinned. 'Rose says you're quite her star pupil. I'm jealous.' Again he tried for the matey tone Jonah despised. He knew what they thought, these government paid hacks, how unequal this conversation really was despite the attempt to make superficial connections. Billy Riley was a similar age to Jonah, in his late twenties or early thirties; but Jonah guessed that was where the resemblance ended. He would put money on Billy Riley's course having been a smooth one from school to college to training in the probation service, not at all like his own checkered one that had set him on the path to this wobbly chair. If Jonah was 'drug addict in the alley', Billy Riley looked like he'd been sent up for a role as 'hipster bloke in pub': lush brown beard, heavy rimmed glasses, weird-as-shit checked shirt and bow tie. Jonah also noted the trilby on top of the filing cabinet next to the exploding spider plant that was sending escapee plantlets roping down the grey wall in a mass breakout. He was never there when Mr Riley left work but Jonah could imagine him walking down the busy high street to Angel tube station, tailored coat flapping, rolled umbrella tapping, content that he'd made a difference. For all the joking about jealousy and Dr Wade, there was probably some hot girlfriend at home and they'd go out for – what did they call it? – tapas? Spicy shit on little plates, cost loads. Yeah, tapas. They'd laugh over Call-me-Billy's anecdotes about the ragtag army of ex-cons he tried to reform, then snuggle down together under freshly laundered sheets for no-kink sex and untroubled sleep.

It would be good to swap lives just for a bit. Even if just for the night with the girlfriend.

Smiley Mr Riley was definitely getting some. And for that alone most of Jonah's fellow inmates would want to give him a good kicking. It didn't take much to earn one.

'Jonah?'

He realised he'd been drifting again in dark thoughts. 'Um, yeah, Dr Wade's been great. She was the one who suggested I try out for small parts – got me an agent who likes my ex-offender CV. Adds credibility, she said.'

'That's new: for an employer to find it a plus. You never told me how that came about.'

'I told Dr Wade about the production of *Henry V* I was in.' Jonah was cautiously proud that he now said it the right way to an educated man like Mr Riley – Henry the Fifth. When he'd first been given the script, he'd thought it was like the *Star Wars* saga, Henry part five. Fucking embarrassing to be corrected. The drama teacher had cut short the laughter and told the others that Jonah was right in that Shakespeare really went in for sequels.

'I remember now. I've got something about that in your file. You were the lead, weren't you?'

Jonah nodded. So many lines to learn but he'd a lot of time on his hands and discovered he had a good memory. Who would've thought? Certainly not any of the teachers who'd given up on him. The king had masses of words; it was like he had Google in his brain and could just keep on pumping out new combinations. For Jonah, who had very little say, or *to* say, in his life, finding the speeches tumbling from his lips had felt like discovering the kick of a new drug without any side effects. 'You should've seen me: I fucking killed that role, Mr Riley. Now Dr Wade's helping me with my application for drama school. She says I should aim for the best.'

Mr Riley spread his hands over the file. 'Then I'm superfluous to requirements.'

Good word 'superfluous'. Old Billy boy had a bit of Henry the Fifth in him. 'That's one of the things I wanted to ask you, Mr Riley.'

The probation officer waved a little impatiently. 'It's Billy. And, Jonah, I have to tell you that I know nothing about acting. Zilch. Nada.'

'Not that, it's just, I mean, do you think I'm too old for this? Am I wasting my time?' He didn't like confiding but who else could he ask?

'On drama school? I can't see why. You're only twenty-seven. Quite a few of my friends have gone back into education to do a masters or retrain. We're all thirty so got a few years on you. That isn't that old, is it? Damn, I hope not.' He offered another of his slightly self-mocking smiles. 'Anyway, they'll not let you in if they think they're wasting a place on you. You do know it's really competitive?'

Jonah nodded.

'I see you did some GCSEs and an A levels while you were at Belmarsh?'

'Yeah.'

'That might not be enough. You'll be OK with rejection if it comes? Not lose it like before?'

'I've got it under control.' He hoped he had. He was sometimes scared of himself, what he might do when pushed.

'If they take you, have you given any thought how you're going to fund your studies?'

Money. It always came back to money. Jonah had done terrible things for it in the not-so-distant past. No longer. 'They have bursaries and Dr Wade says she has a friend, her old landlady, who takes lodgers at below the market rate if they're in the Arts.' The woman was a nutter to pass up income like that but he wasn't going to complain. 'And I was planning to keep with my job at Timpsons for the moment.' Key cutting and shoe mending weren't the most exciting of professions but it was a regular income and his boss had a soft spot for ex-offenders; he didn't mind a bit of crude language as long as it wasn't in front of customers. Jonah knew he was lucky to have found the position.

'That's good. Jonah, you'll probably hear this a lot around acting, so let me be the first …' Mr Riley paused, relishing his punchline.

'Hear what?'

'Don't give up the day job.'

Now Jonah wanted to give him a good kicking too.

Chapter 19

Jonah, One Year Ago

Jonah arrived home at four in the morning expecting the house to be silent with all the good little inhabitants tucked up in their beds. Dumping his jacket on a peg, he was about to go up to his bedroom when he heard someone moving about in the snug. He thought for a moment of Bridget's wish for a ghost but crushed that as fanciful. He pushed open the door to find Jenny stretched out on the floor. Christ, was she all right?

'You OK?'

She looked up, startled. He noticed now (how could he not?) that she was wearing only leggings and a sports bra. Her reply was a cautious nod. Rolling on her side, he had a good view of her toned little backside as she got up.

'Anything I can help with?' He hoped his grin was roguish rather than predatory.

She pointed to the back of her neck and grimaced.

'Cramp?' She shook her head. 'Back pain?' She nodded. 'Want a massage?'

Picking up her tablet, she wrote. *Thanks, but it's not muscle pain. Yoga helps.*

95

'Is that from playing the violin?'

She waved her hand in a fifty-fifty gesture.

'So when it gets bad in the night you have to get up and stretch?'

She nodded.

'Can you get something for it from the doctor?'

The answer this time was a roll of the eyes as if she hadn't thought of it.

'Would distraction work?' Had he really just said that? Must be something about clandestine meetings in the small hours that made his mind go there.

Jenny was no fool. She narrowed her eyes at him and drew a question mark in the air.

'It's just that I heard that there are various ways of relieving pain through natural hormone release.'

Hands went to her hips in an 'oh yeah?' gesture, but she was almost smiling. Good, she didn't feel threatened then.

'And if you wanted to try it, you know where to come. Last door along the corridor.'

She picked up her iPad again. *I'm not a slut.*

He grinned. 'No, but I am.'

Upstairs in his little room he waited until he heard Jenny's door click closed. Shit. It had been too much to hope that on the second night she'd fall for his charms. Until she told him to back off, he'd keep trying. Setting the alarm for eleven a.m., he stripped and dumped his clothes by the door with the pile from the day before. He'd banned Bridget from coming in here months ago so it didn't matter that he was a pig. It had been a total fucking shock to find that she'd considered cleaning his room part of the service. She in turn had been surprised when he'd described it as an invasion of his privacy, telling him she'd always done it for all her tenants. 'I'm the house mother!' she'd protested. He had countered that she was really a 'nosey old cow', which had led them into one of their surreal discussions of politeness. The argument had ended with him agreeing that 'Nosey Parker' was slightly more acceptable and her promising not to come in unless invited. That was the only way to handle Bridget: agree to the things she thought important, hold firm to your own priorities.

Jonah flopped on the bed and let out a sigh of contentment. Next week they were moving on to the big scenes in his storyline so he'd not be at college. That would give him much needed space from Maurice and the other sirens singing him back onto the rocks. Fuck 'em.

OK, calming thoughts before sleep, that's what Dr Wade said. This was probably the nicest room he'd ever been in. He admired the theatre posters he'd got at Christmas as a present to himself: *The Ferryman*, *Anatomy of a Suicide*, Andrew Scott's *Hamlet*. Wouldn't it be amazing to be in a show like that himself one day? Maybe this plotline would give him the exposure that might get him noticed? He switched off the light. See, Jonah, in this darkness you don't have to be scared. No cellmate was going to attack him in his bed, no mother come in to kiss him goodnight. He'd been in the pit and was climbing out the other side, almost at the top. All that was required is taking each day one at a time. Four-hundred and eighty-seven days sober.

Chapter 20

Jonah, Twenty Years Ago

Jonah chucked his school bag on the step of his house. Bins tomorrow. If he didn't put them out then no one would. He opened the side gate and dragged them down the alleyway. They rumbled like a train in a tunnel, which made him the engine driver. Bumping each over the awkward step at the end, he steered them down the cracked concrete path, through the gate, and left them on the pavement. People sneered at bin men but Jonah thought it might be quite a cool job, driving a great big truck and taking stuff to the dump.

Pulling out his key, he opened the front door and let it slam shut. That would tell his mother that he was home. The old lady who had the flat downstairs was deaf-as-a-post-dear when she wasn't wearing her hearing aids so didn't care how much noise he made. She always gave him a little present for putting her bin out, usually a Rich Tea biscuit which Jonah didn't like as it went all gooey in the mouth but he took it anyway. He was always hungry. Mum said he was growing too fast for her to keep up.

Thinking about food, Jonah bounded up the stairs and into

the little kitchen. Their flat was made up of three rooms: bedroom at the front, kitchen and bathroom at the back. He'd picked up some groceries on his way home from school, things that were easy to cook. Dragging the low stool over to the sink, he filled the kettle and put it on. The corner shop had a new Pot Noodle for him to try. Mr Aziz had kept it aside for him and said it was selling at a promotional price, just twenty pence. Jonah wasn't sure he believed Mr Aziz but he was grateful because it meant he still had a little money to buy a banana. They'd had an assembly at school about eating fresh fruit and vegetables so he was trying to include some in what he ate each day, even if it meant eating the yucky peas at lunchtime.

Jonah heard a sound from the front room, a kind of groaning. That meant Mum had company and he was to stay in here. That was bad as he was desperate for the loo. He wasn't allowed in the bathroom in case he met one of her visitors. He should've gone at school but hated the smell in the boys' toilets. He was busting. Could he risk it?

He peeked out onto the landing. If he was really quick he might make it. He was so nervous he could barely pee. Come on, come on. He eventually managed, zipped himself up and washed his hands. Like a hunted creature, he scurried back into the kitchen and only breathed easily when the door was closed. He dreamed sometimes of having his own room, but he doubted he'd ever be so lucky. Mum had explained that she couldn't afford anything better than this flat in Barking. 'We're barking mad about Barking, aren't we, Jonah?' she'd say, then go into peels of raucous laughter.

Jonah didn't mind Barking. His school was OK. He got free meals so that was good. The teachers were kind and patient. They never hit him for getting something wrong or being in the wrong place. He wished he could sleep there too but the teachers all went home at night so he wasn't allowed.

Standing on the stool, he carefully poured the water into the

Pot Noodle and stirred. It smelt really good. Now all he had to do was wait.

He sat down on the stool and got out his homework diary. Mrs Peters had asked them all to make a volcano because that's what they had studied today. It could be a model, a picture, or even a cake. She had said there were good ideas on the Internet how to do this. Jonah had been allowed to check on the class computer before he went home and decided that a model would be best. He'd thought the empty Pot Noodle container could work as a base if he put a cone of cardboard around it. He could perhaps put a little candle inside. The local church had them: he'd seen this when his class went on a multi-faith visit; he might be able to take an old one, maybe? He could ask the priest. And what if he painted the pot red? Then it would look like the caldera (his new word for the day). That would be so cool! Mrs Peters might even be so impressed that she would include his in the class display.

On the scrounge for materials, Jonah rummaged around in the bottom cupboard. A previous tenant had left a pizza box in there. He opened it and sniffed. Apart from a grease stain, it was pretty clean. Now he was in business! With a grin, he rubbed his hands and chuckled softly. He had his volcano and his base. There were no paints but he had a brown Sharpie he'd borrowed from the craft table. If he started colouring now, he might be able to finish the ground today. Tongue tucked between teeth, he scribbled to and fro. The greasy bit didn't take the pen so well but maybe he'd be able to cover that with an orange ribbon of paper to stand in for lava flows?

Pot Noodle! Leaving the Sharpie and box on the floor, he jumped up to test it. One tentative mouthful told him it was as good as it smelt. He sat cross-legged in front of his project and took a few more mouthfuls.

'Jonah, come here a moment!' his mother called.

Jonah froze. His mother never called him in while she had visitors. Had she heard him in the bathroom?

'Jonah?'

Heart thumping, Jonah scooted back into a corner. If she just glanced in, she might not see him. The door to the kitchen squeaked open.

'There you are, lovie! Whatever are you doing down there with that dirty old cardboard?' She stepped on the box, knowing full well that he'd been colouring it. Mum had her ways of showing her displeasure. Her legs were ugly, spotted with horrible ulcers and sores. He didn't like seeing them. 'And eating that rubbish?' She snatched the noodle pot from him and chucked it in the sink. Quick as a snake, she grabbed his arm and pulled him up. 'He does like such unhealthy snacks. I can't seem to stop him buying them.' She gave a false laugh, the pressure of her grip in contrast to the light and airy manner.

'That's fine. Boys will be boys,' said the man in the doorway.

Jonah didn't dare look up. All he could see were polished lace-up shoes and suit trousers with a pale grey pinstripe.

'Now Jonah, my friend here said he wanted to meet you. He is very fond of boys your age and just wants a little chat in the front room, OK?'

It was definitely not OK. He wasn't so young that he didn't know about stranger danger.

She must've seen the refusal in his eyes. 'I'll be very cross if you aren't polite to him. There's nothing to be scared of. I need you to do this for me.' Her fingers were leaving bruises.

Bewildered, trapped, Jonah let her pass him over to the gentler grip of the visitor.

'You can call me Thomas,' said the man, leading him into the front room. 'Just sit next to me and we'll have a little talk.'

When the man had gone, Jonah lay for a long time on his side. His mother came back in, flitting around the room with the frantic energy she sometimes had. Thomas must have given her something.

'See, it wasn't so bad, was it?' She swept the debris of a few days into a rubbish sack – the cans, the takeaway containers, the syringes. Jonah noted bleakly his volcano base and Pot Noodle at the bottom. 'You liked him, didn't you? He's always so kind and generous to me. I wouldn't let anyone nasty near you, I promise.' Dumping the sack outside the door, she came back and knelt beside him. 'I'm sorry if you're upset but you'll get used to it, won't you? Just forget about it. None of it matters. Here.' She handed him one of her precious cigarettes. 'You've always wanted to try this. Have a little puff. It takes off the edge.'

He shook his head. He wasn't here – wasn't thinking – wasn't remembering.

'Don't be a naughty boy, Jonah. Try it! It'll help.'

Afraid what she'd do next if he refused, Jonah drew some of the smoke into his mouth. He coughed. She was right. His mind blurred a little. What did any of this matter?

Then he began to cry. He wanted to die. His mother pressed her cheek against his, crying with him, whispering her apologies, calling him her little man, her sweet angel.

But it wouldn't stop her doing it all again.

A week later, Mrs Peters called everyone up one-by-one to show their models and pictures and say how they did them. Jonah sat at the back in his new hoodie that Thomas had bought for him on his last visit two nights ago. It had a hood with shark's eyes and teeth. If he pulled it down over his forehead, Jonah became the shark; if he pushed it back it looked like he was being eaten by the ring of teeth.

'Jonah, no hoods in the classroom, please,' called Mrs Peters.

Jonah tugged it off reluctantly. He preferred being the shark.

Saleem had a cross-section diagram on a large sheet of paper, arrows pointing to the main parts of the volcano. Masha and her mum had baked a cake with fudge icing – this was the class's favourite as they would get to eat it at the end of the day. Jonno had built a model out of a plastic pudding bowl with a little nightlight inside. It was stuck to a pizza box.

'How clever!' exclaimed Mrs Peters. 'I love how you've junk modelled this, not brought anything specially for the project, except that little light maybe?'

'Dad had that in his odds-and-ends drawer, left over from Christmas,' said Jonno. 'We didn't have to buy nothing.'

'Anything,' correctly Mrs Peters. 'Didn't have to buy *anything*. Excellent. Who does that leave on your table? Jonah, how did you get on with your project? Did you draw me something perhaps?'

Jonah saw the Pot Noodle in the bin. It was rubbish now – and would've been rubbish even if he'd made it. Nowhere near as good as Jonno's. He'd had no labels, no fudge icing, no little night light left over from Christmas. Panic rose as he felt tears threaten. He couldn't cry.

'Didn't do it. Model volcanos are stupid,' he said instead.

'Jonah, that's not very polite. Models are not stupid; they can teach us something.'

They teach that his life was worth only putting in the bin, that Mum loved her smokes and her needles more than she loved him, that he was dirty, and angry, and stupid, stupid, stupid!

'Jonah? You must have done something. Maybe some research?'

He could tell she wanted him to say 'yes' but he hadn't. Rage boiled up from the bottom of his stomach and out of his head. He threw his anger out at all and any target, pushing his table over, kicking his chair. Children screamed and darted out of the way. Mrs Peters tried to approach but he caught her ankle with his toecap and she backed off.

'Children, outside now! Early break,' she ordered sharply. 'Angus, fetch Mr Vaughan from next door.'

Jonah ripped up the diagram with arrows, ground his fist into the chocolate cake and smashed the volcano with the little nightlight left over from Christmas into a million pieces. Now it was him, lying on the floor, ruined. He stamped on the remains and howled.

And then he really was lying on the floor. Mr Vaughan had his hand pressed firmly between his shoulder blades, Mrs Peters was holding his ankles to restrain his drumming feet.

'Hush now, you'll hurt yourself,' she crooned. 'Jonah, you have to stop this.'

The fact that they weren't angry with him knocked the fight out of Jonah. He sagged and began sobbing.

'There now. That's it. Just cry it out.'

Mr Vaughan picked him up in his arms and carried him to the medical room. Jonah put his arm over his face so no one would see him. He was shaking with humiliation and the after-math of his emotional eruption. The teacher placed him on the bed and covered him with a light blanket.

'Stay there, Jonah. I'll sit with you until you feel better. Someone will phone your mother.'

When Jonah screamed and began to fight, they changed their minds about contacting his mother first and phoned social services instead.

They had eventually to call his mother too, of course. There was no easy escape for Jonah. When she learned the serious-ness of their concerns, she did her usual thing of pulling herself together and presenting her best face. She turned it into 'Oh yes, I'm worried about Jonah too, so moody. I don't know what to do with him.' Jonah listened in numb exhaustion as she described how he had stamped on the volcano model she had so lovingly helped him put together, just because he thought it not good enough. 'It's so difficult managing as a single mother. Sometimes I'm scared of my own son – these rages of his.'

Jonah could sense the sympathy in the headteacher's room swing from him to her. Like a sunlamp on the classroom tortoise,

Mum began to stick her head out a bit further, making up more stories about his tantrums.

'I'm afraid, Miss Brigson, that the family support worker doesn't have a space to see you both until next month. Do you think you'll manage until then?' asked Mrs Proudie, the head.

'I'll manage,' she said bravely. 'I'm so sorry about Jonah's outburst. I hope he didn't do too much damage?'

'He upset quite a few of his classmates, I'm afraid. I think it best that we isolate him for the rest of the week. He can go back into his class next week. Mrs Peters suggests he write a letter of apology to the children whose work he ruined.' The head looked at him for the first time in a while. 'You need to say sorry to Masha, Jonno and Saleem, Jonah. They spent a lot of time and energy on their homework.'

Jonah nodded.

'It was very naughty of you to destroy it. Perhaps it's best if you go home for the rest of the day?'

Jonah shook his head.

That wasn't welcome to his mum either. She probably had callers lined up. 'Jonah will be good now, I promise. Won't you, Jonah? Tell, Mrs Proudie. Give her your word.'

'I'll be good.' His whisper was enough for the two women to decide that it was a promise. Mum left saying she'd be back at home time to collect him.

She wouldn't. She always said she hated mixing with the other mums and dads. Stuck-up cows, she called them.

Jonah sat in the corridor outside the head's office. When two children from his class came to collect the register he could hear their whispers and see them straining to catch a glimpse of him. He'd become famous in the small world of the school, drawing hatred in particular for destroying the cake. He wanted to tell someone the real reason why he'd done it, how he had unexpectedly turned into a volcano right in the middle of the classroom, that he hadn't meant to do any of the things he'd done, that he'd just lost it.

But he'd also lost the words. And he was so scared. Mum would still be there in the evening. He was in enough trouble as it was.

Mrs Peters sat with him at lunchtime. She shared her crisps with him as he was having trouble eating the fish fingers and peas today. She asked to see the apologies and swallowed hard when she saw that he had drawn a volcano on each, surrounded by stick people. He'd drawn her a little taller with her curly red hair. He'd just written one word. Sorry.

'Jonah, is there something you want to tell me?' she asked.

He shrugged.

'I've not known you to get so angry before.'

'Sorry.'

'I know you're sorry. I was just wondering what caused it?'

His breath caught in his chest. The hoodie was swallowing him. He stripped it off and threw it in the lost property basket and immediately felt better. He was at school. He was safe. 'I'm fine.'

'Your lovely hoodie!' Mrs Peters took it out and tried to hand it back. 'It's new, isn't it?'

'Don't want it.'

'But your mother will be so sad if you waste something like this!'

He began to shake so folded his arms across his chest. 'Don't care.'

'Right. OK.' Mrs Peters looked at him warily, folded the hoodie and put it in her canvas bag. 'Let's leave that for the moment. This afternoon I'd like you to read a chapter of your story book and write me a paragraph about what you think is going to happen next. Don't forget to look for chances to vary your sentences. Use semicolons if you can, and speech marks – you sometimes forget those. Hold back on the exclamation marks.' She tried a smile but Jonah didn't feel like playing along with this game where everything was normal. 'Right, I'll come by at break to see how you've got on.'

106

Patting his shoulder, she dipped her head into the secretary's office to say she was leaving and someone else needed to keep an eye on Jonah. Masha's mother was on the front desk.

'Oh I'll keep an eye on him all right,' she muttered. 'Spoilt little brat. We worked on that cake for hours.' The other receptionist murmured something about Jonah hearing her, but Masha's mother said she didn't care, that he needed to understand what he had done.

Jonah opened his book at the point where the hero, Jimmy, was fighting a giant werewolf. He read a few lines but none of it made any sense today. He felt so tired, and frightened, and weaponless. No one had leapt in to rescue him and he realised now that they wouldn't. Mum was too powerful.

Mrs Peters had asked for a paragraph on what happened next. *Jimmy got eaten*, wrote Jonah. He remembered that she wanted semicolons and speech marks. *'That was tasty,' said the wolf. 'Bring me another child to eat;'* He thought that was probably the wrong place for a semicolon but he wasn't sure what it did. *So they brought him lots of children!!!!!!!* He liked exclamation marks. He'd only used seven. Sometimes he filled half a page with them if something really dramatic happened. *The wolf got so fat he couldn't fight any more and they killed him. Everyone was happy. Except for the children who got eaten. And the wolf.*

Jonah thought he knew what was coming when he got home – Mum usually slapped him when she was really angry – but he was wrong. She was worryingly calm. The cupboards in the kitchen had some actual food in them and she'd tidied up the front room so that his little bed was neatly made and hers folded away in its sofa mode.

'I'm very disappointed in you, Jonah,' she said in her airy voice, the one that told him she had been using her special medicine recently. She'd float for a bit, then slump, then sleep. He might have a quiet evening. 'To say that I had destroyed your volcano – that's a lie.'

He hadn't said it but he knew to keep his mouth shut. Mum had her own world of truths and lies.

'And they're sending someone round to check on us. We don't need that kind of attention, you understand me?' The floaty feeling was shot through now with ugly streaks of anger. She gripped him by the hair pulling his face up to hers. Her face sometimes looked quite pretty – round and smooth, curly brown hair tickling her cheeks. Now her eyes were almost completely black and she'd scraped her hair back into a tight ponytail. She had spots around her mouth that she hadn't bothered to hide with makeup. He thought they looked like volcanoes seen from space. 'If they decide I'm not a good enough mother, they can take you away from me. They'll shut you in a home for bad children. Do you want that?'

He shook his head as any other reaction would set her off.

She kissed him, pressing her soft cheek against his. 'Good. So when they visit, everything is fine, all right? You're not to mention our visitors.'

He couldn't speak. Even the mention of Thomas made his flesh crawl.

'Promise me, Jonah!'

'I promise.'

She let him go. 'Good. Everything is fine. You'll see.' She wafted away and began humming to herself. Deciding that he'd been dismissed, Jonah went into the kitchen and made himself some pasta with chunks of cheese. He put some in a bowl for her, just in case. Sitting with his back to the cold radiator under the window, he waited for her to go to sleep.

Chapter 21

Months slunk past. At least summer evenings made it easier to stay out. Jonah rarely came home until it got dark. It was amazing how slow you could walk, how many detours you could make, if you put your mind to it. There were refuges that he soon learned about: the local library, though he couldn't stay there too long without an adult; the shopping centre; the park until the gates were closed. You had to watch out for the older boys, but if he ran quickly he was usually OK. Mum was angry that he no longer came straight home, mainly because it meant he missed several of Thomas's visits.

That meant she didn't get paid.

That meant they didn't have money for new shoes, or food.

She said it was his fault.

As July wore away, Jonah wondered bleakly what he would do for lunch during the school holidays. He wasn't looking forward to August.

One night in the last week before the holidays, when he did eventually get back home, Mrs Richardson downstairs invited him to sit with her in the darkened front room. This was where she watched her quiz shows. He'd got to know the schedule and enjoyed the biscuits and squash she got in for him. He wondered what she thought was going on upstairs.

'Your mum has a lot of friends, doesn't she?' she said, a glint of intelligence in her watery eyes. She'd never mentioned it before. Fiddling with her hearing aid, it let out a loud peep like she was stuffing a chick in her ear and it was protesting.

He nodded. '*Who Wants to be a Millionaire?* is on next.'

That was the limit of her probing. She accepted the change of subject. Jonah considered himself like the neighbourhood cats whom she welcomed in on their own terms, never making them stay, feeding them enough to keep them coming.

'Oh good,' she said. 'I like that Chris Tarrant. So clever.'

'I don't think he really knows all the answers. The people who make the programme do.'

Hand shaking, Mrs Richardson spilt some tea on her lap and wiped it away with a Kleenex tissue, which she took from a box hidden by a crocheted cover – *not* knitted, she'd once told him, shocked that he didn't know the difference between a crochet hook and a knitting needle. 'I wouldn't do very well if I were on there but you'd walk away with a fortune. You're a clever boy, Jonah.'

He scratched at a graze on his hand where he'd fallen over in the playground. The teachers had sent home an incident report in his book bag but Mum hadn't read it. He'd got in trouble for not showing it to her. Someone was going to ring. Again.

'Don't look like that! I've never met a brighter boy in my life – and so kind keeping an old lady like me company. You should be out playing. In my day, you could play in the streets.'

'It's getting dark now, Mrs Richardson.'

'So it is.' She looked over to the faded red curtains he had pulled for her when he arrived. 'Goodness: look at the time! Won't your mother have your tea waiting for you?'

When she said something like that, it was the signal for him to pretend everything was normal. He knew all the answers too. 'Yes. I'd better go. Here's the remote.' He pressed it in her bony fingers, which were swollen at the knuckles. Wedding band hung loose like a curtain ring on a pole.

'I'll see you tomorrow, Jonah.'

'Bye, Mrs Richardson.'

Jonah sat on the stairs for as long as he could, then walked up to face his mother.

There was no sign of her in the kitchen. The oranges she had bought to impress Mr Hardy, the social worker, before his last visit, had shrivelled a little, skin going black in places. Jonah dug his fingers into the peel and took it off with difficulty, making a mess of his T-shirt. The juice stung in his cuts. The pieces tasted lovely though. He sat on the floor with the segments on a plate and gorged himself. He had thought to save half for Mum but found he couldn't stop. The taste drove out the sick feeling of eating too many dry biscuits downstairs. He liked the idea that all those good fruit things – vita-somethings – were flowing into him. When he looked down, the plate was empty.

That might infuriate her.

Better destroy the evidence.

He washed the plate and put it away wet as there was no tea towel. His hands still smelt orangey. Washing up liquid didn't seem able to cover it up. She'd notice.

Jonah crept into the bathroom and washed his hands at the sink with her soap. Now he smelt of coconut as well, which was much better. It would confuse her. He could tell her it was a new soap that Mrs Richardson had in her loo. He breathed more easily.

There were no sounds coming from the front room. He knocked lightly just in case. Nothing. She was probably in one of her spaced out moods which meant she wouldn't stir until morning. That made it a good evening for Jonah. Peeking inside, he saw her huddled under a duvet. She was alone. The room smelt sicky and smoky but that wasn't unusual. Her gear was lined up next to her, so he knew she was tripping or sleeping. Either way it was safest to leave her. Taking off his stained T-shirt, he rinsed it out in the bathroom sink, using washing up liquid to clean it as they'd run out of soap powder some time ago. He squeezed it out as hard as he could, remembering how his mum had once told him to imagine he was wringing a chicken's neck. He hadn't liked that idea but she'd spent some years on a farm and told him not to be so squeamish. He shook it out but it still dripped. The only place he could leave it was dangling over the bath taps. Realising he didn't have any clean underpants either for school, he took his off and washed them the same way. They went over the side of the bath. It was unlikely they'd be completely dry the next day but it was better than being called stinker or fleabag.

After a quick brush of his teeth, he was ready for bed. He bypassed his mother and got quietly under his duvet. The room was silent apart from the burble of the quiz show coming up through the floorboards. It was comforting to think of Mrs Richardson down there, probably falling asleep in front of the telly.

Waking to a rumbling stomach, Jonah got out of bed and hurried to the bathroom to pee. He splashed water on his face and wondered what was for breakfast. Mum usually liked it if he made her a cup of tea. Going into the kitchen, he scouted around for something to eat and was surprised to find some Weetabix and just enough milk. He had to stint on that so he could put some in Mum's cup, but if he added a little water, the cereal got soggy enough to eat. He sprinkled some sugar from a little sachet he'd stolen from the coffee shop in Asda. He put the rest in Mum's tea.

Eat first or take her the cup? He decided to eat because if you left Weetabix it bloated into a horrible mush. If you ate it immediately after you put the milk on it kept just enough crunch. It was a skill to know exactly the right moment.

Bowl finished, washed up and put away, he carried the mug carefully into the front room.

'Mum, I've made you tea!' he called softly. She didn't like loud voices in the morning. He knelt down beside her and put it next to her syringe. Normally by now she would be stirring. He reached out to touch her shoulder.

She was very cold, her arm having slipped out of the covers.

He tapped her cheek. That was cold too. He couldn't hear her breathing.

Then he knew.

'Mrs Johnson! Mrs Johnson!' He bolted down the stairs and banged on her door. She took a very long time to answer, probably not yet got her hearing aid switched on. His mind was a scream. He'd slept all night with Mum like that! Slept next to a dead body!

'Jonah?' Her face was all crumpled because she'd not yet put in her false teeth.

'It's Mum. Please! She's ... call an ambulance!'

'Yes, yes, of course. Come in.' Mrs Johnson was flustered but she made the call. She told him to sit in her armchair in front of the blank TV while she made her painful way upstairs to see if there was anything she could do. By the time she came back, the paramedics were at the door. Curled up, hugging his knees, Jonah could hear them talking in the hall.

'Where's the patient?' a man asked. Not Thomas though, so that was OK. Jonah was terrified Thomas would turn up and take him away. No one would stop him.

'Upstairs. Her little boy found her like that. I think she's long gone.'

The stairs creaked as heavy footsteps made their way to the first floor. Mrs Johnson came back into the front room and shut the door.

'Do you have a daddy, Jonah?'

He shook his head.

'Did your mum talk about any relatives? A sister? A mother?'

Another shake. Mum had been fostered by a couple on a farm,

then adopted by some people in Harrow but that hadn't worked out. They'd got divorced fairly soon after and they'd handed her back. I'll never give you back, Jonah, she'd go on to say. It's us together until the end. Mummy and her little angel.

Mrs Johnson huffed and realised she wasn't wearing her teeth. 'Not to worry. I expect the nice ambulance people will know what to do. Lord, I must look a fright.' She left him to repair her appearance.

But nobody seemed to know what to do with him. Mrs Richardson made it clear that she wasn't up to looking after a nine-year-old boy who was no blood relative of hers, thank you very much. The school didn't have a next-of-kin listed on his file. No one stepped forward to claim the body, or the child, so social services took over.

Jonah disappeared into the system.

Chapter 22

Jonah, Present Day

This was inevitable, thought Jonah, to be back here. He hoped he'd escaped the institutions that had boxed him – care homes, police cells and prison – but no: like one of those advertising balloons he'd just gone to the end of his tether to float for a while in an illusion of freedom. Now he was back on the ground with a puncture.

Hello, thin blue mattress, ledge bed, strip lighting and seatless toilet.

Gallant House had been a box too, hadn't it? Bridget would probably prefer it to be called a treasure chest but, like in *The Merchant of Venice*, you should never choose the flashy one. Go for the plain old one with no pretensions: you're far less likely to come to grief.

This was as plain a box as you could get so maybe now he could start the climb up again? That was life: a game of Snakes and Ladders, only with far more snakes and ladders missing rungs so you couldn't climb them anyway.

After his breakdown in the interrogation room, they'd taken him to hospital to get his head injury checked. What had the doctor given him? Something to calm him after his outburst – Xanax probably, and some painkillers. Just paracetamol though so his head still ached. They'd managed with butterfly plasters rather than stitches but he had a lump and bruising from his self-inflicted injuries. Interrogation was called off for the moment. That left him in the cell with his mind cycling in some weird state – balloons and board games. He needed to get his head back on straight and work out what had led to that moment in the hall.

They'd argued but he didn't think many words were said; as he remembered it, the row had taken the form of a tussle. She'd attacked him first – he was pretty clear about that. Whether she had known what she was doing though, that was debatable. Her mind had been scrambled for a good few months now, her behaviour obsessive. They'd all seen it but no one had found the right intervention. If what he did in the hallway was his way of handling her, then clearly he'd chosen his strategy badly.

If she survived, maybe she'd now get treatment? Never waste a good crisis, one of his counsellors had said.

You're thinking about her, Jonah, but what about your own future? That fucking persistent inner voice was back like a buzzing in his ear. Your career will go down the shithole if you get charged for this.

He knew – of course he knew. There had been no sign of his agent, though she had to know by now. She'd probably dropped him already. It was fine to have a reformed convict on the list, but not a relapsed one. Any whiff of violence against women these days, even without any formal charge, was enough to put a male actor in the doghouse with no path back.

So it was either back to key cutting or prison.

116

Chapter 23

Jonah, One Year Ago

Jonah was grinning as he jogged home to Gallant House. His agent had left him a message. He had an audition for a new TV series for a streaming service, not a background character but one of the main parts. There was a hotly tipped young director who wanted to do a British version of *Narcos* and Jonah was up for the leader of a drug ring that was sending fifteen-year-olds out as expendable couriers to supply their clients. Once again his so-called authenticity was playing in his favour.

The news had made him think that maybe he should try out for some more villains in the autumn stage productions? He'd assumed he wasn't up to the mark for Shakespearian roles but the academy had taught him there were some sick guys he might stand a chance of playing in the right production. Iago – he acted like a drug pusher to Othello, feeding his obsession about his wife. Probably too soon to hope for that? Don John from *Much Ado About Nothing* – another manipulative bastard. More likely? The Donmar Warehouse had the play on their list of forthcoming productions. He should mention it to Carol, his agent. He could feel that his star was rising and maybe, just maybe, he'd get the breaks to make this a career. A role on stage would be a great experience and really improve his CV.

Letting the front door slam, he dived straight into the shower. The fortnight shoot for his storyline had just finished and everyone was pleased with how it had worked out. Jonah had been surprised to find his character got away with his thefts. The main victim had been an old stalwart of the soap who had been considered by the producers as dead wood. He'd been given a flashy farewell as he died of an accidental overdose, thanks to Jonah's character supplying an impure drug. The writers were kicking around the idea of having Jonah's character up for trial next season. Again they were pumping him for real life stories but he didn't mind if it meant more airtime.

Whistling, Jonah cleaned himself thoroughly with citrus body wash, and wrapped a towel around his waist. His dream of escaping to his own flat looked increasingly realistic.

He dressed quickly in sweatpants and a T-shirt. They'd wrapped up filming early so he had time to cook himself a meal and get down to some of his much-neglected course work. Carol was urging him to stay on the degree for as long as possible; she said it made him sound truly reformed when she told filmmakers he was now putting himself through the rigours of RADA.

Rigours of RADA? Good one, Carol. He liked being surrounded by people who knew how to use language. Maybe he'd get there one day himself. His own speech was still salted with the curses he'd learned to use in care and in prison and he knew now after reading so many plays and scripts that this emptied out the impact. Fucking this, fucking that, fucking nothing. It was more effective to hear one swear word from, say, Bridget than a string of them from him. In his defence, he thought, he would not have survived without adopting the same speech patterns as his peers. Say 'rigours of RADA' at either place and you'd get your face smashed in.

He looked through the contents of the fridge. Knowing he

didn't have time to shop, Bridget added his order onto hers and he settled it as part of the rent. Before it had always been easy to distinguish his things from his landlady's as Bridget had a few staple meals she rarely strayed from, and she usually cooked vegetarian. He'd not thought to ask what the arrangement was with Jenny. He'd better go and find her before he stole her chicken pieces.

At first there was no answer when he knocked on her door. Thinking he could hear movement inside, he tapped again. Of course, she wouldn't be able to tell him to enter.

'Jenny, it's just me. I just wanted to know if the chicken in the fridge yours? I was thinking of doing a stir fry.'

The door opened a crack and a hand appeared signing 'no'.

'Are you OK?' He seemed to be asking her that a lot recently. The sign repeated.

He pushed a little at the door and it swung open. Jenny's face was tear-stained and she was bent over like an old lady.

'Can I get you something?'

She shook her head. Then she stretched back out on the floor and let the tears run down her cheeks.

'Your back again?'

She gave him the thumbs up.

He was getting used to entering a room and finding her stretched out on the rug. 'Has it ever been this bad before?'

The wafting gesture suggested that it had once, but not for a long time.

'Have you got some painkillers? It looks like you really could do with some.'

She pointed to the bathroom. He went in and found her pill dispenser. She had the strong ones – prescription opioids. He felt an echo of his old longing for them but forced it away. This was about Jenny. Today's capsule was empty so he took two pills from tomorrow and brought them back to her with a glass of water.

'I think it's an emergency,' he said when she looked doubtful.

She took the pills in one gulp.

'You lie there and wait for those to kick in. When was the last time you ate?' She was looking drawn, lines around her mouth and top of her nose from setting her face against the pain. 'Want to share my stir fry?'

Wearily she nodded. He didn't think she'd be eating much, so the chicken should feed them both. 'OK, come down in about twenty minutes. It should be cooked by then.'

The stir fry took fifteen. He plated up the multi-coloured meal, pleased with the contrast of the red peppers against the pale bean shoots and chicken. Cooking was another thing he'd learned in prison. It was much easier doing this for two rather than hundreds. As Jenny still wasn't down, he went out into the kitchen courtyard and snipped a little coriander in the herb bed. The vine had its roots down here in this odd corner of the garden. He patted the stem appreciatively. It was twisted like a hank of steel wool, turned around itself many times. The leaves were now the size of side plates. He remembered Bridget saying you could cook with them but he wasn't sure how you'd do that. Eat them in a salad? He tore off a strip and tasted it. It was OK but lettuce was better. The little globes that would swell into grapes were just beginning to form.

There was a rap at the window.

Good: Jenny had made it to the kitchen. 'Coming!'

As he turned to head inside he noticed that the lid covering the old well was open. The well wasn't a thing of beauty, just a low stone wall that reached his knees, the shaft covered over by a hinged trapdoor. If there had been a bucket and pulley system it had long since gone. He peered inside out of habit, caught a glimpse of his head outlined against the sky, then closed the safety barrier. It was dangerous to leave it like that. An animal could fall in – or a kid if one strayed into the garden. Norman was having someone to stay, wasn't he? He'd have to mention it to Bridget, though why she opened it in the first place he couldn't imagine. Maybe Norman had been poking around with her as

120

part of their historical investigations. Those two were thick as thieves at the moment. He remembered reading something about the digging of the well in one of Bridget's chapters when she'd still been able to con him into reading that weird shit she wrote.

Back in the kitchen, he snipped the coriander over the meal and presented Jenny with her plate.

'Thank you,' she signed.

'Feeling better?'

She held up finger and thumb. A little. Her eyes were haunted by the memory of the pain but she was in the floating stage of the pills that he remembered too well. He could feel the ghost of the pill on his tongue. Forget it. Not going back there.

'Can you take some time off?' he asked to distract himself.

And lose my place? She wrote.

'They can't fire you for taking sick leave.'

But what if they hire someone to fill in who's better than me? What if they decide having a mute violinist is too much for them?

'Then you sue them for discrimination – you could rake it in.'

He'd said it like a joke but she obviously took offence at his bald statement of this home truth. Her eyes were sparking. If she'd been a cat she would've scratched him. But he couldn't be bothered with tiptoeing around the truth. A spade was a fucking spade.

He swallowed his mouthful. 'Don't get me wrong: you've got the talent as far as I can tell. But it's worth facing up to how the world sees us.' He poured them both some water from the jug on the table. 'I'm an ex-con. That got me into RADA as some bleeding-heart liberal wanted to give me a chance. I expect there wasn't a dry eye in the house after my audition and sob story. I'm sure there were a million other better candidates but I look good on the books.' She was obviously shocked by that revelation, eyes rounded so that he could see a full ring of white around her brown irises. 'What? No one told you? I thought you would've guessed when you met my probation officer.'

121

She shook her head. She'd stopped eating. He wasn't having that: he nudged the hand which held her fork.

'Don't panic, Jenny: I'm house-trained. Anyway, usually I'm up shit creek when I go for jobs, but bizarrely in television my drug offender background gives me an edge when I'm trying out for roles in hard-hitting drama. It gives them a story for their publicity people, they can pimp me out to interviews and shit. Look at Jonah, our tame ex-con. Fucked up life, drugs and gangs, and now he's all shiny and new. I'm not happy I lived through that crap, but I'm happy it plays well for me now. You could make your story work for you, couldn't you?'

Jenny was still staring at him as though he'd sprouted a horn in the middle of his forehead.

'You really didn't know?' He rotated his head from side to side. 'I would've thought it was obvious. Got these in prison. Like them? I'm Frankenstein, see? Society's monster. And these.' He held out his spiderwebbed hands. 'I'm a tarantula, hiding in corners, nasty bite. You quickly learn that it's safer to look like the big bad wolf than the lamb in there. It's camouflage.' That wasn't quite the truth. He'd learned to look mean long before, when he was in what was laughably called the 'care' of the local council. 'They are all roles, just like acting. I don't think the real me is like any of those images. The real me probably doesn't exist and I'm just a collection of parts these days.' He hadn't meant to tell her that. She could think of him what she liked; it was his own opinion that mattered. 'I think it's why I'm so fucking good at what I do.' And he was. He had the agent and the casting call to prove it. Today he was feeling pretty fucking proud of himself.

'And look at you,' he continued, anger swinging round to her, sitting there so defeated and pathetic, like his mother did, 'you're a shit hot violinist. Minority – disabled – ticking so many boxes for their numbers they'll be begging you to work for them. You should be making those albums where you drape yourself naked over rocks, modesty preserved by a bit of silk or something.' He

122

grinned. 'Yeah, I've seen those classical magazines at the newsagents even if I don't know what the music sounds like. You can't miss those cover girls who hug their instruments and look like they're getting off on it.' Her furious expression was priceless but these musical babes were such hypocrites: pretending to be so refined when really, they were selling wet dreams to rich blokes in Surrey who could buy the soft classical porn without a blush. 'The public would go for you, big time.'

Jenny pushed her plate away.

'Hey, don't waste good food!'

She was tapping furiously. He read over her shoulder. *Thanks for the career advice – for a career about which you know nothing. So I sell myself as a sex object and maybe people will listen to my music? Great. That's so why I studied and practised all these years. If I can't play while keeping my clothes on, then I'm not going to play.*

Jonah held up his hands. She clearly didn't understand his brand of teasing. 'Sorry. I was just telling you how I see it. Sex sells for guys as well as girls. If you've got it, why not use it? Someone else will if you don't. You're streets ahead of all those buck-teethed only-their-mother-loves-them guys who make up half the orchestras I've seen on TV.'

I know sex sells, but I don't sell sex, she wrote primly.

Why was he bothering? 'Yeah, I know, you're the good girl. Eat your food and shut the fuck up, Jonah.'

Chapter 24

Jonah, Present Day

'How are you feeling now, Jonah?' asked DS Foley. She'd done her hair differently today, loose at the back, two strands from the front in slides above her ears. It made her look softer, more feminine. He wondered if they'd decided to play the cliché of good cop bad cop.

'I feel like shit.' From the reflection in the glass he knew he had two black eyes to add to the lump on his forehead.

DI Khan was observing him, chair pushed slightly back and at an angle, hands loosely linked on the knee of the leg he rested on the other. Had Khan actually brushed his hair today? Maybe the superintendent was visiting?

Mind games were wasted on Jonah. He knew too many acting tricks to be caught out. 'How about you: are you OK, Sergeant Foley?'

'Yes, thank you, Jonah.'

'She's not the one sitting here looking like they've been in a bar brawl.' Khan's voice was acerbic, unpitying. He'd have to remember that tone for his bad cop routine.

'My colleague realises he stumbled on a hot button topic so we won't return to your childhood today,' said Foley.

'Good, 'cause my childhood seriously sucked.' Even now he shuddered just saying the words. Some places you never went back to if you wanted to stay sane.

'Instead, I'd like to ask you about some of the things that we found in your bedroom.'

OK, this was safe territory. There was nothing there he felt ashamed of, except perhaps the mess. He smirked at the idea of the forensics team picking through his dirty laundry.

'We found some clippings.'

He had a scrapbook of reviews of his performances. 'Yeah? I suppose it seems a bit up myself but I wanted a record of what I'd done.'

'Would you say you were misogynistic? That you hate all women, Jonah? Or is it particular ones that you dislike?'

'What?' How had she gone from a scrapbook to misogyny? Yeah he knew the word – he was at RADA for fuck's sake.

'You're pretty brutal to the women in your scrapbooks.'

He tried to think what she could mean. He'd noted that one negative reviewer was a fucking cow but that was about it. 'I'm not following. What do you mean? My comments on the critics?'

'You regard women as critics?' She no longer looked soft; DS Foley was looking as hard as fucking nails at the moment.

Jonah knew better than to fall for generalised comments like this. They'd have him agreeing that genocide was OK in certain circumstances if he wasn't careful. 'You'll have to give me an example.'

Slipping on latex gloves, she reached into a document case and brought out a red WHSmith scrapbook and put it on the table between them. 'Take a look.'

As Jonah could not remember seeing it before, he didn't fall into the trap of touching it.

'Show me.'

'All right.' Slowly she turned the pages. Someone had gathered news articles about Bridget, printouts of the early reviews of her performances, her marriage announcement, a report of her husband's death, candid pictures, studio portraits. That wasn't too bad but what was truly sickening was what had been done to the images. Every picture of her had a slash across the neck and eyes blacked out.

'Fuck. That's screwed up.'

'This was in your room.'

'I've never seen it before.' What was going on here? Were they trying to frame him for something?

'There was a second. Do you want to see that?'

Maybe it was the scrapbook about his career? He could show them the difference between him, the sane gatherer of reviews, and the freaked-out scrapbooker. 'Yes.' God, he could do with a smoke.

She got out an identical book but the contents focused on Jenny. The person had gone right back, gathering articles about her from an Essex newspaper. He only had time to read the headlines as Foley flicked through.

Girl 14 left for dead. Strangler still at large.

Strangler victim might never recover voice, say doctors.

Silent Girl wins county music competition.

Essex Pride and Joy: Our Silent Girl gains place at Royal Academy.

Jenny wasn't named in the reports of the crime, but it wouldn't take a genius to put together that the mute girl in the county competitions was one and the same as the victim, especially not if you lived locally. Again the collector had gone crazy with a magic marker, striking across Jenny's neck in the photos. This time the eyes were left untouched but the mouth had been made into an ink spot.

'I didn't do this. Had you checked for prints?'

'There are none.' She got out the scrapbook he did recognise, blue with a cartoon squirrel on the front. 'Is this yours too?'

'Hang on, I said those weren't mine.' Fuck her, that was a clever trap. 'That one is mine. Only that one.'

She opened it and someone had gone through and drawn over his carefully collated collection of pictures. Bolts had been drawn on his neck, mocking his tattoos, and a line struck through his face.

'They've ruined it!' He felt violated. 'Who did this?'

'Yours are the only prints on this scrapbook, Jonah.'

'It wasn't me! I'm proud of my career; why would I fucking mess with it like that?'

'You've got a lot of hatred inside you, Jonah. It's all here in Dr Wade's report.'

Dr Rose Wade was turning on him now, was she? His records were supposed to be private. He folded his arms across his chest. He wanted to cry at the ruin of his archive but, fuck, he was twenty-nine, not a kid anymore.

'She says you have a problem with older women.'

Now Jonah felt exhausted. 'Not like that.' He waved at the scrapbooks. 'I have a problem with mothers, not all women. Anyway, I thought we weren't going to talk about my childhood?'

'Mothers? You see Bridget like a mother?'

'Bridget is a crazy cow so, yeah, she reminds me of my mother.'

'And Jenny? Do you hate her too?'

'I didn't say I hate Bridget. Detective, stop putting words in my mouth.'

She wasn't giving up on this line of enquiry, coming at him from another direction. 'I have here testimonies from your class-mates at RADA. A common theme is that you get through girls like toilet paper.'

'I thought it the other way round,' Jonah muttered.

'Excuse me?'

'They sleep with me for the thrill then chuck me out the next morning. No, "have breakfast and stay and chat, Jonah". It's all: "oh, my flatmate will be back soon, thanks for the shag".'

'You've slept with men too.'

'Yeah, I know. I was there.'

'Do you feel differently towards your male lovers?'

It was the first interesting question she'd asked. Did he? 'No.'

'What do you mean by "no"?'

'I'm answering your question. No, I don't feel differently about them. I think the truth is that I don't feel much about sex with men or women. It just is.'

'So why do it?'

'They expect it of me.'

'So you take out your anger on their pictures?' She pushed the scrapbooks closer to him again, daring him to touch them.

He touched his bloated eye sockets rather than the mutilated pictures. 'Those aren't mine. The one that is – I didn't vandalise it.'

'These were in your bedroom at Gallant House. Who else could've put them there?'

'Yeah, that is the question, isn't it? I can think of at least three people: Bridget, Jenny and Norman.'

'Norman?'

'Norman Stratton. He lives next door and has free entry to the house through the back.'

'You're accusing the GP who lives next door?'

He remembered this now, the slippery twisting of anything he said when in interview. 'No. I'm just telling you who comes and goes in the house. My bedroom isn't locked and I've not been in there for days now. Where did you find these?'

'You tell us.'

'For Christ's sake, I don't know because they aren't mine!'

'They were under the bed with the one you do say is yours.'

'Then they could've been there for a while. I haven't added to mine since last December. I shoved it under there and forgot about it. It's now, what, April? That's four months for someone to mess with them.'

'You want us to believe that you didn't notice these lying under your bed for four months?'

His mood teetered on the edge; he could go with hot anger or cold fury. Try to keep your cool, Jonah. 'You really are good at your job, aren't you, DS Foley?' He could do hard if she did. 'I did not say that. I'll repeat it for you. I said that I hadn't looked at my scrapbook since December. It could've been tampered with at any time since then – three months ago, two weeks, yesterday, how the hell would I know?'

'So why then is the last entry a review of your performance in a TV drama shown in March, just six weeks ago?' She flipped through to the last filled page. A clipping from the Daily Mail had been pasted in, a picture of him – ironically, one of his character behind bars in the season finale. It was the only picture not defaced.

'I've never seen that before.'

'You haven't seen the review?'

'Yes, but not in there. Only online.' His mind whirled. Had he put it in and forgotten? He really didn't think so.

'These scrapbooks suggest you hate Bridget, hate Jenny and even hate yourself.' DI Khan had decided to join in. 'So who do you hate most, Jonah?'

Part 3 – The Moor's Room

Acciaccatura – crushing; very fast note
'crushed' against another

Chapter 25

The House that Jack Built – Chapter Six – My First Deaths

I wept when the undertakers carried out the Admiral, ripping him untimely from my drawing room where he had laid in state for two days. Dead at fifty-nine, I'd expected him to live longer and enjoy his golden evenings with me. I went into mourning, dropping the leaves from the vine and turning the grapes sour in endless weeks of rain.

It took a while for us all to adjust to the new balance of power in my halls. Admiral Jack's wife acted as if nothing had changed, ordering the servants around as if she still captained the ship. Her eldest son's wife watched her and bided her time before staging her mutiny. Through her manoeuvres in parlour and kitchen, warning salvoes over the tea tray, the admiral's wife realised she had to beat a retreat. Her son found her a small house in Greenwich with a view of the river and she left, taking her unmarried daughters with her. We all breathed more easily.

My new master was another seaman, but we were now at peace and he saw his future in the merchant navy. He captained an East Indiaman. She came a close second to his love for me. A picture of her hung in the hallway and I admit she was a beauty: three masts and taut lines stretching from stem to stern. Her belly swelled with silks, spices, cottons and porcelain. She wore him down, his face weather-beaten and lined from so many hours standing under the hot sun on her decks, but he was happy with her, and the others that he came to own over the years. He had a fleet by the time he finished.

His wife's belly also swelled with alarming regularity. A shore leave always resulted in a babe nine months later. Four of them died, sighing out their last little breaths in the nursery on the topmost floor – little nestlings who never made it out of the nest. They were buried in a plot together near the Admiral, their grandfather close by to steer them into the next life.

Nine, however, survived and stretched my capacity to the limits to house them in comfort. Captain Jack Junior ordered an extension be built on the rear so the kitchen could expand. Children tumbled into beds, two or three apiece. The washing tub was always full of the baby's napkins. The pump on the green no longer sufficed so he called in a water diviner. Find water, demanded the wife, or they'd have to move to a more convenient house with modern amenities. She grieved me then; I'd thought her my friend.

The diviner was an odd fellow. Dressed in an old scarlet coat of a soldier and black breeches frayed at the hem, he arrived on a mule from Kidbrooke. He walked up and down my lawns, his bare feet stroking me with a seductive touch. I fell in love with him despite his look of a vagabond and gypsy, despiser of settled abodes. The hazel twigs crossed in a corner where I had hidden a spring deep beneath the lost maids, rebels, cave dwellers and dinosaurs. I kept my secrets even from the Admiral but this lover wheedled them from my clutches. Labourers were called in to dig a shaft. At first it hurt as they pierced my surface, but the gush of water came as a release and I forgave them. They bricked the sides of the shaft and built a well housing to protect it. I now had maids clattering and rattling buckets into my depths several times a day but I grew used to their pillaging. The water, which carried the taste of the heath, was my gift to the Jacks. They all absorbed a little of my darkness as they washed, shaved, and cooked with it.

Chapter 26

Jenny, One Year Ago

Sitting at the back of the rehearsal room during a break, Jenny read through the latest chapter Bridget had lent her. She was getting a little obsessed with the story, taking it everywhere with her, even finding herself dreaming about it on the nights when she did sleep. Over the last few weeks, odd things had been happening in her room – things she could be imagining – like possessions a hair out of place, drawers not quite closed, more flower petals where there should be none. All had a rational explanation: she'd forgotten where she'd left things, neglected to shut the chest of drawers properly, let in a draught that carried the petals. But that just didn't fit what she felt was happening. When she read these chapters, it seemed possible that the house was talking to her too as it did Bridget. She'd never lived anywhere with a personality. It wasn't frightening, more frustrating, similar to how she felt when she so frequently couldn't make herself understood. The more she read, the more she suspected that the answers were here. What was the house – Bridget? – trying to tell her? That the house was haunted? Or cursed? Did it explain the strange noises at night?

And so often the story cycled back to death.

Chapter 27

The House that Jack Built – Chapter Seven – The Well

Captain Jack Junior did not keep himself just to practical improvements. He lavished his wealth on the rooms where they received visitors; he furnished a study and library for himself, gave his wife a morning room and new portraits for the drawing room. Such things have to be paid for so he went to sea again in his big-bellied ship, this time embarking on the most lucrative trade of them all: opium. He carried the poppy from India to China and, when the authorities refused to see any more of their people chase the dragon in opium dens, the British Imperial forces sent their gunboats. Free trade forced by canon barrel meant soft Turkish rugs on my floors and tiger skins sprawled in the library.

And did I care where the money came from? Of course not. I never had. My task was to stand the test of the centuries, keep my roof tiles intact and protect the infant Jacks as best I could. That was no easy job and I saw many losses. Two of them went as Company men to India and promptly died of fever. A girl followed, seeking a husband, poor thing. One son, the youngest, took to religion and moved into Whitechapel to preach to the poor. He and his wife swooped in occasionally like the pinch-faced house martins who lodged under my eaves, fouling the ground beneath. I rejoiced when they emigrated to the New World.

Two of the sisters made conventional marriages to self-important men and soon regretted leaving me. One stayed to look after their mother during the father's long absences. She wore out her lonely watch pacing the balcony, wishing she could see action and have adventures. The cruelty of inheritance meant that the roving spirit came to sons and daughters in equal measure but only the boys could satisfy their urge to see more of the world. Unfairly she considered me a cage and grew bitter. I let mould grow in the corner of her box room where the gutter leaked.

The eldest son, however, the one who stood in line to own me when his father died, was a wastrel. He amused me, spending his money on the prostitutes of the high-class bordellos in Covent Garden and pretending to his mother that he was merely going to his club. I could smell the perfume on him and saw the state of his linen when it was dumped in the wash tub. The maids and I kept his secrets; they because they were handsomely tipped, and sometimes, given gold when taken against the wall of the washroom by this randy son of the house; I kept my counsel because I was wooing my next lover. I understood his wandering eye. If he resented me like his sister then he would mistreat me and I knew better than to invite that kind of attention. I'd be knocked through, split up, sold to the highest bidder. So I kept him sweet with my silence. When his father was reported dead in the port of Hong Kong, I came to him. Respectability descended on him like a cloak, hiding the true man beneath as he managed the Jack shipping company. He married late in his thirties. His wife spent her years covering up the legs of the furniture, while he tucked pound notes in the garters of dancing girls.

This most lascivious of the Jacks hid a darkened heart under his curly moustache and sideburns. The maids no longer vied to be alone with him in the washroom as he'd lost his youthful glamour. One poor soul from the workhouse was pushed forward by the others. She endured, because life had taught her that, and she hid the swelling belly under her apron. The other servants pretended not to see. The babe came early to this fifteen-year-old Mary – a seven-month gasping thing born on the flagstones of the washroom. Mary wrapped it in swaddling and looked for a place to rest the little boy's head. I opened the well shaft and beckoned her closer. The babe was a Jack after all, even if a bastard one. She dropped him in with a whispered prayer and considered joining him. It would have been better if she had done so on that cool summer night; she should've taken the quietus I offered.

The conspiracy of servants broke their silence when they saw her the next day sans bump, sans child, sans everything. Her reason gone, they called the police. I tried to keep the lid on her secret, I really did. Poor Mary. They opened the well housing and poked the ink black water with a bill hook. A little bundle came up on the third time of asking. Mary screamed then, as they dragged her away, that he'd been dead when he went in. I did manage to keep the truth about that from them and she was merely committed to the madhouse rather than to the gallows. From being born in one institution, Mary ended her life in another. Some people never really have a chance.

Chapter 28

Jenny put the chapter aside with a shudder. Bridget had left it for her on her bed and given no warnings of the content. That poor child, mother and son both.

The well was still there, Bridget had pointed it out on her introductory tour, but Jenny sincerely hoped the little body had been buried elsewhere. Surely it would've been put in the churchyard? But wasn't there something about unchristened children not getting a grave on consecrated land during Victorian times? *Tess of the Durbervilles* has taught her that. Had they buried the little bastard baby in the garden then like a family pet? That thought was too macabre. Surely they would've made better arrangements than that? Was that the origin of the ghost who visited her room – a damaged child?

'Hello, Jenny. How are you?'

So Harry had decided to pay her one of his 'we're still friends' visits.

She signed that she was fine, which was a lie because she could barely hold her violin today and she'd already taken all of her prescribed painkillers meant to last the week. She'd made an emergency appointment with her new GP.

'Great. You're looking well.'

She looked crap but she smiled anyway.

'We're having a party tomorrow night. Please come.' He must've noticed her less than enthused expression. 'It's a proper party with a meal, conversation and music, very grownup – for my thirtieth birthday.'

Of course it was. How could she forget? Once she would've been meticulously planning the event for weeks in advance.

Harry rubbed the back of his neck. 'I want to introduce you to someone. I think you'll get on.'

She wondered what he meant. Was it a blind date kind of thing when he could finally pass on the baton of feeling responsible for her; or was it a totally insensitive invitation to meet a new girlfriend about whom he was serious? Either was possible. *Who?* she signed.

He grinned. 'If I tell you, that'd spoil the surprise. He said he knows you already.'

Not a girlfriend then.

'Intrigued? You'll have to come and find out now, won't you?'

'Going out?' asked Jonah.

He had caught Jenny looking at her reflection in the long mirror at the turn of the stairs. It had the most flattering light in the house, muted by the vine leaves fringing the oriel window. The long green dress looked good on her against her skin tone – her goddess look as Louis called it.

'You look great.' Jonah swung like a little boy on the bannister at the bottom, to and fro, to and fro – odd from someone who liked he chewed razorblades for breakfast. He was clearly in high spirits.

'What's up?' she signed.

'I got the part!'

Thumbs up. Not that she knew which role he meant. Their paths didn't cross much in the house with them both working long hours. 'What part?' she signed.

'God, did you escape me raving about this? Lucky you. It's for an evil drug lord of some crap estate with my own entourage of henchmen.' He laughed. 'It's such a great break – so well written. I'm so fucking proud of myself I want to do something – cartwheels, but I can't do those. Fuck, and I've just got an evening planned catching up with my homework like some kid. I should get drunk, get laid, something.'

Thinking quickly, Jenny signed a question.

'Come with you?'

This was too difficult to sign with him just at the beginner stage. She pulled her iPad out of her evening bag. *I'm going to a party at my old flat. I'd appreciate the company. My ex has arranged for me to meet someone he thinks I will like.*

'Prick.'

And that was why she forgave him for his bluntness. Jonah got why that was as an attractive a prospect as a root canal.

Instead I can introduce him to someone I think he'll like – my movie star housemate.

'Not a movie star – not yet! OK, give me a moment. I'll just slip into something more comfortable.' He grinned at the hammy line and raced up the stairs.

She began to fret that maybe she'd implied this was a date. No. Looking back over the messages she'd typed, he couldn't possible think that. Harry had taught her never to get involved with a housemate. Not that she liked Jonah that way. They came from such different directions on absolutely everything.

It only took him five minutes but he returned in a clean dark blue shirt and smelling of aftershave. 'I hope I don't disgrace you?'

For Jonah, he looked good, like a wolf pretending to be a German shepherd dog. The collar hid the bolts and the cuffs were a little long so you didn't even notice the spiderwebs immediately.

Thumbs up.

He offered her his arm in an old-fashioned gesture. 'My lady, your carriage awaits.'

She laughed.

'I do not jest,' he said in his best RADA manner. 'It's the train, but it does have carriages.'

A rattle of crockery heralded Bridget's arrival from the drawing room. Had she been having tea in there alone? 'Off out, dears?'

'Yes, Mrs W. We are.'

'Together?'

'Jenny's invited me along to meet some of her friends.'

'That's nice. I'll leave the chain off when I go to bed.'

'Thanks.' Jonah was already steering Jenny out of the door. He heaved a sigh of relief when they got to the gate. 'I thought she was going to ask to come with us for a moment there.'

Jenny shook her head.

'I know – she never leaves. But she looks like she wants to, doesn't she?' He glanced over his shoulder. 'I bet she's watching.'

Jenny shied away from thinking about that. Sometimes she thought she would become Bridget one day – shut in, obsessive, trapped. She patted her shoulder bag, checking she had her heels as she was wearing Converse lace-ups for comfort and speed – her getaway gear.

'Don't you wonder about her sometimes?' said Jonah. 'I used her as a character study in loneliness in an improv class the other day and people found it hard to imagine someone like that existed. I called her Eleanor Rigby to disguise her real name, but they thought I wasn't describing a real person. Got it in the neck for that as it was supposed to be observation from life.' He offered her a cigarette and she refused. 'But the thing is, Jenny, people are weird as shit. You can't find a character in a book or film without being able to find an even more extreme example out here.' He waved the roll up to the millionaire houses. 'There was this guy I knew who was inside for stealing. What did he nick, you ask?' Jenny was amused by the way he carried on his mono-logue as if she was participating. 'I'll tell you. Railway station signs. He wanted every single one from the British rail network.

He had them hung all over his house and stacked in the shed. In prison, he started nicking labels off doors – name plates, warning of biohazards, No Entry. He put that one on his own cell so you have to admit he had a sense of humour. And when he gets out, what do you think he's going to do? Go collecting all over again. Waste of time putting him away. It was a compulsion. They should just let him do it and bill him.'

He looked down at her. She squeezed his arm to show she was listening.

'I guess we all have our obsessions. I'll make a wild stab and say that yours is music?'

She nodded. It was her secret world, like another dimension she could go to as soon as she started playing or put on some music. Life was flat without it.

'All music or do you have particular pieces you play over and over?'

Good question. Her profession meant that she was always moving on to new repertoire but she did have a few pieces that she returned to like comfort food for upset. She nodded.

Jonah laughed. 'I've got to get better at asking you questions because I'm not sure what you just agreed with. You have some special pieces?'

Smiling, she nodded again.

'Sometime I'd like to hear them.'

'And you?' she signed.

'My obsession?' Jonah looked out over the rooftops. 'I've had such a fucked-up life so far, Jenny, my current obsession is not going back there. I'm five-hundred and one days sober – that's drugs and drink, so don't let me fuck up tonight OK? Tell me to step away from the sherry trifle if it gets out of hand.'

She gave him a firm nod.

Chapter 29

The House that Jack Built – Chapter Twenty-Two –
My Lost Boys

They say the first decade of the twentieth century was one long golden afternoon where men in straw boaters punted ladies in white dresses along placid rivers, interspersed with games of cricket on the lawn. Perhaps it was like that for some. For me it was an era of comings and goings, steamer trunks standing in my halls, raised voices from bedrooms as young men searched for belongings and blamed brothers for stealing them.

The senior Jack, father of these boys, was a straight-laced man, who took over from his wastrel father and honed the shipping concern ruthlessly to keep a step ahead of the competition from America and Germany. As the century changed, Bertram Jack declared a new leaf was turned under my roof. His long-suffering mother was given a cottage in Richmond but she surprised us all a year later by running off with a painter from Kew, a younger man in need of a patroness. I enjoyed that letter, read in aghast tones over the eggs and bacon. The lady and her artist lived a glorious rackety life in Paris thereafter. Against all predictions, her painter stayed with her until her death. Sadly for him, he was more talented in the bedroom than on canvas, but Widow Jack did a sterling job fanning the flames of his belief in himself. They were happy.

Her bewildered son, Bertram Jack, paced the halls in frustration as his parents and children scattered in moral disarray like the sticks in a game of jack straws. He called his children ungrateful, unchristian, and prayed long and loud for their salvation. And so the jack straws trembled. The eldest son grew his hair long and took to a smoking jacket, aping his hero, Oscar Wilde. He got caught by the opium his family had so long shipped to other countries and moved in a set of disreputable friends. In the end he had to be packed off as a remittance man in some forgotten spot in the empire. Money was cabled on the understanding he never darkened English shores again. He settled for the sunshine instead and was as content as a Jack could be away from me.

The will was rewritten by his censorious father in favour of the next boy down but that son disappeared into the Antarctic. The next two joined up straight from school, heading out in the British Expeditionary Force at the beginning of the Great War. They did not survive the trenches to join the Jacks in the local churchyard. Two white military crosses in a Normandy cemetery was their destiny.

Only one boy remained.

Chapter 30

'Jenny!' Harry opened the door wearing a '3 today' badge somebody had got him. Against her good sense, she felt the old pull of attraction to him, his goofy sense of humour and love for life. It's the last throes of a fever, she told herself, you're almost over it. 'So glad you made it. Oh, and you've brought a friend.' He looked a little alarmed at the scary guy at her side.

'Hi, I'm Jonah Brigson, your friendly, neighbourhood gate-crasher.'

Jenny elbowed him and pointed to herself then Jonah.

'You're dating?' guessed Harry, looking shocked.

'I wish,' said Jonah with a snaggle-toothed grin.

Frustrated, Jenny got out a pencil and scribbled on the back of the birthday card she'd got Harry. *We both live at Gallant House. Jonah's an actor.*

'Cool,' said Harry. 'Hey, Luke, set another place, will you? Jenny's brought a plus one. Come in, come in!' He stood back. Jenny was amused to note that the guys had made an attempt to clean up. Was that air freshener she could smell? Even the pile of mouldy trainers had gone from by the door. Harry must've been watching her because he said:

'Yeah, we got a cleaner.'

She patted her chest in surprise.

'I know. Pigs might fly and all that, but your leaving was a kind of "come to Jesus moment" and we're reformed fellows. Cleaning up after ourselves sucked and, as some of us are earning proper wages, we had no excuses. Anyway, we've got a lovely Brazilian lady who sorts us out.' The way he said this suggested that there was still plenty of the old Harry left. 'Everyone, this is Jenny and Jonah. Jenny, you know most people here but you haven't met Matt, or at least not for a few years.' He pointed to a man sitting at the far end of the table. Matt had reddish wiry hair slightly thinning on top and a few freckles across a narrow nose. 'Matt plays the violin too. He's taken Lucy's place while she's on maternity.' He had to be the guest Harry wanted her to meet.

'Jenny, great to see you again.' Matt smiled as if she should know him.

Where had she met him? He rang no bells with her. Perhaps they'd been in the same orchestra at some point?

'I've put you next to Matt so you can catch up. Jonah, where shall we put you?'

'Next to the prettiest available girl,' said Jonah, 'Or guy. I'm not fussy.'

Everyone took it as a joke and laughed.

'OK then. Brian, move your chair along. Brian plays the tuba but you can't have everything. He's a nice guy otherwise – and pretty too, according to his mother.' Brian looked like he'd spent rather too much time being kicked at the bottom of a scrum. 'It'll have to be a stool, is that's OK? We're out of chairs. We're using the camping gear Luke got for Glasto.'

The table was laid for ten. Jenny hoped that the meal was something easily divided or she was going to feel guilty for messing up Harry's arrangements.

Luke appeared from the kitchen carrying another set of cutlery. Asian in extraction, he was a good-looking guy with straight dark hair cut sharply, front styled in a flip back, and big dark eyes. That coupled with an incredible talent on the cello made him something of a heartthrob in the orchestra. He'd definitely make the charity calendar if the orchestra ever did one. 'Hey, Jenny.'

She waved.

'Jonah. Pleased to meet you. What do you play?'

'The spoons and the occasional triangle,' said Jonah catching on fast.

'Jenny said he's an actor,' Harry corrected.

'Oh great. Stage or screen?'

'Mostly screen. I'm in *Blue Light Run*. Small part but recurring character.'

'I think I've heard of that.' Luke said it to be kind. Not many people in the orchestra had time to follow soaps.

'I'm still at RADA, end of my first year.'

'Isn't that really hard to get into? You must be good.' Luke looked at him askance, clearly wondering about Jonah's age. He appeared older than everyone in the room, though Jenny knew now that he was only twenty-nine.

'Before RADA I served four years at Her Majesty's Pleasure,' said Jonah. 'You have at your table a convict, reformed.' He swept a bow, Mephistopheles meeting Faust.

There was an awkward silence. Harry was looking at her as if to ask what trouble she had got herself into now.

'That's rather a good conversation stopper,' said Matt, rescuing the mood. 'None of us can top that. What've you cooked, Harry?'

'*Moi?* Cooked?' said Harry in shocked tone. 'We have, I'm pleased to say, the best curry in Kennington heading our way. According to the app, it should be here any moment.' The doorbell rang. 'Great timing.'

Harry and Luke went out to deal with the delivery. Feeling as though she had just led the bull right into the china shop, Jenny sat down. It gave a pleasant frisson to what she otherwise expected to be a trying evening. She nodded as Matt offered to fill her glass with red wine. Drink was good.

'Not sure it goes with curry. I could get you a beer if you prefer?' he said. 'There are some in the fridge.'

She shook her head in an 'it's fine' gesture.

'You lived here until recently with these guys?' He motioned to her former housemates. In addition to Harry and Luke, three were present, plus their current girlfriends. Jenny couldn't remember the girls' names but that was OK: not speaking had its unexpected benefits.

She nodded.

'You went out with Harry for a while?'

That seemed a bit personal for a first conversation. She nodded cautiously.

'Sorry, just I found that hard to imagine: the Jenny I knew with the brass section's Casanova.'

She raised her brows.

'His reputation precedes him. I remember him from school.'

What was it with this guy? He was acting like he knew her very well and it sounded like they'd gone to the same school. She was going to have to take a leaf out of Jonah's book and be blunt. She got out her iPad.

Sorry but where do we know each other from?

Matt gave her a sympathetic look. 'I suppose I shouldn't be surprised you forgot me. It was a difficult time for you and your mother.'

Oh God, he was from then. She swallowed. *Harlow?* she mouthed.

'Yes. I was one of your mother's students. Matthew Upshaw. She gave up teaching for a while as you'll remember so you didn't see me again until, well, until today.'

If she could just box up that period in her life and put it in the attic so no one remembered it was there, she would do it in a blink of an eye.

'I imagine you're now wishing you'd never seen me ever again,' he continued as the curry containers did the rounds of the table. 'I'm sorry, Jenny. But we'll be working together so I asked Harry if we could, you know, clear the air, away from the orchestra? Make the reintroduction low key.'

The thought edged in that Matt's request had been responsible for her invitation; Harry hadn't intended to invite her to his thirtieth at all. Breaking a poppadom into tiny bits she was fiercely glad she'd invited a gatecrasher. She only hoped now that Jonah did not behave himself.

Matt refilled his glass. He was drinking white. 'We used to play duets together. Do you remember that? The Telemann Canonic Sonatas?'

She shook her head.

He looked disappointed in her. 'I understand. It was very rough what happened to you. You really don't talk?'

She shook her head again.

'I know they had you on a ventilator after the attack, according to the news reports. They didn't use your name, of course, but we all knew at school it was you. You know how it is. Did that damage your vocal chords? You used to have a lovely singing voice.'

What planet was he from where he thought she could talk about this over lamb korma and chicken tandoori?

She grimaced and put her finger to her lips in a shushing gesture.

He nodded sagely. 'Understood. I was warned that you keep it quiet – you don't want the notoriety. It must be really hard even though it was fifteen years ago.'

She was reminded of one of the lines from the Harry Potter films, Hermione telling Ron he had the emotional range of a teaspoon. She was sitting next to her own Ron Weasley.

'I'm pleased though that it hasn't held you back. Knowing, you know, about it all, I followed your career with awe – even saw you on TV once. You stand out and the cameras kept going to you, did you know that?'

Jenny shook her head.

'And I thought, there she is! The violinist from my town who made it. It gave me hope for my own chances getting into a top-flight orchestra. You've been in Philharmonic for how long?'

Safer ground. She held up two fingers.

'Two years? Wow. You must be good.'

Shrug.

'Oh, come on, Jenny! I've heard great things about you. You're regarded as the reliable backbone of the second desk strings.'

Why did being a reliable member of the second row sound like an insult? She wanted to brilliant, outstanding, original.

'I think I'm placed right behind you so I'll be watching your every move. Don't let the newbie down.' He patted her wrist and pulled a tub of mango chutney towards himself. 'Want some?'

Jenny found the meal interminable. Matt kept trying to engage her in conversation but she really wanted nothing more than to escape from him. She didn't remember him but he did remind her of what she had been like at thirteen: eager to please her mother by joining in with duets, loving the music that filled her home life, enjoying the company of the (usually) older students that came for lessons. They made her feel talented and grown up – head-turning stuff at that age. Faces long forgotten flashed through her mind; there had been Harry, of course, and a Rachel, a Claire, two Toms, and a Ben that she could remember with some distinction. They'd been at her fourteenth birthday party and played a version of 'Happy Birthday' written as Beethoven might've orchestrated it. She'd laughed until she got hiccups. The other students were rather mixed together: earnest faces, polite voices, well brought up boys and girls often coming in uniform direct from school for their lessons. She could ask her mother, of course, if she remembered a Matthew Upshaw but that was something Jenny knew she wouldn't do. Mum loved any sign that

152

Jenny was willing to talk about what happened, claiming Jenny's blocking out of that time was bad for her psyche.

Psyche: that was the Greek for moth. She'd read that recently in a retelling of myths when researching for a piece they were recording. Jenny twisted the stem of her wine glass so the red caught the candlelight. Sometimes she felt that she was nothing more than a moth battering itself against a lantern. What earthly good would it do to open the door and let it fly into the flame?

A roar of laughter from Jonah's end of the table drew her thoughts out of the dark place to which they had fluttered.

'So no one bent down to pick up the soap around him again,' concluded Jonah, proving he was telling some blue joke or anecdote. Jenny smiled, feeling fonder of her housemate than ever before. Trust him to lower the tone of a gathering. He was a very good bull.

'And did you really do the tattoos yourself?' asked Brian's girlfriend, an inexplicably beautiful girl with sleek blonde hair and a Page Three figure. Inexplicable in that compatible couples, in Jenny's experience, tended to gravitate to people of the same attractiveness score.

Jonah was enjoying the attention. He held out his hand. 'No. Got them in exchange for favours, if you know what I mean.'

This was met with blank faces.

'Really? You guys are so fucking naive! What else do you think we have to exchange in prison when we've no money? A young guy like me and a lot of bored old lags: use your imagination.'

Jenny was and it wasn't taking her to nice places.

'One of my friends was a good artist. He did these, and these.' Jonah rolled his neck to show the bolts.

'You were lucky not to get Hepatitis,' said Brian's girl. 'Or worse.'

'Viv, you're right. But don't worry: I got myself tested. I'm clean as a whistle, ready to be blown.' He winked.

153

His neighbour looked shocked, not sure if she should show that she got the innuendo or ignore it. Jenny recalled now that Brian's girlfriend's name was Vivienne and she was a health visitor. You would've thought she'd be less easy to embarrass about bodily functions.

'Did it hurt?' Vivienne asked, opting for ignoring.

'Hell, yeah. But that's part of the point: to hurt yourself on purpose rather than let others hurt you against your will.'

'I hadn't thought of it that way.' Vivienne bit her bottom lip. She was thinking but the gesture was also a very sexy one. Jenny wasn't sure she could carry it off herself. She'd probably just appear constipated. Brian wasn't looking too pleased, though, that Vivienne's attention was fixed on Jonah. His naan bread was pulp. 'I've got some troubled families on my list and some of the parents have whole sleeves of tattoos, which I've always found odd considering how cash-strapped they say they are. I'd thought it a fashion thing but maybe it's a statement?'

'You should ask them, Viv. You might learn something helpful about their lives.' Jonah scrapped a foil dish of rice onto his plate. 'Lots of us at the bottom of the heap have people assume they know us but we all have our stories to tell.'

'That's profound,' said Brian in a mocking tone.

'I've been known to have deep thoughts. Staring at four walls with only a farting cellmate for company can make you reconsider your life choices, you know, Brian?'

'I don't know, actually, not having served a prison sentence.'

Jonah turned back to Vivienne. 'Your boyfriend's a prick.'

'Hey!' Brian pushed back from the table, chair clattering to the floor.

'Bri!' Vivienne was also on her feet. 'Don't!'

'You want me to sit here and let him chat you up all evening? Whose side are you on?'

'I wasn't chatting her up, Bri,' said Jonah, thoroughly enjoying himself. 'I came with someone else in case you haven't noticed.'

154

'Jenny?' Brian made a dismissive gesture. 'She wouldn't go out with someone like you.'

Why wouldn't I? Jenny looked round for something to throw at Brian so she could participate in this ridiculous argument.

'Why not?' Jonah got slowly to his feet, a much more menacing gesture than Brian's outraged leap.

'Guys, guys, it's my birthday!' pleaded Harry. 'There's red wine, curry, and we've just had a new carpet.'

Brian was now red in the face and roaring. 'Because she's got better taste than to shag an ex-con!'

'Maybe she likes a bit of rough? Maybe Vivienne does too. Ask her.'

'That's a totally inappropriate question,' said Vivienne.

'See, she does,' crowed Jonah. 'Dead boring in the sack, is he? Poor—'

Brian's fist put an end to his next words. Jonah ducked, showing he was used to fighting. His knuckles ploughed into Brian's gut. The big guy folded, wind knocked from him, possibly the shortest fight in history, making Brian look foolish to have started it. Jonah had miscalculated, however, if he thought that would win him the match. Vivienne took the glass jug of water and poured it over his head.

'You bastard, you provoked him!'

Jenny was worried that Jonah would retaliate. Instead, he looked amused. He grabbed an end of the tablecloth, spilling drinks and plates, to wipe his face and chest. 'You noticed? In my defence, I'd have to say he was asking for it.'

'Get out of my way! Get out!' Vivienne pushed past him. 'Bri, are you all right? Oh, darling!'

'The fucker's just winded. No harm done,' said Jonah, getting a packet of cigarettes out of his back pocket. 'I think I'd better go. Happy birthday, Harry. Nice meetin' ya'll.'

He was already in the hallway when Jenny caught up with the fact that her escort home was leaving. She grabbed her handbag and dashed after him, exit impeded by having to squeeze past everyone's chairs.

'Jen, you don't have to leave!' called Harry. He was on his knees, blotting a red stain from the carpet. 'It wasn't your fault!'

The front door slammed. Jenny didn't bother changing shoes but opened the door and ran after Jonah. He had paused at the gate to light up.

'Sorry, sweetheart, but those guys really got on my nerves.' He waved the smoke away. 'Don't leave just because I made myself unwelcome.'

She grabbed his sleeve to kick off one shoe and slip into her Converses.

'Really? You want to leave with me?'

He was her lifeboat from yet more talk with Matt. Foot wiggled into the second one and she scooped up her heels and stuffed them in her bag. She could feel eyes on her from inside the house, spying on what was going on at the gate. She offered him her arm, an echo of his gesture back at Gallant House.

'My carriage awaits?' Jonah laughed, then swooped down and kissed her on the lips. 'There: that'll give your jerk ex something to think about. Can't believe you wasted time on that smug bastard.' He placed his fingers lightly on her elbow. 'Take me home, m'lady.'

When they arrived in the cool, dark hallway of Gallant House, Jenny put down her bag and placed her hands flat on Jonah's chest.

'What's this?' Jonah rested his lightly on top of hers. He would be able to feel her trembling. She'd decided on the train that she was going to prove her old friends wrong. They seemed to regard her as some Vestal Virgin still worshipping at the shrine of Harry. That wasn't her. Not any more. Harry needed exorcising once and for all. She needed to take something for herself, some human comfort.

156

She went up on tiptoes and kissed Jonah lightly, letting him decide which way this was to go. He could say goodnight and they both could part with no embarrassment, or he could take the signals she was sending and run with it.

'Has my luck changed?' Jonah brushed her cheek with his thumb.

She nodded.

'You know that I don't do "love", right? I just do the casual thing?'

That's all she expected. 'Yes, I understand,' she signed.

He caught her hands as she finished, pulling her further into the house. 'It won't be awkward, I promise. Tomorrow, we'll go on as before; tonight is just a …'

An interlude, she thought.

'A space out of time. That's what sex is. You don't have to think about it after.' He picked her up, cradling her across his body. 'I don't know about you but I don't want to go upstairs. Want to get snug in the snug?'

The teasing tone was just what she needed to take away the gravity of her decision. She nodded.

'Thank God, as I don't think I could carry you upstairs.' He pretended to stagger under her weight as he kicked open the door to the snug.

She poked him.

'Just joking. You're as light as a feather.'

She rolled her eyes.

He placed her on one of the sofas and began unbuttoning his shirt. 'What falls faster: a tonne of feathers or a tonne of rock?'

She shook her head at him.

'If you don't answer I'll stop here.' He paused over the fourth button. 'And if you get it wrong, I'm the winner and get to have my wicked way with you.'

She pointed to herself.

'And if you win, you get to have your wicked way with me.'

157

She giggled. It felt good to treat everything like a joke.

'Seriously, not another bit of flesh until you answer.' He bent over her and kissed her before pulling back. '"Jonah, don't be so cruel!" you cry. But I'm not budging.'

She got out her iPad. 'They both fall at the same speed. Duh!'

Jonah grinned and took the tablet from her. 'Did I say they were both all wrapped up nice and tight?' He started on the zip at the back of her dress. 'No, I did not. Just imagine: one rock plummeting to earth.' He pushed the zipper to the bottom. 'And all those feathers scattered to the air so that they fly away on the breeze.' He whispered kisses all over her shoulders, neck and breasts – feather-light. 'I win.'

When dawn peeked in through the vine leaves, Jenny stirred. She was lying squashed against the sofa back with Jonah sprawled beside her. He was on his front, one arm trailing on the carpet. The light showed that his tattoos did not stop at his neck. Spread across his shoulder blades was a bird. An eagle? She shifted to take a closer look. A phoenix rising out of a nest of flame. It had to have been professionally done as the reds and yellows weren't the muddy colours of the prison made ones he showed off so readily. She let her finger trace them a millimetre from the surface of his skin. He was lean and fit under his shirt, a better body than she had been expecting. Actors were probably told to tone up. She realised that his habitual stance was a little hunched, like he wanted to guard himself against attack. Another thing they had in common. Smiling, she leaned forward and kissed the phoenix.

'Mmm?' He stirred, rolled and fell off the sofa. He lay on his back and laughed. 'Look at me with my cool moves!'

She tickled his stomach. He batted her hand away, then caught it and kissed the fingers. The moment hung between them for a second before he let go and sat up.

'I'd better go upstairs.'

He didn't mention Bridget's name but neither of them would want to be found like this by their landlady. Their clothes were strewn across the snug. His boxers were draped on the TV and her bra on a table lamp.

'Thanks for a lovely evening, Jenny.' On his knees now, he kissed her. 'I enjoyed being with you.'

He was saying goodbye. Jenny grabbed her dress from the back of the sofa and pulled it over her head.

'Friends still?' he asked anxiously.

She smoothed it down. He'd warned her what this was. No stupid expectations of a relationship. Besides they didn't suit. She pushed back her wayward hair and smiled.

'That's my girl. You deserve so much better than me.' He leaned forward and kissed her tenderly. 'But I'm here, OK, for those times when you can't get what you deserve?'

She caught the back of his neck and pulled him to her for her kiss. How could she tell him that he was wrong? He wasn't some second best, bottom-of-the-bargain-bin man? Getting out her iPad now was just not going to work. She rubbed her lips over his cheeks, his nose, and then his mouth, savouring him.

'God, you're sweet. You'd better keep away from me or I might get addicted.' He gently unlinked her hands and stood up. 'Back to normal, remember? This was a time away from reality.'

She nodded and blew him a kiss.

He laughed. 'You're something else, Miss Jenny Groves, something else entirely.' And he left.

Chapter 31

Jonah, Present Day

'How would you characterise your relationship with Jenny Groves, Jonah?' asked DI Kahn.

Jonah rolled his neck. They'd have to charge him or let him go soon. It would've usually happened already as they had already detained him for over twenty-four hours, but the little side trip to the hospital to check his self-inflicted injuries had stopped the clock on that. His actions had given them a few more hours to question him until they maxed out their time limit and had to decide if to apply for authorization to continue holding him.

'Jonah?'

'Sorry, can you repeat the question?'

'How did you get on with Jenny Groves?'

'Jenny and I were cool.'

'So you would say you were friendly?' asked DS Foley.

Did the police know that they'd slept together? Did it matter?

'Yeah, we were good friends. Just mates, you know?'

'Did you want to be more than mates, Jonah?' She said it in that consoling way, intimating that she knew all about frustrated hopes.

Jonah rocked on his chair, realised that gave away too much, so sat back down firmly. 'We were mates. End of.'

'Did you look into her past? Maybe so you could understand her and know how best to relate to her?'

They were fishing for him to own up to the creepy scrapbooks. 'No. I knew she'd been hurt. Obvious, isn't it? The not-talking thing is a bit of a giveaway. But her past was hers to share or keep to herself.'

'You were sometimes asked to research characters for your coursework. Perhaps you made a study of Jenny Groves?' suggested Khan.

'Why are you talking about that as if it is in the past tense? I've still got a year to go at RADA.' Act like an innocent man and maybe you'll convince the audience.

'I'm talking about past actions. Did you research Jenny Groves?'

'No. I've already answered that question.'

'But your tutor said you used her as an example in a mime class.'

Fucking Maurice. So that's what the police had been doing in his twelve-hour break: interviewing everyone who knew him. He shrugged. 'So?'

'So you studied her. Closely. Intimately.' Khan didn't do the innuendo well. He should've left it to his sergeant with her husky voice.

'OK, this is how it is. I'm an actor. I watch people. I observed the way Jenny got round the problem of not being able to speak. I thought it beautiful.' There: he'd given them the truth. The word 'beautiful' felt unnatural on his lips, not part of his usual vocabulary. 'I observed her – just as I observed Mrs Whittingham – I used her in a class too. Are you going to arrest me for that? I observed the guy on the train opposite me – the old woman feeding the pigeons in Trafalgar Square – I'm even observing you both now in case I ever have to play a tight-arsed policeman and his scary sidekick.'

Foley smiled acerbically at her superior. 'At least I get scary.'

'Yeah, you look all soft then you bite, like a fox. You're the threat in the room.' Jonah made a snapping motion with his teeth. He knew it would either rile her or bring her a little over to his side: either reaction would be interesting.

'Jonah, where were you fifteen years ago? asked Khan, flicking through the manila file. They knew the answer, of course.

Jonah wrinkled his brow as if thinking. 'Fifteen years ago? I was what? Thirteen? Fourteen?'

'That's right. Where were you?'

'I'll have to consult my engagement calendar.' He was now acting out in his head super important businessman, not a role he ever expected to play on screen. 'I moved around so much, I find it hard to remember. Places to go, people to see.'

'Then let me remind you. You were taken into care when you were nine.'

'Oh yeah, I definitely remember that. Got beaten up the night after my mum's funeral by another fucking foster kid. Happy days.'

'You were moved from that house to a children's home in Romford. You didn't settle.'

That was an interesting way of characterising his reaction to the relentless bullying he'd experienced from the other boys. He had been younger than most, and vulnerable. That had been one of his most important life lessons: don't let the fuckers see you're hurting.

'After that, you were put with a foster family in Harlow. You stayed with them for a few years.'

He remembered the Walshes. They'd been OK. He'd actually gone to school fairly regularly and got on well with the other foster kids, an older girl and a younger boy.

'Were you aware that your foster sister was having music lessons?'

'Yeah. She tortured us with her Grade One violin for a year until she gave it up.'

162

'Do you know who her teacher was?'

Where were they going with this? 'No idea. Enlighten me, Sherlock.' Why was he acting so cocky? He didn't understand himself sometimes. It was like he had behavioural Tourettes.

'Nikki Groves, Jenny's mother.'

'Really? Small world.' Was he surprised? His life was such a tangle of awfulness, of course they'd dug that up. 'Though I suppose there are only so many violin teachers in Harlow so maybe not so much of a coincidence.'

'Did you know Jenny Groves before she moved into Gallant House, Jonah?' asked Foley.

'No. Did she go to my school then? The intake was about two hundred each year so I didn't know everyone. I spent most of time off my head.' He fantasised about a cigarette. He could feel himself drawing the smoke into his lungs and expelling it in the police officers' faces.

'No, you didn't attend the same school.'

'OK then. I didn't know her.'

'And you didn't know anything about the attack on her at the time? It was massive news, locally and nationally: I find it hard to believe you didn't notice.'

He wasn't sure what they wanted from him. 'No, it must've passed me by. We didn't live in Harlow itself but in Nazeing.'

'Nazeing?'

'Yeah, it's a funny little village a couple of miles away. Nothing happens there. I wasn't the kind of kid to take much notice of the news.' He'd spent those two years getting drunk on the allotments if he remembered rightly. Cheap cider bought from the local Spar where the bored assistant turned a blind eye to underage drinkers. It was why the Walshes eventually handed him back. They couldn't curb his habit because they were powerless to isolate him from himself. He'd been in a deep self-hatred and drank to escape. He'd tried to keep it out of their house though, as he respected them.

163

'Jenny Groves was attacked in her bed on the night of her fourteenth birthday. The assailant silenced her by strangling her and left her for dead. He's never been caught.'

Shit. He'd suspected something like this. They were trying to frame him for a sexual assault and an attempted murder fifteen years ago. This was fucking reaching. He must've really pissed them off. 'I didn't know Jenny. You have my DNA. You won't find it at that crime scene.'

Khan tapped the file. 'Unfortunately, the samples taken from that crime were tested by a company that has since been proved to have lax laboratory procedures. Their evidence has been discounted and people convicted on the strength of it have been released on appeal.'

So they didn't have shit.

'Why are you asking me this? I was thirteen years old!'

'Why did you move so abruptly?'

'Let me introduce you to local government bureaucracy.' Hatred for their complacency filled him. They didn't have a clue. 'I was put in Nazeing by Essex County Council for a few years then transferred to Redbridge. None of it was my choice. It should be in the file. When there, I got into trouble with some older boys and served my first period in a juvenile detention centre; the rest, as they say, is history.' He waved away the cycle of burglary and drug offences and increasing time in prison.

'Odd that you should mention history,' said Foley.

'Is it?' He was so tired of this. He just wanted to rest his head on the table and sleep – or was that weep? 'Look, are you going to charge me with anything? I'd thought I'd left all this behind but my life is going up in flames the longer I sit here, and you're asking me about a crime committed when I was a kid!'

'I'm mentioning it because someone remembers that crime very well, despite it being fifteen years ago.'

'I imagine Jenny does.' Just like he hadn't forgot a single second of any of the assaults he'd suffered as a child for all his efforts to blank them out.

'And her attacker. Have you been leaving flowers on her pillow? Have you been sending threats to Jenny, telling her to keep quiet about what happened that night?'

'What?'

Foley put Jenny's phone on the table between them. It was held in an evidence bag but he recognised it from the music notation cover. 'We've had our people going through this. Jenny's been getting messages from an unrecognised number. We think it's from a burner phone, no way of tracing the source. They refer to details only Jenny and the assailant knew about the incident. They mention the flowers.'

'Nothing to do with me.' Jonah took his hand off the table as he could see his fingers quivering slightly. This was getting deadly serious.

'Jonah, did you assault Jenny Groves when you were fourteen?'

'No.'

'When she moved into your house, did you fear that she would recognise you and threaten her?'

'No. Have you even thought through what a coincidence that would be – her moving into same house as her old attacker? I lived there a year before she was even mentioned.'

'Not so big a coincidence if you engineered it – kept tabs on her all these years and suggested her as a suitable housemate once the opportunity arose. Did you pretend to be her friend, start an intimate relationship with her, so that you'd have more power over her? Did she come to realise who you really were?'

'No. Did Jenny accuse me of any of this?'

Khan sighed. 'Jonah, you know full well that Jenny can't say anything. You made sure of that, didn't you?'

OK: a line had definitely been crossed. 'I want a lawyer.'

Chapter 32

Jenny, Eight Months Ago

'I'm sorry, Jenny, but I can't increase your prescription. You've already taken all the tablets meant to last you till the end of the month. That tells me the Tramadol has become the problem, and that can become more serious than even the neck pain.'

Small and neat like a sparrow, Dr Chakrabarti was looking at her with that compassionate expression that meant sweet FA in the face of the agony that gripped Jenny. How would the doctor like to live with the sensation of an iron spike being driven into the base of her skull?

She tapped out her pleas. *I can't live like this. I'm in constant pain. I can barely write. I can't hold my violin.*

'You're a professional musician, aren't you? Yes, I can see that that must be a problem. I can sign you off sick while we try to manage your pain issues. And we might need to think about other delivery mechanisms.'

Jenny wanted to lunge across the corner of consulting desk and scratch Dr Chakrabarti's soft brown eyes right out. Christ, I didn't know I was like this, she thought in despair.

Please. I'm at my wits end. I just need the pills.

'I can't in good conscience deal them out like sweeties. These are powerful medications.'

Exactly: that was why she wanted them. *PLEASE!*

The doctor resettled the stethoscope around her neck, untangling it from her reading glasses that hung by a beaded chain. 'Jenny, I'm not cutting you off as I might in other circumstances.'

Jenny breathed through her nose. Keep calm. *Other circumstances?*

Dr Chakrabarti looked uncomfortable. 'Where a patient appears to have become addicted to their opioid tablets. I'm just saying that you need to adopt other strategies to manage your pain so that the drugs can do their job. If you misuse them, there is a danger your addiction will spiral out of control.'

Inside Jenny was screaming. For the doctor she acted rational. *What strategies?*

The doctor gave a relieved smile, like a sheepdog herding a recalcitrant ewe into the right pen after a long struggle up and down dale. 'Ideally, we get you on a lower dose – or wean you off entirely. There's a pain management clinic at the Queen Elizabeth Hospital. I'll see if I can get you an urgent appointment.'

How urgent is urgent?

'Hopefully in a couple of months or less.'

I have to carry on working. She wanted to add angry emojis to the message, expletives and exclamation marks. Her fingers were clenched, struggling with the impulse.

'You have to manage your dosage more carefully. Rest. Reduce the amount of time you spend doing activities that hurt your neck.'

Which part of 'professional musician' had the doctor not understood? This was useless. Jenny got up to go.

Dr Chakrabarti turned back to her screen and tapped a couple more keys. The printer began to whirr, giving Jenny hope. 'Look, Jenny, here's a repeat prescription. I've given you just enough for seven days. You'll have to come by once a week to pick up a new one so I can see how you are handling the tablets. Opioid addiction is not to be waved off as a minor problem. Research it if you don't believe me. The statistics in America are terrifying. More people die from it than gun violence. It's getting a grip here too. Believe me, you won't want to go down that slippery slope.'

Jenny took the printout and left. All she could think as she went to the pharmacy in the surgery was about taking those pills immediately.

Floating home on a Tramadol, life didn't seem so grim. She'd obeyed Dr Chakrabarti and resisted downing two or three just to kill the pain that she'd suffered from for the past three weeks. She worried that her body was growing resistant to the drug but this tablet was working just fine, reassuring her.

I can do this. I can handle this. The pill gave her a little pulse of pleasure. She plucked a rose from an overhanging bush. As it sprang back, it showered her with petals from blooms that were going over. The scent took her back to childhood, to making rose perfume outside her family's apartment block with Angela, the girl from the flat upstairs, which meant sitting on the little communal lawn cross-legged and bruising rose petals into a tub of water.

Her mind drifted, not so much like a petal but more like a dandelion seed. It bumped over the roofs, the tree tops and up into the cloudy blue sky. A Bulgarian harpist had told her the night before that there was a whole valley in her country devoted to growing a particular rose that produced the world's best essential oil. Japanese tourists came thousands of miles to see the fields when they were at their height – an inland sweet-smelling scarlet sea. She would sit and play to them surrounded by blooms. That sounded almost like a Haiku. You couldn't pick them by machine as that spoiled the petals. You had still to do it by hand.

Jenny imagined herself there, going down the rows, plucking red, pink, and white petals, surrounded by the perfume of roses.

Inland scarlet sea
Sweet-smelling and hidden thorns
I pick them by hand.

She counted the syllables against her thigh. Now she was brushing her fingers over the velvety flowers, like Maximus in *Gladiator*, touching the corn that represented home. Strains of Hans Zimmer's *Rhapsody* wound through her mind. She imagined who might be standing in the lit doorway as she walked through the field to her house.

She loved Tramadol.

What nonsense was she spouting? This was the drug speaking. Her thoughts dropped back to Earth. Was she addicted? What could she do if she was? The pills were her lifeline.

Unexpectedly, homesickness and hopelessness overwhelmed her. She sent a text to her mother, interrupting Nikki's stream of consciousness on the WhatsApp chat. Mum was wittering on today about politics, not an arena Jenny wanted to enter into. Too depressing. The lunatics had taken over the asylum on the world stage.

Her mum's response was instantaneous. *How are you darling?*

Should she tell the truth? They'd last got together in August for a holiday in Portugal during the orchestra's annual break. It was now late September. Her summer had been a slow torture. She'd survived her concert programme on pure grit. Everyone remarked on the strain that showed on her face and how much weight she had lost. Maybe it was due to her silence, but people felt they could state the bleeding obvious to her. In Portugal, Mum had fed her little custard tarts – a local delicacy – with the devotion of a penguin who walked a hundred miles to the edge of the ice sheet to come back with a fish supper. At work, new friend Matt, the guy she'd sat with at Harry's party, had tried to get her to eat, badgering her after every rehearsal to go with him to the nearest café. These hadn't felt like invitations to a date but genuine concern. Harry had shot her worried looks from the brass section but, as they weren't talking (hah!) after his birthday party, he hadn't said anything directly to her. She wondered if he was the one behind Matt's Mother Hen act. The two, friends old and new, seemed bent on conspiring to interfere in her life. She didn't want either of them to see what was really going on inside.

You need looking after, said her subconscious Harry. You're a mess, Jen. You need to hook up with a nice caring guy like Matt and stop spending time with the ex-con.

Shut up, Harry. You always were a snob.

Perhaps she should be grateful rather than resent the fact that people cared? Look at Bridget. She cooked extra at most meals and put it in the fridge with a label suggesting Jenny do her a favour and finish it for her. Not wanting to upset her, Jenny gave most of these dishes to Jonah who had a robust appetite. He always said he was missing out on a few meals from when he was little so was making up for it now. He never put on weight.

Jonah was a godsend, Jenny admitted to herself. He was the only one who didn't nag at her or tell her to take better care of herself. His help was more practical: gentle back rubs and cuddles when she got overwhelmed. They'd fallen into a comfortable 'friends with benefits' pattern over the summer that had become her one haven. He was the only one with whom she could relax.

Mum was waiting for a response. At least, with messaging, pauses to think up plausible lies were less apparent than in direct speech.

Fine. Looking forward to the autumn programme. Couple of short tours next season – Germany, Russia.

Exciting. How's your neck?

Still there. Nothing to report. Certainly not that the doctor feared she was becoming addicted to her medication.

Good. You'd let me know, wouldn't you?

No. Of course.

Any concerts you think I'd like to attend?

Great: her mother had moved off the subject of her health.

They could message about music until the cows came home without Jenny feeling suffocated. A little image of dusky nights and cows plodding up a country lane, bells rolling, rambled through her brain. *How do you feel about Berlioz?*

The house was chilly when Jenny came in. She'd noticed that it seemed to have its own internal weather, not respecting what was going on outside; was it the ghost from the well keeping it at his own temperature maybe? In the world of Blackheath, it was a muggy day, hot when the sun escaped from brief cloud veilings. It sprawled in the sky and panted down at the dry common like a Golden Retriever overcome by heat. A young family played rounders in the distance, cries of children sounding like starlings. In Gallant House, however, autumn had already set in. No Indian summer allowed beyond the doorstep. An arrangement of chrysanthemums occupied the telephone table, outrageous gold and red globe heads shouting into the gloom. Nature saved up its most flamboyant flower for the last months of the year.

She let the door bang – a habit acquired from Jonah.

'Is that you, Jenny?' called Jonah from the snug.

Who else would it be? He got his answer when she didn't reply. Dumping her bag in the hall, she went into see him. He was standing by the doorway that led to the balcony. Pendulous grapes hung around him, turning him into some latter-day Bacchus. He even had the *joli laid* grin of the statues.

'How did it go with the doctor?'

She gave him a thumbs up. It wasn't accurate but she didn't want to talk about it.

He grinned. 'Watch this.'

He turned and did a kind of limbo dance under the nearest bunch of grapes. His tongue whipped out and he snagged a fruit, clamping on it with his teeth. He chewed and swallowed before springing up. 'And they even taste good. Try one.' He picked one of her and beckoned her over. As she approached his smile broadened and he put it between his teeth with his

171

usual 'I dare you' twinkle in his grey-blue eyes. Sometimes she didn't feel like playing along but today, with the buzz of her pill still working, she was feeling mellow enough. She leant forward and took it from his lips. The taste of sun-ripened grape burst on her tongue.

'Good?'

She nodded.

'But they don't taste half as good as you do.' He pressed himself against her and whisked his hands over his favourite spots for his mouth to cruise. Jenny could feel herself softening and warming, natural pain-relief flooding her. She leant forward, again this time for a kiss.

There was a cough behind them. 'Oh, excuse me, I see I'm interrupting.' Bridget made to scuttle away.

Jenny would have leapt apart from Jonah but he held her firmly to his side. They'd kept their relationship away from Bridget but she had to suspect something was going on.

'It's OK, Mrs W, we were just playing a team game they taught me at RADA.' So smooth, Jonah, so smooth. 'You must've played it – the one where you pass something between people, an orange or a balloon. We were trying that with grapes.'

If she bought that as an excuse, then she was an idiot. 'No, I don't think I have played that, Jonah. Does that mean the grapes are ripe?'

'Yes. Want one?' He reached up and plucked another grape and held it out.

'Only if I don't have to join in your game,' said Bridget, showing she was on to him.

'No, that's between consenting adults only.'

She took the grape and tasted it with a serious expression. 'You're right: they're perfect. Rather too many pips though. I wonder if they'll make decent wine?'

'You're asking the wrong person, Mrs W.' He stepped aside so she could inspect the vine from the doorway. Jenny noticed

Bridget didn't venture outside, not like she and Jonah did on a regular basis.

'Norman will know.'

'I haven't seen so much of our trusty neighbour, Mrs Whittingham. Is he ill?'

'Norman?' She picked another grape and rotated it in her fingers, not eating. 'Oh no. He's fine. Fully retired now. He's spending more time with his guest than we expected. They're getting on like a house on fire.'

Jenny thought that a peculiar expression. The last thing you'd want is a relationship that burned down the building you lived in.

'Have you met his new friend yet?' asked Bridget. 'Lovely young man. Single.' She gave Jenny a significant look.

Jenny shook her head. Was Bridget trying to set up a date?

'Me neither. I think Norman's abandoned us.' Jonah's tone was abrasive, rubbing up on Bridget's loneliness. The Tuesday gatherings had lapsed over the summer without their core members: Jonah too busy filming and Norman too … well no one was sure what he did now with his days. 'They've not come to a Tuesday, have they?'

'His friend works and doesn't get back in time, Norman explained. I'll invite him to supper one evening, revive my Tuesdays, so you can both meet him. It looks like he's lodging there long-term. I'm so pleased Norman has company.'

'What's he like, the friend?' Jonah squeezed Jenny's backside out of Bridget's sight. He'd intimated already that he thought Norman was possibly homosexual. Jenny could tell he was wondering if this was the truth about next door.

'Very nice. Polite. He's a medical student, which is why he's so busy. Norman will be such a help to someone starting out.' She put her hand to her forehead. 'I'm sorry, I'm not so good with names these days. I make up mnemonics then forget what I was thinking. Norman tends to just call him "his boy".'

Jonah squeezed again. Jenny knew without him saying anything that he was thinking 'toy boy'. 'Good for Norman.'

Bridget ignored his suggestive tone, her tactic for anything that ruffled her refined world. 'I'd better get on. I was going to pick some apples. Jenny, I just called in here to say I almost tripped over your bag in the hallway. Please don't clutter the entrance.'

Jenny nodded and signed 'sorry'.

Bridget left them.

'Well,' said Jonah.

'She knows?' signed Jenny.

'Must do. I don't suppose she cares – unless she's jealous.' He grinned wickedly. 'She doesn't know that we've done it in almost every room in the house, except hers. We'll have to find a time when she's in the garden.'

Jenny could feel herself blushing. It had been Jonah's idea to shock the living daylights out of the waltzing ghosts by a sexual marathon around the house and grounds that summer.

Not living daylights, she corrected, deathly daylights.

Her own favourite was their encounter in the drawing room at midnight under the disapproving gaze of Admiral Jack's wife. The secrecy and fear of being discovered just made it more fun. Jonah was a risk-taker and she found she was too.

She looked up at him hopefully.

He laughed. 'Sorry, babe, no time now. I'm expected at the studios at four. And aren't you going to Kris and Louis' wedding planning meeting?'

She nodded. She had a day off and was catching up on her chores.

'Say I said "hi" and if either of them needs a best man: I'll be there.'

'Louis chose me as his,' she signed.

'Really?'

Jenny grinned and decided to write the rest down. *Because I can't make a rude speech about him.*

'Clever! So Kris will have to dig up a Trappist monk to get even?'

What Louis doesn't know is that I've arranged for a slideshow that speaks for itself. His sisters were very helpful.

'I bet they were.' He checked his phone. 'Gotta go.'

When Jonah left, his energy drained from the room and the cold seeped back. Better move that bag, thought Jenny. She picked it up from below the coat pegs, feeling the familiar twinge in her neck. No more pills allowed today. Irritation scratched inside her. You'd have to be crawling along the edge of the corridor to trip over it. Bridget probably just didn't like the clutter. She should've said that rather than make Jenny sound like she was creating hazards on purpose.

Going up to her bedroom, Jenny dumped the bag on the bed. An overblown chrysanthemum lay on the pillow, many of the petals already turning brown. Not again. She'd asked both Bridget and Jonah months ago if they were leaving these little tokens for her and both vehemently denied it, though Jonah said he'd wished he'd thought of it to freak her out. He'd suggested the next stage should be a dead bird or frog as if the house had a ghost cat leaving offerings for her owners. He referred to the mysterious flower-giver from then on as Spooky Moggy. That helped exorcise her fear.

Jenny picked up the chrysanthemum and threw it in the bin. That would annoy Bridget but right now she couldn't be bothered to take it down to the compost heap. Petals remained on the pillow so she brushed those into her hand and dumped those too.

It had to be one of them, didn't it? Flirt with the idea of a ghost though she did, she couldn't quite see it carrying whole flowers to her pillow. It could still be Jonah in a clever double-bluff. He might be waiting for the moment for her to run to him one night again and then laugh himself silly at her expense for being so gullible in believing the house was haunted. That would turn the sequence of flower gifts into a joke. She hoped it was that.

If it were Bridget, though, then Jenny had to attribute that to senile moments or, more worryingly, malice. There were a few sharp edges still in her relationship with her landlady. Bridget wanted to mother her and Jenny had told her that she had a perfectly good one of her own. That hadn't gone down well. Finding Bridget in her room one day, standing at the window with her bucket of cleaning materials, had been a shock. She'd asked to do her own tidying but Bridget had insisted that, as Jenny had the en suite, she let Bridget continue to keep an eye on things. Jenny wasn't sure what Bridget thought she'd do in there – guesses ranged from leaving the bath running till it over-flowed, to snorting cocaine off the vanity unit? – but there were some things on which the landlady would not give way. This was one. They did agree that Bridget would not come in without invitation while Jenny was in the house and she had also agreed to have a lock fitted, a little bolt on the inside so Jenny could feel safe at night from intrusion.

There was a snake even in Eden, Jenny reminded herself. Everything had a price.

She propped herself up against the bedhead and pulled her laptop out of her bag. Dr Chakrabarti had suggested she do some research so she would. Typing in *Opioid crisis* she was rewarded with a blizzard of hits.

I'm not like these people, she thought, after having read a few case studies. I'm taking the pills for my pain, not for the buzz. I'm not a drug addict any more than a person taking heart medicine or Lithium tablets.

I'm not.

Chapter 33

Louis and Kris lived in Pimlico in a maisonette not far from the Thames, a couple of suburban roads north of the riverbank. They had the upper floors, and if you stood on the flat roof over the extension you could just about see a glimpse of the buildings on the southern side of the river. This was where they were holding the wedding planning meeting, completely against building regs and the wishes of their neighbour underneath. But what the insurance broker under them didn't know wouldn't hurt him.

'Unless we fall through onto his Aga. Can you imagine fitting an Aga in Central London?' asked Louis. 'It was so heavy they had to hire a crane to lift it in over the roof.'

'Electric rather than gas or oil,' said Kris. He didn't seem bothered to be sitting so close to the edge without a balcony rail, even with his balance issues. He reminded her of Jonah in that. Maybe it was an unwritten requirement for living with Bridget?

'What's the point of an electric Aga?' Louis raised his hands to the heavens. He'd chosen the chair nearest the house wall. Heights weren't his thing. 'They are supposed to be in country kitchens with Jill Archer knocking up a batch of scones for the village fête.'

'I haven't cured him of his *Archers* addiction,' said Kris mournfully.

'That'll never happen. It's fascinating. The characters go through personality transplants at regular intervals like aliens have taken over their brains, just so the story can keep on rolling with some dramatic tensions. The story of simple country folk.'

Kris topped up his beer from the large glass bottle of some local microbrewery. 'People in real life aren't like that. Someone who starts life an arse ends it as one, in my experience. Take my best mate, Ralph. I love him dearly – he saved my life – but he can still be a total shit to women. You have to love him despite his failings.'

'Ah, so you should give up trying to change me then and take me warts and all,' said Louis triumphantly. 'I'm stuck on *The Archers* and you'll just have to adjust.'

Jenny tapped the pad which was lying on the garden table they'd carried out of their kitchen sash window.

'Jenny is calling us to order. Quite right, darling. We've confirmed the venue and the colours for the flower arrangements. So how much do we spend per head on our guests? The caterers sent a menu with options.'

'What about cancelling the caterer and doing a bring-and-share supper?' said Kris as an opening gambit.

'What about eighty quid a head, not including alcohol?'

While they wrangled their budget, Jenny flicked through her messages. Her mother had reverted to politics. She interjected an 'I know. Aren't they all awful?' which would do for any political statement her mum might make. Louis pushed a glass of white wine into her hand. She sipped it without looking. It tasted crisp and cold – perfect.

'We'll still be paying off the wedding when we draw our pensions!' argued Kris.

'You already have a pension.'

So there was still some way to go in this argument. She tuned out again and went through the messages from unfamiliar numbers. No, I haven't been involved in an accident which wasn't my fault. No, I don't want to find out more about PPI mis-selling. No, I don't want to know more about your amazing broadband deal. She hit delete on all of them. Then she came across another with a weird opening line. *Do you like my flowers?*

Was the joker going to unmask himself? It had to be Jonah surely, as Bridget didn't text? She tapped on the message.

Do you like the flowers? I enjoy putting them where you lay your head. Do you think of me when you look up at the canopy at night? Do you miss me?

Something about the tone set her teeth on edge. *Who are you? This isn't funny!*

An admirer.

Her hand jolted, spilling the wine. Oh my God, the answer was instantaneous. The person was waiting on the other end. Even though they weren't right beside her, it brought them so much closer.

'Jenny? What's wrong?' asked Louis.

She must've given away that she was alarmed. Turning the screen to face them, she showed them the message.

'You have a secret admirer who leaves you flowers?' Louis was trying to work out why this was upsetting her.

'Sounds more like a stalker,' said Kris. 'Creep.'

Jenny nodded fervently.

'Flowers in your bedroom?' Louis was anxious too now.

'Have you told Bridget?' asked Kris.

Jenny set down her wine and picked up her iPad. *Yes. Neither she nor Jonah have owned up to it.*

'But it has to be one of them?'

Who else could it be? The house is never empty. Bridget's there all the time.

'Then this must be Jonah's idea of a joke,' said Kris, gesturing to the messages. 'He has a cruel sense of humour at times. Do you want me to talk to him?'

Jenny shook her head.

'I know. I'll send the reply for you.' Before she could stop him, Louis composed a response.

Take your limp dick and fuck off, you flower fetish crazy guy.

Jenny grabbed the phone off him but it was too late. Kris was laughing.

Not funny, guys!!!! she scribbled on the notepad where they were planning their wedding.

'No, it's not. If he does it again, I'll sort him out for you,' promised Kris. 'What about thirty quid a head, that's including booze?'

They slipped smoothly back into discussing their wedding reception, leaving Jenny with that incendiary message winging its way through the ether. Thanks to the bloody frustrating fact that she couldn't talk, she hadn't explained the connection to the earlier message about the attack on her years ago, so why should they be worried? But she was. She didn't like the fact he had her number; she hated the thought that it might be Jonah. He was in the house with her; she believed they liked each other; they had an intimate relationship. This flower thing wasn't a joke for her and he had to know her well enough to get that. What did it mean? She needed space to think – puzzle it all out.

Jenny gestured that she was going in to the loo.

'OK, sweetheart. I'll guard your wine for you,' said Louis with a wink.

'Are you all right?' asked Kris.

No, all wrong. What did it signify that she was sleeping with a guy who could torture her like that? Jenny pointed inside and clambered back over the sill. Pain lanced through her as she bent to squeeze through the gap. Damn her neck.

Reaching the bathroom, she leant against the sink and took some breaths. Managing her pain, Dr Chakrabarti would call it. Her eyes watered and she felt like sobbing but feared if she started she would be unable to stop. Splashing some cold water on her face, she dabbed herself dry with the black hand towel. Focus on that, not the pain. Such a guy colour. Her gaze drifted to the bottles lined up on the shelf below the window. Nestled against the shaving foam was a tub of Kris' prescription. His pain killers for his ongoing discomfort after amputation. She picked it up and shook it. Practically full. The case studies she'd read online edged into her mind, how the desperate began stealing from medicine cabinets when visiting friends, or going around houses with an estate agent on the pretence you wanted to buy them and taking from strangers. The ideas had been planted …

Oh my God, you aren't! Her conscience squawked with outrage. Jenny, this isn't you!

No, Kris was a hero and friend. He didn't deserve this from her.

I need it more than him.

You do not!

I can't function. He has Louis. He can get a repeat prescription. No one would question a veteran.

This is wrong and you know it!

Somehow her internal moral compass had gone awry, needle swinging north-south-north-south without settling. The tub ended up in her handbag without her even remembering the moment.

Put it back.

No.

Now her inner voice arguing with inner conscience sounded like a toddler.

You'll hate yourself.

I already do. So, so much.

There came a knock on the door. 'Jenny, are you all right in there? Louis and I are sorry if we made a joke of your stalker.'

It was Kris. Too late to put it back now. He might hear the rattle. At least, that's what she told herself.

She opened the door and gave a wan smile. Stealing made her

feel like scum but she didn't have the will power to stop. She pointed to the door.

'Heading home?'

She mimed being tired.

'Yeah, we understand. We can be a bit much for anyone. Thanks for your help with the wedding. I've knocked Louis down to a reasonable price per head so we won't have to sell our first born.'

She gave him a thumbs up. She was such a fake friend.

'Are you really all right? You look …'

She raised a brow.

'I suppose that's not a very flattering thing to say, but you look bad, not your usual self at all.'

How accurate. She mimed sleep again.

'Good idea. Get some rest. Do you want us to stump up for a cab for you?'

She shook her head. Ouch.

'Fine. See you soon then. We've made an appointment at the suit hire place. Want to help us choose? It'll be one morning next week.'

Another thumbs up.

'I'll text you the time and place. Maybe your mean old boss at the café will let you have the time off?'

She smiled, as he meant her to.

'Jenny's just heading off!' he called to Louis.

Louis came in carrying the wine she had left. 'Did he tell you what a tight-fisted bastard he's been?'

She didn't feel like this teasing but had to play along. She shook her head.

'We'll be eating burger and fries from McDonalds if he has his way.'

'Nothing wrong with a Big Mac. My army mates would appreciate it far more than that salmon crap you want.'

Jenny put a hand on each chest and mimed pushing them apart.

'Yeah, yeah, we won't come to blows about it. I love the idiot too much,' said Kris.

'Love you too.'

She waved goodbye and left them to their good-natured sniping.

The tub of pills deep in her bag broadcast a beacon of shame all the way home to Gallant House.

Chapter 34

Jenny couldn't believe what she had done. When she arrived for her shift at the café the next day, pain-free thanks to a couple of Kris's tablets, she wondered about producing the tub tomorrow and pretending she'd picked it up by mistake. She'd taken several. How would that look to Louis? Couldn't she just forget it and put it down to a one-off lapse? Kris would cope.

Racked by this moral dilemma, she avoided Louis by cleaning tables as far from him as she could. The only music running through her head today was Chopin's *Funeral March* which blended into close cousin Darth Vader's theme tune. Fortunately, Louis was too busy to notice her avoidance tactics. He'd made the mistake of putting Vlad and Ryszard on the same rota and they had inevitably had a screaming argument in front of customers. The two student cellists were highly strung (hah!), in competition with each other and from countries that were traditional enemies. Louis should know better.

Her rehearsal meant she had to leave an hour before the usual end of shift and, thankfully, no time for a gossip. She signalled 'must dash' with her body language, putting on her jacket as she headed for the exit.

Louis still managed to catch her on the way out.

'Just a second! How are you, Jenny? Feeling rested?' He looked at her, noting the relaxed lines on her face. 'You seem better.'

She gave him a thumbs up.

He hugged her. 'I had to grab you just to say that we really appreciate everything you're doing for us.'

She signalled a zero.

'Not nothing! You keep Kris and me from throttling each other over party favours. Grumpy old man.'

Jenny dug up a smile and signalled, 'Which one?'

He laughed. 'Both. Kris misplaced his meds but didn't notice till this morning when he needed them.' He picked up her violin and helped her strap it over her shoulder, which was good as she didn't have to meet his eyes. 'I suspect our new cleaning company are responsible so I've told him not to leave them out where anyone can see them. There's a thriving black market for that stuff.'

'Is he OK?' she signed.

'He will be. He's got an emergency appointment with his doctor. Hadn't you better run?'

Jenny kissed him on the cheek and headed out the door. It was official. She was a thieving scumbag – and she hadn't even confessed when she'd had a huge throbbing opportunity to own up. These were her friends: they'd be shocked but they would've understood if she had come clean. Now she'd hidden it, the damage if they found out would be irreparable.

And the humiliating fact was that she'd left the tub at home so she'd never intended to own up, had she?

In a break during the rehearsal for that evening's concert, while the percussion ironed out some problems with the conductor, Jenny went back to researching opioids. She couldn't face herself if she stole from a friend again. That was a line she wouldn't cross, not twice. Louis' mention of a black market, though, suggested there was another, less impactful way of getting what she needed. She'd heard stories of the dark web but had no more hope of finding her way there than the average person. Her web skills were limited to a Google search. But the world was her marketplace online. Maybe there would be a semi-legitimate grey market she could tap into? She tried a few search terms and came up with a site in the Middle East. If she gave her credit card details would she be scammed? What would arrive – if anything – in the post? Would the order get confiscated by Customs? There had to be laws about this, didn't there? God, she was such an incompetent criminal.

'Penny for them?' Matt sat down beside her and handed her a chai. He'd come to know her likes and dislikes over the summer and understood she had a weakness for a milky chai in the afternoon.

'Thanks,' she signed.

He signed back: 'My pleasure.' She'd told him he didn't need to do that because she had two working ears but he'd enjoyed learning the signs from her. He reminded her of Jonah in that way, though Jonah was more adept, having an aptitude as a quick study.

'What were you doing?'

She wondered if he would understand the signs for 'Mind your own business'. Instead she went for 'Nothing much.'

'When are you going to invite me round to your amazing house?' he asked, unwrapping a chocolate bar. 'Harry told me you've ended up on Blackheath in a mansion, miles from the rest of us.'

'He's not seen it,' she signed.

'He looked it up online and got the street view.'

'Spying on me, is he?'

'You know Harry. Once you're in his circle of friends, he feels responsible for you.'

She rolled her eyes. Harry was such a mixed bag, sometimes the spoiled boy, sometimes the old fusspot. He'd been the same in school when they first met; he'd been a few years above her, everyone's favourite. She'd assumed the 'spoiled' part would drop away with maturity. She was still waiting.

'Have you heard he's got a new girlfriend?'

Jenny had told herself that she had long since moved on, but it was still a jolt. 'A girlfriend? Or someone he's shagging?' she signed.

Matt laughed and looked around a little embarrassed. 'That sign is a bit graphic for doing in public.'

No, shagging is too graphic for doing in public, not the sign for shagging. She didn't bother trying to communicate that. Matt was nowhere near fluent enough to understand a signed joke.

'Don't you want to know who it is?' asked Matt, returning to the safer ground of the girlfriend news. Orchestras were terrible for their backstage gossip.

'OK.' He knew that gesture.

'Su-Lin.'

She mimed the flute player.

'That's the one.'

That made sense. Su-Lin was quiet and Harry had told Jenny that he found silence restful. Su-Lin, whom Jenny wished she could hate but really couldn't, was that way because she chose to be. Harry would have no competition in his 'This is Harry' Show. Jenny didn't give it long, unless Su-Lin had bedroom skills to keep him interested enough to stop sleeping his way through the orchestra. She mimed that she was happy for them.

'You're not, but that's OK. I know he hurt you. He told me why he dumped you. That was harsh.'

'He did?' she signed.

'He was always a bit freaked out by knowing you'd been the victim of a violent assault. After you told him the details, he worried that you'd have flashbacks.'

That wasn't what he had told her, but she could believe that was one of his reasons. Harry, as he had gaily admitted, was selfish at heart.

'He doesn't want there to be any awkwardness between the three of you. He wondered if you'd like to come out for a drink after the concert? I volunteered to be your escort so he said that was OK.'

Still feeling hurt that Harry had rejected her for something she really could not help, she signed, wishing irony was easy to convey in gestures: 'So he's not a fan of Jonah, my last escort?'

'What?'

She'd made up a sign for Jonah which involved a whale swallowing him whole. She'd forgotten that was a private thing between them and not immediately apparent to an outsider like Matt. She spelt out his name, frustrated by the slowness of communication with Matt.

'God, no! He thinks your housemate a menace and probably a threat to society.' Matt gave a lopsided smile that actually made him seem fleetingly attractive. 'I thought Jonah hilarious. I'd like to meet him again.'

'OK,' she signed.

'OK what?'

She mimed going for a drink. After all, the alternative was to sit at home, hating herself.

Matt had suggested they went to one of the bars in the Oxo Tower which led to an awkward walk down the Embankment. They'd fallen into twos, Harry with his arm around Su-Lin in front, Matt and Jenny trailing behind. Su-Lin was a tall, willowy girl originally from Hong Kong. She had a river of long dark hair, that slipped and slunk over her shoulders whenever she moved her head. Why didn't it get tangled or knotted, frizz up in humidity like Jenny's did?

That's because she's worth it, sneered her internal voice. It sounded less like Harry now and more like her evil twin whispering the worst things. Not that it ever hadn't been self-generated. If she ever went back to counselling the psychologist would probably have a field day with her interior life. Who internalised the voice of an ex who really never cared that much about her to start with?

'Adès was a harsh bastard in rehearsal but he really brought it off tonight, didn't he?' said Matt. 'The Stravinky piece was really tight.'

All Jenny could do was nod her agreement. Her pain was back. She'd taken all of her prescription pills for this week, Kris' were at home, so she was now left clenched in the jaws of agony. The intense rehearsal followed almost immediately by the concert had taxed her beyond what she could bear.

'Something the matter?'

She couldn't hide much from Matt. She signed that she was in pain.

'Again?'

'I'm so worried it might stop me playing.' The symbol for this message was pretty apparent even to someone who didn't know BSL that well.

'Oh Jenny. What can I do to help?' He slid his arm around hers, knowing not to press on her shoulders.

She was about to sign 'nothing', then wondered. She got out her phone and typed a message. It was the best thing to write on at night while on the move.

'Do I know anything about black market sources?' He looked shocked. 'Me? Whatever made you think I would?'

That had been a misstep. *Sorry. I'm desperate.*

He didn't back off as she expected, but went silent, the tension rippling through his arm where it touched her. 'This would help you?'

She nodded, eyes pricking with tears. Was someone going to reach out and help her with this?

'I suppose … I suppose I could look into it. I have some friends … well, it doesn't matter about the how. What do you need?'

She typed out the brands that would do.

'I'm embarrassed to ask this but you would pay me, right?'
Of course!

He nodded. 'Yeah, of course you would. This is OK, isn't it? You're not going to do something stupid, like overdose?'

Without pain relief I'll have to stop playing. My life would be over. I am my music.

'Yes, I understand that.' His voice was a whisper. 'Music is our life. I wouldn't do this for anyone, you know,' he added, more in his old way.

Harry must've caught that. He turned around. 'What are you doing for Jenny, Matt?'

'Sharing my spare strings,' said Matt quickly, showing he could think up plausible lies with admirable swiftness.

Harry looked disappointed by the answer as if he was expecting something more salacious. Which it was, if he'd heard the truth. 'Oh. OK, the first round is on me. What do you want?'

To go home to bed and bury her head in the pillow. She typed on her phone that she'd have Barcardi mojito and turned it round for him to read.

'Trying to bankrupt me now?'

She nodded.

'What goes around comes around. Just wait for your turn. You in those swanky digs with next to no rent, must be raking it in.'

She mimed laughing. Everyone knew the violinists were the worse paid members of the orchestra.

Matt went for a pint of craft beer and Su-Lin pointedly ordered a fizzy water. Harry kissed her approvingly and then elbowed his way to the bar. '*Mein host!*' It wasn't a German themed bar but Harry had his own way of commanding attention. 'Two pints of your finest, please, then we'll do the girlie drinks with umbrellas and shit.'

Jenny wondered how Su-Lin could stand him. Then again, how had she?

Matt guided us over to a table with a view of the Thames.

This view was why the bar was so pricey. The old heart of the City lay across the dark waters, St Paul's dome glowing white over the orange glare of the other buildings. City cruise boats passed, lit windows showing diners and party-goers enjoying the mild evening.

Harry came back with a tray of drinks, expertly holding them over the heads of the other patrons. Few musicians made it into the profession without some time spent as a waiter.

'Here we are: two craft beers brewed in Islington, one fizzy water from Evian, and one mojito with enough lime to make a saint turn sour. How's that bastard you share the house with?'

Dig, dig, dig, why don't you? thought Jenny. She hadn't realised that a hidden part of this evening's agenda was to get back at her for the ruined carpet and birthday party. Matt was mistaken if he thought Harry was trying to smooth the way; he was rubbing her nose in it.

She pondered her answer, then wrote:

Spectacular.

Let Harry make of that what he would. His imagination probably wouldn't be far wrong.

'You see, Su-Lin,' said Harry to his companion, as if she'd asked, 'Jenny's shacked up with this ex-con. He came to my birthday party – uninvited, I might add.'

I invited him.

'Yeah, I remember. He came to cause trouble – didn't have a clue how to behave with civilised people. He was the one who gave Brian that bruise.'

'What bruise?' asked Su-Lin guilelessly.

'Just below his ribs. Jenny's guy didn't pull his punch. It could've done real damage. As it was Brian couldn't play without pain for some weeks. He thought about suing.'

And did he mention that he threw the first punch?

While Jenny was writing this, Matt got there first.

'That's hardly fair, Harry. Brian started that fight.'

191

Harry waved that away as if it were unimportant. 'And Jenny here never even apologised for bringing a dangerous man right into my party. An ex-con for Christ's sake!'

Jenny now understood that maybe Harry hadn't proposed this evening at all; it was sounding more and more like Matt's well-meaning but misguided idea to reconcile them.

'You can't hold Jenny to blame for the actions of someone else,' said Matt. 'I'm sure she's sorry he did what he did.'

She really wasn't. *How much damage was done?*

'The carpet was fucking ruined,' said Harry. 'That cost us three hundred quid to replace.'

How to respond? She really didn't want to apologise. Instead she went for:

'Look, Jenny's sorry – and as I said, how was she to know that Brian and Jonah would come to blows? Friends again?' asked Matt hopefully.

'I've always been Jenny's friend,' said Harry heroically. Su-Lin looked at him in adoration. Jenny wondered how long that stage of the relationship would last.

'Jenny?' asked Matt.

She nodded. As she hadn't specified what she was agreeing to, she felt OK taking the easy way out. Note to self: no more after concert drinks with Harry.

'I'll get the next round to celebrate.' Matt got up. 'Same again?'

'Yeah, mate: that microbrewery knows its stuff.'

'Thank you, Matt. That'll be lovely,' said Su-Lin.

'Another mojito?' asked Matt.

Why not? thought Jenny. The alcohol was dulling the pain, making her head bearably fuzzy. She could almost not be here at all. *Yes please.*

Chapter 35

The next week, Jenny had to miss a shift and a rehearsal due to neck pain. Kris' stolen pills didn't seem to touch it, which she took as suitable punishment for her theft. All she could do was lie flat on her back in her bedroom and wait for the firestorm to pass. Was this her life from now on? All those years spent qualifying only to be cut short? She wanted to scream with frustration, break the windowpane with her shrillness, but, of course, she couldn't even do that. There was no Jonah to comfort her because he was now shooting his part at the gang leader, which meant a fortnight spent in Liverpool for location filming. Bridget tiptoed in and out, brought her meals and drinks, even left pages of her history of the house by Jenny's side as if that would comfort her. She didn't feel like doing anything, not even reading.

If this goes on, thought Jenny, I'll have to go home. By home she meant her mother's house. It would be a total signal of defeat. Grown up life will have proved a test beyond her and she would retreat to being the teenager in her bedroom again.

Her phone pinged. Jenny lifted it up to read the message. It was from Matt's number.

Missed you last night. Everyone's asking after you. How are you?

Then I have some good news. I got what you asked for.

Joking? She hadn't really expected him to turn up anything.

No, serious. My contacts came through. They say they are the real thing. He'd already lectured her on the danger of taking unverified drugs and extorted a promise she wouldn't try that route. He was now keeping his side of the bargain. *Do you want them?*

YES!

Do you want me to come to you?

Thank you. Thank you.

I'd prefer not to be seen if that's OK? I feel awkward.

So did she. She knew that she was pushing a decent guy into being her drug runner. *Text when you're outside. I'll let you in. Can you come immediately?*

Be there in half an hour so we can get the Jenny show back on the road.

You are a

With the promise of relief so close, Jenny smiled as she lay on her back. She was already anticipating the loosening of the grip of pain across her back and up to her skull. She even managed to sleep for a little.

The phone pinged again. *I'm outside.*

Jenny rolled onto her side then carefully stood up. Making her way downstairs, she listened out to noises that would tell her where Bridget was to be found. From the burbling of the radio in the kitchen, it sounds like she was cooking. Jenny quietly opened the door and beckoned Matt inside.

'Hello, sweetheart.'

She pointed upstairs and put her finger to her lips. Matt grinned and followed her without a word.

Once in her bedroom, Jenny put the bolt across.

Matt gazed around the room with interest and went to the window. 'This is some place you've got here. Mine looks like a broom cupboard by contrast.'

Jenny wasn't feeling up to small talk. She tugged his arm.

'Oh sorry.' He reached inside his jacket and pulled out a brown padded envelope. 'This is part of the batch. I kept the others behind in case I got stopped by the police. I can't imagine why anyone would stop and search but I was feeling absurdly guilty.'

'Sorry,' she signed.

'No don't be. I'm only too pleased to help. I read the instructions. No more than two a day, OK? You have to promise me you'll keep to the rules.' He held it out of her reach.

Like hell she would. She nodded.

He handed over the envelope. She dived into the bathroom, ripped open the packet and took two with a gulp of tap water. Pain shrieked in her skull as she did so, protesting as she bent down. She breathed through it, feeling like a lion tamer whipping the pain back into its cage.

'Jenny?'

Oh shit, Matt was still here. Of course he was. Just when she wanted to relish the feeling of being pain-free all on her own. She stood up, ran her hands through her dishevelled hair and came out. The drug was already beginning to take just the edge of her agony and lighten her mood. She could pretend to be human.

'Did they work?'

She gave him a thumbs up and a thank you.

He smiled. 'That's great. So, er, about the payment?'

She got out her purse, hoping she had enough cash.

'It cost me five hundred quid.'

She dropped the purse. She didn't have that much in her bank right now, let alone in her purse.

'Yeah, it sounded a lot to me too but it's not on the NHS, is it? I wasn't sure of the going rate. Not my world.'

Jenny felt awful. She hadn't thought. She'd plunged her friend into debt without even giving him a budget for his illegal supply of drugs. God, that was almost funny if it weren't so disastrous. How could she have been so stupid?

'Jenny, you're worrying me. You look really upset. Can't you pay me today?'

She shook her head. Ironically, that no longer hurt.

'Can you … er … pay me ever?' He was catching on fast. His voice sounded a little hoarse. What difficulties had she made for him?

She would pay him back. Eventually. Maybe. She grabbed her iPad to write an explanation. He pushed it down gently.

'Look, I think I get it. It's too much. I'm a novice at this and I made a mistake. It's my fault. I should've driven a better bargain.'

She shook her head again. Not Matt's fault.

'I could, you know, take some of the hit, if that'd help? You pay part, I pay part.' He toyed with one of the chrysanthemums Bridget had left in a vase to cheer her up.

She looked up at him. What was he offering?

'I really like you, Jenny.'

Yes, it was what she thought.

'I'd do this for a friend. I can earn the money somehow – do some more hours.'

If she earned it another way, wasn't that what he was too shy to suggest?

'I moonlight as a hospital porter, did you know?'

No, because she'd never asked him about himself. What kind of friend did that make her? A shitty one.

'It was a guy at work who told me how to get hold of them. I can get more – hopefully for less. He must've thought I was a clueless clown, not bargaining.' He pulled a self-mocking face. 'And I can see you're hurting. I just want to help you.' He reached out and touched her cheek. 'I know I'm not good looking or anything, but I do care about you. Really care. Let me look after you.'

Jenny swallowed. She wasn't really here was she? The painkillers cushioned the present, muffling ugly edges and tones. Jonah always said sex didn't matter.

196

'Will you let me take care of you?'

She nodded.

'OK then.' His hands went to the front of her blouse. 'Remember: I love you.'

Lying next to him, Jenny found she couldn't feel much about anything. She recalled her proud words to Jonah months ago, that she didn't sell sex. She wasn't sure what had just happened here, but it had been dangerously close to that. She'd gone to bed with her friend, not because she wanted him, but so he'd do something for her. And yet, her slippery conscience was giving her a pass because it was the only way to get hold of the tablets.

She turned her head on the pillow to look at him. Matt had his hands behind his head and was smiling at the ceiling. At least someone had enjoyed himself. He must have felt her gaze because he shifted to run his hand down her arm.

'You're gorgeous.' His fingers went up rather than down to caress her cheek, then down to her jaw, her neck …

She flinched back.

'Sorry. Does that still hurt?'

No, she was just sensitive about the scars. She held still, hoping he'd get her point.

'I'll kiss it better.' He leant forward and pressed lightly on her throat with his lips. Even that soft touch was too much. She wriggled free and bolted for the bathroom with not a stitch on her.

She retched into the sink. Oh God. Oh God.

A minute later there came a gentle tap on the door.

'I'm really sorry, Jenny. I didn't mean to upset you.'

She wiped tears away.

'I'll go now. I promise I won't do that again. I just want you to feel good about yourself – show you that even the scars are beautiful. See you later, OK?'

She waited until she heard the bedroom door gently close.

When she came out, she saw that he had straightened the covers and picked up her clothes for her. A piece of folded paper lay on the pillow.

You owe me nothing. Love Matt

Jenny crunched up the note, stood at the window and screamed soundlessly.

Chapter 36

Bridget

Bridget heard the front door close softly. That was neither of her lodgers. She'd suspected Jenny had a guest when she heard whispering in the hallway but she'd merely turned up the radio and tried to ignore it. If Jenny wished to have a gentleman caller in the middle of the day that was her affair entirely.

Bridget stirred the quince jelly, watching how the orange gloop coated the back of the spoon. Would it ever set? Such a tough fruit when picked, skin unyielding, pale green with unhealthy freckles. Cutting it up was a trial and she'd almost given up as the knife had refused to saw through. Only the thought of Christmas Day with homemade quince jelly to go with an interesting array of cheeses kept her persevering through the stages of cooking, straining and now adding the sugar. She checked the recipe again. Wait until the jelly wrinkles when dropped on a plate. She tried the test again. That would do. More folds than wrinkles but she was feeling irritated by the whole process.

What's wrong with me? I'm normally so patient when cooking. She poured the mixture into the sterilised jam jars, already aware that it was going to be a failure. Am I jealous of Jenny?

With a lowering sensation, Bridget realised she was better when her lodgers were male – she didn't feel in rivalry with them. Jenny was undoubtedly pretty and young. Bridget, pouring amber liquid into glass jars, imagined herself like that old witch in *Sleeping Beauty* checking the mirror to ask who was the fairest in the land. A terrible anti-feminist stereotype, she knew that, but somehow the patterns engrained in childhood persisted. What chance had she, being raised as she had?

Bridget dumped the pan in the sink and splashed water into the bottom. Her mother had been so proud of her ballerina daughter, coming to every recital, making her tutus from yards of pink net and sequins. Her father had attended the major shows, dressed in his Marks and Spencer suit and tie otherwise reserved for weddings and funerals. They never said it aloud to her, but she knew she had pleased them both as their only child. So delicate. So light. In touch with a civilised world of composers and choreographers with foreign names, a culture unimaginable in their little housing estate in High Wycombe. They had boasted so often about her to the neighbours she had come to see herself as the street's golden child, the chosen, and held herself aloof. Poised as if *en pointe*. Then the shattering diagnosis and a few years of flat-footed disappointment. Her advantageous marriage had revived her parents' hopes. They passed away within a year of each other, still waiting for grandchildren. She'd stop reminding them of her age, preferring to leave them with the illusion that late forties was not too late for family. They so didn't want her to be alone. The fact that Paul was not up to the job was never mentioned. Perhaps they assumed she'd see to it herself, get what she needed from someone else? And she had done so in her own way, but that had not included children. A slight story, not one worthy of her history book, lower middle-class girl makes good. No, she wouldn't include that.

Setting the jars aside to cool, Bridget took off her oven gloves and returned to her manuscript. A drop of jam marred one corner, blurring out the last word. She wiped it off. *Trenches*. So many Jacks lost to that stupid war, more killed than in their reckless exploring. If given the choice, better to die in the Antarctic, a hero, remembered for ever smiling in your photograph, dressed in sealskin anorak and gloves; better that than posing in uniform at the dusty city studio before deployment, then drowning in Flanders mud? So much grief for the women left behind. The streets of London must've been salty with their tears.

Bridget looked out of the window at the shadows in the garden under the lilac tree, the well with its open cover and soothing depths. The Victorian father of the baby who had been lost down the well-shaft had paid dearly in grandchildren for his sins. That individual died, she had discovered from veiled references in the family archives, when rutting between the legs of his latest in a long supine line of mistresses. Nobody mourned. From her research, it was clear that he'd become an embarrassment with his dyed hair, moustaches and corset to hide his paunch. Only one grandson – the youngest – had survived the war to go on to be the father of Bridget's mother-in-law. Still, it was a tale worth telling, those two generations after the wastrel, the ones who took us from the lamplit nineteenth into the neon glare of the twentieth century.

Chapter 37

The House that Jack Built – Chapter Twenty-Three – Ghosts

When the tide of fighting withdrew, Bertram was left high and dry with a grown daughter and an infant boy, his wife having died in the lowest point of the war in 1917. Thanks to Bertie, she had made one too many forays on her no-man's land of childbirth. Gallant House was plunged into gloom, ashes cold in all the home fires. The lone daughter was unable to stand it any longer. She could not move around the hallways without hearing the ghosts of her dead brothers whispering, echoes of ball games in the attics on wet days, laughter on the lawns as they cart-wheeled. She declared she was leaving to make a home with her grandmother and her artist lover in a place with no memories. Bertram called her ugly names and sent her to perdition. She said she was going to her salvation as by then the house had become a place fit only for the most deadly of the pure in heart.

I sighed for them both. They would never understand each other and the damage the preceding generation had done to them both. The boy from the well had his revenge on the legitimate seed. I could hear him sniggering in the dark as they fumed and fretted. What my Bertram did not understand was that if he wished for saints then his children were doomed from birth to disappoint him; that the blackness was imbibed with the water. It might now come through lead pipes into the kitchen (no one ever touched the old water supply after the baby had been dragged from the well), but the source was ever the same: the heart of Blackheath.

Chapter 38

Bridget put her pen down. She'd only changed a few words this time. Was the book finished yet? She had reached her own era and circled back but it was hard to imagine exposing it to public view, no more than she would throw open the front door and invite all-comers inside. She could do with a second opinion.

Perhaps the wish had summoned her? Jenny came in and headed straight to the kettle.

'How are you, dear? Feeling better?' Bridget asked.

She nodded but kept her face turned away. Surely the girl should be feeling more cheerful having just cavorted in the middle of the day between the sheets with a gentleman caller? Did this younger generation not enjoy sex?

'I've made quince jelly for Christmas. Do you want to invite your mother to spend it with us?'

Jenny paused, wiped her sleeve over her face, then reached for her phone to type an answer. *Thanks but we usually spend it with friends.*

'You don't fancy a change? I'm sure Jonah would love to have your company.'

I'll mention it to my mum but I don't think she'll like to let them down.

Bridget almost suggested the friends come too but held back. That would sound just too desperate, extending an invitation to complete strangers. She doubted very much Jonah would spend the day with her and Norman, he had already warned that he had other plans. 'Just a thought, dear.' She pulled the newspaper towards her and leafed through until she came to the article she wanted to clip for her scrapbook of recipes. *Ten things to do with windfalls* – that meant apples rather than money. 'I've been wondering about sending my book to a publisher. What do you think?' She said it lightly, hoping to hide her eagerness.

Was that a sigh? That was not very nice if that were so. Jenny hung her head over the mug where she was making tea directly in the cup rather than using a pot.

'I'm a little nervous showing it to an expert,' continued Bridget. Jenny took out the teabag and put it in the compost bin under the sink. She took her mug to the table and pulled a scrap of paper towards her.

You should do that. I like it so why not? But I've heard that publishers get sent lots of books. It's like trying to get a role as an actor – lots of auditions and only a few roles.

'You think it will be rejected?'

Jenny wobbled her hand in a 'maybe' gesture. *Your book might catch someone's eye but it might stay on the slush pile. Before you send it off, ask yourself if you really want to go through all that rejection?*

Bridget thought that might be the longest note Jenny had ever written her. 'I suppose you're right.'

And they might ask to meet you.

Her cheeks flushed. 'Then I'd just invite them here. This house is the star of the show, after all.'

Do you love it so much?

Bridget's gaze travelled round the kitchen. 'I'm not sure love is the right word. I can see its flaws.'

Jenny raised a brow.

'I'm not talking of the patches of damp or areas that need redecorating. I know very well – as you should after reading my account – that the house is built on dark deeds. That's rather the fascination. I sometimes think it's wicked at heart – and it makes us that way too.' She laughed. 'And why am I talking to you like that? Listen to the mad old woman! It's bricks and mortar, nothing more. You might say I spend too much time infusing it with personality.'

Jenny shook her head. *It's memories and history too. I like it here.*

'Really? I did wonder how you in particular would feel when I gave you that first chapter.'

She drew a question mark.

'Black ivory. The house that Admiral Jack built was paid for by the proceeds of the slave trade.'

Jenny's brown sugar eyes widened in shock. *That's what black ivory means?*

'Yes, dear, a euphemism. Opium and slaves – the truth about the British empire. I think it came to haunt the Jacks in the end. Why else is the place now in my hands – the daughter of a grocer from High Wycombe? And who else lives here now: a working-class lad from East London and a black girl from Harlow. None of us are taken from the top drawer. I think the house, if it could speak, would probably say we were more suited to the kitchen than the drawing room, don't you?'

Jenny was now looking around the walls as if they might collapse in upon her.

'I always agree with Feste the fool from *Twelfth Night*: the whirligig of time brings in his revenges.'

Jenny pointed at her question mark.

Bridget silently lamented the lack of literary education among the young that had been standard in her generation. 'In modern speak, it means what goes around comes around. We three are what this house deserves.'

You think we are the revenge?

'Aren't we?' And Bridget realised she still had another chapter to write.

Chapter 39

Jonah, Present Day

His court appointed solicitor shuffled through the statements. 'They've held you since Saturday night. That means they've taken all the extensions they can and they will have to either charge you or let you go.' Keith Gooding looked rumpled and tired in his sweat-stained shirt and shiny tie. Jonah doubted he appeared much better than the solicitor because he was still wearing the same clothes in which he had been arrested.

Jonah crumpled his empty cup, then regretted it as the cheap plastic split. No refills now. 'If they charge me, what're my chances of getting bail?'

'Pretty good. Your previous convictions were for drug-related offences, not violence. If they charge you with assault, and I'm not convinced they will, we can argue that it was an isolated event due to the extraordinary circumstances. The fact that your victim had herself just assaulted another woman in a drug-fuelled frenzy, I would argue, backs up your claim that it was self-defence.'

'It really was. She was out of control. I barely touched her.' That's how Jonah liked to remember it so he was persuading himself it was true.

'I'm not advising you to misrepresent the truth, of course, you must be open and candid with everyone ...'

Yeah right, thought Jonah, like that had always served him so well in life.

'But it would be better for your case if you avoided any implication that bodily contact was made before you offered first aid, even the mildest form of restraint as she went for you.' Her dark eyes burning, pushing at him to get out of the way; his hands at her throat to stop her. 'OK, yeah.'

'There is no forensic evidence to contradict due to the fact that all agree you had close bodily contact with the victim when you gave mouth to mouth resuscitation. Any bruising can be attributed to that.'

That glossed over what had made resuscitation necessary in the first place. Jonah wondered if the lawyer thought him guilty or innocent. 'I didn't do it.'

The lawyer gave him a tight smile. 'Then we shouldn't have a problem, should we?'

Jonah couldn't believe that he was actually walking out of the lockups at Lewisham police station. The police had caved pretty quickly once the lawyer got involved and they released him with the warning that he was still a person of interest in their enquiries and that he should keep himself available.

'Always am,' he'd quipped to the officer on duty.

What Jonah found even more difficult to believe was that his theatrical agent was sitting in the reception area, waiting for him.

'Carol?'

'Jonah?' She got up and moved closer to give him a hug. 'You poor old thing!'

He held up a hand. 'I wouldn't. I'm wearing the same clothes I was arrested in.'

She patted his arm anyway. 'No charges?'

'Not at the moment. The solicitor is just having a chat and

asked me to wait here for him.' He glanced through the doors to the street. There was a cluster of paparazzi lurking. Under other circumstances, he might've taken this as an encouraging sign that his fame had reached sufficient standing for him to merit the treatment. 'I thought you would've done a runner?'

She grimaced. 'Jonah, I knew you were trouble when I took you on. You didn't do it, right?'

'Fucking right.'

'Then if we handle this intelligently, then it should play in our favour.'

'So I'm still on your books?'

'Yes. And don't worry about RADA: they can't expel you unless you're convicted. How would that look? They were already aware of your past convictions so can't play all shocked that the police unfairly persecute a man just because he's got a record.'

Yeah, he could see how that would come across. Carol was doing a good spin, making the police look lazy as they went for the most obvious target. He just had to broadcast his innocence and hopefully this could blow over, even help him in an ironic way, sharpening his edgy reputation.

Having finished his conversation, Keith Gooding came over and Jonah introduced them. The lawyer shook hands with Carol. 'Nice to meet you, Ms Travis. I've just been informed that Jonah shouldn't go back to Gallant House until Mrs Whittingham allows it. In any case, seeing how it is the scene of the crime, it would be better if he steered clear. He'll be allowed back briefly with a suitable escort to collect his clothes and personal belongings but in the short term he needs somewhere else to stay.'

'I'll sort that out for him,' said Carol.

'Good: I hoped you'd say that. Jonah, I'll be in touch. Keep out of trouble, OK?'

Jonah shook hands, wondering why he hadn't had the sense to call in a suit earlier. Decades of distrust of authorities probably explained it. But he wasn't that vulnerable kid anymore; he was an actor with a profile and people investing in him. That gave him some power and he should seize it. 'Thanks, Keith. Much appreciated.'

'And obviously, don't try to get in touch with Mrs Whittingham or Miss Groves without first clearing it with me. I believe both are still hospitalised.'

'OK, fine. Wasn't planning to. Anyone got a cigarette?'

They both shook their heads. Bummer.

'Ready to go, Jonah?' asked Carol. 'I've a taxi waiting.'

'Can we go by a shop? In fact, could you lend me a tenner? I didn't have time to grab my wallet when they arrested me.'

'No problem.' She took his arm just above the elbow and led him to the main exit.

'We're walking right through them?'

'You bet. Try not to look guilty.'

'Shit, I was born that way. What should I look like?'

'Defiant?'

'Yeah, I can do that.' Holding his head up, he strode towards the black cab, smiling slightly as the flashbulbs flared.

Chapter 40

Jenny, Six Months Ago

Jenny tried to enjoy the wedding, she really did. She'd survived the ceremony held at the registry office but was finding the reception at the Victory Services Club near Marble Arch a trial. Even with Matt as her date fending off most requirements to be sociable, she was dreading the moment when she'd have to stand up and do her 'speech'.

'Jenny?' Matt whispered. 'Are you OK?'

She shook her head. Would she never get away from this suffocation? Everywhere she looked things were being strangled: chairs under fabric covers and noosed with ribbons, tables swamped in fine linen. Even the flower arrangements had curls of raffia garrotting them, red blooms swooning from the vase.

'Nervous?'

Her finger touched her neck: their private signal that it was the pain that was getting to her.

He looked around to check that they weren't being overheard at their spot on the table in the centre of the dance floor. While the caterers changed the place settings for the toast, Kris and Louis were chatting with family members so had abandoned them for the moment. Kris's best man, Ralph Shaftesbury, an old army colleague, was laughing with some military types at the bar. A big bear of a guy, he'd carried the wounded Kris out of the combat zone on his back. His slim, much botoxed wife with threaded eyebrows and an expression of permanent surprise had disappeared to the Ladies, though Jenny suspected she'd really gone outside for a fag. Kris had said Ralph was a shit to women and it looked like the wife agreed.

'I thought this might happen,' Matt murmured. 'I got something a little stronger, just to help tide you over.' He pressed a single foil wrapped tablet in her palm, clipped from a strip. 'I was told we have to be really careful with this. It's Fentanyl – a synthetic opioid so much stronger than what you've been taking.'

All Jenny heard was 'much stronger'. She popped it from the foil and downed it with a swallow of champagne.

Matt tried to take the glass from her. 'I don't think that's quite the idea.'

She attempted to keep it away from him.

'Jenny, behave!' Matt looked around, flustered by her reckless move. 'I went to a lot of trouble to find something to help you and you repay me like this?'

His tone reminded her how well and truly under his thumb she had become. Her grip on the glass loosened.

'Here, take my water. Drink that.' He brushed his hand up and down her arm. Nausea curled in her stomach.

'Everyone all right?' Louis was beaming as he returned to the table. He liked to believe the fiction that Jenny was happy in her new relationship. So well matched, both musicians together, he said, as if repeating a mantra until he believed it.

Jenny gave him a weak smile.

Louis tapped a fork on a champagne flute. 'Ladies and gentlemen, if I can have my husband back, we are about to cut the cake!'

This garnered great cheers from around the room. Jenny was

reminded that a wedding audience was the most forgiving you could hope for and, besides, her presentation was already recorded. All she had to do was stand up and press the button.

The tablet had really kicked in by the time her moment arrived. Louis was about to pass over her but she held up her hand.

'Oh? What's this? Are you going to play us something, Jenny?'

She nodded and with a flourish produced a remote that brought a screen unfurling from the ceiling.

'Uh-oh. That's not what I meant. I was thinking the violin.'

She grinned and started the presentation. A montage of photos of Louis from a baby and up to date began to flicker across the screen. She'd chosen some of his best recordings to accompany it, including 'My Funny Valentine' when the pictures of him and Kris together began. That produced a roar of laughter. She finished with a photo Matt had uploaded for her at the beginning of the reception: Louis and Kris saying their vows a couple of hours ago. That got a cheer.

Louis was twinkly-eyed when she finished. 'I'm speechless,' he said.

Kris got up. 'In that case, I have to say, that is the best best man's speech I've ever heard.' More laughter. 'Louis and I just want to say a big thank you to everyone who has helped make today so special for us.' He went on to give the usual round of appreciation to various people who had been involved before adding: 'And we'd both like to say an extra special "thank you" to our friend Jenny, who always listens when we talk to her, and is always there for us.'

Jenny scribbled something on the back of the menu and passed it to him.

'She says that we don't give her much choice.' He grinned then bent down and kissed her cheek. 'You're a gem, darling.' He concluded his speech with a thank you to the two families in the room, all of whom had supported the wedding wholeheartedly. That got a big cheer too so he announced he was quitting while he was ahead and took his seat.

During this speech with all its focus on his girlfriend, Matt was playing with a lock of her hair, twisting it around his finger so that it tugged a little uncomfortably on her scalp. She brushed his hand away once attention moved on.

'Careful,' he murmured.

She went still. He often threatened to withdraw his help in getting what she needed if she rejected him. Their relationship was the definition of unhealthy, of course she knew that: her so dependent and him so possessive. It didn't mean that she could see a way out of it. If she had more money, then she could seek out her own supply and cut him loose. That's if he'd accept that. She'd got worried recently that he wouldn't react well to her ending things.

So instead she smiled apologetically and gestured that she was going to the Ladies.

'OK. See you in a minute, beautiful.'

She hurried away, only able to breathe more freely when she got to the cloakroom area. Finding a sofa there, a man's jacket discarded on one end, she sank down. There was no one around. Thank God. Her shoulders slumped and she collapsed against the arm. She no longer had to pretend. The satin bodice of her orange dress dug in under her bust. She couldn't wait to get out of it later. If only she could manage that so she was alone when she did.

Shifting, she felt a lump in the jacket digging into her side. A wallet. Over the past few months she'd taken to stealing just a little, here and there, in the hopes of getting enough money together for her own drug supply. Bags at the café, untended backpacks in rehearsals … Could she? Most people didn't notice if twenty pounds vanished. They'd just think they'd spent it and not realised. If anyone saw her, she could claim she had found it on the floor and was looking for a name on a credit card to find the owner. That was plausible.

Before she had really made up her mind, her fingers were

already unfolding the wallet and checking the cash pocket. Over a hundred. The owner wouldn't know. She slid out forty and tucked it in her bodice.

'What the hell do you think you're doing?' It was the other best man, Ralph the bear; he had just come out the gents and caught her. 'That's my wallet, you fucking slut!'

She pressed it into his hands, panicking. 'Sorry, sorry!' she signed.

Of course, he didn't know signing. He grabbed her by the wrist, looked over to the reception where the dancing was just getting underway, clearly contemplating dragging her before Kris and Louis. She tugged, but he was ex-army and it was about as equal a struggle as a bear with a salmon hooked in its claws. She tried a new tack. Putting her free hand flat on his chest, she met his eyes. Please. At least that was what she hoped he would read in her expression.

His gaze dropped down to the notes tucked in her bodice. 'Come with me.' He pulled her to a stairwell and they went up a flight to an empty landing. She was getting a very bad feeling about where this was going. He pushed her up against a wall. 'You can't tell me why you took that, can you? But we both know it's not yours. That's my money.'

She fished in her cleavage to retrieve the notes.

'Ah-ah. Too late. I don't want that back now.' His eyes turned hard. She could well believe the stories Kris had told about him. He'd come through Iraq without a scratch. 'How about you earn what you took, then I won't say anything to anyone?' His hands slid under her skirt and hooked his thumbs in the waistband at top of her tights. 'Fair exchange?'

She swallowed and did nothing as he pulled all layers of clothing down.

'Nod if you agree – or I'll take you back down there and tell the whole room what I caught you doing.'

She nodded.

216

When he left her, Jenny stared for a while at the white wall opposite. He'd told her she'd been a good girl. He liked women who didn't talk back so she was his perfect lay. If she wanted to do it again, she could message him. Forty pounds was selling herself cheap. He'd even pay more if she acted like she enjoyed it next time. He'd then stuffed his business card where she'd shoved the money. She could feel the edges digging in but couldn't move to get rid of it.

On the wall opposite, there was a little map and instructions what to do in the event of fire. She imagined lighting a match and setting fire to a curtain, sitting here as she watched smoke fill the stairwell. She could go to sleep and not wake up ever again.

'Jenny?' That was Matt, calling for her. Oh God. If he found her like this, he'd know what had happened and then he'd freak out. She picked herself off the floor, hauling up her knickers and tights, and hurried along the corridor, trying doors. She opened one that hadn't been shut properly and slipped inside. A suitcase lay open on the bed. From the dress suit hanger on the wall it had to belong to one of the guests who had come here to get ready. If she was lucky, they'd stay downstairs long enough for her to hide in here and clean herself up. She went into the en suite and inspected her appearance in the mirror. Her neck was reddened where Ralph had bitten her. God, why did some men thinking playing vampire was sexy? She pressed against it with a dampened face cloth. She was never going to be able to explain that away to Matt.

Perhaps that was why Ralph had done it? His revenge? She sensed he never did anything without calculating all the angles first.

A large-size men's toiletry holder lay unfolded on the counter top, different compartments neatly arranged for shaving equipment, toothbrush and toothpaste, a few first aid items. Spotting a pack of plasters, she unzipped it and took one out. Could she claim she'd been stung by something? It would have to do. She ripped the packet open and stuck the pale plaster over the mark. Stupid racist plaster manufacturers: it lit up like a neon sign against her darker skin. Matt was never going to excuse this. He'd still want to know where the marks came from. She stuffed the plaster box back inside the wash bag and something rattled.

Kris's tub of pills. She was in the bridal suite. How perfectly fucking perfect.

In a second, she untwisted the lid and tapped two out onto her palm. She met her eyes in the mirror. She hated herself.

And then a second pair of eyes met hers. Kris was standing in the doorway.

'What the hell do you think you're doing?'

Chapter 41

In the taxi home, Matt was glaring at her.

'Where did you go? I was stuck on my own for over half an hour.'

Buzz, buzz, buzz: he was like a wasp in her ear. A mosquito under the net.

'It was embarrassing, sitting there, not knowing anyone.'

Jenny wasn't listening. She was replaying the awful moment when Kris realised that, not only was she planning to steal two tablets from him, but she was also responsible for the theft two months ago. Where were the words to explain? Locked up inside – so fucking far out of reach. She'd dropped the pills on the counter and wept but he wasn't sympathetic, accusing her of going so low that he didn't recognise her.

'I felt completely abandoned!' said Matt

Then the moment in the bathroom had got a lot worse. She'd thought that Kris hadn't been aware that she'd just had sex with his best man in the corridor while Ralph's wife was downstairs. How great was that, at a wedding of all places, with promises of eternal love in the air? But she was wrong. He spat out that news of that escapade was why he'd come looking for her. He'd already been primed to tear a strip off her for going so low.

219

Kris's face was flushed with rage. 'It's my fucking special day and my best man comes up to me with a nod and a wink, thanking me for providing you as the entertainment. I know Ralph – I know what that means. How could you, Jenny? I trusted you.'

That seemed to be the cry of the evening: how could you? Yes, how could she? It had been surprisingly easy. Particularly after she'd made a grab for the pills she'd dropped and downed them in a dry throat. That had shocked Kris more than anything else she'd done: he ranting and her still going ahead with the theft right in front of him. Brazen didn't even begin to cover it. She'd been able to retreat into a lovely floaty feeling where nothing very much mattered anymore, not even a shattered trust.

'You've got a lot to answer for!' said Matt as the taxi took Waterloo Bridge over the Thames. She imagined rapping on the glass partition for the driver to stop and then leaping over the edge into the silent black water. Mary Wollstonecraft, a feminist heroine of hers, had tried that sometime in the eighteenth century after being shafted by the men in her life, but some do-gooder had rescued her. Maybe Jenny would get lucky and die. She laughed soundlessly.

'What were you doing?' Matt leaned over and sniffed her. 'Are you drunk?'

Not drunk enough.

'And this? What's this?' He had moved her hair and found the plaster. 'Jenny?'

She turned away, watching the lit buildings flicker past, imagining the lives going on inside on this disaster of a Saturday night. People loving, lying, arguing.

'We'll have this out when we get home,' he said, grip tight on her wrist.

Odd how he called her bedroom 'home'. They never went to his broom cupboard of a room in north London, always sneaking into hers like they were doing something illicit. Jenny was almost sure Bridget wouldn't mind but so far their paths hadn't crossed.

Bridget had become very distracted recently, spending long hours sitting alone in the drawing room, working, she claimed, on her book. Jenny had done everything she could to keep Matt away from Jonah, knowing exactly how any encounter between them would go. She'd stopped sleeping with Jonah when she started seeing Matt – she did have some standards; she wasn't a slut even though Ralph said she was.

Was she?

You've just had sex in a stairwell for money. Do you care to reconsider?

Matt was now worrying about the taxi metre. 'It's already on eighteen quid. Do you have any cash? Of course you don't. You're always coming to me for handouts.'

Jenny dragged the forty pounds out of her bodice and slapped it on his palm.

'Where did you get this?'

She returned to looking out the window.

'You should never have let Kris put us in a taxi. I said we'd go by train.'

That had been when Kris had marched her downstairs and collected Matt from the reception, saying Jenny had asked to go home. While Matt fetched their coats, Kris had told Jenny that she'd have to live with the knowledge that she'd spoiled the wedding for him but he wouldn't let her spoil it for Louis. He'd make her excuses but she had to go at once before he lost his temper with her. The final words he'd hissed, while he fixed a smile on his face for the other guests' sake, was that he had obviously never known her properly, never wanted to see her again, or hear from her. People often lost touch with old friends once married; now would be a very good time for her to live up to that cliché. He'd expect her to find a different job while they were on honeymoon.

I need help, she'd wanted to say, but she'd stolen from a veteran, messed up his friendship with Ralph, ruined his big day: who was she to ask for anyone to care?

221

The taxi pulled up outside Gallant House. Matt handed over the exact money, not even rounding up to include a tip. Jenny could hear the driver cursing as he pulled away. She shivered. It was sleeting. Bridget had put up holly and some twinkling white lights but only in one window. The house had swallowed Christmas cheer like a python and was still digesting.

'Inside,' said Matt.

There was a light on in the snug. That probably meant Jonah was home. Once she could've gone in there and wept on his shoulder and he would've hugged her without asking awkward questions. She felt a deep longing for such easy, unearned comfort.

'Upstairs,' hissed Matt.

Taking her high heels off, she followed him meekly up the steps. Once in her room, she dropped the shoes in the wardrobe. Matt didn't like mess.

'I want to see what you're hiding.' He pointed at the plaster.

Maybe this was her way out of this relationship? Maybe he would be so disgusted with her that he would dump her? That would risk her drug supply, but there were other men, weren't there? A business card still pricked her breasts. She walked into the bathroom so she could see what she was doing. Wetting the band-aid, she slowly peeled it off. Matt stood behind her. At first, he didn't seem to know what he was looking at.

'Is that … is that a bite mark?'

She nodded.

His face flushed scarlet and Jenny felt scared for the first time with him. 'You little bitch! After all I've done for you!' Breathing hard, he pulled her over to the bed and pushed her down on her back. 'Who was it, Jenny?' His hands ringed her upper arms. Alarm flared, hot and searing.

She couldn't answer – not that it would've helped.

He dropped on top of her, driving the breath from her lungs. 'You … you … you …! But I love you!' He couldn't find a curse strong enough. For a second time that night, a man was between

222

her legs. On this occasion, she wanted to scream, push him away, but couldn't. His mouth was on her neck, biting down with every thrust. Heart labouring, breath shallow, she could feel herself blacking out. Oh God, this time she'd die – she just knew it. The panic would kill her. But then he lifted his weight up to unzip and shove aside their clothing, allowing her lungs a full gasp of air. 'I love you, Jenny. Don't you get that? Why do you treat me like I don't matter?' He didn't care or notice her panic. Jenny thrashed but couldn't get free. He heaved and sobbed, telling her how much he loved her, how much he hated her hurting him. Then he lay spent on her chest, head nestled between her breasts. She could feel his tears. Her neck stung. He'd added his bruising bite to the mark Ralph had made, trying to overwrite the touch of another man.

Her skin had turned chill by the time he separated from her. He stumbled into the bathroom, not looking back. She could hear a bath running. After five minutes, he came out.

'You need a bath. Come on.' He held out a hand, acting as if he hadn't just … just what? Raped her? It fell in some confused place between agreement and refusal. He'd taken her silence for consent. Maybe it would be easier to pretend, like he was, that it hadn't happened? Jenny stood up, her skirt falling back to her knees. Shaking, she reached up to take off her fine gold chain necklace and, whilst she put that away in her jewellery box, she slid the business card inside.

'Jenny? I'm not angry anymore. I know you can't help being how you are.' Matt was smiling now in a sad way, like a kindly priest who had caught a nun *in flagrante*. 'I noticed you were a little bruised. Let's soak the pain away.'

Numb to the core, she took his hand and went into the bathroom.

Chapter 42

Obedient to Kris' wishes, Jenny handed in her notice at the Festival Hall café and found another job a few buildings away at the National Theatre restaurant. It was the least she could do to show she was sorry. She kept herself apart from her new colleagues so was barely noticed as she cleaned up and carried trays. The cloud she moved in was grey, muffled by her drug habit of starting each day with three tablets and topping up as and when needed. Neither she nor Matt mentioned the night after the wedding. He continued to supply her with pills; she pretended to love him. It was like she'd split herself in two. Part of her was a marionette dancing merrily away while he pulled the strings; the other, her real self, looked on in dumb horror. She couldn't think how she'd got here or, more important, how she could get out. Her only peace was when she'd just taken a pill. Matt had continued to get the more powerful Fentanyl for her, possibly because somewhere at bottom he felt guilty about what he had done. It worked to make life just about bearable as she drifted semidetached, not feeling too much of anything.

Christmas at home passed in a blur. Her mother noticed, how could she not? She nagged at Jenny to get help for her pain, and Jenny promised she would, though what shape that help would take meant very different things to each of them. January was wearing away and Jenny took no pleasure in her music any longer, but still she had to play. Bills had to be paid or she would've dropped out of this too. What was the point of it all: sawing away on strings and wood to make these meaningless sounds? The enchanted kingdom was just dust and ashes.

Habit stepped in when will power failed. She took her place on stage and set out her score on the music stand to join the other strings as they tuned up for Wagner's *Die Walküre*. Jenny wished she wasn't playing such a demanding piece. It lasted for five hours, full of tension from the start, continuing through three acts, to the tempestuous conclusion. The only good point in her grim mood was being paid double rates for Wagner. Incest, murder, fiery death, sung by opera soloists guesting with the orchestra – Jonah would laugh if she told him the story. He thought posh people were weird listening to this stuff for entertainment.

She felt a tap on her shoulder from Matt's bow. Turning round, she saw that he was passing her a tablet. That time already? Gratefully, she downed it with the bottle of water she'd hidden under her long black skirt.

The conductor entered to the applause of the well-fed, well-dressed audience. Not many black faces out there, thought Jenny dreamily. A sea of middle-aged white people.

The conductor bowed, turned to the orchestra, then held himself poised, making sure he'd made eye-contact with all instruments involved in the orchestral prelude. And flick up. Away they went, sounding like a hive of upset bees. She could see them swarming out of the f-holes of the violins and violas around her. Flying overhead now. Oh my God, they were swarming. Her bow stilled. One landed on her knee and stung her. She slapped at it with the hand that held the bow, hitting the music stand with a discordant clang, scattering her music. The conductor's gaze flicked to her as pages flew.

What was she doing? There were no bees. Scooping up the music, she tucked her instrument back under her chin and pretended nothing had just happened.

She managed to keep with the score all the way through to the interval between Acts One and Two. The soloists filed out for a brief break.

'What was that about?' asked her neighbour under the cover of the applause.

She mouthed an apology.

Matt tapped her again with his bow. 'Jenny, you've got to hold it together better than this.'

Oddly it looked like his mouth was moving separately from the words he was saying. She pinched the bridge of her nose. Something was very off about her senses.

'You lost the timing in "*Ich weiss ein wildes Geschlecht*".'

She snorted. *I know a wild race*. How ironic: wild women. Wouldn't it be amazing to turn into one of them, a Valkyrie? Picking over the dead to choose which man deserved to be in Valhalla?

'Jenny, snap out of this!'

She waved over her shoulder. Yeah, yeah. The conductor and soloists returned and the second act passed at a gallop. Jenny thought she probably played it – most of it. The conductor kept looking her way and then she would try to match the bow strokes of the violinist in front. It reminded her of primary school concerts where she would pretend to blow her treble recorder – that was until she learned to play properly. She couldn't bring herself to add to the discord until she knew what to do. Giggles bubbled up in her chest as the famous refrain of the Valkyrie ride emerged in the first duet between Wotan and Brünnhilde. She kept thinking what Jonah would make of this glamorous lady in a sequined gown warbling 'hojotoho' so seriously to call her horse. It was never good to have an emperor's new clothes moment in the middle of an operatic concert. The event relied on everyone taking it seriously.

Control yourself, Jenny.

It was no good. The laughter took over. She bent her head and bit her tongue hard, hoping to stop it with pain. More and more members of the orchestra were aware of her misbehaviour. Their turned heads would be signalling it to the audience if this carried on, and that would not be forgiven by the conductor.

She managed to make it to the opening of Act Three. Just before they started playing again, Matt passed her another tablet, his expression quite frantic.

'Take this, for God's sake. You've got to pay attention, Jenny – or at least look as if you are!' Sitting behind her, he had a grandstand view of her muffing her part.

Was it her imagination or was the conductor giving her an especially hard stare as he called them to attention? This was the most famous part, familiar even to the people who wouldn't be seen dead in a concert hall as 'The Ride of the Valkyries'. The opening notes ran up her spine like fingers playing the strings on the neck of the violin. Her earlier mockery vanished as the excitement caught her in its spell. She sat still, unable to do anything but let the music surround her, push her onwards, thoughts kaleidoscoping in her head. Then the soprano hit a high note that released the pressure inside her. Jenny wanted to leap into the audience, be met with upraised arms, crowd surf until she burst out into the night sky, flying far away. She stood up, letting her violin fall to the floor. The other violinists watched her out of the corner of their eye, all still bending and bowing as if her rebellion was not really happening. Drifting past them, she walked to the edge of the stage. All eyes were now on her but no arms were upraised. No one greeted her. They did not understand how amazing this was, how she had burst from her skin and was flying. She tilted forward, preparing to jump.

A stage manager got to her first. She was dragged into the wings, orchestra still playing away though the performance was a little ragged around the edges and Wotan missed a cue. Joyous

227

laughter rumbled up from the pit of her stomach, shaking her. The stage manager propelled her into a little dressing room.

'What the heck are you playing at?' she hissed right in Jenny's face. Jenny recognised her as Millie, an old hand backstage. 'I hope to God you're ill?'

That was funny: hoping someone was ill.

'What's wrong with you? Are you drunk?' The woman peered more closely at her. 'Your pupils are like pin pricks. Oh God, what did you take?'

Jenny smiled and curled up in the armchair. Inside, she was still flying.

'You're out of your head, aren't you?' The woman – Millie – strode to and fro like a metronome. 'I can't cover this up, Jenny. Everyone saw you behaving like a lunatic.'

Lunatic. Affected by the phases of the moon. Like a werewolf. Jenny giggled and snapped at Millie. Such a silly name for a woman in a responsible position. Millie. Silly. If only she could speak and share the joke but her attacker had put pay to that so long ago. So many years of silence. Time lost forever.

She was suddenly really, really sad. Something broke inside her. She could hear the snap. Had to get out. Had to.

She got up.

'Jenny, stay where you are!' called the stage manager. 'I'll call the medics.'

Didn't want the medics. Didn't want anyone called. She wanted Jonah.

Pushing past Millie, Jenny went through a fire escape onto the Embankment and began walking. If she kept going, eventually she'd reach Greenwich. Then she could turn up the hill and be home.

'Jenny!'

Hojotoho, she thought. What nonsense. Hojotoho. Find me a horse and bridle and I'll ride home in the sky.

'Watch it, lady!' exclaimed a statue artist. Pretending to be

Charlie Chaplain in gold, he'd been knocked off his plinth by her erratic passage along the path by the river.

'Sorry, sorry,' she signed. She offered a hand to help him back up which he didn't take.

'You're mental!'

She nodded her agreement and strode on, kicking at the long folds of her black skirt. More witch than Valkyrie.

The path petered out somewhere near the Globe. She got lost in the backstreets near Borough Market and wandered in a circle, ending up by a replica Elizabethan ship. Maybe she could sail away? She rattled the gate but it was closed.

'Hey, funny lady, you lost?' called a couple of young men outside a pub. They appeared to be Malaysian or Thai, maybe. Clean looking. Puffa jackets and knitted black caps. She was reminded she felt cold.

She nodded.

'Want a drink?' One held up a pint, cigarette in the other hand.

She patted her pockets. She'd come with nothing.

'I'll buy you a drink,' he offered.

Grinning, she staggered over to them and pointed to her throat and drew a line across her throat.

'You don't want to talk? Not a problem, lovely lady.' He passed her his beer and she took a deep draught. They laughed and started clapping: 'Go! Go! Go!' She finished it and wiped at her mouth. 'OK, that means another round,' he said, handing her his cigarette to hold as he went into the pub to order.

She ended the evening curled up against the embankment wall along the Thames with her new friends, burrowing into them for warmth. They talked over her head in another language, not bothered that her appearance with them was completely random and unexplained. When the pub closed they stayed on. They had no idea of her name, or she of theirs, even though they'd told her. Students from Bangkok, they said, travelling the world. That sounded nice. Why had she never had a year out?

She had had a year out – spent it in her bedroom when she was fourteen after the attack.

'Have one of these.' One of the guys slipped something into her mouth. It was a little roll up. 'Just Spice. Nothing illegal.'

She puffed inexpertly, having never been a smoker, then snuggled nearer her friend. The edge had well and truly been taken off her evening. Everything was …

Jenny woke up with a police officer standing over her.

'Miss, Miss, are you all right?'

She looked around her but her friends had gone. Fear gripped her. Her blouse was undone but bra in place. Her head ached. What had happened? Sitting up, she gathered the edges of her blouse together.

The officer crouched beside her, trying to get a clear view of her face. Her patrol partner was standing a little further off, talking in his radio. 'I can't leave you until you tell me you're OK.'

The orange light of the city glowed in the sky behind the officer. Jenny had no memory of what had happened but she was fairly sure she wouldn't want to remember. God, was she in some gap year traveller's newsfeed as the slag who was so far out of it that she let people do whatever they wanted to her?

'Miss?' The officer cleared her throat. 'Er, you seem to have something written on you.'

Jenny glanced down in horror. The officer shone a penlight, making sure not to catch Jenny's eyes in the glare. On the swells of her breasts, there were two sets of initials. 'I think someone's tagged you. We see that from time to time. Were you out with a hen party?'

Jenny couldn't get past the horror. She pulled herself up by the wall, revealing her once smart outfit of black skirt and blouse.

'I'm sorry,' she signed.

'Ray, we've got a deaf one here,' the officer announced, leaping

230

to conclusions. Turning her back so Jenny couldn't lip read she went on. 'Looks like she got wasted and then dumped by her so-called friends. No sign so far of anything worse than the tagging took place. What do you want to do with her? She would be classed as vulnerable with her disability.'

God, how she hated people talking about her as if she were mentally retarded.

'Has she got a handbag with her?' The man sounded bored. Scooping up drunks and stoned addicts was all part of his ordinary life.

'No. Probably had that snatched while she slept it off.'

'Tell her she can report that when she sobers up. Explain to her that we'll contact family or friends and escort her to a taxi.'

The female officer turned back. Jenny was too humiliated now to admit she'd heard their exchange. The police community support officer got out her notepad and wrote down what her colleague had just said. *What number do you want me to call?*

Jenny thought briefly of Matt but he'd never let her live it down, never forgive her. His annoyance would cost too much. She then realised that she had little choice. She couldn't remember any mobile numbers and there were only two landlines she knew off by heart. Deciding her mother really didn't need to know about this, she gave them the number for Gallant House and prayed that it would be Jonah who would answer.

'Bridget's bawdy house,' chirped Jonah. He always did that, claiming when challenged that he said 'boarding house'. 'What service can I render?'

231

Chapter 43

'Have I got this right, Jenny: you overdid your medication, walked out in the middle of a concert, got drunk with a couple of strangers who then drew on your breasts?'

Jonah brought her a mug of tea and tucked a blanket around her on the snug sofa.

She nodded.

He clinked his mug against hers. 'Cheers. Welcome to my world. I can't count the number of times I've woken up with a dick drawn on my forehead. Want to let me have a look?' He pretended to peer down her blouse but she clamped her hand to her buttons. 'What did they do? Snoopy faces around your nipples? That's what I would've done.'

She didn't want him to go around imagining anything quite as graphic as that so she pulled up her shirt to give him a quick flash.

'Dickless fuckers. Just initials up there? They're probably gay.' He patted her shoulder. 'Let me know if you can't wash it off and I'll help.'

She rolled her eyes.

'Or will your boyfriend object?'

She looked down at the tea. He must've used Bridget's full fat carton for the milk because there were ugly white bits floating on the top.

'What does that look mean? Don't want me to meet him? Are you ashamed of me?'

She shook her head. He had sounded like he expected her to agree.

'Ashamed of him?'

She gave the smallest of nods.

'Then why stay with him? You can do better than that.'

No, she couldn't. Matt was what she deserved.

There came a ring on the front door.

'Who the hell could that be? It's seven in the morning.'

Jenny flapped him frantically to answer it before Bridget came down.

'OK, OK, I'll get it.' He opened the door and Jenny heard a brief conversation on the front step. Footsteps headed back her way.

'Jenny, this guy says he's your boyfriend.' Jonah didn't sound that convinced.

'We met before,' said Matt defensively. 'At Harry's birthday party.'

Jonah laughed. 'Oh right. Yeah, that evening is engraved on my memory but I'm sorry if I've forgotten you.'

Matt's expression was dark. 'Jenny, I've been searching for you all night! You left these behind. I can't believe you were so cavalier about your instrument.' He produced her violin and her handbag.

Her violin! She hadn't given it a thought. That made her realise just how far she had fallen.

Jonah, as usual, quickly assessed the situation. 'Jenny was taken ill. She's only just got back. I'm sure she would've got a message to you if she could, but you had her phone.'

'Are you her spokesman now?' Matt's tone was sneering.

'I can usually tell what's she's thinking. If you know her so well, you'll realise she's had a rough night.'

'I know that. I was there when she disrupted one of our most important concerts of the season.' Matt turned to her. 'I've been told to tell you that you're not to come back. The conductor refuses to work with you whatever your excuse. No one will work with a second violinist who can't keep in her bloody seat!'

'Hey, what part of "rough night" didn't you hear? Jenny had a freak-out. It happens to the best of us. Give her a break, OK?'

'Tell this idiot to go away,' demanded Matt.

Jenny rested her head back wearily. All she wanted right now was to tell Matt to leave her alone.

'I live here, mate, and you don't, so if one of us leaves, it's going to be you. Jenny, do you want Matt to stay?'

Knowing she'd pay for this later, she shook her head.

'Right, there's the door, Matthew. Be through it in twenty seconds or I'll kick you out myself – with great pleasure.' He snagged the bag and violin off Matt's shoulder. 'I'll take those.'

'Don't think I'll do another thing ever again for you!' shouted Matt as he stormed for the exit. The bell jangled in the backdraft as he slammed it.

'Did he just break up with you?' asked Jonah, sitting by her feet.

She shrugged, numb to everything, even the news that her career was in ruins.

'Good.' He began massaging her toes. 'You don't need a wanker like that in your life.'

But she did.

Chapter 44

Matt didn't call or reply to texts. She understood the message: not so much that they were finished but that he was punishing her. He'd wait for her to crawl back. Not that she cared, apart from the fact that she had run out of all drug supplies, legitimate and black market. It also appeared that she had somehow lost her job. Dismissed for behaviour unbecoming to a second violin. That was almost laughable if it meant anything other than the total wreck of her career.

Jenny sat for a long time in her room gazing out at the view of the heath. She heard Bridget try the door mid-morning but still she sat. She had a bizarre sense she was a doll, not a person, unable to move unless someone did it for her. Perhaps the baby from the well would come and play with her? Shift her arm, move her head, lay her flat.

'I just wanted to clean the sink. I'll be back later!' called Bridget.

Eventually, Jenny stirred herself to check her bank balance and cache of stolen money. She had about a hundred and fifty as most of her direct debits had already gone out this month and Christmas had been expensive because she'd wanted to get Mum a nice present. It could've been nearly two hundred except she had thrown the forty pounds at Matt and not asked for change.

They both knew she stood knee-deep in debt to him so it hadn't felt appropriate to claw back ten quid.

What have I become? she wondered. I'm an addict. But the prospect of going back to Dr Chakrabarti and confessing this and seeing her weekly legal dosage cut off, was too much. She couldn't deal with that today. She had a shift at the restaurant later, and she'd have to figure out how to get hold of her own supplementary supplies as Matt was choking them off.

Ice slid down her spine as she had a flashback to his … his rape? Why couldn't she call it what it was? Intellectually she knew what had happened between them hadn't been consensual but she couldn't bring herself even all these weeks later to admit it. She would still be with him if he allowed because he gave her what she needed and she knew, oh she knew, what that said about her.

Better not to think of her own opinion. What would Jonah say? He'd say sex didn't matter, that she should move on, pick herself up. His advice always seemed so matter of fact. Life's shit: deal with it. She wasn't living some Victorian existence where fallen women had to hang their heads in shame or go around with a scarlet letter on their chest. She had to be better than this. So what would recovery of some sense of agency in her own life look like? Getting some money to start with. The violin leaned by the wardrobe. It was worth several thousand and was insured too. Could she claim it was lost and get the money? That would take weeks. Too long, and what if they discovered her deception? Could she pawn it? Sell it?

She shuddered. The violin was the last thing she would've thought she'd consider parting with, but what choice did she have?

Her gaze went to the jewellery box with the business card tucked inside.

'You're looking lovely,' said Jonah, meeting her on the stairs a few weeks later. 'Going somewhere nice?'

She nodded. The drape of the plum silk dress accentuated her curves. Little diamond studs glinted in her ears and a diamond teardrop necklace rested on her collarbone. She knew she looked high-class and expensive.

Jonah leant against the banister, happy to talk. Their paths hadn't crossed much recently. He was flying high as his storyline in the soap was being very well received by the pundits and public. 'Who with?'

'Boyfriend,' she signed.

'Not Matt?'

She shook her head. After taking her up on one date, where she'd met him at a hotel for a night, Ralph had confessed he couldn't make it a regular thing in case Kris or his wife suspected. She wasn't to worry though, Ralph had said: she would be much in demand in his circle once the lads knew the arrangement. His friend, Bobby Williams, worked in a big legal services firm in the city and often required arm candy, as Ralph so flatteringly put it. She would then expected to go back to Bobby's flat with him, of course, and provide different services, but she could at least pretend that it was a normal relationship. Her own sugar daddy. Better than standing on street corners touting for customers. Lots of girls were doing it these days – always had, as Ralph so bluffly put it.

That was weeks ago now.

'Going out to dinner?' guessed Jonah, tapping her earring.

She nodded.

'If you get back early, look for me in the snug. You can tell me about the new guy. I'm planning a quiet night in. It's been mental.'

She smiled noncommittally.

'How's the music business going?'

The toot outside announced the arrival of her taxi. 'Must go,' she signed.

'Taking taxis? You must be doing well.' He held the door open for her. 'Leaving me all sad and lonesome.'

A taxi paid for by Bobby so she looked perfect on her arrival at whatever venue they were attending tonight. She waved and slid into the back seat.

'Where to, love?' asked the driver.

She passed him the address through the little payment slot.

'Green Park? OK then.' He pulled away.

Jenny looked back. Jonah was standing in the doorway, looking down at his mobile. A ping from her phone drew her attention to the screen. An unregistered number.

I won't bring you flowers anymore. Sad M

Spooky Moggy to Sad Moggy. He'd outed himself, probably in a lame attempt to cheer her up. Why revive that joke now, even with its sardonic Barbra Streisand reference? She hit delete. Not funny, Jonah.

Bobby was suitably impressed with her appearance when she slid out of the taxi and wobbled a little on her killer high heels on the cobbles. They were at an exclusive event at the Royal Academy and drop off point was in the courtyard, hence the unfortunate nature of flooring for ladies. Flaming torches lit the entrance, giving it an *Amadeus* atmosphere. A snatch of Mozart's *Requiem* played in her brain, tricorn hats and black cloaks whisking around corners, manic, desperate laughter. For a moment Bobby's undistinguished features were cast in saturnine shadows; but then he went back to being the slightly florid, paunchy guy in his mid-years who hadn't been able to find, or not wanted to be bothered, with a wife. At least she didn't have adultery on her conscience.

'Babe, you look gorgeous,' he said. He had the familiar estuary accent, a reminder of where she came from herself. 'Come inside. You must meet everyone. Our firm is sponsoring the event so you can imagine that we'll be in high demand tonight!'

She took his arm and tried to add some genuine warmth to her smile. He'd paid for her to go to a beautician in preparation for the evening so her makeup suited her skin tone perfectly. Her lipstick was a luscious plum colour that complemented the dress; eyelash extensions flattered, and shaped eyebrows accentuated, her dark eyes. If she hadn't been here for mercenary reasons, she might even have enjoyed how she looked. In the opera music she used to play, there were a lot of women like her, the Musettas with their protectors. Had they ever felt this wretched? There probably was an aria for it. What the hell was she doing here?

On reaching a waiter standing at the top of the stairs with a tray, Bobby selected a champagne glass for her and whiskey for himself. Strains of a jazz band wafted from a room further in. The walls were hung with a series of life drawings, some graphic representations of grizzled flesh, others just a couple of lines capturing a sleek form.

'We asked for the caterer to complement the theme of the exhibition,' said Bobby jovially, 'but I think he went a little over-board.' He plucked an hors d'oeuvre in the shape of buttocks from a tray. 'Salmon and thyme puff?'

Obligingly she ate it from his fingers.

'I hope to God everyone finds it witty rather than crass,' he said, clearly worried an event in which he had a hand in the planning was going to bomb. He had just enough self-knowledge to be aware of the possibility. He did not regard himself as infal-lible – the nicest thing about him – and Jenny had discovered that much of his air of talkative bonhomie was a mask to hide his nervousness.

Jenny knew her part. She squeezed his arm reassuringly. He didn't like her writing or signing so that left these wordless gestures.

It was in fact very funny, decided Jenny, the number of human torso gestures a talented chef could make out of the food. From the snatches of conversation she caught, the guests were chatting far more about the food than the exhibit of Twentieth Century Life Drawing. Two champagne glasses later, she was finding it highly amusing too. She offered Bobby a little gateau topped by a cherry.

'You minx,' he said appreciatively and snapped it from her fingers with a growl. 'If I had my way, we'd leave right now.'

She was not eager for the moment so just patted his arm consolingly.

'I know, I know, I'm one of the hosts. Let's go over to Carl. He's a banker from Switzerland. Great guy.' Everyone was a great guy or lovely girl with Bobby.

He steered her into the next room where the band was set up. The singer was mid song and it wasn't until Jenny paid attention to him that she realised it was Louis.

Of course it was. He did this kind of event on a regular basis.

She tugged on Bobby's arm, hoping to divert him into another room.

'Settle down, you insatiable siren, we'll be at the flat in no time. I just need to talk to a few more people. Take a look around the room and memorise a few poses. We'll try them out later.'

She grimaced and he laughed. He'd worked out that she had a prim side to her nature and loved to take teasing pokes at her in public for being new to the game.

'Carl! It's been too long!'

Carl turned and shook his hand, then swept an assessing glance over Jenny.

'Meet my lovely companion, Jenny.'

What was it about names that zinged through the air over the rest of the conversation like a kind of dog whistle? Jenny felt the exact moment that Louis spotted her in the crowd.

'Charming.' Carl kissed her knuckles. He had the sleeked-back black hair and gaunt face of a man who would be a shoo-in for a vampire role if in a wild moment he decided to throw in banking and hit the stage. Even his accent lent itself to that impression. 'What are you doing with this one, my dear? Just give me a call when you tire of him.'

Oh God. Jenny didn't think he was joking. She silently added to her mental picture of him; a fiendish cackle and hand rubbing.

'She won't do that,' said Bobby with an edge to his voice. 'She can't talk.'

'My God, you lucky man.' Carl leant forward. 'I wish my wife would suffer from the same malady. She's bending my ear about buying somewhere in the Cotswolds for the weekends. Don't you have a place out that way?'

The two men discussed property near Burford, paying no more attention to her as their thoughts turned to their first love: investments. Jenny felt safe as long as she could hear Louis still singing. Hopefully, Bobby would wind up the conversation before this set was over and allow her to entice him away.

Her luck did not hold. The jazz band went into an instrumental number.

'Jenny?' A gentle tap on her shoulder told her that Louis had found her before she could escape. She would have to pretend.

She turned with a big smile and waved her hands in admiration at his smart evening wear.

'You look good too – amazing in fact.' His gaze went to Bobby but he was still deep in conversation about the future of property prices. 'No Matt?'

Jenny hadn't seen Matt for weeks. She shook her head.

'I heard a rumour …'

Oh God. Which one?

'Did you … did you lose your job? I messaged you but you didn't reply.'

Of course she hadn't because she had a promise to keep. That was her penance. Jenny signed that she was sorry.

'They were all talking about it at the Festival Hall. It was a little confused by the time it came to me but there was something about being out of it …? That didn't sound right. Not the Jenny I know.'

But he didn't know her, did he?

'I've really missed you. Kris said people can be funny once you get married, think you need space, but nothing's changed.'

Hadn't it?

'You're always welcome at ours. How about lunch one day? Come to the café. We'll catch up. I haven't even told you about the honeymoon yet.'

Bobby was paying enough attention to hear something that sounded like a date being set up with his girl. 'Hello, and who's this?' He held out a hand.

Louis shook it. 'I'm an old friend of Jenny. In fact, she was my best man.'

Alert level dropping, Bobby smiled. 'Great. I heard you singing earlier. Reminded me of ol' Blue Eyes himself.' Did he have to be such a cliché? 'Carl, this is ...' He paused, realising they hadn't got as far as names. 'Sorry, didn't catch your name.'

'Louis,' her friend supplied.

'Good to meet you,' said Carl with every indication he didn't mean it. Why would he want to meet the hired help?

Louis got the message that he was intruding on the business between the two men. 'I'd better go back. Lovely to see you again, Jenny. You can tell me all about ... er ...'

'Bobby,' he said. 'Bobby Williams.' Then he did that embarrassing wink and gunpoint thing with a double click of the tongue, but got the timing a little off.

Louis manfully avoided laughter. 'Yeah, Bobby, you can tell me how you got together when we meet up. I'll message you.'

She smiled. She had perfected one that said everything and nothing.

'I'll send Kris your love, shall I?'

Thumbs up.

'See you later then.'

As he moved away, a waitress arrived with a fresh supply of hors d'oeuvres. 'A little dick anyone?' she giggled. 'Really, they're raspberry Swiss rolls.'

'How appropriate,' murmured Carl, taking that in good humour. 'I bet Roger paid you to come over and say that, didn't he, the bastard?' His gaze went to a man on the far side of the room who had a blonde girl in a dress with plunging neckline on his arm. 'Bobby, look, I think it's winding down here. How about I round up a friend and we go back to your flat together, just the four of us? I think this conversation should carry on in a more relaxed setting, don't you?' But his eyes were on Jenny.

'Excellent idea. It will be like Cannes all over again,' said Bobby. 'My thoughts exactly.'

Chapter 45

The next day, as she dug in her purse to pay the taxi home, Jenny resolved to sell the violin.

The night in the flat after the reception had proved to be her breaking point. The events scared her and she vowed never again to be in that vulnerable situation, not when she couldn't control things. Being helpless was her ultimate fear.

The taxi pulled away and she took a breath of cool early morning air. Carl's guest had turned out to be a high class call girl whom he often employed when in the city and what followed had been quite tame compared to what might've been. As she lay awake on fine cotton sheets next to Bobby, Jenny realised how close she had sailed to disaster. 'The friend' Carl called could've been another man, or several, and she might've ended up in the middle of something for which she was completely unprepared. Instead, the four of them had had drinks, chatted and retired in their couples to separate bedrooms at about midnight. But there had been a moment at a minute to the hour when everything had balanced on a knife edge, where Carl hinted and Bobby parried. The call girl, Camilla, not her real name, had looked supremely bored by the idea of sexual fun and games; Jenny expected she'd looked sick.

'My little Jenny is shy,' Bobby had declared proudly. 'Maybe, Carl, when she knows you better?'

Jenny thought the real reason Bobby refused was that he was feeling unsure about how he himself might perform in a four-some. He was repressed English under the act and that had saved her.

'Maybe later then?' Carl had kissed her knuckles, letting his tongue touch her skin.

Gross. Suddenly pudding-like Bobby had seemed a safe haven and she had been almost relieved to have sex with him in a straight forward way.

Back in the hall, carrying her shoes, Jenny took her decision. She had not consciously chosen this life of being a paid-for mistress, not thought through how much of her self-respect she would have to surrender, how she would have to become someone else to be successful. Where had her addiction sent her? She couldn't even recognise herself anymore. No more of that, please, even if it was easy money. She'd prefer to lose the violin than all her self-respect. The only thing more important than either was the cash for her drugs.

Up in her room, she wriggled out of her dress and hung it up on the satin-padded hanger. Seeing it hanging there, empty, it wasn't hard to draw a parallel with herself. A beautiful nothing – that's what she'd become. Until now she'd not thought much about gender roles in society. Naturally, she'd called herself a feminist, assumed equality was a no-brainer, but that reception, her place in it to be available, seemed like something from a past era: women paid to please men, to be treated like toys in the world of international business men who bonded over their ability to buy beauty and bed it. That world should be long gone but it lingered like persistent rot. You only had to look at the men in power to see this. She wished she could work up the energy to be angry about it. Putting the plug in the tub, she started running a bath. How she hated to be their puppet, assumed to be up for anything as long as she was bunged a wad of cash. Adding a dose of bubble bath, she swished her hand to create foam. The road ahead led into the dark. Once the violin went, she would have nothing. If only she could turn aside. But how to live with the pain?

She sat back on her heels to turn off the taps. It was only then that she saw the message scrawled on the mirror in plum lipstick.

BLACK BITCH

And she was back in the worst night of her life.

Chapter 46

Jenny, Fifteen Years Ago

Jenny cleaned her teeth in the bathroom, bobbing in a happy dance with her reflection to put more effort into the process. The chocolate cake had caught in the crevices of her molars and she was worried about getting cavities. So far she'd made it to fourteen without a filling and she wanted to keep up her good record. At least her complexion had cleared up from the latest outbreak in time for the party.

'I won't be late. The concert should be over by eleven,' her mum called from by the front door where she was putting on her shoes.

Jenny spat out the toothpaste and splashed it away with a blast of the tap. 'OK! I hope it goes well!'

'Your dad said he'd ring so if the phone goes it'll probably be him.'

'OK!'

'I know it's your birthday but if you do have any homework …'

'I know, I know.' Jenny came out of the bathroom and leant over to give her mum a goodbye kiss. 'I'll get to it, I promise, Mum. Thanks for the cake.'

Her mum looked up at her and smiled. 'My pleasure, darling. It was fun, wasn't it? They're a nice bunch. We'll go somewhere at the weekend, prolong the festivities.'

'That would be great. See you later.'

'I hope not.' Her mum slipped into her jacket. 'You should be asleep by then. You've got my number if anything happens?'

'Of course I have. Go on: you'll miss your lift.'

Her mum waved and headed out the door. Almost as it banged closed, the phone rang. Jenny hurried to the phone in the lounge to catch it before it clicked to the answerphone.

'Hello?'

'Jenny! It's your dad here.'

'Hi, Dad. Where are you?'

'Toronto.'

'As in Toronto, Canada? What are you doing over there?' Jenny twisted the springy cord around her finger.

'Interviewing for a job tomorrow. African studies at the university.'

That was the first she'd heard that he wanted to leave Nigeria. 'Oh, er, great. Good luck.'

'I didn't call about that. A little bird told me it was my girl's special day.'

Her mum had probably had to remind him. 'That's right.'

'I can't believe you're a teenager already.'

'I'm fourteen, Dad.'

'That's what I meant. I've sent your mum some money for you to spend as she couldn't think of something for me to buy for you in Lagos. She suggested you'd like some sheet music. I thought that safest.'

Jenny's spirits developed a slow puncture. 'Great.'

'I put a card in the mail today too. Sorry that it will arrive a little late but I think you will like it. I picked it out myself.'

When normally he didn't? 'I'll let you know when it comes.'

'So, tell me, how did you celebrate?'

248

She started on an account of her birthday party with the music students singing 'Happy Birthday' in the style of Beethoven, how witty it had been. There had been a whole crowd of them, most were older than her but who had got to know her through their lessons and at music camp last summer. She had a bit of a crush on one boy in Year 9 who was about to take his grade eight theory. Harry had bought her a card, a corny cartoon one of a kitten like she was ten or something, but it still had pride of place in the front room.

Her dad's replies to her chatter were 'hmm' and 'ah-ha'. Was that the sound of typing in the background. 'Dad, are you doing your emails?'

'Oh, er, something urgent has just come in about arrangements for tomorrow. I had to reply immediately.'

She pressed her head back against the sofa cushions, feeling a little sad and lonely now. 'Are you going to fly through London on your return?'

'I'm sorry, Jenny, but I'm going via Paris. I have a colleague I need to see.'

'Right. OK.' Disappointment bloomed. 'I'd better go and do my homework.'

'On your birthday! What a good girl you are! How are you fixed for the summer? Do you want to come and spend a couple of weeks with Marissa and your brothers?'

'Will you be there?' She'd gone last year and found she was an unpaid nanny to her father's new family with him barely in evidence.

'Oh, in and out as usual. It depends if I get the new job. If that comes through, then I will be arranging our move. I'm a busy man, Jenny. I cannot drop everything, you know that.'

Why couldn't he? 'I'll talk to Mum.' And find a way of refusing. 'You're always welcome here, Mum says.'

'What, Harlow?' Her father chuckled.

'We could go on holiday in England together. Or I could meet

249

you in Paris? I'm fourteen now. I can do the journey on my own on the Eurostar.' She could just imagine having him to herself as they walked through the Louvre or drank citron pressé at a café in the Champs Elysees. Her language text book was full of such little transactions, buying drinks and tickets. She could try them out. French was one of her dad's languages.

'Fourteen! How did that happen?' And so he passed over the bait, not taking up her suggestion. 'Let me know about the summer when you know your availability. Marissa loved having you last year.'

Of course she did. His wife spent most of the time meeting her friends for coffee in Lagos' most upmarket air-conditioned malls while Jenny played hot, sweaty garden cricket with the boys. There was nothing wrong with Marissa, apart from the fact that she saw a sibling relationship as cheap labour. As eldest of five, Marissa had probably been on the other end of that treatment herself.

'OK, Dad. Good luck tomorrow.'

'Thanks, Jenny. Love you!'

'Love you too.'

Did he? Did he love her? The evidence seemed to be very slight on that front. If her mother hadn't kept badgering him to keep up at least this minimal contact, he would probably have dropped her altogether, like he had Nikki ten years ago.

She went into the kitchen and helped herself to another slice of the cake in the fridge. It would probably give her new spots but she didn't care.

'It's my birthday and I'll cry if I want to,' she sang, bending the lyrics of one of her mum's favourite tunes from the Eighties. 'You would cry too if it happened to you.' Putting the plate down, she grabbed a wooden spoon. Homework could wait. She was going to have a kitchen karaoke. She couldn't be bothered to get out the PlayStation and use one of the games Mum had bought her to encourage her vocal skills. A spoon and the radio would do. A few Justin Timberlake tracks and a Beyoncé later, she was feeling much better. She gave up at 50 Cent, not knowing the words well enough to keep in time and that annoyed her as she liked to be perfect when singing. The others had sounded good though. She might offer to sing something at her school spring concert. They expected her to play the violin, of course, but it would be fun to surprise them with something contemporary. Maybe a Britney track? 'I'm Not A Girl Not Yet A Woman'? Would that suit her voice? She could wear a really cool outfit and shock everyone so they all had to reassess their assumptions about her. The boys might notice and then …

She kissed the kitten card and carried on humming tunes while she completed her homework. Nothing too heavy, just ten Maths problems and some French vocabulary for a test tomorrow. That done, she could practice her violin pieces for her lesson with Mum on Thursday. They'd taken to making it official as otherwise they both just put it off, Mum for paying students, Jenny because … well, it was Mum, wasn't it? She loved the Telemann she was learning at the moment. It was a duet, which was so much fun as you wound in and out of the melody with someone else. It made her feel like she was full of bubbles. She and Mum would have a lovely time together when they did that later in the week. Mum had been teaching it to lots of her students too because it was on the exam syllabus so the apartment was continually resounding with the happy tune.

With a sigh of contentment, bad feelings generated by her father's call played away, Jenny put her beloved violin back in its case. Mum had really pushed out the boat to buy this one for her thirteenth birthday a year ago, forgone getting a car so she could afford the loan. Best birthday present ever! It was a huge step up from Jenny's previous instrument that had been a cheap new one made in China. Mum hadn't wanted to fork out on a special violin until Jenny had settled on her choice of instrument. But the violin was the one for her. She was her mother's daughter.

251

Brushing her teeth again, Jenny got ready for bed, choosing clean shorts and a T-shirt from her chest of drawers in honour of her birthday. She put the old ones in the laundry basket. Coming out of the bathroom, a noise from her mum's room caught her attention. She peered inside and saw that the net curtain had knocked a box of tissues to the floor as it billowed in the breeze. Picking the box up, she put it back on the sill and reached up to close the window. Jenny ran through her mental tick list. She'd remembered to leave the chain off the door so her mum could get back in, and checked the door was locked as Mum had instructed her to do when she was on her own. They lived on the fourth floor of a block of flats so it felt a safe place once the entrance was fastened. Any intruder would have to be Spider-Man to get in.

With a smile, she got into bed and reached for the bedside light.

It was the hand that woke her. A hot hand stroking her cheek.

'Mum?' She turned towards it, expecting to see that her mother had come in to say goodnight, but then sensed something else entirely. Alarm rocketed. A stranger was lying on the duvet next to her. He smelt of men's deodorant and cigarettes. She opened her mouth to scream but the palm smashed over her lips and his weight slid over her.

'Sssh, sssh. No need for that. Don't make a sound. You want this, I can tell. Be a good girl. It's just you and me, nothing to fear.'

It was pitch dark. She couldn't see anything in this dark cave in which they were enclosed. The blackout lining she'd asked for in her curtains to keep out the streetlights was working too well. She thrashed and screamed in her throat against his grip.

'So beautiful,' he whispered. 'Your voice singing to me – so lovely. I love listening to you. Sssh.' His hands went to her throat, squeezing. 'You have to keep quiet now. Let me do this.' He shoved the duvet aside.

252

The horrible unexpectedness of it all stunned her. It had to be a nightmare but she knew it wasn't. Thoughts whirling super-fast looking for a way out, her brain divided into the part that analysed the situation for the exits, while the other just screamed in horror.

As he adjusted his flies, his hand let up momentarily.

'Mu—' She didn't get any further.

'No! Don't spoil it! Shut up, you little black bitch!' He grew angrier at her continued resistance. There was a sweet taint to his breath as he panted in her face. The next few minutes were horrific. She almost didn't care what else was going on, the viola-tion secondary to the compression on her throat; the caring would come later if she survived. Her body focused on living through this. No air made it past his grip. Her consciousness faded in and out. She clawed at the back of his hands, but he was wearing gloves. She couldn't break skin. She couldn't …

The doctors said later she must've blacked out when he pressed down so hard that he damaged her larynx. Impossible to say if he had been intending to kill her or this was just the way he liked it.

Her mother's return prevented her death. Her assailant must've heard the door, and, it was assumed, hidden elsewhere in the flat. Her mother sensed something was wrong even as she crossed the threshold because she could see down the single corridor that ran from the front to the back of the flat. She immediately noticed that Jenny's bedroom door was wide open. Thankfully, she came straight in and found Jenny half-dragged from the bed. Nikki was too distressed to check she was safe from attack herself; her only thought was to summon an ambulance. That short interval gave Jenny's assailant a chance to slip away.

No search of the apartment was made until the police came looking for forensic evidence. They'd found Jenny's cake out of the fridge and worked out that her attacker had been in the flat some time while Jenny got ready for bed. She had inadvertently locked him in with her. The other possibility was that the window she'd closed in her mother's room had been big enough for a man to climb through if they had a head for heights and didn't mind scrambling up the balconies. Whichever way he'd entered, he'd acted as if he owned the place. He helped himself to the birthday cake, a neat slice put on a plate, then left by the washing up bowl when finished. Then in a mercurial mood change, he'd dropped the rest of the cake on the floor and stamped on it. The impressions of his trainers had been clear in the chocolate frosting and added to the file, as well as the DNA traces they'd found. They asked Jenny, when they were finally able to interview her, if she'd heard anything, but of course she hadn't. She'd been humming along to Britney, doing her homework in her bedroom.

That all came later. At the time they were searching the flat and coming up with these theories, Jenny was in hospital with tracheostomy, hooked up to numerous machines to breathe for her. She'd been rescued from brain damage only by the quick actions of her mother and the paramedics who had come in response.

They had saved her life, her brain, but not her voice.

It didn't matter. She never wanted to sing again.

If she did, Jenny believed, he might come back.

Part 4 – Return to the Fair

Notturno – a piece written for the night

Chapter 47

'OK, Jonah, we need to start spinning this – and spinning it in a direction that helps you,' said Carol. 'How do you feel about doing a feature on your past with a journalist friend of mine? I promise she'll treat you fairly.'

Jonah sat back on the sofa, reflecting how much had changed in the past few hours. From a bare interview room, he was sitting in a boutique hotel not far from Baker Street station. The room was furnished in red velvet like a nineteenth century whorehouse, though with the address maybe they were trying more for a Sherlock Holmes vibe? If so, they missed. They should've gone with greens and browns for that. He knew what his expected role was here though, just as he understood what the police had wanted from him and he'd withheld it. Everyone wanted his story.

'I'm happy to do anything you suggest, Carol,' said Jonah. 'But how does it help to get my past out in the media again?'

'It's already out there. What do you think the press has been doing for the last thirty-six hours?' She paced by the window, probably to get away from his tobacco smoke. He'd do a lot for Carol, but this was something he couldn't give up. His last addiction, even if against hotel rules. 'What works in our favour is that the news cycle is ready for a new phase, having exhausted the "we told you so" angle.'

'"We told you so"?' He leaned his head back and blew a plume of smoke into the air.

'Yeah, it's amazing how many people suddenly claim to have predicted that employing a guy so soon after he came out of prison was a mistake. That's the leopard-can't-change-his-spots people who occupy the right-wing tabloids and morning chat show sofas. Don't worry about them: when it's proved you're innocent, they'll swing right round to spout the opposite. No one'll blink an eye.'

'Fine. I'll be guided by you then.'

Carol paused by the room service tray and poured herself a tea. 'Want a top up? I can order something stronger if you like?'

'I don't drink.'

'Oh yes, I forgot. That's good though. And how many days sober?'

'Eight-hundred and forty-eight.'

She topped up his tea, forgetting he hadn't said yes. 'That's great, Jonah.'

'You know sober means drugs, don't you? I haven't drunk alcohol for much longer. I didn't like what it did to me.' Drink had made him mean, particularly with women.

She obviously hadn't known, but she tried to cover it. 'Still good.' He stubbed out his cigarette and she sat down. 'Let's get to what you might say then. The police let you go with no charges?'

'Correct.' He liked that word: so powerful.

'There was no evidence to connect you to either attack?'

'Correct. The first one was something that blew up between Bridget and Jenny – nothing to do with me.' Though it had been, of course. It was true though that he hadn't been in Jenny's bedroom when the confrontation between the two women had taken place. He'd been downstairs doing the equivalent of putting

258

his fingers in his ears and whistling, knowing that no good would come of him intervening. 'The second wasn't a real attack at all when she came at me. I think it was a desperate call for help before she collapsed from her overdose. She couldn't breathe for herself – that's a side effect of too much Fentanyl. I was just the unlucky bugger who caught her.'

'So do you know why the women were fighting? It seems very odd. I mean, it's come out, of course, that Jenny is an addict. Did Bridget get in her face about this? It had to be hard for her having that in the house with her own problems.' Carol was spinning her fictitious scenario, persuading herself by her own replay of that night. 'Did she threaten to throw her out and Jenny refuse to leave?'

'I don't know. I wasn't there. You should suggest your journalist friend interviews her too, get the full picture.' He began rolling a new cigarette.

'Who?'

'Either. Whichever one is in a position to communicate.' He licked down the edge of the paper but held off lighting it. 'The police didn't keep me in the loop over their condition. The overdose was a serious one though. I'm not sure she's conscious yet.'

Carol made a note. 'I'll see what I can find out. Jenny has a mother, doesn't she?'

'Yes. Nikki Groves. A violin teacher in Harlow.'

'And Bridget? Who does she have?'

Jonah rubbed his eyes wearily. 'Bridget? I don't think she has anyone.'

Chapter 48

Bridget, Three Days Ago

Bridget went round the house closing the curtains. Spring had arrived again but it still got dark fairly early. She didn't like the idea of having lights on inside and not knowing who could spy on them from the heath. The silent watchers were never far away. A sixth sense told her that the house was always under observation, not that she thought they were there for her this time, or not just her. She'd felt someone else in the house with her when her tenants were out. A ghost? It wouldn't surprise her. She didn't think they were interested in her but she'd found dead leaves in places she'd swept. The well lid was so often off when she was sure she'd replaced it. Drips of water trailed down corridors where no one had passed for hours. Was it too fanciful to think that the things she'd tried to hide were escaping their confines? Had she all these years been trying to hold water in cupped hands, black heath water, and inevitably it would slip and spill, ruining everything?

In the garden, the lilac was just budding. She'd clipped some of the lower blooms earlier and put them in the hallway. Not that she knew why she did that. The sight always made her feel despairing as it marked out that yet another year had passed and she had not made any progress. By now she had hoped at least she would have a book published, something to show for all her time devoted to this house, the sacrifices she had made to keep it, but she still hadn't gathered the courage to send off the manuscript. There seemed to be absolutely no purpose to her life. Worse: she had given her soul for ... for what? For a pile of bricks and mortar that no one would care for when she was gone.

Music was coming from Jenny's room – not from her violin but some awful female pop singer. The instrument had disappeared a few weeks ago. Bridget had looked through all possible hiding places in her tenant's room and drawn a blank. Something catastrophic must've happened. Jenny's neck injury had likely got too much for her, just as the arthritis had stopped Bridget's career in its tracks. The expensive clothes hanging in the wardrobe suggested that Jenny was following a different path now, again like Bridget's own story. Jenny appeared to have found herself a well-heeled man. Good for her. It made the difference between sinking and swimming away from a career wreck. And to be honest, it was time Jenny moved on. She'd got behind with the rent and no longer supplied Bridget with what she needed as part of the house family now she was shut up in her bedroom most of the time. This was sad when Bridget had such high hopes for Jenny. She didn't comment on the chapters Bridget offered her and barely communicated when they crossed paths in the kitchen; she seemed to be function on emergency power only, with none of her usual *joie de vive*.

Maybe, thought Bridget, she should put the word out through Rose and Norman that she was looking for another person working in the arts? One who would need the protection the house offered, another nestling ejected from their nest who needed picking up off the ground? It would be nice to have a few to select from to make sure she made the right pick next time.

The music switched off and there came the sound of a toilet flushing – a fairly sure sign Jenny was going to bed. There would be little chance of her emerging again tonight. Bridget drifted down the corridor and paused outside the box room door. There was a light on in Jonah's bedroom. Loneliness had taken great bites out of Bridget today. She needed to speak to someone and he never turned her away. She tapped gently.

As she had taught him to do, he opened it without saying anything. His eyes went from curiosity to resignation in a fraction of a second. He'd been expecting Jenny, had he?

Bridget nodded and walked away, knowing he would follow.

Chapter 49

Jenny, Three Days Ago

Jenny held the tub of pills in her hands like she was holding her own heart. They never seemed to last, no matter how many she bought. And she'd bought a crippling amount of late. After a few false starts, she'd eventually found a contact at the National Theatre who was able to show her how to access the black market. They'd bonded a little over their shared powerlessness in the face of their dependency. This transaction like many others, had been carried out under Waterloo Bridge, and had been surprisingly easy. A guy had rocked up on a bike, asked to see her money, then they'd done a quick hand over. No one had jumped out and arrested them. No one had even cared.

This was the last money from her violin. After these were gone, she'd have to go back on the game or steal enough for another fix.

Or could she ask her mother for a loan? Jenny revolved that thought as carefully as she studied the tub of anonymous pills. She'd not gone that route yet because it had felt so much worse than the shady ways of getting the cash together. It was shaming to admit that this wasn't because she had morals against it – God, she'd surrendered all of those, hadn't she? – but because she knew her mother would probe. This was not a behaviour she wanted brought into the light.

She had three choices: face the excruciating pain, continue with this shambolic life of getting money any which way, or …

Maybe I could just take them all at once and not wake up? she mused. She was surprised that this wasn't a bleak thought. In fact, it was attractive – easy. She rattled the bottle. There was more than enough.

But then her mum would suffer. She'd be left alone and blame herself. Jenny couldn't do that to her. She loved her too much to put her through that agony.

OK, no easy way.

Suicide deferred for another night, Jenny rationed herself to just one pill and lay back on her bed. She'd sleep now. Her body slowly relaxed, bones melting into the mattress.

One-two-three. One-two-three.

The bloody birds – ghosts – bats – whatever – were at it again. Thanks to Fentanyl, Jenny didn't feel scared; she felt pissed that her nice slip into rest was ruined. Damn – damn – damn! She'd go up there and chase them out: just see if she didn't! Shoving feet into mules, she stomped up the rickety stairs to the attic. A faint silvery wash of light came from the moon through the dormer windows. Full moon. Time of lunatics, Jenny thought grimly. I'm a bloody lunatic tonight. I just can't bear it any longer.

The sound was coming from the far end of the long attic, the space directly over her room. This had once been a dormitory for maids, at other times a nursery for children; now it served as the house lumber room. She pushed past steamer trunks, an abandoned cradle, boxes of papers Bridget had amassed in her research, until she reached a space curtained off at the end.

'That's it. That's it!' Bridget was moaning. 'Yes!'

Jenny abruptly changed her mind about what was happening. Common sense told her to step away; impulse had her pull aside the curtain.

Bridget was riding a man, back straight as a ruler as she sought her climax. The man had his face turned away from his partner which meant he was looking directly at Jenny as she stood in the gap between the curtains.

'Jenny!' gasped Jonah. 'Fuck!' And he started laughing just as Bridget reached her peak.

Jenny fled. The scene somehow just did not compute – it seemed so ... so wrong. Neat, calm Bridget clawing at Jonah's chest in climax, howling like an abandoned thing.

I'm an utter fool. Embarrassment, rage, jealousy – Jenny couldn't work out what she was feeling but it was ugly and raw.

By the time she reached her own room, bits and pieces Jonah had said over the months began to take on new meanings. How could she have been so blind for so long? Jonah had dropped enough hints, telling her how sex meant nothing, how Bridget brought into the house what she needed, that he was used to supplying what people asked of him. He'd said that with an odd note in his voice but she'd failed to care enough to dig any deeper, too wrapped up in her own business to ask the awkward questions. Her mistake had been to assume that because Bridget was in her sixties that she had stopped having sex. No one else came into the house, apart from Norman who was reputably gay, so it had to be Jonah, didn't it?

She ran the cold tap and splashed her face, hoping that would drive the image out of her brain. Bridget. Jonah.

It didn't work.

Anger won the upper hand. Jonah wasn't the victim here. Look at it another way: he'd been shagging Bridget while he'd been doing the same to her. How he must've laughed at the situation: both women desperate and he having it away with the two of them, keeping the other in ignorance. How stupid did that make her look? She hated him – hated Bridget – for making her feel such an idiot!

I can't think about this! Can't bear it! Jenny grabbed the tub of pills. A handful and then she'd not have to face this. She picked up her water goblet.

'No!' Bridget knocked the tub out of Jenny's hand. In the mirror, Jenny glimpsed her landlady whirl around in a flash of lithe white body and scarlet silk dressing gown, barely belted at the waist. She smelt of sex and brandy, eyes wild. Jenny had never seen her like this before, so out of control. 'You will not waste those pills on this pathetic show of jealousy!' Bridget snatched them up off the floor, breasts gaping as she leaned forward. 'How dare you stand there and act the tragic heroine?'

She had her pills. A heat built in Jenny's chest, a hum under her ribcage, a rumble that was the prelude to a storm.

'You have no right – no claim on Jonah! You with your rich fancy man – don't you think I know what's going on? Have you told Jonah what you're doing?'

Jenny wrestled for the tablets.

Seizing Jenny's hair, Bridget pulled her head round with surprising strength to face the mirror. She pinned Jenny against the sink with her body. 'Face facts, dear: you're nothing but a cheap whore!'

Jenny tried to grab the tub back from Bridget but the woman's grip was unbreakable. Her dark eyes burned with fury as her gaze met Bridget's in the mirror. Their enraged expressions were alike.

'Jonah is not yours!' screamed Bridget, spittle flying and hitting the polished surface. 'I saw him first. He's been my lover for two years.'

Jenny didn't care about that: she cared about getting her last tablets back. She'd suffered too much for them. The rumble became a deep growl formed in her throat, animalistic, inhuman. She raked at Bridget's arm, breaking skin.

Bridget shrieked. She picked up the water carafe on the vanity unit and upended the contents over Jenny's head. 'You slut!'

'Mmm—mine!' roared Jenny. It hurt like the scrape of a knife as damaged larynx forced out the sound. Her first word in fifteen years.

'No, mine!' Bridget smashed the carafe over Jenny's head.

Chapter 50

Jonah, Present Day

Carol came back with the news that Jenny had been released from hospital twenty-four hours after the attack, having had ten stitches to her scalp and mild concussion. She'd been picked up by her mother and taken to her old home in Harlow where she was reportedly incommunicado.

That was the first time he'd heard rehab called that.

Should I ask Keith if I can visit her? Take her flowers or something? he messaged. *She likes flowers.* Besides he knew a thing or two about coming back from an addiction. It was a hard road and Jenny would just be entering the very early stages. That's if she wanted to get clean.

He could imagine Carol thinking over the publicity angles: housemate rushes to bedside of his friend as soon as he could after release from police custody. If Jenny agreed to see him, it would do a lot to bolster his claim of innocence. It would show she wasn't scared of him. Then all he'd have to do was demonstrate that he wasn't responsible for what happened to Bridget. That was a matter really between Jenny and their landlady. He'd just been caught in the crossfire and fended off Bridget's frenzied attack. Yeah, that would fit the facts.

Make sure the police clear it first, messaged Carol.

Neither of us are charged with anything. It's Bridget who's in trouble.

Still check. There's just enough doubt about your role. It's a delicate balancing act coming out of this smelling of roses.

So Jonah shot off an email to Keith and started looking up ways to get to Harlow. A couple of hours later, he got his reply.

The police would prefer you not to see Jenny but I pointed out that both of you were currently regarded as victim and witness, not perpetrators. Until they change their mind over charges, that is the official position. You are free to see Jenny.

Great. Jonah tapped on Jenny's number and sent her a message.

Hi gorgeous. I hear the Wicked Witch of the West did a number on you. Can I call round with supplies of chocolate/flowers/witty repartee? Jonah

Only after he had sent it did he recall the last time Jenny had seen him. Oh bugger. Well, plough on, Jonah, as if there was nothing to be embarrassed about. So what if he'd earned his place in the house by offering the owner a little thrill in her sex-starved life? It had meant nothing. If Jenny was going to be all messed up about it, then that was her problem.

As a displacement activity, while he waited for her reply, he opened the mini fridge and took out all the alcohol. Waiting was oddly nerve wracking. He hadn't realised how much he'd come to value his friendship with Jenny. He wasn't used to caring about someone. Turning a can of beer around in his hand, he caressed the top. He'd so loved beer once upon a time. He picked up the telephone and rang room service.

Five minutes later came a discreet knock on the door.

'Thanks for coming, mate. Can you put these somewhere else please?' Jonah handed over the unopened bottles. 'I'm on the wagon. Can't be handling the temptation, you know?'

'Of course, sir.'

Jonah patted his pockets wondering if he needed to tip the guy. He wasn't used to this sort of thing.

The man held up a hand, part demurral but also ready to accept a tip should it come. 'Really, sir, it's my pleasure. Is there anything else I can get you?'

Jonah handed over a couple of pound coins. 'No, thanks. I'm fine.'

Closing the door, he wondered how much the guy would make selling that little detail to the tabloids. Jonah hoped he'd get more than the measly two quid he'd rustled up. That was rather the point of making a fuss about the alcohol – a bit of Jonah brand management that Carol would like. It was either that or read lies about himself being holed up in a drunken stupor in his room, refusing calls. Feed the press a crumb and they'd make a loaf.

By the time he returned to his phone, he discovered that the message he'd been waiting for was already in.

Yes. Please come.

That was brief, even for Jenny. The phone binged again with the address.

I'll be there asap.

Two hours later, Jonah was ringing on the buzzer for Flat 12, John Clare Road, Harlow.

'Hello?'

'Hi. Is that Jenny's Mum? It's Jonah – Jonah Brigson.'

'We're on the fourth floor. I'll buzz you in.'

Jonah gave a cheery wave to a hardy member of the local press who was still staking out the victim. At least the guy's watch had paid off. He was already on his phone so there would be more journalists when Jonah left. He realised he'd come empty-handed so as a last-minute gesture he dropped his bag in the doorway to stop it closing, and broke off a sprig of lilac from a bush in the communal gardens. That was the kind of behaviour that went with his image so he wasn't too worried that he'd been photo-graphed doing so. He gave a thumbs up to the watcher.

Nikki Groves was looking out into the corridor for him.

'Sorry, had to get some flowers!' he said.

'Come in, please. Let's go through to the kitchen.' Nikki took the lilac from him, making no remark as to the origin of the clearly stolen bloom. 'I'll put this in some water and explain the situation.'

That sounded ominous. Jonah followed Jenny's mum, looking out for the similarities. They had the same small build but Jenny was more full-figured, presumably inheriting that from her dad's side. Nikki had a neat crop of straight brown hair and warm cinnamon eyes very like her daughter's. She moved shyly, another thing she had in common with Jenny. Neither of them liked to make a great entrance, keeping their gestures small and ever-so-slightly hesitant.

She put the lilac in a squat little jug, a good choice as the heavy bloom threatened to overturn the normal vase she tried first.

'I think I should explain that I have you here under false pretences, Jonah. It wasn't Jenny who invited you, but me. I saw your message on her phone and replied on her behalf.' She gestured to the new phone lying on the counter. The police must've kept the old one but she'd managed to retain the same number.

'Oh. That's awkward.'

'Isn't it? Cup of tea?'

'Yeah, thanks.' Jonah paced to the window and looked out on the estate. Some kids were kicking a ball in the car park below. He had a sudden yearning to go and join them; it would be so uncomplicated compared to this emotional chess he was having to play with Jenny. A couple of cars pulled up and cameramen began hauling equipment out of the boot. No way could he leave so soon after having just arrived.

Nikki filled the kettle. 'Jenny's not communicated with anyone except the police and that only the very minimum to make her statement about what that woman did to her. She's drawn right back into herself like she did when ...' She didn't finish the sentence, getting a little lost in her own kitchen as if she couldn't remember how to switch on the hot water.

Jonah took the kettle from her, settled it on the pad and flicked the switch. 'Yeah, I understand. I know about Jenny's past.'

'So I thought a visit from one of her new friends might shake her out of this.' Her tone was bright and brittle. 'That lovely boy Harry called round but she refused to see him, but of course that's difficult, what with him ending things with her.'

'Harry came here?'

'Do you know him?'

'A little.' Jonah gulped back a laugh. 'I wouldn't describe us as friends.'

'We've had flowers, of course, from all sorts of people but she won't come out of her room to even look at them. I've had to put them in the lounge.'

'Do you mind?' Jonah gestured to the sitting room which he could see through the open door on the far side of the kitchen. 'Please.'

He had a quick check of the bouquets. Harry's looked like he'd picked it up at the station. There was a pretty florist-made one from Louis and Kris, as he expected, and another from the tedious Matt. The largest and most expensive came from someone signing himself 'Bobby', which wasn't a name Jonah recognised. They made his own offering of a stolen lilac look rather pitiful. He went back to Nikki.

'Milk? Sugar?'

'Yeah, thanks. One.'

She poured the tea and handed a mug to him. 'I'm sorry, Jonah. I've put you in a bad position.'

He was used to those. 'No, Mrs Groves …'

'Nikki, please.'

'Nikki. Anything I can do to help. Jenny's a great girl.'

Nikki's lower lip trembled and she sniffed, trying to hold back tears. 'Sorry, sorry, I get like this. It's just so hard …'

'So hard seeing someone you love hurt?' He felt like that might've been a line in a TV episode he had been in and winced.

Nikki nodded. 'She's just been so unlucky. Every time she makes progress something kicks her in the teeth. She lost her job with the orchestra, did you know that?'

Jonah wondered how much of the story Nikki had heard. 'I did, yeah.'

'She didn't even tell me!'

'Perhaps she didn't want to admit failure to you?'

'But I love her no matter what happens!'

'Of course you do.' Jonah didn't have much experience of unconditional maternal love. He could imagine it was a burden to receive. 'She knows that.'

'I'm not expecting you to produce a miracle, but if you could just talk to her?'

'I'll try.'

'Take her a cup of tea, will you?' She handed him a second mug, this one decorated with a Mozart wearing sunglasses.

'OK. Let's see if she'll let me in. Maybe it's best if you stay back here?' There might be parts of the conversation he really didn't want her to overhear on his side, like when he apologised for letting Bridget ride him like a jockey at Ascot Ladies Day.

He carried the two mugs down the corridor to the door with a blue flowered sign in childish handwriting saying *Keep Out*.

'Not that one,' said Nikki. 'She sleeps in the box room now.'

Of course, she would. The old one would be forever tainted by what happened there.

'It's the same flat?' asked Jonah.

Wearily, Nikki leaned on the doorpost to the kitchen. 'Maybe we should've moved away after the accident. But Jenny refused to go out, panicked if I tried to make her – and housing association flats like this are hard to come by. We just locked the door on it all.'

And that wasn't a symbol of all the crap Jenny had had to deal with?

Jonah knocked with his foot. 'Hey, Jenny, it's me. Make yourself decent because, ready or not, I'm coming in.' He balanced a mug on the top of a radiator to turn the handle. 'There you are, gorgeous.'

Jenny was looking up at him from a small armchair by the window, knees up under her chin. They'd had to shave a little of her hair to make the stitches so she looked fairly battered and bruised, but at least when the hair grew back no scar would be visible.

'Jonah,' she signed.

Thank God she still used their special symbol. It gave him hope he'd been forgiven.

'That's right, love. Your mum sent me bearing tea. She's a nice lady.' He set her cup down on the window sill and looked for somewhere to perch. In the end he settled on the floor with his back against her bed, putting himself below her. The body language lessons at RADA were really proving their worth of late in his real-life drama. 'The police kept me in for thirty-six hours.'

'Why?' she signed.

'Because of what happened in the hall after Bridget attacked you. They took one look at my ugly mug and thought I had to be guilty of something. Bridget collapsed on me and I bruised her a little doing mouth-to-mouth.' Jonah scrubbed his face, feeling a forgotten sense of embarrassment. 'Look, I'm sorry about what you saw in the attic – not what I did, but that you saw it.'

She looked away.

'What Bridget and I got up to up there – that meant nothing to me – just a … a transaction, part of my rent.'

Jenny grimaced and pointed to herself and made a zero sign.

'Not like that. I enjoyed it when we were together – I wanted to have sex with you. I never wanted it with her. It was just something I did. It wasn't the sex I had with you though which

274

meant something; it was our friendship. I haven't ruined that, have I?'

She bit her lip, still looking out the window at grey skies and tower blocks. Like her mother she had the tendency to tears but also tried to hide them. He could feel the struggle like he was going through it himself. She had never been one to play on his sympathies purposely; she'd earned them because he did feel sorry for her. Life appeared to have picked her out for fucking cruel treatment.

'Why?' she signed.

'Why what, gorgeous?'

'Why does sex mean nothing to you?'

That wasn't quite the question he'd been expecting but it was easier to answer than questions about Bridget. He'd worked this out long ago. 'It's survival. I thought you understood.' It was hard to raise this down the corridor from a room where horrible violence had once happened. 'My first experiences taught me that sex is mostly a barter, sometimes an abuse. I've not changed my mind since.'

'I don't understand.'

Jonah didn't feel the boiling anger he usually experienced when talking about his past. He was speaking to another victim, not one of those in authority who had failed to protect him when he was a child. 'I'll see if I can explain. I might not make much sense. First thing to know was that my mother was an addict and slept around to buy drugs.'

Jenny nodded. 'I know the feeling,' she signed.

'You didn't? You did?' She was taking it so seriously, he could tell. Jenny would have hated that particular fall off her high horse. 'Welcome to the slut club.'

She almost smiled. 'I'm like your mother,' she signed.

'You're nothing like her; you're more like me,' he said quickly. That was something he was sure about. He wouldn't be sitting in the same room as her if he believed she had anything in common with his monster of a mother. 'You wouldn't hurt someone else to get what you want, would you? You sold yourself. She sold me. Big difference. She passed me on to one of her customers and the abuse only ended when she died.'

Jenny had tears trickling down her cheeks now. Finally, someone was crying for the poor lost kid that he'd been. 'I'm sad for you,' she signed.

'Yeah, so am I, bloody sad. I never had a chance really. Someone should've taken me away from her earlier but they preferred to ignore the signs. I know I'm ten million ways fucked up but I'm wired to see sex as abusive when the people involved aren't equals. The only way to survive it is to not let it matter. Our abusers? Sex matters too much to them and that's what twisted them up so they could do that to someone else.' He let the silence stretch between them so she could consider his words. 'You know what I say?'

She shook her head. 'But you're going to tell me,' she signed.

'Fuck the lot of them. Do what you must to survive but dump the guilt.'

'I stole from people I love.'

'If they love you, they'll forgive you – at least they do in the movies.' Another corny line he must've borrowed. He grinned in self-mockery: he had little experience of receiving forgiveness from anyone; no wonder he was reaching for Hollywood schmaltz for inspiration. 'Anyway, the Jonah sermon is over. I'm sorry that crazy cow went off like she did. I didn't expect you both to fight over me.'

'Not over you,' signed Jenny.

'Oh, come off it!'

She pushed up her sleeve and showed him a patch on her arm. 'We fought for this.'

Chapter 51

Jenny, Present Day

Jenny could tell that Jonah didn't really understand. He knew of her reliance on painkillers but not how close she'd come to overdosing. Her craving for them was stronger than any weak feeling she might have for another person. Their landlady had saved her from that even while Bridget brained her with the water carafe – one of the more bizarre ways to deter a would-be suicide: try to kill her yourself.

It was impossible to sign this so she uncurled to reach for her iPad. She'd had nothing to do but think the last few days and had put a few things together. She moved beside him so he could read over her shoulder. *It was a really bad night for me. I was on the edge before I saw you. She caught me about to swallow too many painkillers and snatched my tablets.*

'On, Jen … I'm so not worth it.'

This time she did smile. Men! *Don't flatter yourself, Jonah. You were only one tiny part of my meltdown. But I can't make sense of what she did next – why overdose in my place? The police said she collapsed in the hall having taken six of my tablets.*

'The only explanation I can think of was that she probably

thought she'd killed you. Head wounds bleed like a bitch. She didn't want to face the consequences.'

So it was remorse? But she didn't sound the least bit sorry when she took them off me – more triumphant.

'I didn't say she was sorry, just that she knew she'd gone too far hitting you. Can you imagine Bridget going through the humiliation of a trial? She'd have to leave the house for one thing. They only got her out this time because they carried her out on a stretcher.'

But I've been wondering if maybe it was accidental? I don't think she knew what was in the tub. I got it on the black market and it wasn't labelled. Inside was Fentanyl rather than Tramadol.

'So?'

Bridget has chronic pain too, doesn't she? Maybe she was in pain after the effort of hitting me.

'Yeah, like that makes me feel so sorry for her!' Jonah gave a choking laugh. 'She left you bleeding in the bathroom: what a hero!'

I don't think either of us was thinking clearly. First I embarrassed her by interrupting your …

Jonah took the tablet as she so clearly didn't want to write a crude word. *SAGA holiday.*

'What?' she signed.

'Sex and games for the aged.'

Jenny rolled her eyes and took back the iPad. *If she thought she was taking her usual dose then maybe she overdosed accidentally? She must've run out of her own prescription. Pain can drive you crazy.*

'Jesus, I didn't know it had got so bad for her. She never mentioned it to me. The arthritis?'

She nodded. *I think so. But it just doesn't add up. She should've called an ambulance if she regretted it, or finished me off if she didn't.*

'There you go – back to my explanation: she's crackers, rattling around in that house on her own all day, and now we have to factor in the addiction. Don't go looking for reasons where there aren't any. It was impulse.'

Jenny still wasn't satisfied but it was unlikely they'd get any further with their guesses. *The good news is that I've levelled out since coming home.*

'Really? That's great!'

My doctor here has known me since I was little and has been really helpful. She's changed the way I take my painkillers. Apparently my GP should've done this as soon as she saw there was a problem. The patch gives me a steady dose of pain relief so no more lottery of downing pills scored on a street corner.

'You wild child, you.' He sounded admiring – that was so Jonah.

I think I went mad for a while there. I wasn't rational and couldn't imagine an alternative. I should've asked for help so much earlier.

'Few of us do ask before we have to, darling.' He took the iPad and put it on the bed behind them. 'I need a cuddle. It's been a stressful couple of days.'

She had to smile. So like Jonah to give her the comfort she needed by phrasing it as a favour to himself. She leaned into him.

He put his arm around her shoulders. 'And, Jen, I have to mention something.' He pulled her hand onto his lap and laced fingers with hers.

She made a circle with her free hand to indicate he should go on.

'Why aren't you in worse shape? I've been through withdrawal and, damn, girl, you either have one robust metabolism or you are sneaking some extra patches somewhere. I think I should look.' He made as if to peep down her shirt.

She tugged free. 'Am not!' she signed.

'Then I have to ask: how're you doing it? Because you're not acting like any recovering addict I've ever known – no shivering, sweating, throwing up, wishing you were dead.'

279

'I don't know,' she signed.

'How many pills were you taking each day?'

'Seven or eight.'

'Steep but hardly the habit of a real druggie. In fact, I'd call it pretty tame, you lightweight.'

She pulled the iPad onto her lap and wrote: *It never seemed enough but I couldn't afford more. The effect was very hit and miss. Sometimes the relief worked, sometimes it got worse.*

'You should ask your doctor about it.'

I will, but I really do feel so much better now.

'So why've you been giving your poor mum the heebie-jeebies by not communicating to her?'

Jenny shrugged. She couldn't tell him the real reason; she still hadn't come to terms with it herself, wondering if she'd only imagined it. Her throat still ached.

'You need to give her a break, let her know not to worry.'

You're right.

He snatched the tablet. 'At last: someone says I'm right about something! I'm gonna send that to myself.'

She chuckled, a little coughing sound coming from her chest.

'Hey, you made a sound!' Until now her laughter had always been silent.

She shrugged.

He put his head to her chest. 'It was lovely. Do it again!'

She pushed him away. She wasn't ready for that. 'There's something you can do for me, Jonah,' she signed.

'Anything legal, babe, and probably a few illegal acts too.'

She rolled her eyes.

'Oh come on, you can't tell me, you as a fully paid up member of the slut club, that you haven't thought of that too – you, me, a bed …?'

She smiled and shook her head. 'Not that kind of favour.'

'Shame: they're the best sort. OK, I'll be serious. What do you want, darling?'

She took the iPad back. *I need to fetch my stuff. Will you come back with me to Gallant House? Just you and me. I don't want my mum there.*

He grimaced as he read the message. 'That's a toughie, as I'd prefer to burn the place to the ground, but OK. I'll have to check first with my lawyer that I can.'

The police said they'd cleared out. It's no longer a crime scene. Our tenancy is still running as Bridget hasn't said it isn't.

'They told me I wasn't welcome but, technically, there's no reason they can give us to stop us going in, is there?' Jonah kissed her knuckles. 'OK, I'll take you. When would you like to go?'

How about now?

Chapter 52

It felt very wrong letting themselves back into Gallant House, forbidden, like kids sneaking home past curfew. Neither of them had ever been inside without Bridget in occupation and the house felt the lack. Jenny could sense it was lonely, with its long untrodden corridors and closed doors, dust settling on untouched bannisters, neglected ledges and tables. In a strange way, Bridget had been its soul, hadn't she? thought Jenny. She had channelled the dark energy that lurked here, drawing it to herself like the lightning rod on the roof; she'd been the ghost in the machine. If she didn't return, what would happen to the empty house?

No one had cleared up the flowers on the hall floor. The water had evaporated but the lilacs had browned and drooped. Jonah knelt down and picked them up. Striding past Jenny, he threw them out the front door into the gutter. She kicked the shards of glass against the skirting.

'Horrible things,' he muttered.

'I thought you liked lilacs?' signed Jenny.

'Hate them – too highly scented.'

'But you got me lilacs.'

'Stole – from your communal garden – because I thought you liked them.'

'I hate them too,' admitted Jenny.

Jonah laughed. 'Christ, what a pair we make. So, what do you want to do now?'

'I'm going to pack my stuff,' she signed.

'Want a hand?'

Jenny thought of the Bobby-bought clothes hanging in her wardrobe. Jonah would no doubt make a few jokes about her call girl career if he saw those. She wasn't quite ready to treat it so lightly. She'd lost herself for a few months and not yet found a path back, though maybe she was now at least facing the right way? 'No, thanks. Hadn't you better pack?' she signed.

'I suppose I should. I might look around first though: while the cat's away, this mouse will play. I'll leave you to it.' He wandered off, whistling a snatch of something she thought might be the Danger Mouse theme tune. 'Watch out for Spooky Moggy!' he called over his shoulder just before he disappeared into the snug. He was probably going for a smoke, knowing him.

She wanted to summon him back to remind him he'd already sent her a message owning up to Spooky Moggy weeks ago.

He had, hadn't he? To be honest, those last weeks were a horrible scar on her memory, with only the pain, fear and embarrassment clear, like stitches across a wound.

Jenny tugged on her braid, unravelling the strands that pulled on her injury. She no longer had that phone – the police had taken it into evidence in case anything connected Bridget to the harassment of the flowers and the messages she'd told them about. She could only remember the text had been signed 'Sad Moggy'. Jonah liked to flog a joke way beyond death so who else could it have been? She'd confront him on the way home, tell him to cut it out. Shrugging it off for now, she went upstairs and into her bedroom. It had the stale smell of a room that had been closed for a while. The curtains were drawn. She pulled them back and tried to open the sash but failed as usual to lift it. The cord must still be broken. The room looked pretty sad in the twilight,

283

bedcovers rumpled and the pillow dented from where she'd last lain down. There were even a few blood spots on the white carpet between the bed and the bathroom.

From the creaking overhead, it sounded like Jonah had gone back upstairs to visit the scene of his amorous encounters. If she had her way, she'd burn that daybed. Jenny started piling scattered clothes on the duvet. Bridget should know better than to use a vulnerable guy like Jonah. He might not like that label, but that's how his experiences had left him, wide open to more abuse by people who exploited his low self-opinion to use him for sex.

She hadn't done that as well, had she? She'd certainly looked to him for comfort.

Not liking where her thoughts were going, she connected her new phone to her speakers and let it blast through her 'Most Played' tracks. She had been wandering in a desert lately, her love of classical music vanished like a mirage as she tried to approach it. Her spirit felt dry-as-dust too as a result. Could *Petrushka* return her to the ocean? That Russian ballet was the last concert she remembered playing and enjoying. She'd connected to the piece, lost herself in it in a deep dive. She was scared she couldn't recapture that. Had she really lost all hope of a career in classical music? What would she do now? Stay in Harlow? She didn't think she had the gift to teach violin like her mum, so what could she do?

Never mind that now. Concentrate on the task at hand, Jenny, she told herself. Tidy this part of your life away so you don't have to think about it again.

Taking her suitcase from under the bed, she began folding up her clothes from the wardrobe. There were some lovely pieces here, especially the plum satin evening gown and an embroidered lace over nude sheath. If she sold all the designer clothes, would she get enough to buy back her violin from the dealer on the Portobello Road? He might not yet have found a purchaser. Doubtful that they'd be worth that much second-hand. She wasn't

284

sure if she actually owned the jewellery. She'd have to ask Bobby and wouldn't that be awkward? They'd never officially ended their arrangement. He'd been pestering her to go out again with him. He'd even sent her a bottle of champagne, saying they could drink it together at a romantic night at the apartment, just the two of them, underlined. She dug it out of the bottom of the wardrobe. It had a great yellow ribbon with streamers on the neck. He'd guessed rightly that the night after the exhibition had scared her away and she'd need some coaxing back. The bottle might be worth a few quid, though, as it looked a superior vintage. She cut off the label from him with her sewing scissors and threw it in the bin, and put the bottle aside for last minute packing.

But enough of Bobby. She wasn't going back to that life. A holdall would have to do for her underwear and T-shirts. She dragged this out from the bottom of the cupboard and turned to her dresser. Pulling out the top drawer, she stopped.

Someone had removed the underwear, every single lacy scrap and sensible cotton brief. The police? They were the only ones she knew to have been in here since the attack. But why? It hadn't been a sex crime that had taken place in this room, just a straightforward assault. She opened the next drawer down in case the police had done a search and simply mixed things up. All her bras, stockings and tights were missing too.

'Looking for these?'

Spinning round, Jenny found Matt standing by the bathroom door with a black thong dangling from one finger. She hadn't seen him for months and he looked more neatly groomed than she remembered, hair recently washed, clothes a bright white Tee and new dark jeans; that should make him look nice and normal, that was until she saw that his eyes lit with malice.

'I see I've left you speechless?' He gave a humourless smile. 'But then you always are. That's one of the nicest things about you.' He took the panties to his nose and sniffed. 'And your scent. Did I ever tell you how much I like that?'

Jenny closed the drawer slowly. Matt here? But why? His presence made her skin crawl – it always had a little, she realised. 'How did you get in?' she signed, fingers trembling. How far away was Jonah?

He looked down at her hands wryly. 'So predictable.' He made his voice a falsetto. 'How, Matt, why, Matt? That's how I imagine you sound in your head, while to the rest of the world you're silent. You had such a grating accent when you were thirteen – so ill-fitting to your gift! I did the world a favour breaking you of that, even though it was an accidental outcome. I have to admit you've been a good girl staying quiet all these years, much better behaved than recently.'

What was he saying? Jenny shook her head, not knowing what she was denying. Being good? Everything? Even being here with him?

'Why so shocked, Jenny? You must've known. Come on: we've been together for months now.'

Did he mean …?

'We had something special all those years – you and me. I knew when we first met that we had to be each other's first, both would follow our music step by step, our lives linked. That night was sublime; it's never quite been as good since. We've never gone quite so far in our sharing.' He plucked the elastic string he held between finger and thumb, making it snap, snap, snap against his palm: pizzicato on thong, so bizarre and so wrong. 'But you took it so badly, retreated so I couldn't reach you. I had to wait. But maybe you were right. It was too soon: you just fourteen and me only seventeen. We had to nurture our talent first. I admit that I'd never be half the musician I am now without your example to pull me along, challenging me to keep up. I'm a patient man.'

Even while pretending to pay attention, Jenny looked frantically around for exits, for a way of summoning Jonah. Window – door – all blocked.

'And so I waited, watching, and timed my move to when you

286

finally saw that you needed me. And we could've been the perfect duo – even your friend Louis saw that. He told you but you didn't listen.'

What did he mean by saying he'd been watching? She'd never noticed Matt until Harry's party – or was this all his own fantasy? 'Why are you here? I thought you'd finished with me.' she signed.

'You want to know why I'm here?'

He was acting so strange – too calm, almost removed from the situation; except for his angry mauling of her underwear. She had to keep him talking. She nodded as her stomach clenched with sick anticipation.

'Don't you realise by now? Christ, I take it all back: you're so dumb!' He turned slightly away but before she could move for the door, he was back, finger in her face. 'I live next door, right under your nose, you stupid bitch. I've watched you coming and going for a year now. I've never stopped watching you.'

Oh God. He wasn't just angry or jealous; he was insane. She pointed in the direction of the GP's house.

'Yes, I'm living with dear old Norman. He's got more than a touch of senile dementia; that's why his partners at the surgery eased him out so quickly last summer. Didn't you wonder about that? Thanks to a couple of embarrassing misdiagnoses and mutterings about patient complaints, it was "adios and here's your gold carriage clock, Norman".'

God, that poor man: he must've been so lonely and confused, wide open to the first con artist who happened upon him.

'It was around the same time I convinced him, easily enough as it turned out, that I was the grandson of an old friend and he invited me to stay with him. He was feeling adrift and needed someone to cheer him up, the pathetic old sod. He felt like he was being useful – and he so loves feeling useful.'

This was all building to some crescendo, wasn't it? Matt had a plan for being here and had had time to prepare while she'd been in Harlow. Jenny wondered how long she could stall him and keep him talking. Did he know she wasn't alone? Jonah would come looking for her eventually. 'Go on,' she signed.

'You want to hear the full story, do you?' He moved to the door and pushed the bolt across. Chills ran down Jenny's spine and she began to wonder if he ever intended to let her out again. 'I suppose we have time and you should know, because it's all your fault for moving in here. Norman would never've met me if it weren't for you.'

Jenny tracked his movements, trying to keep away from him, but he was getting closer as he prowled. She couldn't afford to get cornered. Could she go across the bed and get out of the door before he caught her?

'I think dear old Norman got a little intimidated by me.' He sounded so philosophical about it all, as if they were discussing something quite ordinary and not his terrorising of an elderly man. 'But I never took his hints that it was time I should leave and assured your nosey landlady that he was perfectly content with me. She kept asking me to dinner to meet you. That would've been a laugh, wouldn't it? Obviously I refused and, as for Norman, he's happy with the arrangement now. And you should thank him. He's been supplying Bridget's medical needs for years until they shoved him out of his surgery. He still knows a thing or two and told me how to get all those pills for you – well, for me technically, but it didn't matter to you, did it, as long as it was you who shovelled the stuff down your ungrateful throat? You took the pills like a little baby bird, beak open, cheep, cheep, cheep, Matt: feed me, feed. You didn't care how I got them or how difficult it was for me.' A thought seemed to connect out of nowhere. 'Have you been blowing those guys? Of course, you have! They paid enough to have you any way they liked, didn't they? You, on your knees, lips all slicked up in that tramp lipstick I found—'

He was getting angry again. She had to get him back on the less explosive subject of Norman. 'Why is Norman happy now?' she signed. What had Matt done to him?

'Forget him. I want to talk about you. Just tell me one thing: why, Jenny?' Realising he was still holding the thong, he dropped it as if it now disgusted him and made a lunge for her. She tried to dodge but he seized her upper arms before she could escape and dragged her to him. He looked into her eyes, trying to root out her secrets. 'Why did you do it, Jenny? I loved you: why wasn't I enough?'

She couldn't sign, couldn't write, all she could do was raise her eyebrows in a question. This wasn't the Matt she remembered, at least he had only been this way once … the night after the wedding reception. Oh please, God: not again! She couldn't bear it! Her body shook in his grip, adrenalin pumping for fight or flight, but there seemed no chance of escape. He was so much stronger than her.

'You're looking at me so scared, so innocent! No shame or guilt! You don't know what you've done, do you?' He laughed mirthlessly. 'What a joke. Let me remind you, you worthless little whore! You should've come back to me – I'd've taken you back even then – but instead you spread your legs for God knows who else – the clothes, the taxis, the late nights. I watched you – tracked you through your phone – and you're that stupid, you didn't even realise that I'd activated a tracker app months ago. You were sharing your position with me every second of the day and night. You never once looked over your shoulder to see me watching you with those men, on their arm smiling so obediently, letting them touch you, going up to bed with them – one, two, it didn't matter to you.' He bent forward and rested his forehead on her shoulder. His skin was clammy. 'You gave them what should've been mine. I've loved you forever, Jenny, and you keep on turning me away – ruining everything!'

She tried to push him off but that only resulted in him tightening his grip. Her hands began to tingle as he cut off the blood supply like a blood pressure cuff.

'I waited for you to come back. Warned you I'd leave no more gifts, told you that you'd made me sad, but you didn't come to me. Then that woman hurt you and I wanted her dead for daring to touch you – wanted everyone in this house buried, gone! So I've been waiting. I've decided I can't let you do this to me any longer. It's got to stop.' Looking wildly around, he grabbed the scissors from the dressing table and held them to her throat. 'This time I'll make you mine for ever, then burn this fucking place to the ground.' His voice broke and he started to push in the blunt ends, weeping as he did so. 'You've made me do this! It's your fault!'

Bewildered, it had taken too long for Jenny's brain to catch up with the fact that she was in mortal danger and not just facing rape from him. Drenched in a cold sweat now, she bent over backwards, putting a little gap between herself and the blades. She opened her mouth and screamed just as a clashing chord burst out from the speaker. 'JONAH!'

Chapter 53

Jonah

Leaning over the balcony, Jonah threw his cigarette butt into the open well in the courtyard below. The structure creaked and the handrail gave way, sliding down to rest on the floor with a clunk. Maybe crazy old Bridget did have a point about this being dangerous?

Not his problem any longer. He was moving on. This would be his last visit to the house.

He nodded a farewell to the ugly sofas. He had a good memory of them, thanks to his first time with Jenny. In fact, she was the source of most of his happy reminiscences about this place – her and Kris when he'd been here doing his singer-songwriter thing, hanging out in the garden to practise or coming into Jonah's room late at night to ask for an opinion on a new composition. It hadn't been a bad place, much better than so many he'd lived in. Jonah wandered into the kitchen and checked in the fridge. Bridget had put some leftover salmon quiche in a plastic box. He mentally counted how many days it might have lurked in there. Too old?

Oh sod it: live dangerously. He polished off the slice. It tasted

291

fine so if salmonella lurked, so be it. No one had predicted he would die of food poisoning – violence, booze, drugs, yes – so it would be kinda funny if was a quiche that ended him.

He padded upstairs, trainers making hardly any noise. Jenny was playing her music really loudly. He didn't like the piece she had on and he wondered about teasing her into changing it for a bit of Eminem or Bastille, which he knew she quite liked despite being a classical babe. Then Bridget's bedroom door distracted him. The chance was too perfect to pass over. He turned the handle and stepped inside.

The first thing he noticed was the heavy drapes at the window cutting out the last light of the day. He groped on the wall for the switch. A chandelier lit up, dazzling: curling cupped flowers on silver stems from a centre point. The room was surprisingly decadent. He'd imagine Bridget lying in some nun-like bed with a white counterpane, more like Jenny's. This was still decorated how it must have been during her marriage: heavy four-poster, blood red velvet hangings with gold fringe, a mountain of satin pillows. You'd get lost in there if you tried to have sex, thought Jonah, overwhelmed by the womblike atmosphere. Complete turn off. Maybe that was why she preferred the simplicity of the daybed upstairs? He'd've struggled to get it up in here.

He wandered to the dressing table and pulled open a drawer on the right. Ointments and hairpins, a nest of beads and artificial flowers. Next one down held an upmarket label maker, stapler, and collection of pens and pencils. Bridget was something of a hoarder with old labels and receipts all stuffed inside in no particular order. The one below that contained her manuscript, as did all the ones on the left-hand side, some yellowed with age. Jeez, Bridget, how many of these things do you have? He counted at least five before he gave up. From the front page, they all looked pretty similar. He shut the drawers with a snap.

That music still blasted from Jenny's room. How the hell could she listen to that crap?

And here was Bridget's en suite. Jonah had been the only one to use the bathroom in the corridor as both the women had their own. He'd thought that a great deal because it made it as good as his. Jenny's had been a nice black and white affair, a modern version of Edwardian taste, bath big enough for some fun and games. So what was Bridget's like?

Oh my God: black and gold! He laughed with pure glee. This shrieked of 80s excess. His and her sinks – kidney-shaped bath with jacuzzi – separate walk-in shower with dolphin-shaped taps: priceless! It was the kind of place that would suit a Trump tower. He walked over to the huge mirror-fronted cabinet and grinned at himself. He looked about as at home in this monstrosity as a mutt at Crufts. He bared his teeth in mock growl.

'OK, Bridget, what other secrets are you hiding?' he murmured, opening the cabinet.

Row upon row of bottles confronted him like a mini New York skyline. At first he wasn't sure what he was looking at, then he read the labels. They were all for painkillers but the prescriptions were made out to other people: Jenny was here, as was Kris. The dates on some of these went back years. He even saw several ancient ones in the name of Paul Whittingham, her husband, as well as for Bridget herself, all issued by Norman, though that supply had stopped when Norman retired a while back. They were all empty. Had she been taking them from the bins, hoarding them for some insane reason of her own? But why keep them? Then he found a strip of tablets at the top shelf with Jenny's name on them and a recent date: a week's dose. There were some pills left under the foil.

Hang on …

She hadn't …?

He went back to the label maker in the desk drawer with Jenny's prescription to compare. It was set up to print off what looked like a standard pharmacy label.

The vicious old cow! She must've been taking the prescriptions belonging to her tenants. Rage boiled inside Jonah. When Norman's prescribing rights had been removed by his concerned colleagues, she'd taken to nicking Kris's pain relief, then Jenny's, and probably putting some placebo, or lookalike pill, in its place on her daily spring-clean because she was too fucking scared to score her own supply. Kris had been dosing himself on paracetamol or bloody vitamins and wondering why his old injury was playing up so badly. No wonder Kris had moved out because his pain got so bad! And then it had been Jenny's turn. From the looks of these shelves, Bridget had a couple of years to perfect her sleight-of-hand and no one had suspected a thing because, well, who would? She was so nice, wasn't she? So motherly. Welcome to the house. We're all one big happy family. You, young man, I need for a good shag; you, little girl, because I can screw you over for your medication.

Bitch.

Taking the box of painkillers to the window, he looked out at the garden and wondered. It was only then that he began to realise the full extent of what Bridget had done to Jenny. Her life had collapsed around her like a house of cards all thanks to her desperation to get pain relief. Bridget had floated around Gallant House on the drugs that belonged to someone else, killed her own pain but pushed Jenny into a cesspit of despair. Jenny had lost her job, her self-respect … fuck, the prim girl who blushed at talk of sex had been thrown on the game. That was Bridget's work.

Jenny deserved to know.

Jonah threw open the door and strode down the corridor. Music still blasted from Jenny's room. He tried the handle but the door did not budge.

'Turn the sodding music off, Jenny! I've got something important to show you!'

The only answer was a thump and a bang. Had she fallen?

'Jenny? Jenny?' Bloody music seemed to be even louder now. Thumping on the door wasn't getting any response.

Then someone screamed his name.

Jonah kicked the door in and saw Jenny wrestling with a man – that ginger-haired tosser, Matt. He'd pushed her to the floor, clenched hand at her throat. He was choking her.

'No, you fucking don't!' Jonah hauled him up by the back of the shirt.

Matt came up stabbing at Jonah's stomach. The blow wouldn't have hurt it if Matt hadn't had a pair of scissors grasped in his fist. Fire speared through Jonah as he looked down in disbelief. The scissors were sticking out of his abdomen – so wrong, too surreal, like some gory special effect.

'You screwed her too, didn't you, you bastard!' Matt shouted and started kicking at Jonah, aiming mainly for the head as Jonah had collapsed and curled around his injury, clutching the plastic handle of the scissors. He could barely see through the pain as Jenny got up on her knees, groped for a champagne bottle and brought this down over Matt's head. It didn't break, but Matt did – at least his skull. He sprawled out cold on top of Jonah, his fall driving the scissors an inch deeper.

Jonah screamed.

Chapter 54

Jenny

Jenny staggered to her feet. Jonah was curled up, cursing, screaming and sobbing. He needed help but she couldn't even call an ambulance for him. Maybe he could manage if she got him a phone? Hers was lying near Matt. She knelt, then stopped cold. The things Matt had said finally began to make sense. He'd admitted the attack on her at fourteen, hadn't he? Or had he fantasised about it and put himself in the scene because he was obsessed about her? Both were frighteningly possible. One thing was clear: he was out of his mind with jealousy and had just tried to kill her and Jonah. She'd never be safe from him.

Jenny's mind went briefly to the prospect of a trial and testimony. All her past being dissected again – her name getting out as, God, there weren't any other black voiceless violinists were there? People trolling her on social media – telling her she'd got what she'd deserved, you black bitch. If there was a foul insult out there, c-word, n-word, it would come her way in such a disgusting torrent that she'd have to hide again. She couldn't stand that. Just couldn't. She just wanted it all to go away.

Her gaze slid to the door. Matt had dropped a bag on entry

just inside. A mood of unreality stole over her. Ignoring Jonah's sobs, she knelt to open it. It felt like a message sent from … from Fate? Matt had packed lighter fuel and matches. An odd feeling swept her; it was as if someone else was in control of her and she was just observing. The solution was obvious. She took out the fuel and matches, spilled the liquid over the bottom of the curtains and lit the match. Her drapes went up with a satisfying 'whoosh'.

'What the fuck, Jenny?' groaned Jonah. 'Are you trying to kill us?'

Disorientated, she realised she'd done this in the wrong order. She should've made Jonah safe before torching the place. Too late now though. Still functioning in a cloud of unreality, she cast about for her next move. OK, she'd have to make a belated attempt at the first part of the plan. Taking her plum silk gown, she made a stabilising bandage for the scissors, tying it around Jonah's middle. Pulling them out now would risk massive blood loss: she remembered that much from a first aid course members of the orchestra did so they could work with school kids. Smoke was already gathering, flames eating at the ceiling, blistering the white paint black. She grabbed Jonah under his armpits and started dragging him to the door.

'Shit!' He yelled. 'Stop it, you mad cow! I … can … walk,' he gasped.

That would be better for both of them. Jonah clutched his abdomen and struggled to his knees. She supported him as he got to his feet.

'You're fucking insane.'

She knew that.

'Are you going back for him?'

She shook her head.

'Because I don't think … I can manage … the stairs on my own.'

It took so long. She was having problems breathing as she

acted as his crutch on the steps. They managed to get as far as the hallway before Jonah passed out. Crap, she was hoping he'd call the ambulance for her. She opened the front door and dragged him onto the path. At least he was safe. Then she went back into the house, half expecting, half hoping, to see Matt at the stop of the stairs. She gripped the bannister so hard it hurt. For a moment, her emotional fog lifted and she felt a sharp stab of regret – maybe guilt? It was difficult to know what she was feeling. Then reality finally managed to punched through her numbness. This was happening for real. Matt was lying helpless upstairs as the fire took hold and she was to blame.

My God, did I really mean him to die?

Oh God, oh God. Was there still time to go upstairs to try to rescue Matt?

Then a billow of black smoke obscured the oriel window, taking the decision away from her. Her fire-making had worked too well. Chances of her carrying Matt out were vanishingly small. She'd probably end up killing them both. Instead, she picked up the old landline and dialled the emergency services.

'Which service do you require?' came the voice.

Jenny struggled, gulped, tried to summon the sounds she had managed twice now.

'Caller, which service to you require?'

'All. Urgent.' The sound was ugly, more growl than words.

'All of them?'

'Yes.' She put the phone back in the cradle. Smoke was filling the hallway. There was no choice now of going upstairs and surviving so she went out to be with Jonah and watch Gallant House burn.

The fire service arrived very quickly, already summoned by a neighbour. Before she could even wave to get their attention, competent-looking men in uniform swarmed her.

'Is there anyone left in the house?' asked one.

She nodded. 'One. Front bedroom.' She pointed to her window where flames and smoke billowed.

'Inhaled the smoke, did you?' The fireman beckoned a colleague. 'Get some oxygen over here. Team, we've got someone trapped inside. Adult or child?' He was talking to her again.

'Adult,' she rasped.

'OK, Miss, you sit still and my colleague will look after you until the ambulance arrives.'

Jenny hated watching the firemen risk their lives to enter the house but she could hardly admit her guilt, could she? A second engine arrived and there were now firehoses trained on the front of the house. Flames had reached the attic. At least the daybed would be a goner.

The police and first ambulance arrived together. Jonah was stretchered away and left on a blue light run. He'd relish the irony, she thought, doing it for real, rather than just for the cameras. A policeman hunkered down next to her while a medic checked her over.

'We know you, don't we, Miss?'

She nodded.

'You're the lady who can't talk?'

She gave him a thumbs up.

'We'll need to know what happened here.'

Another thumbs up – agreement to questioning.

He exchanged a look with the medic. 'The paramedic wants to take you into hospital to get you checked over. We'll catch up with you there, all right?'

Jenny nodded, but her gaze went to a spot beyond him. The firemen, who had entered the house fully suited and booted, were now emerging. They were carrying a shrouded body.

'Do you know who that is?' asked the policeman.

Jenny coughed, took a sip of water. 'M … matt.'

The policeman looked at her in surprise.

'Upshaw.'

'Matt Upshaw? Housemate?'

She shook her head. Her throat ached. These words felt like fingernails being bent backwards but she had to explain the essentials or they'd arrest Jonah again. Or maybe her? 'He … attacked … us.'

'Officer, I really have to take her now,' said the paramedic as his colleague arrived with a stretcher.

Jenny waved it away. 'Walk.' Leaning on his arm, she crossed over to the third ambulance just as the second carrying Matt hurtled away, sirens screaming. Did that mean there was some life left in him? She didn't know if she preferred him dead or alive – not because of doubt about what he deserved but because she'd have to face up to being a killer if she'd succeeded in ending his life.

As the ambulance doors closed, Jenny looked back and saw the roof fall in over her bedroom. Sparks wheel up into the sky like the ghosts of the Jacks escaping. Bridget should've been here, she thought. A fitting end for the admiral's cursed house.

Sitting in the examination cubicle alone, Jenny hugged her arms to herself. God, what had she done? The sense of unreality that had cocooned her was retreating. She'd asked them not to phone her mother. Instead, she had sent a message from a borrowed mobile that hers was out of juice and that she was staying up in town with Jonah. She hoped news of the house fire remained a local London item, rather than make the national newsfeed. Technically, what she told her mother was true: her phone would not have any battery left, having been burnt to a cinder, and she was staying in hospital to see how her friend did.

On arrival, the doctors had poked and prodded her, noted the shallow cut on her throat and bruising on her upper arms. Checking with the uniformed police officer who had followed her to hospital, they'd asked if she needed a rape kit but she'd shaken her head and with that they'd left her alone. A pile up on a local dual carriageway had demanded their attention in A&E.

'Knock, knock.' A plain clothes police officer put her head around the curtain. 'Jenny? I'm Detective Sergeant Foley, can I come in?'

Jenny beckoned her closer.

'My colleague, Constable Morningside, who looked after you at the house, said you have recovered a limited ability to speak?'

Jenny breathed through her nose, preparing herself. 'Single ... words.'

If Foley found this suspicious, she kept her tone rigorously polite. 'Thank you. We just needed to know as we have a female voice on the emergency call. Is that you?'

Jenny nodded.

'You spoke to my colleagues last time you were interviewed, but I've been working the earlier assault case for CID. Do you know what that means?'

Jenny nodded.

'This is the second time in a week that we've been called to Gallant House. The first time there were two casualties – yourself and Bridget Whittingham. This time we have one casualty – Jonah Brigson – and one body.

She'd killed Matt?

'You told Constable Morningside on the scene that the man's name is Matt Upshaw. Is this correct?'

She'd murdered him.

'Jenny? Is that correct?'

Trembling, she nodded. Oh God. She'd done this.

'OK, I've already run a check through our case notes and I found a Matt Upshaw listed as being part of the same orchestra you played for, yes?'

She nodded, going into automatic as her brain tried to process his death.

'Can you tell me anything else about him? Next of kin, for example?'

Jenny squeezed the bridge of her nose. God, this was a nightmare – one she had helped create.

301

'Jenny, I know this is difficult …'

Jenny mimed writing.

'You need something to write on?' The police officer ducked out of the cubicle and came back with a clipboard and pen. 'Here you are.'

She had to pull herself together just enough to answer the questions. She could fall apart when the police left.

Matt Upshaw was my ex-boyfriend but tonight he also admitted he'd been stalking me since we broke up. He was waiting for us in the house. He attacked me and when Jonah tried to stop him, Matt stabbed him with my scissors.

DS Foley was quiet for a while after reading this. 'What were you and Jonah doing in the house?'

Collecting our belongings.

'We'd told Jonah it wasn't a good idea to go back there.'

I asked him to keep my company. It was my idea.

'And Matt was waiting for you?'

That reminded Jenny. *He admitted to living next door so he could spy on me. Please will you check on Norman, our neighbour? I'm worried Matt might've hurt him too.*

Foley nodded. 'OK, I'll get right on that. I imagine the fire brigade have already checked on nearby houses. I'll see what I can learn.'

The sergeant went out beyond the curtain to make her call. Not that this posed much of a barrier as even in the hubbub of A&E, her side of the conversation could be clearly heard.

'Norman – no, didn't get a last name. A neighbour. I can go back and ask if you need. OK. Thanks.' There was a long pause. 'You have? Norman Stratton. Right. I'll let her know.'

DS Foley came back in, her expression a little less suspicious than before. 'I'm afraid you were correct, Jenny. The fire brigade found the occupant of the neighbouring house dead in an upstairs bedroom.'

'Fire?' Oh Christ, had she killed Norman too?

'No, he'd been that way for some time. But it's an unattended death so there'll be an investigation.'

Poor Norman. Jenny forced her brain to think through what this meant. Had Matt killed him when he no longer had a use for him? Had her breaking it off with Matt triggered this too? Was she partly to blame?

'I've checked with the doctors and they're happy to discharge you. I'm going to arrange for you to be transferred to our station so we can question you properly: is that OK? You aren't under arrest but you are clearly key to our enquiries, at the very least as a witness.' Foley was leaving the door open to ramping that up to suspect, was she? Jenny had to hope Jonah didn't mention that little scene he saw of her with the lighter fluid.

How's Jonah? She tapped the pad to get Foley's attention.

'He's in surgery.'

Can you interview me here? I want to be with him when he wakes up. She did care about him, but she also had to make sure he didn't say anything.

'How about we take you to the station, you answer some questions and we take your statement, then we bring you back here?'

Jenny nodded, unable to think of a reason worth annoying the police officer. An innocent person would do all they could to help law enforcement, wouldn't she?

303

Chapter 55

Jonah

Jonah came back to consciousness with a strange impression that he had no stomach. Not in the sense 'no stomach for something' but just that there was a gap in the middle of his body, a Teletubby with the TV screen removed. He'd always found those children's characters sinister; now he knew why.

'Jonah, can you hear me?'

Fuck, it was DI Khan.

Jonah blinked. 'Give me the pretty nurse again.'

'The nurse said you came round immediately after surgery and went under again.'

Jonah had a vague memory of that, of someone giving him something to drink and telling him the operation had gone well.

Scissors. In stomach. It came rushing back but bits were missing, like how he'd got here, snipped out of his recall.

'Jenny?'

'She's fine. They let her go hours ago.'

She hadn't stayed to see if he survived? But what did he expect: no one ever did stay with him. Sod it, he was getting self-pitying. Man up, Jonah. It's you against the world as usual.

'She helped you out of a burning house and called an ambulance. Did you know she can speak?'

He shook his head. 'Can't.'

'Just a few words. If she makes herself. She called the ambulance. She also said you came to help her when she shouted for you?'

He phrased it as a question. Jonah thought back. He'd not heard anything over that fucking awful music she'd had on with its clashing chords. She could've been the one shouting, but he'd not stopped to think, just reacted. And his reward? A pair of scissors in the gut. Again, not an end for him that anyone had imagined: him playing the hero.

'I need to ask you some questions. I know you're feeling rough ...'

'Had scissors shoved in your belly, have you?'

Khan shook his head. 'No, but I got glassed in a bar brawl once.' He turned his head to display a scar under his chin. 'A bit to the left and I would've been dead.'

Yeah, he looked the sort to have survived some rough stuff. 'So you're telling me not to be a fucking pussy and answer your questions?'

'It would be very helpful. You may not know this yet, but a man died in the fire.'

So Jenny had done for Matt, had she? Jonah wasn't sure what he thought about that. Totally didn't go with what he thought he knew about her. 'You're right: I didn't know.'

'Can you tell me what happened?'

'I'll have to be brief because this hurts.'

'What? The memories?'

Mock a man when he's down, would you, DI Khan? 'No, talking.' He silently added 'you prick'.

Khan gave a wry smile, probably knowing what was unsaid. 'OK, tell me what you can.'

Shit: they weren't getting to understand each other, were they?

'We went back to pack our stuff. We split up – Jenny headed off to her room and I went out for a smoke on the balcony.' Jonah wondered if he should talk about what he discovered in Bridget's room. But how to explain why he was snooping? 'How bad was the damage?'

'I'm not sure they know yet. They've contained the fire to the first floor, and there's extensive smoke and water damage.'

So it was possible Bridget's bathroom survived. Let them carry out their own investigation. It wasn't his responsibility to do their job for them. 'I was heading along the corridor to tell Jenny something when I heard a thump. I thought she might've fallen. She didn't come when I knocked so I kicked in the door. Matt – the guy who died – was on top of her. I thought he was raping her – strangling her – something. I didn't see that he was armed. I pulled him off and that was when I got stabbed. Hurt like fuck. He kicked me, shouting crazy stuff – I really thought he was going to kill me – but Jenny got up and bashed him with a wine bottle. He fell on top of me. Next thing I know was that the room was on fire and Jenny was hauling me out. I can remember going down the stairs with her help but then nothing.'

'Do you know if the room was on fire already when you entered?'

Jonah had a choice. He could tell the truth of Jenny's little arsonist moment or …

'No idea. I was focused on Jenny. Matt would've killed her if I hadn't got there just in time. He probably wanted to kill us both. Set fire to us too. The guy was fucking insane.'

Khan settled back on the visitor chair, making it creak. 'Tell me what you know about Matt Upshaw.'

'Is that his surname? I know next to nothing. Jenny dated him for a while. He had an unhealthy attitude towards her, controlling, you know? She got to know him thanks to a guy from the orchestra called Harry. You might have better luck with him.'

Khan nodded. 'OK, Jonah, thanks for answering my questions.

There'll be more, but we'll leave those until you feel better.'

'So I don't need to call my lawyer?'

'Not this time.'

On the next occasion Jonah woke up, Jenny was sitting beside him.

'I thought you'd gone home?' he murmured.

She shook her head and signed, 'They took me in for questioning.'

Jonah felt absurdly pleased she hadn't abandoned him. 'The police said you talk now.'

'Some ... words.' Her voice was deep and gravelly, like Scarlett Johansson after a week's bender, almost masculine.

'Matt died.'

She looked down.

'I didn't tell them.'

'I must explain,' she signed.

'You don't have to.'

'I must.' She thumped her heart.

'OK, tiger, explain.'

She tore the lid off a cardboard box of tissues and took a pen from the clipboard of notes at the end of his bed. Of course, she'd lost her iPad too, hadn't she? *He said he was my rapist when I was fourteen. He raped me in December. He was going to kill me last night and burn the house down. I lost it. I'm sorry.*

It took Jonah a moment to take in what she was saying. 'OK, then he deserved what he got. But do you believe him? That he's been stalking you all this time?'

She shuddered and bit her lip, not looking at him.

'Jenny, it's not very likely, is it? After all these years?' He wondered what he would've felt if someone had claimed he was Thomas. He'd probably torch him too, just to get rid of that possibility. He remembered then that during his earlier interrogation the police had talked about messages Jenny had been

307

receiving. 'Did he send you those creepy messages – put the flowers on your pillow? He was Spooky Moggy? God, I'm so sorry I joked about that.'

I think so. He meant Sad Matt in a text that outed him but I totally didn't get the reference. He's been living with Norman. Norman is dead.

Jonah swore. 'He was the fucking lodger! Did he kill him?'

Jenny gestured that she didn't know.

'But he would've been able to come and go like Norman did, through the garden.' Jonah wished he felt more up to this set of revelations. His brain felt too slow at making the connections. 'Did Bridget know what was going on?'

Another wavering hand gesture of uncertainty.

Who knew what went on in the world of Bridget? She'd probably been too high on her pills to notice. Which reminded him.

'Jenny, there's something else. I was coming to tell you when I stopped Matt.'

'I stopped Matt,' signed Jenny, almost indignant.

'Yeah, well, I stopped him first time. You just did a better job. I found something in Bridget's room – lots of somethings.' He held her gaze, hoping she'd be able to take the next bit of news. 'I now know why you aren't in withdrawal. Bridget has been stealing your meds, swapping them for lookalikes or sometimes just nicking a few here and there if she thought you wouldn't notice. And she'd done the same to Kris. I don't know how far it goes back. Probably did the same to her invalid husband as I saw some bottles with his name on them. She was a hoarder.'

Jenny gaped.

'That's not a good look, darlin'.' He gently lifted her chin to close her mouth. Her eyes brimmed with tears. It was like another pair of scissors in the gut to see the thoughts going through her brain.

'Bridget?' she growled. 'Did this? To me? Made my treatment useless?'

'You, and Kris.'

Jenny leapt up.

'Hey! Where are you going?' She was already out of the door. Christ, she was going for Bridget. Their landlady was here in Intensive Care in the same hospital.

You stupid sod, Jonah, he berated himself. Ripping the IV out of the back of his wrist – fuck – he got to the floor, wobbling on his bare feet. He felt awful but if he didn't stop Jenny … Hobbling, holding his guts as he set off, he saw the lift doors close on Jenny's tearstained face. No way could he manage the stairs. He called the second lift and watched the floor counter mark her passage. It stopped at third floor just as his ride arrived. He got in. Porters with an elderly patient tried to follow him. 'Fuck off,' he snarled.

'How rude!' said the lady as the doors closed.

The pain was so intense he feared he'd pass out. He rested against the wall. Third floor. He read the guide by the button. Yes, that was Intensive Care. Could he get there in time?

The doors slid open and he was faced with what looked like a mile of corridor. He wasn't going to make it, was he?

'Hey you, twenty quid if you wheel me to Intensive Care,' he said to a guy hanging around by the drinks machine.

'You what?' The man had an Arsenal shirt on.

'Come on, mate, you wouldn't leave a fellow Gunner's supporter in agony, would you?' He didn't confess he supported West Ham.

'I suppose not.'

'Grab a wheelchair and take me to Intensive Care. I'll pay you twenty quid.' The fact that all his money was God knows where was also something he failed to mention.

'OK.' The guy took hold of one of the wheelchairs waiting by the lift. 'Where's Intensive Care?'

'Fuck if I know. Follow the signs.' Jonah eased himself down on the seat.

'Do you know you're bleeding?'

Jonah looked down. The back of his hand was oozing blood but, more worryingly, so was the area around his stitches. 'That's why I need Intensive Care.'

That worked a treat. The man hoofed it down the corridor, shouting 'out of my way' when they met any visitors or outpatients. They arrived at the doors of the unit.

'Thanks, mate. My wallet's upstairs. Do you wanna wait?'

'Forget that, man. You get yourself some help, OK? Want me to stay?'

'No, thanks. I'll be fine. Minor wound.'

With a nod, the man turned on his heel and walked back the way they'd come.

With a deep breath to brace himself, Jonah stood up and walked into the hush of the critical care unit. He could see Jenny. She was standing at the window looking in on a room beyond. He could just make out Bridget lying in the bed, hooked up to a ventilator. He hobbled over and put his arm around Jenny, using every last bit of his grit.

'What were you going to do, love? Stand on her tubes?'

'Jonah?'

God, he loved hearing her husky voice. 'Yeah, darlin', I'm here. You can't ruin yourself by taking revenge now. Look: she's punished enough.'

'Not nearly enough. Oh Jonah.' And now she turned and wept on his shoulder. And her sobs were guttural and noisy. Finally, she'd found a voice.

How long did it take for someone to have a complete meltdown? It felt like hours but it was probably only a minute or two. This was not a role he was used to playing: the shoulder to cry on. Jonah looked up on hearing voices approaching and remembered that he was bleeding.

'Jenny?'

'Yes?'

'Is it OK if I pass out now?'

'W-what?'

Disengaging himself from her, he leant against the wall. 'Some nutter fucking stabbed me, remember?' He lurched sideways, steadied, then slid to the floor. 'Be there when I wake up, OK? Don't let them arrest us.'

Chapter 56

Jenny

Jenny didn't get her wish to keep her mother out of this. Nikki arrived at noon, having located her thanks to the police. Jenny was sure there was probably a law against breeching her confidentiality, but too late now.

'Jenny? Are you all right?' Nikki whispered. She looked down at where Jenny held Jonah's hand on the cover. 'What on earth happened?'

I killed a man. Jenny wasn't sure if she could live with that knowledge. He had to be her attacker – had to be. That was the only thing that could justify it even a little. Here was someone who might know. 'Mum?'

Nikki reeled, couldn't find anything to hold on to so moved a couple of steps to the window to lean against it. 'Your voice!'

'Some … words. Not many.'

Tears dripped down Nikki's face and she gave a half-sob. She came forward and kissed her daughter's head, gripping her tight. 'Oh God, darling, I can't believe it! So many years!'

Jenny slipped her hand free of Jonah's. 'I still find it easier to sign,' she signed.

312

'Of course you do, darling. But it's a start, isn't it?' Nikki pulled up a chair and sat beside her. 'Is Jonah going to be OK?'

'He was stabbed by the man who attacked me. That man died in the fire,' she signed. The one I started – the one that makes me a murderer. She didn't sign that.

'Then I can't say I'm sorry for him. Who was he?'

Jenny pulled over a pad. *Matthew Upshaw. He said he was an old student of yours.*

'Matthew Upshaw? No, I don't remember him.' Nikki shook her head, little treble clef earrings wobbling.

'Three years older than me,' signed Jenny. 'He said he came for lessons just before the attack at home took place. He claimed we played the Telemann together.'

'That does sound possible. I'll look in my records for him.'

Jenny preferred to write this next bit. *He said he was the one who attacked me back then.*

'What! If that's true, then we must tell the police.'

Jenny put her hand on her mother's wrist then wrote: *I'm not sure it's true. Please, please let it be him.*

'I'll look him up right now.'

'How?' she signed.

Nikki frowned then clicked her fingers. 'I know: I'll phone my accountant. She's done my books for twenty years and has a list of all my students. If there's an Upshaw on the list, she'll be able to tell me.' She rose to go. 'I can't believe it! You mean that evil man got in because he was one of my students? Oh God, I'll never forgive myself.'

Jenny left her mother to her frantic conversation with her accountant. She could hear enough 'Oh my God's and 'Yes, really's to guess the tenor of the exchange. Jenny went back to her watch over Jonah. He looked so defenceless lying in this hospital bed, no longer the worldly-wise cynic but an aged and exhausted child who had seen too much. That wasn't a bad description of him.

A strange woman came in to stand by her side. The fact that she had managed to get past the police guard suggested she was known to Jonah, if not to Jenny.

'Jenny Groves?' The woman's tone struck her as brisk and professional.

Jenny nodded.

'I'm Carol Travis, Jonah's theatrical agent.'

She gave a little wave.

'Is he going to be OK?'

Jenny nodded, but added a fingers crossed. His journey to the third floor to stop her doing something stupid to Bridget hadn't helped his prospects for a full recovery.

'May I?' Carol gestured to the second chair.

Jenny made a 'be my guest' gesture.

'You can't help feeling fond of Jonah, can you? He really does have the most appalling language, and can be very rude on many occasions, but I've always sensed his basic decency.'

Jenny didn't think she needed to respond to that.

'Did he really dive in to save you from your attacker?'

Jenny nodded.

'But you knocked the guy unconscious and then he died in the fire while you carried Jonah out?'

Close enough. That was the story both she and Jonah had told the police and it seemed to be sticking. She just had to hope her fingerprints didn't turn up on the lighter fuel and matches. Still it was her room. Who was to say they weren't hers in the first place and that Matt just used them? She'd kept her details to the minimum. I was packing. He attacked me. Jonah saved me. I saved Jonah. Room on fire. We escaped. Sorry, I couldn't carry two men out on my back. Look at me: I'm five foot four and nine and a half stone. I would've gone back but the fire had taken hold. I phoned for help and went outside to let the professionals handle it. She was working on convincing herself that this was the truth. If she said it enough times, maybe

314

she'd forget the pyromaniac moment, persuade herself it hadn't happened?

The alternative was to look in the mirror and see a killer. The only thing that would make that something she could live with was the knowledge that Matt had deserved it.

'It's an amazing story. Is it OK to tell the reporters? They're salivating for more details. Jonah's hot stuff at the moment. I'll pass any press release by you or your representative, of course.'

Jenny didn't know what to say.

'Jonah could come out of this with his career enhanced. You want that for him, don't you?'

Jenny nodded.

'And in return I could see what I can do about getting you your career back. I know some people in the music business. London Philharmonic, wasn't it?'

'Yes,' rasped Jenny.

Carol smiled. 'Interesting: you do speak a little. If you can say a few more words, I can get you an interview with the right people. Though the signing works too, now I think about it, so different. If publicity can help you, I can fix that for you. It's what I'm good at. In fact, I know some people who represent musicians. I can arrange you to meet them. Your story is solid gold.'

All this because Carol was desperate to get permission to tell her hero story about Jonah? Jenny would've agreed for Jonah's sake without the pay-off for herself, but she'd be an idiot not to take the hand that offered to help her up off the floor.

'Thank you.'

'So, we're agreed: I'll run my press release by you and in return I'll see what I can do for you?'

'Yes.'

'I'll go write it then and be back in a minute.' Carol stood up and gave Jonah a pitying look. 'Poor guy. You be good to him, Jenny, OK?'

Jenny wasn't about to tell her they weren't like that. She wasn't exactly sure how they were, so she just smiled and waved goodbye.

Her mum returned as Carol left to write her press release in a corridor somewhere.

'Who's that?' Nikki asked.

'Jonah's agent.'

Nikki smiled with glistening eyes. 'So strange to hear your voice. It's going to take me a while to adjust.'

'It's not … the same.'

'No, but it wouldn't be would it? You were a child when you lost it.'

Jenny went back to signing. Her throat hurt from overuse. 'What did the accountant say?'

'There is no Matthew Upshaw in my records – no Upshaw of any kind. I asked her to check on my Matthews in case the surname is a lie and when she went through all of them I was sure there was no match. I remember them all and know what they're doing now.'

The fragile ground under Jenny crumbled. 'So he wasn't your student?'

'Not unless he went by another name entirely.'

Jenny picked up the pen. *But he knew about you – my singing – the Telemann – the party.*

'It doesn't mean he wasn't the intruder; just that he didn't get in because he was one of my students. Maybe the police can find out more. Have you told them about this yet?'

Jenny shook her head. She hadn't because it would sound like she had motive for murder. Which it was.

'When you do, ask them to check his background.'

Then Jenny remembered. *Harry knew him. I'll ask Harry.*

'You still talk to Harry?'

Jenny made a so-so gesture of uncertainty.

'That's good. He'll certainly talk to you. He came by with flowers so you can message him to thank him and ask him if he knows anything helpful that can clear this up. If Upshaw was a local boy, it would make it more likely he was the one.'

Jenny nodded. A movement from the bed drew her attention back to Jonah. Another Essex boy lay in front of her, one who the police had told her at the station last night had potentially known her as a teenager. The police had been very suspicious about his behaviour, said he'd kept a nasty scrapbook on her, but she'd dismissed that. Jonah was capable of doing rash things but he'd proved he was one of the good guys last night, hadn't he?

What if she was wrong?

God, was she seeing potential enemies everywhere now? Screw your head back on, Jenny. Bridget stole from you, Matt assaulted you, Jonah tried to save you, and you're the mad woman who set fire to the house. And don't forget Norman. Matt might've done away with him and, even if he didn't kill him, he never called anyone when the old man died. There were white hats and black hats in this tale and Jonah was so far the only one wearing the white.

'Jenny?' Her mother touched her arm making her jump. 'Sorry, love, but you looked a million miles away in a not very nice place. Will you contact Harry and let me know what he says?'

'I haven't got his number. My phone is toast,' signed Jenny.

'I've got it. In fact, I'll just pop out and get you a replacement phone. I'll feel so much better if I can keep in touch. I'll write his number down for you.'

Jonah stirred. 'Mrs Groves?' His voice was as gruff as Jenny's.

'Nikki, Jonah, dear. Call me Nikki. Can I get you anything?'

He opened his eyes. 'I really feel like some chocolate cake, but I think I'm banned from solids.'

'How about chocolate milkshake?'

A boyish smile broke out across his face. 'That would be amazing.'

Nikki leaned forward and brushed his cheek with gentle fingers. Jenny was amazed when he didn't flinch away. 'My pleasure, Jonah.'

317

Chapter 57

Bridget

Bridget stirred. Her limbs felt so heavy. What was wrong with her? This wasn't right; nothing was familiar. A machine hummed beside her. The light was too bright: it hurt her eyes to open the lids so she closed them again.

The second time she woke a nurse was leaning over her.

'Mrs Whittingham – Bridget – can you hear me?'

Bridget blinked.

'You're in Intensive Care at the Queen Elizabeth Hospital. You've been unconscious for five days. We're giving you something to help with withdrawal symptoms but I expect you still feel rotten.' The nurse – dark-skinned with a thick Jamaican accent – moved competently but flatfootedly around the bed, checking the drip and the monitors. 'You were on a ventilator until last night so your throat is likely to be a little sore?' She offered Bridget a drink with a straw. 'There: that's better, isn't it?'

Bridget pushed the cup wearily away. 'What … happened?'

'I'm afraid I can't tell you. The police will be in later and I'm sure they'll fill you in on all you need to know. We removed the catheter earlier – I don't suppose you remember. Do you need a bedpan?'

Bridget shook her head. People had been doing things to her – intimate things – and she hadn't been aware.

'Push the buzzer when you do. Do you want to sit up a little?'

'Yes.' That seemed the first step to recovering some sense of normality.

The nurse raised the head of the bed with the control and showed her how to adjust it herself. 'Now you no longer need intensive treatment, we'll probably move you onto a ward in a few hours. Just sit tight for the moment.'

And she bustled out, her generous backside straining against the seat of her scrubs.

What a motherly person, thought Bridget languidly. My opposite in so many ways. She would've loved a child but Paul refused to countenance a bastard. She hated him for that sometimes. Her gaze went to the window with its view of the brick wall opposite and ventilation units. She appeared to be on one of the upper floors. If she wasn't so floaty, she'd feel … what? Frantic about not being at Gallant House?

Her fingers explored her neck. The nurse was correct: she was feeling sore and sick. What had happened? Fragments came back: her and Jonah caught on the daybed in the attic; her storming down to confront Jenny and somehow being sidetracked by the pills Jenny waved in front of her. They'd fought, hadn't they? Had she … had she struck Jenny? Oh God. She remembered screaming and blood as the Wicked Queen in the mirror had emerged and struck down her rival.

But that had been her, hadn't it, in a mad, mad moment? Bridget, what have you done?

And then what? She'd panicked, taken a handful of pills to … to what? Dull the pain – dull reality? She couldn't remember. She'd been beyond rational, spinning out of control. Normally that number of tablets would just take the edge off but she'd entered a confused fugue state where she felt beside herself, watching this harridan storm through the house. She'd met Jonah in the hall and he'd asked about Jenny and questioned why she had blood on her hands – she remembered that much. He'd tried to get past her to go up the stairs.

Then what?

She felt like she might've flown at him, trying to push him away, stop him seeing what she'd done. She'd been screaming.

And then he'd fought back, hadn't he? He'd throttled her, yelling at her that she was not his fucking mother, that she couldn't fucking hurt him again, that she mustn't hurt Jenny.

Was that what had happened?

It all felt so dreamlike, so impossible.

The next time she opened her eyes two scruffily-dressed strangers were at her bedside. One – the man – looked positively thuggish. Her heart raced in panic.

'Nurse! Nurse!' She groped for the buzzer.

The man passed it to her. 'Mrs Whittingham, I'm Detective Inspector Khan, and this is Detective Sergeant Foley.'

These were the police?

The motherly nurse came in. 'Is everything all right, Bridget?'

'I think we just startled her,' said Khan.

'These visitors are from the police, Bridget, like I said. You can ask them your questions.' The nurse plumped up her pillows and patted her arm reassuringly.

'Sorry.' Bridget tried to regain her poise. 'Water, please?'

The female officer passed her the cup. 'May we sit down?'

'Please do. How can I help you?' The nurse left the room.

'Mrs Whittingham, you should know before we go any further that we are placing you under arrest for the assault on your tenant Jenny Groves. Charges pending.' The sergeant ran through the usual caution, words Bridget had only ever heard in Radio Four dramas.

'Jenny? I assaulted Jenny? That can't be right.' It was the Wicked Queen from the mirror.

320

'It is of course your prerogative to maintain your innocence but you should be aware we have substantial forensic evidence of the assault, including your fingerprints on the weapon, Miss Groves' blood on your hands when you were brought into hospital and her witness statement.'

'Is she all right?'

'Miss Groves had to have ten stitches to her scalp and stayed in hospital for a few days with concussion, but yes, otherwise she is expected to make a full recovery.'

'This doesn't feel real,' murmured Bridget. It struck her anew that she wasn't in Gallant House, that they'd brought her somewhere else. She was so far from her things, her writings and her perfectly arranged rooms. What were these drugs they were pumping into her by the drip? She wanted her pills. Panic surged again. 'I have to go home!'

'Mrs Whittingham, we aren't here to question you about the assault as that can wait until you're stronger. I'm afraid we've come to tell you about subsequent events that have taken place while you've been in hospital.' The female officer injected a tone of concern into her forthright manner.

'What events? What are you talking about?'

'There was a fire at Gallant House two nights ago. It happened when your tenants returned to collect their belongings. They surprised an intruder, and in the resulting altercation the first floor caught fire.'

'What? No!'

'The fire brigade was able to contain it to your tenant's room and the attic. The rest of the floor and the rooms below sustained some smoke and water damage, I'm afraid. As it's a crime scene, we've barricaded off the house. Because you were unconscious, I understand that your family solicitor contacted your insurer. They've sent people to tarpaulin the roof. It is quite secure and safe from further damage.'

'My house? My house burned down?'

321

'Only a section of the upper floor. In the course of our investigation,' the woman continued in a brisker tone, 'we had cause to examine your bedroom and bathroom, looking for evidence of what the intruder might have been doing. Mrs Whittingham, would you care to explain why you were in possession of so many prescriptions for painkillers, only a few in your name?'

'My house,' moaned Bridget.

The police officers exchanged a look. 'Did you know a man called Matthew Upshaw?'

'What has he to do with anything?' She clawed at the IV port at the back of her left hand. 'I want to go home – I want to see.'

'That won't be possible just yet. Please, Matthew Upshaw? I should explain that he died in the fire.'

'Someone died in my house? But why? What was he doing there?'

'But you know who he was? He lived next door.'

'He's Norman's boy? The lodger?'

'Yes, he was.'

'That wasn't the name he gave me.'

The female policeman glanced at her colleague, who gave her a slight nod. 'When did you last see Norman Stratton, Mrs Whittingham?'

'Norman? Why? Has something happened to him too?'

'Please just answer the question.'

'What day is it, did you say?'

'It's Saturday. You were admitted to hospital exactly a week ago.'

'So long?' Bridget raised her right hand to brush aside a strand of hair that had fallen across her cheek. It felt lank and unwashed. 'Then I last saw Norman a week ago Tuesday. I called round to ask if he wanted to come in for one of my gatherings but his tenant said he was busy. Ah, no: so I didn't actually see him, did I? It must've been the Tuesday before that then. We had a cup of tea together in his kitchen.' It was the furthest she ever went from her home. 'He said he didn't feel up to socialising. I was worried about him, actually; he seemed very out of sorts.'

'Then I'm sorry to have to tell you that Mr Stratton passed away a few days after. He was already dead, we think, when you called in.'

'Norman? Dead? No, that can't be right!' But why would the police lie about something like that? 'Matthew hid that he was dead from me?'

'From everyone.'

'But why?'

'So he could go on living there with no one the wiser. He was obsessed with your tenant, Jenny, and it appears, also with you and Jonah Brigson.'

'Obsessed with us?'

'We found cuttings in his room. He'd made a scrapbook on you and Jenny Groves, and defaced the one Jonah had compiled on his career. We believe he then planted them under Jonah's bed immediately after the first assault to direct our suspicions towards Jonah. He wanted Jenny for himself, you see, and saw Jonah as a threat.'

Bridget shuddered. 'Do you mean to say that this … this creature has been watching us from next door all this time? But why?'

'That'll be one for the psychologists. What we do know is that he started a few years ago obsessing about Jenny and then his paranoid fantasies spread out to those closest to her – which means the inhabitants of Gallant House. We found scrapbooks on other people who were close to her – her friends from work and the orchestra – but nothing as violent in their imagery as those in the books on you three. Mrs Whittingham, I have to ask this. Everyone tells us that you were in the house the whole time. Did you on any occasion see him come and go? For example, did you see him leave flowers on Jenny's pillow over the past year?'

'That was him? No, no, I didn't. I swear it.'

'Did you notice any signs that he'd been in the house?'

Bridget thought back to the drips on the floor, the well cover, the strange noises which she'd imagined were ghosts. She'd sound foolish to admit that she'd put these down to the house 'talking' to her through its past occupants. 'Nothing that raised my suspicions, no.'

'OK,' said the male officer. He was the senior person, wasn't he, even though he held himself back through most of this? 'Now, what can you remember of the night of your own collapse from an overdose.'

'I overdosed, Inspector … sorry I've forgotten you name?'

'Inspector Khan. Yes. On Fentanyl – your tenant's black-market pills.' He said this without any hint of judgement but that sounded so sordid. Bridget wondered at herself: how low had she stooped?

'I didn't mean … how on earth …' Bridget touched her neck.

'Opioid painkillers are well known to suppress breathing. You only survived because Jonah Brigson gave you first aid,' said Khan.

'He did?' That wasn't how she remembered it. 'I thought he strangled me?'

'Did he?' Khan leaned forward, a spark of interest in his eyes.

'I … I don't remember clearly.'

'Why would he strangle you, Mrs Whittingham? Your argument was with Jenny, wasn't it?'

'But he was holding me by the throat, forcing my chin up?' She could remember the pain of that. She'd already been struggling for breath, hadn't she, disorientated, before he'd touched her?

The officers didn't say anything, waiting for her to decide her version of events. Her memories were so fragmentary, so distorted. 'He was resuscitating me, you say?'

Again they said nothing. One step more with these accusations and she could send the boy back to jail – and for what? She really couldn't remember. What kind of witness would she make at a trial? And the humiliation, consider that. She would prefer to plead guilty to everything they charged her with and drop allegations against all others to free herself from that.

'Yes, yes, that sounds like Jonah. He's a kind boy and provides what I need. He would've tried to help.' She preferred that version of the story than the one where she had provoked him to a murderous rage. 'Tell him I'm grateful. And tell Jenny I'm sorry. I really don't remember what happened but if I hurt her, I truly regret that.'

DI Khan stood up. 'Thanks, Mrs Whittingham. That's all for now. We'll take a more formal statement when you're recovered.'

'Do I need a lawyer?'

'It's not our place to say.'

'Please, I have no one else to ask.'

'Most people in your position find it helpful to have legal representation,' said the female officer carefully.

'I see. Thank you. I'm sorry for being such a nuisance.'

They left and she had the room to herself again. So much lost. Soon she'd be down on a ward where she'd have to remember she had an audience. Here though: here she could cry and no one would see. No one.

Chapter 58

Jenny

Jenny waited for Harry in a coffee shop on the other side of Charlton Park, a short walk from the hospital. Her mum had urged her to contact him but Nikki had probably just meant her to send a message. Jenny, however, wanted to do this face-to-face. Harry was too good at ducking her texts, a behaviour learnt at the end of their relationship; this time she wouldn't let him wriggle free from her questions. She had to know the truth. She couldn't rest until she knew for a fact who Matt had been to her.

And if it turned out Matt wasn't a local boy after all? What would she then do with the knowledge that she'd killed him? Turn herself in to the police? Punish herself in some other way? Kill herself …? Oh God, oh God, oh God. She needed Jonah – someone – to tell her she wasn't an evil person and didn't deserve this.

Her silent crisis was disturbed by the attendant who brought her coffee to the table. Jenny forced herself to smile and pay attention to her surroundings, rooting herself in the everyday things, not her inner torment. She couldn't be in meltdown when Harry arrived. The contrast between where she was and what she felt inside couldn't be starker. Normal life carried on around her in the Old Cottage Coffee Shop. It was one of those quirky gems that provided an antidote to the chains. It looked little more than a large shed from the outside, members of the Royal Family painted in the windows, waving to the passers-by, but within it was an Aladdin's cave. The red walls were crammed with antique pictures and shelves of mismatched crockery; the furniture was equally eclectic. She suspected the owners had gone around collecting any old donations left for upcycling on the pavements of the posher ends of London, all done with a sense of humour. You're here to have fun and relax, the café said.

If only.

Her coffee came with a heart in chocolate powder on the frothy surface. She stirred that in. No mixed messages for Harry when – if – he arrived.

A predictable fifteen minutes late, Harry breezed into the place, jingling his keys.

'Jenny, sorry I'm late. Had difficulty finding the place.' Both these sentences were lies. Harry didn't want to be here. Even if he didn't know what Jenny was going to ask, he had to be aware that he had engineered her first meeting with the guy who had gone on to try to kill her.

'Sit down please.' Jenny signalled to the waiter to come over for her guest's order.

Harry sat down in the chair and dropped his bike helmet on the floor. 'My God, you can speak!'

'Few words. Still hard.'

'But, wow, that's amazing. I think I guessed you might have something left.'

The waiter interrupted at this point – just as well because Jenny suspected he was going to go into one of his 'if only you'd done what I'd said earlier' speeches about getting professional help with her voice. She got out her replacement iPad.

'Do we need that now?' said Harry, giving her one of his soulful looks. 'It's so great to finally talk.'

I need it.

He held up his hands. 'OK. You're the boss.'

Did you hear about Matt?

Harry looked away. 'Yeah. Actually, the police have been interviewing us all about him. They came to the rehearsal this morning, totally messed up the schedule. Why didn't you come back to the orchestra, Jenny?'

She paused in surprise. *How could I?*

'You had friends there. We would've helped you.'

But I was sacked.

'Says who?'

Jenny stared at him.

'Said Matt?'

She nodded.

'That's what the police told the managers you believed to be the case.'

How do you know what they said to the managers?

'I know one of them well.' That was Harry code for 'having slept with'. 'She knows I'm your friend. Anyway, it all came out. They thought, when you didn't come back, that you'd effectively resigned. Sure, there would've been some comeback for your weirded-out moment, but there are processes, didn't you realise?'

She hadn't but she should have.

'The orchestra doesn't just ditch people, not if they're in trouble. And you were in trouble, weren't you? That bastard was controlling you. We all saw him giving you drugs and stuff. We've told the police, but Jenny, he was isolating you – classic abuser behaviour. I didn't get it at the time, but I do now. I should've got in contact, reached out. I'm sorry I didn't. I left you alone with him.'

The waiter returned with his black coffee. 'Anything else, guys?'

'Not at the moment, thanks,' said Harry.

Jenny didn't interject, but it was so like him to take charge and speak for her. He'd always run the show when they were dating. Jonah never did that to her.

Harry, I need to know how you got friendly with Matt. He said he knew you from school.

Harry looked awkward. 'Yeah, he said that to me too but I didn't remember him. You recall what it was like, don't you? I was a popular guy in the upper school and sixth form – knew loads of people. I didn't want to hurt his feelings by saying I'd completely blanked on him.'

But he was a musician. Wouldn't that make him stand out?

'He was several years ahead of us. I mean, I was flattered that an older boy remembered me in what, Year 10 or whatever it would've been when he was in his final year?'

Jenny made a note to ask her mother to check with the school. She was beginning to think that Matt either went through Harlow without anyone really noticing him, or he'd never been there.

What did you tell him about me, Harry?

'Me? Nothing!'

She didn't believe him so she just stared at him. Harry wasn't good if you turned the spotlight on his lies.

He stirred the coffee even though he hadn't added sugar, then put the spoon down with a sharp tap. 'Look, OK, when you started going out with him – I didn't force you to, remember? – I did have some chats with him to help out.'

'Help out?' she rasped.

'He was worried he'd upset you by touching you in a way that triggered your fears. He wanted to know how I'd managed … well … you know? He begged me to tell him. I did it as a favour to you both.'

So Harry had betrayed her confidence and compared notes on having sex with her. That was vile. Perhaps it had been too much to hope that he wouldn't eventually tell someone. He'd just chosen the worst possible person.

How many details did you give him? Jenny, when she had been in love with Harry and thought him the one, had told him everything she remembered about that night, even some of the silly details of listening to Britney and having a kitchen karaoke.

'I just told him how not to scare you. Honestly Jenny, I hardly remember everything you said. It was years ago that you told me that stuff. I remembered about the … the physical side though: not to give you the sensation of being crushed or trapped, that kind of thing.

So nothing about the evening before – what I did – the singing – the music practice?

'Why would I tell him about that? I didn't even remember it until you mentioned it just now. What were you singing?'

It doesn't matter. Jenny looked across the table at Harry, trying to work out how much of the truth she was getting. Everything about him had been so important to her ever since she had her crush on him at thirteen; finally getting to go out with him after college had been a teenage dream come true. She didn't think she'd forgotten a single important thing he'd ever told her. But she could well imagine him being far more careless with her confidences. Forgetting them would be totally in character.

Did you ever write down what I told you?

He looked squeamish at the thought. 'No, God, no! What if someone came across it?'

She nodded. Exactly.

'I only told that guy what I thought would help. I'm sorry he turned out to be a psychopath but you can't lay that one on me.'

Jenny didn't grace that with an answer. She sipped her coffee. So, if Harry hadn't told Matt, maybe Matt had been her attacker after all? She tried that out, enjoying the bright relief for a brief moment, the sense of justification.

Then her mood clouded. But that just didn't feel right and was why she wasn't accepting what Matt had told her last Saturday night. There had been no physical similarities between her assailant and Matt, nothing to trigger any alarms earlier. From her sketchy memories at fourteen, he'd been a bigger man than Matt, more Harry's size.

She looked at Harry. What if …?

330

This was stupid. She was beginning to suspect any boy who had ever been within ten miles of her in Harlow. Harry was an idiot, selfish, controlling in his own way, but that didn't add up to a violent sexual predator. She surely would've seen that in him over their years together? People couldn't hide that stuff for long. It leaked out like fluid in an old AA battery. No, Harry's sin, if you wanted to give it a name, was breaking a promise to keep her most private fears a secret.

Jenny decided she'd got everything she could from him. She needed to be alone.

Thanks for coming over, Harry.

'Least I could do.'

How's Su-Lin?

'Oh, you know ... ended a while ago. I'm going out with Laura now. Oh yeah, you don't know her. She took your chair in the orchestra.'

Jenny gulped. Right. OK.

'Sorry, that was tactless. But I'll tell the managers I saw you. I mean, there's a chair in the third desk of the violins now, isn't there?'

That was the only seat in an orchestra in which she could never sit. She shook her head. *I'll get in touch with them. No need to get involved, Harry. I'll be fine.*

He drained the last of his coffee. 'Good. Great. Luke sends his love, by the way. How's that bloke, Jonah?'

Jonah had moved up a peg or two from 'dangerous ex-con' to 'bloke', most likely because Harry had been reading the positive news spin Carol had been giving her client.

'Recovering,' Jenny said. 'Saved me.'

'Yeah, then you saved him. Quite the story.' He picked up his cycle helmet and gave it a quick tap-tap. 'You're looking good, Jenny. Apart from the ...' He pointed to the shaved patch and scar. As if she didn't know it was there! His tactlessness was so awful, she laughed.

331

'Yes, I know. Bye, Harry. Thanks.'

He leaned forward and kissed her cheek. 'Stay in touch, babe.' And with that, he was gone, forgetting that he hadn't paid for his coffee. Or maybe he still remembered she owed him for the mojito? It would be like Harry to keep a running tally in his head. He was capable of bearing a long grudge.

'Was everything OK?' The waiter asked as she signalled for the bill.

'Yes, thanks.' She waved her bank card over the contactless machine.

But, of course, it was nowhere near.

Chapter 59

Khan and Foley found Jenny at Jonah's bedside the day after her coffee meeting with Harry.

'Miss Groves, you are a difficult person to track down,' Khan said with evident irritation.

Jenny pointed to her position then to them with an 'evidently not' wave of her hand. Had they come to arrest her, she wondered?

'You've got her phone number, mate,' said Jonah grumpily. He had complained to her that his stitches were pulling so was feeling particularly short-tempered this morning.

'Mr and Mrs Upshaw have come to Lewisham police station,' said DS Foley. 'They wish to speak to you if you would be happy to spare them a few moments. There's no obligation on you at all to do so, but we promised to pass the message on.'

It took Jenny a moment to work out who they meant. 'Matt's parents?'

'Correct. I take it you've never met them?'

She shook her head.

'They're under the impression you were the closest person to their son. They've persuaded themselves that the incidents of the night when he died have been exaggerated, or that he was not himself. They look on you as their best chance of hearing about what really happened to their son in his last moments.' Foley dug her hands in her pockets. 'I wouldn't advise seeing them. It'll be distressing to both parties.'

And pass up the chance of getting the truth about Matt, whether he'd been her attacker all those years ago? She had to.

Jenny took her tablet. *If it can help them get closure, I'm OK to see them.*

Jonah grabbed the screen from her. 'What the fuck, Jenny? Are you a masochist or something?'

She shrugged.

'If you're going ahead, I really wouldn't advise seeing them on your own,' said Foley.

Jenny looked at Jonah, who groaned. 'OK, OK, we'll see them together. Jenny, as you know, doesn't do much talking. I can tell them everything they need to know.'

And leave out the stuff they really don't. Jenny shivered as she remembered the matches. She'd killed him.

'If you're sure?'

'Yeah, yeah. This whole thing is mad, by the way.' Jonah collapsed back against the pillows.

Khan folded him arms. 'Here's another "by the way". Bridget Whittingham is awake. She spoke to us the day before yesterday.'

Jonah closed his eyes. Jenny thought he looked more exhausted than ever, like he was preparing for yet more blows but wearily braced for them.

'She thinks you might've got a choke hold on her, Jonah,' said Khan.

'That's not true,' said Jonah. 'I fended her off and then offered CPR when she collapsed. She must be confused.'

Did she remember attacking me? wrote Jenny.

'Partially. She says she's sorry for the harm she did you,' said Khan.

Really? Remorse for messing up Jenny's whole life? An apology wasn't enough, Bridget. Jenny didn't say any of this though, not to the police. She'd wait until they were alone so she could vent to Jonah.

334

'Do you believe her?' asked Jonah, returning to the earlier accusation.

Khan considered his words carefully before speaking. 'I think no one is telling us the full truth, but tell me something I don't know as a policeman. With you, I'm dealing with an actor who knows how to deliver his lines. Miss Groves here says very little about anything. We could pursue her for drug offences, but what would be the point? She's most clearly the victim and how would that look: going after the one person who doesn't seem to have lain a finger on anyone else? Besides, she's receiving treatment. Why derail that? We have no hint that she supplied others.'

Jenny hadn't even considered that her drug buying habits would put her at risk of prosecution, other crimes having loomed so much larger in her conscience.

'We looked hard for signs that you had been involved, Jonah. Your record suggested we would be fools not to, but came up with nothing.'

'Because there is nothing,' said Jonah, a hint of anger in his voice.

'That leaves us with Bridget Whittingham, caught red-handed in the old-fashioned sense having struck Miss Groves. She also had an extraordinary collection of painkillers in her private bathroom. Your name was on some them. Does that mean that she stole them from you?'

This question was directed to Jenny, who nodded.

'We've also got confirmation from Kris Cameron that his medication was tampered with. Mrs Whittingham appears to have had a longstanding drug habit which she successfully masked.'

And what about Matt? asked Jenny. That was the one she really wanted to know about – her attacker, her victim.

'He remains an enigma. We have his computers and, when our overworked digital detectives can get to it, they'll look back and see what he was up to.'

So, she wasn't going to get quick answers that way. Mr and Mrs Upshaw were her best bet.

'Are you bringing any charges of any sort against Jenny and me,' asked Jonah, cutting to the chase.

'No,' said Khan. 'Not at this time.'

'Not ever?'

'Come on, Jonah, I can hardly promise you that.'

'Meaning you think you'll see me back in the interview room in the not-too distant future?'

'On TV, certainly. In my nick? That depends on you.'

'Eight-hundred and fifty-three days sober. Shit, maybe fifty-four? I'm losing track of time in here.'

'I wasn't thinking of drugs.'

And with that Jenny knew Khan thought Jonah guilty of assault on Bridget but didn't consider he had a snowball's chance of pressing charges with all the counter facts. But if Jonah had tussled with Bridget in an attempt to get upstairs to help her, in Jenny's book that was no crime.

Jenny coughed to bring attention back to herself. *Tell the Upshaws we'll see them this afternoon at 3 p.m.* She wanted Jonah to have a chance to rest.

'Fine,' said DS Foley. 'In that case, I'll accompany them.' Before Jenny could protest, Foley added, 'I want to listen in. They might say something useful that goes to explain Upshaw's actions.'

Jenny nodded. You and me both, she thought.

The first word that Jenny thought of when seeing Mr and Mrs Upshaw standing outside Jonah's private room was 'pitiable'. Hand in hand, they were miniature versions of Matt: Mrs Upshaw with faded ginger hair, Mr Upshaw with his wiry frame but several inches shorter.

This wasn't a good idea after all.

'Please, come in,' said Jonah, scraping together some manners for once in his life. They'd arranged the chairs so the Upshaws would sit on the other side of the bed from Jenny, Jonah as referee in the middle. DS Foley stayed by the door, watching the scene with acute interest. Was she really watching Jenny? Did she suspect?

'Thank you for seeing us.' Mr Upshaw held out his hand then half withdrew it, unsure of his welcome.

Jonah held his up and shook hands firmly. 'No problem.'

Jenny felt a shiver at disgust at herself shaking the hands of the parents of the man she'd killed. Matt brought it upon himself, she told herself, he really had; but it was hard to believe it when she saw the people who mourned him.

Mrs Upshaw was reluctant to let go of her hand. 'You're as pretty as Matt said.' She only let go to wipe her eyes with a crumpled tissue. Jenny, pleased she had something she could do, offered her a fresh one from a packet she kept in her shoulder bag. God, she felt a complete fraud. 'Thank you, dear.'

Mr Upshaw cleared his throat. 'If you wouldn't mind, could you please tell us how Matthew died? We don't believe the lurid version we've been reading in the press, you see. You were there. You know the truth.'

Jenny nodded and reached for her iPad, but Jonah pressed it gently down.

'You know Jenny has trouble talking?'

'Yes, we know all about that. Matthew often told us that she'd been the victim of a horrendous attack on her when she was only a child. He said she'd been so brave,' said Mrs Upshaw.

Often told them? How long had he been talking about her? As far as she was concerned, her relationship with him began around nine months ago at Harry's doomed party.

'We've agreed that I'll give you an outline of what happened and answer any questions that I can. Jenny will cover the ones that only she knows.' Jonah leaned a little forward, regretted the resulting pain, so relaxed back again. His voice deepened to best sincere mode. Khan was right: he was an excellent actor. 'I'm afraid your son was upset when Jenny ended their relationship. You might say that he lost it.'

Mrs Upshaw shredded another tissue. 'We're sure he didn't

mean to do anything bad – he just didn't know how to handle his emotions. I'm so sorry.'

Jonah didn't challenge that over-generous interpretation of the facts; there was no point. 'When he heard us enter the house, he came in to confront Jenny. They argued and he turned on her.'

Mr Upshaw shrank in his chair. 'But I brought him up never to raise his hand to another person, especially not a woman.'

Then the lesson hadn't stuck.

'I'm afraid there's no doubt about that. I found him assaulting Jenny and pulled him off. In the confusion he stabbed me with scissors.' He looked briefly across to DS Foley. Was she getting this? 'To save me, Jenny had to hit him over the head with a bottle, knocking him out. By this time the room was on fire.'

'Oh God, so he did attack you!' Mrs Upshaw had clearly been hoping for another explanation.

'He wasn't in his right mind at the time, Mrs Upshaw. Jenny,' continued Jonah, 'managed to carry me out. She tried to go back for Matthew – I doubt she could've carried him but she would've tried. Unfortunately, the fire beat her back and the firemen arrived too late. Your son wouldn't have known anything about it, Mrs Upshaw. He would never've woken up.'

Jonah was being incredibly tender towards the grieving mother. Jenny was surprised by his tact.

Mrs Upshaw swallowed a few times to master her voice. 'Thank you. Yes, that is good to know.'

'Mrs Upshaw, Mr Upshaw, I know Jenny has some questions she'd like to ask you.'

Jenny had already written them down so passed them to Jonah to ask. He was doing such a good job at hitting the right notes, firm but not harsh.

'She wants to know how long you've known about her? When did Matthew start talking about her to you?'

This appeared to trigger happier memories for the couple. They looked at each other and smiled sadly.

'It was Christmas a couple of years ago, wasn't it? He said he'd seen the girl of his dreams and that she played the violin like he did,' said Mr Upshaw.

That was the year her orchestra had appeared in a televised Christmas special of festive music. Had he just seen her on screen to start with?

'But he said it was too early to introduce us. He didn't want to scare you off. Like tickling trout, that's what he said, like tickling trout,' said Mrs Upshaw.

'I used to take him fishing as a lad up in Scotland,' explained the father.

Jonah glanced at the next question and adapted it. 'Are you from Scotland then?'

'My parents were, from Perth. But we moved south when we got married, didn't we, love? Matthew was our only child.'

Jenny felt sick at herself. She'd taken their family from them. It was hard to remember what Matt had become when she imagined the boy knee-deep in a Scottish river. His parents seemed nice, ordinary people. There were no signs to indicate how he would turn out.

'And where did he grow up?' asked Jonah.

Please let it be Harlow, Jenny begged silently.

'We live near Bath and had a few years in Bristol too when he was little,' said Mr Upshaw. 'I worked as a mechanic and Mary here did hairdressing at home. That meant she had plenty of time for our son. And he needed it when he got into his music – all those competitions, and concerts.'

'I said I was more like his taxi driver than his mother when he was a teenager,' said Mrs Upshaw, then sobbed. 'Oh God.'

Jenny could feel answering tears in her own eyes. How was she going to live with the guilt of what she'd done?

'He loved his violin and his computer, in that order. It made him a solitary boy, I suppose, outside of orchestra practices.' Mrs Upshaw sniffed and dug in her bag for a new tissue. 'And there was that trouble at the music school he went to – a boarding school. He won a scholarship – we thought it the answer to our prayers but it turned out a nightmare. I'd lost hope that he'd ever recover from that. What he must've seen!'

Jonah asked the question Jenny wanted. 'What kind of trouble?'

Mrs Upshaw wiped her eyes. 'Teachers interfering with the children – that's what we used to call it then.'

'Child abuse?'

'Matt always said it wasn't anything to do with him, but he was so closed off from us after his year there. We kept him home, didn't we, dear? We could hardly get his out of his bedroom.' She turned to her husband for comfort, for reassurance they'd done their best. 'And it soon came out and the music school closed after the scandal. But Matthew found it hard to relate to people afterwards.' She reached out and patted Jenny's hand where it lay clutched in Jonah's on his lap. 'That was why we so delighted that he met you. It's not your fault but he was inexperienced with girls. I can't remember him bringing any girls home, or even talking about any before you, can you, Roger?'

Mr Upshaw shook his head. 'He probably leapt in with both feet and decided you were the one. That's what broke him.' Mr Upshaw's voice hitched on the last word.

'Have you ever been to Harlow, or did Matthew visit it as a boy?' asked Jonah. Foley was looking at him hard now.

'Harlow? Where's that? Suffolk?' asked Mr Upshaw.

'No, Essex. It's where Jenny comes from.'

'Ah, no. Not that I know. He never had a competition there, did he, love?'

Mrs Upshaw shook her head. 'No, dear. And I would know. I always took him as he didn't like coach travel with the rest of the orchestra. He said they teased him and the boys in the percussion section were rough. It was a relief when they all grew up and behaved like adults, not playground bullies.'

The conversation ran on a little longer but Jenny had learned what she needed, maybe too much as it made her feel even worse about what she'd done. Matt hadn't only abused her as her boyfriend; he'd also likely been abused. But it was also emerging that Matt had been fantasising when he claimed to be a past student of her mother and to have gone to school with Harry, constructing a version that he wished had happened to replace his own bad memories. It sounded extremely unlikely that he had had the opportunity to assault her as a teenager. But questions remained. How had he known what happened? Had Harry lied about what he told Matt?

There was one other possible source, of course. Her rapist.

Chapter 60

Jenny discovered that it wasn't so much love but a twisted shared secret that brought her closer to Jonah. By their tacit agreement, she didn't go back to Harlow but stayed in his hotel room while he was in hospital and visited him daily. He said he knew she was teetering on the edge of doing something rash in response to her crisis of conscience, and she was a bloody idiot; he refused to let her go it alone. When he was discharged four days later, it was to her he went back, all with Carol's approval and drip-feeding of the press with the news. This love-plucked-from-disaster storyline was sending Jonah's profile rocketing and doing Jenny no harm too. The Philharmonic had invited her back for a re-entry interview but so far she was resisting. There were two reasons: one was that she was out of practice and not up to a full-time orchestral position; the second was that the guilt was crushing her. It felt like waking up each day paralysed and having to force herself to move her injured spirit, finger by finger, until she became something vaguely human again. Only in Jonah's company did the darkness recede. If she went back to the orchestra, the terrible void inside her would be worse as there'd always be the ghost of Matt breathing down her neck if she sat in the violin section again. She'd decided to give herself a month to regain her sanity or ... not.

Jenny and Jonah lay together on the brothel-chic double bed off Baker Street and listened to the traffic pass outside. He was on his back, her curled into him on her side. Neither showed any signs of getting up although it was noon.

'Decadent – yeah, that's the word,' said Jonah.

Jenny gestured between them.

'Yes. We're lounging here on someone else's tab – thank you, Mr Tabloid Journalist with your exclusive deal – with nothing we have to do, no demands on either of us, and no crazy person after us.'

The bedside phone buzzed. That was either reception or Carol: no one else contacted them that way.

Jonah picked up the receiver. 'No rest for the wicked. Jonah and Jenny's bower of bliss. What, now? OK, fine. Send them up.' He put it down and reached over to pat her butt. 'Shake a leg, sunshine. The police are here. They've got some news.'

Jenny pulled the sheet over her head. They were coming for her.

'You can stay like that if you like. Personally, I find you very fetching with no clothes on, but you might feel a little disadvantaged if they decide to drag us out in handcuffs.' He headed to the bathroom and next thing she heard was the shower.

Jenny couldn't joke. Some days she looked at Jonah's razor and considered taking that way out. But she couldn't do that to him, or her mother. Better prison than that. She left him to deal with the initial pleasantries while she took her own shower. She massaged her throat. Though she was saying more and more as she got used to her raspy voice, she still hadn't acclimatized to the necessity most people felt to talk all the time, say six things when buying a pint of milk, including: thanks, thank you, bag? please, no problem, that'll be 10p, have a nice day. People chattered away without thinking about their words at all. She still had to consider if it was worth saying each one, like a miser with her coins.

Dressed in loose trousers and a white T-shirt, she joined Jonah and their familiar detective duo in the lounge area. She sat next to Jonah, showing which side she was on, which was 'us against the world'. Was this love? She wasn't sure. But it certainly was loyalty.

She'd tell him that later: I'm in loyalty with you. He'd dig that.

'Jenny, Jonah, thanks for seeing us,' said Khan. The first names had been creeping in but today they seemed a full-blown declaration that both of them were no longer under suspicion for anything.

'You mean we had a choice?' asked Jonah, lighting up. 'Anyone?' He offered his cigarettes around, which was a close as he got to politeness over smoking.

'No thanks. Don't smoke,' said DS Foley, moving to the open window and leaning against it. Whether this was purely to get some fresh air, or a police ploy to observe them, Jenny didn't know.

'I will if you don't tell anyone.' Khan took a cigarette and accepted a light. 'Karen here hates it when I smoke.' He grinned at his colleague.

'You'll kill yourself,' she murmured, but without much rancour. It did sound like a genuine dispute between the two of them, and not something for Jenny and Jonah's benefit.

'OK, right, I'd better tell you why we're here,' said Khan. 'You'll remember I told you that we had detectives looking into Upshaw's digital archive? Well, they've bumped it up to priority thanks to the press interest.'

Carol's publicity scheme had unexpected benefits.

'And what did you find?' asked Jonah. He laced the fingers of his free hand with Jenny's and let them rest on his knee.

'We've been wondering how Upshaw knew about what happened to Jenny when she was a teenager – how he knew things that weren't in the public domain. And I think we have an answer.'

'You do?' asked Jenny. Her heart leapt into overdrive. Had they

344

got Harry to confess he'd been the source? Maybe, despite his denials, they'd found emails from him?

'Matthew Upshaw had, I think it's fair to say, an unhealthy interest in sex crimes and violent pornography.'

Jenny wasn't shocked. It would be more surprising to find the opposite now.

'He regularly deleted his browser history but as I'm sure you'll know, nothing is ever really gone. He visited sites showing snuff videos and violent rape.'

'Snuff?' Jenny thought she'd heard the term but wasn't sure.

'As in snuffed out,' said Jonah, her guide to the wicked world. 'They're films where people are killed or kill themselves.'

'For real?'

'Well, yeah. It's the ultimate sick stuff.'

'There is no evidence he acted any of it out, unless you can tell us differently, Jenny?' asked Foley.

Jenny huddled closer to Jonah. 'Just once.'

'He raped her,' said Jonah, puffing out a plume of smoke like her guardian dragon considering toasting an annoying knight, 'after he got angry at a wedding reception in December. And I suppose he was heading that way again on the night he died.'

'You reported this?' Foley directed her enquiry to Jenny.

'No,' she said.

Foley paused. 'Would you like to make an official statement now?'

'No point.' Jenny thought of his parents. She owed them at least that much. To add rapist to the list of crimes would make their lives even more intolerable.

'OK. Don't rush into a final decision. This isn't a time limited offer. You have my number.'

Jenny nodded.

'There's more,' said Khan.

'Always is,' said Jonah, tapping the glowing end of his cigarette into a cut-glass ashtray.

'We found a conversation in a chat room for people with shared interests in this material. He had explicit exchanges over the years with a person called NeroXX. In this message chain, NeroXX mentions your case from fifteen years ago, Jenny. He knew who you were – told Upshaw you'd become a violinist. Upshaw liked that because he was already one too. With Upshaw's encouragement, NeroXX goes into some detail about what happened that night. He never comes straight out and says he was there, but either he was, or he knows the person who was. We think that set Upshaw off on a mission to track you down. He wanted to repeat the experience.'

Jenny whimpered. Oh God, so it definitely wasn't Matt. Jenny could feel the void yawning beneath her. She'd killed a mentally-ill man who was innocent of that first assault at least. She tried to tell herself that it would've been worse than it already was to find she'd been sleeping with the guy who'd attacked her. But what excuse could she have now for setting the fire? She'd taken him out as a threat with the bottle – the rest was just revenge.

'And do you know who NeroXX is?' asked Jonah. Even in her turmoil, Jenny could tell from the tenseness in his grip that he was aware of her emotional distress and trying to hide it from the police. It was a warning not to give away too much. These were not friends, no matter how matey their tone.

'Yeah, actually we do – but that's thanks to another case. NeroXX is Clive Lee, currently serving fifteen years in Belmarsh for child abuse. You didn't meet him, did you, Jonah?'

Jonah flicked two fingers at Khan, using his extravagant rudeness to keep the focus on himself. 'As you well know, sex offenders are kept away from the rest of us in case we do to them what they did to others.'

'What did he do?' asked Jenny quietly.

Khan looked over at her. 'He raped and strangled his girlfriend's sister. She was eleven at the time. Also, she was mixed race like you which goes to pattern if you weren't the only victim.'

Black bitch. Jenny could still hear the whisper. She began to shake.

'It's OK, love. He's in prison – can't touch you,' said Jonah, putting his arm around her. 'Has anyone asked him if he did the attack in Harlow?'

'We interviewed him yesterday. He's a cool customer. Said he remembered the case, admitted he'd discussed it with Upshaw, whom he knew as Vio5, but claims he can't remember how he knew so much.'

'Have you reopened the case?'

'We've passed the information over to Essex. They'll take it on from here as it falls into their area. I just thought you should know that, if it was him – and that seems very likely to me – then he's already off the streets. Like Jonah said, Jenny: you don't have to worry about him.'

'Not for ten years or so,' said Jonah. 'Then he'll probably be released to go his merry perverted way. We should get him for this – lock him up for longer.'

Jenny didn't want it all raked up. In fact, she'd sooner forget everything and start again as if today was the first day in her life – no assault, no Matt, no fire-setting.

'I'll give you the contact of the officer in charge at the Essex end. But as for the case involving Gallant House, what we now think happened was that Upshaw heard about you from Lee and looked you up. Upshaw found the link that you were both violinists irresistible, began to fool himself that you were in some way his perfect match, so worked his way towards you, making career choices that eventually brought him into your circle. He had a whole fantasy life running with you as his girlfriend even before he met you. Then he got to live out his little dream – all his Christmases come at once because you were in no position to refuse him. He saw your vulnerability, took advantage of it and made himself indispensable by providing your painkillers, little knowing that Bridget Whittingham was aiding him there by stealing the real stuff from you. The more pain you were in, the more you needed him. That was the poisonous combination that led to the confrontation at the house.

'We've one big gap, though, which we are interested to fill. You say you broke up with him in January?'

Jenny nodded.

'How did you manage when he was no longer supplying you?'

'Jenny, don't say anything. You might incriminate yourself,' said Jonah quickly.

'This interview isn't under caution. It's just information gathering,' said Foley.

'Yeah, right, like that makes any difference.'

Jenny thought about writing something down but decided no permanent record was better. 'I sold my violin. Bought online.' They already knew she had black market pills in her possession and had said they weren't charging her so she doubted that would change their minds.

'I didn't know you'd done that!' said Jonah. 'I assumed that …' He trailed off, thinking twice about mentioning her time as a sex worker. 'Do you mean your violin didn't go up in smoke?'

'I sold it a few months ago to a dealer.'

'Dealer?'

Jonah, of course, only thought of one kind of dealer. 'In *violins* – a shop on Portobello Road.'

'Any chance we can get it back?'

She shrugged, trying to disguise the fact that his suggestion felt like a cup of water offered to a person stumbling out of a desert. If she got it back, she could play again, escape into her music.

Jonah seemed even more enthusiastic than her. 'Let's look into that, Jenny. You can't be without your violin – your old one or a new one. We'll fucking sort it, I promise.' He stood up.

Taking this as their dismissal, the police left, promising to be back in touch if there was any progress to report.

'So that's the last we'll hear from them,' said Jonah cheerfully. 'The police are rubbish at keeping victims informed. They're losing interest with their rapist slash murderer being dead. No one to prosecute and Bridget won't stand trial.'

Inspired by having a straightforward way of helping her, Jonah went to the Portobello Road armed with a full description of her instrument. He returned in triumph, holding the case up like the World Cup when she answered his knock on the door. He kissed it, then her. 'He hadn't sold it.'

She signed an only slightly mocking 'You're my hero.'

He laughed and slumped on the sofa in front of the TV. 'God, that feels good: one thing sorted out of this mess. Go practise, woman. I want to watch the footie.'

And she did practice – and it was one of the best moments in recent days. How could she ever have sacrificed this? She must have been insane to think she would ever be empty of her music. As she played through her favourite repertoire, she could feel the notes filling her up from her toes to the top of her head like a spring of water. The void receded for the moment. A little awkward at first, muscle memory reasserted itself. It felt so wonderful, she had to share it. She went into the lounge and stood in front of the TV.

'Hey!' grumbled Jonah.

She just smiled.

Jonah zapped the screen. 'It's OK. They were losing dismally as usual. Go on then, gorgeous.'

And so she played him the theme from Schindler's List again.

He grinned. 'You are so, so sexy when you play. Your eyes light up.' He looked around the room. 'We've not done it yet on a windowsill. Are you up for it? I am.' His expression left no doubt what he meant.

Maybe music wasn't everything to her after all? 'What about the press?' she asked, putting the violin down.

'Fuck the press.'

She signed that she'd prefer to fuck him, which made him laugh.

Some while later, as they sat on the sofa together to eat pizza, she asked the question that had been working its way from the back to the front of her mind.

'Come with me?'

'Where?'

'To see Clive Lee.'

'Jenny ...'

'I have to know. I killed over this ...'

'You did nothing to be ashamed of, Jen.'

She was ashamed, but knew he wouldn't understand that. She had to see the whole picture so she could persuade herself there was a way of living with the guilt. 'I can't just leave it.'

'He's unlikely to tell you anything.'

Jenny sipped a juice. 'He doesn't have to. I think I'll know.'

'You remember what he was like?'

'Enough.'

'But he can claim that you invented those details after visiting him – it could mess up any evidence they gather.'

'It's not details. I remember an impression. Nothing I can swear to in court. This is for me, not justice.' That might be the longest speech she'd yet made.

'OK. But let's not give him time to work out how best to torment you. How about I ask to see him? I can claim I'm researching a role for a new TV drama. If he likes boasting online, he'd probably like to do so in person. I can say you're my research assistant, take the spotlight off you.'

Jenny gave him a sceptical look. 'Won't he know me?'

'Might – might not. It was Matthew who obsessed about you. Lee knows your name but I doubt he knows what you look like now. He won't necessarily click to the fact that it's you until we ask our questions. We might wrong-foot him into saying something unguarded.'

When he mentioned being in the same room, it became more real. Jenny began to get cold feet. 'This is a bad idea, isn't it?' she signed, going back to the means of communication that she found most comforting.

'Probably.' Jonah ruffled her hair. 'The best ones usually start that way.'

It appeared that Clive Lee didn't get many visitors. Jonah had contacted the booking line and expected a refusal but word came back that he was more than happy to allocate one of his monthly slots to a couple of strangers who wanted a chat.

Jenny was consumed with nerves as they approached the visitors' centre by taxi. This would be the crisis point of her life, she felt, the final unveiling of the mystery that had eaten away at her. She wasn't sure she would survive it so clung on to Jonah's practical approach to visiting a monster. He had talked her through the procedures, what to expect, what she could take in, having been on the other side of it. She'd forgotten that this was his old prison.

And who should they meet coming out as they went in but Billy Riley, his probation officer.

'Jonah! How are you, mate?'

Jonah accepted the handshake with Billy adding a second grip to his elbow – the power-shake of world leaders and probation officers.

'I'm good, Mr Riley.'

'Billy, call me, Billy. And Jenny is with you!'

'Billy.' Jenny was treated to another power-shake but this one a little less vigorous.

'I've read all about what happened, of course, in the papers. Terrible business, but glad you're looking so well. And Jonah, the career! Amazing! When I signed you off my list, I had high hopes, but you've exceeded them.' He then remembered where they were standing: in front of prison gates. 'At least, I hope all is well?'

'Yeah, great, Mr Riley. How's the doc?'

'Rose?' Billy blushed. 'Did you hear that we'd moved in together? She's expecting our first child.'

'That's great news. Say I said "hi". Jenny and I had better hurry. Got an appointment.' Jonah gestured inside.

'Of course. Well, good luck!' Billy hurried off to the bus stop where his service was just pulling up.

'Dickhead. He and Rose told the police stuff about me that should've remained private,' said Jonah, his smile going feral.

'It doesn't matter now,' said Jenny, leaning against him. That blast of ridiculous normality had proved helpful.

Jonah cast one last dark look at the back of the bus and then looked down at her. 'You're right. He's part of my past. Do you still want to revisit yours? Are you sure you want to go through with this?'

'Yes.'

'OK.' He took her hand and they walked into the visitor reception.

'Mr Brigson!' said the officer on duty with every sign of genuine pleasure. 'Our celebrity graduate!'

'Hey, Mr Ravensbrook, how's things?' Jonah signed his name into the log and presented his passport for identification.

'Same old, same old. We miss you in the annual play.'

'I bet.'

'But it's a thrill to see you on the screen. I nearly choked on my dinner when I caught you in *Blue Light Run*. You know where to go?'

'Yeah, thanks.'

When they moved on to the next stage in the security process, Jenny raised a brow.

'Him? He was OK as far as the screws go. Big supporter of the drama programme.'

The visitors' room was predictably institutional, reminding Jenny of a hospital canteen. An attempt had been made to liven it up with a small soft play area for children and craft table, but no children today as it was the segregated prisoners' turn to have visitors. Jenny was a little unnerved to find they'd be sitting at the same table. No glass partition and telephone between them like you saw in films.

A bell went somewhere in the depths of the building and the prisoners started filing into the room. They wore orange vests over casual grey sweats to distinguish them from the visitors. None of them were handcuffed – again an image she'd expected from TV but had proved misleading. Wardens stood along the walls, with one behind a desk who looked like the senior man on duty, but that was it as far as security went. She realised with a sudden twist of panic that she didn't know what Clive Lee looked like. He could be any of these men. What was she getting into?

Jonah stood up as a middle-aged man came into the room. 'That's got to be Clive. I had a look at his mugshot before we came.' Lee was white, heavy build with badly cut black hair, thinning on the crown, ordinary looking. That shocked her most: she'd expected her monster to show the signs outwardly. At Jonah's movement, Lee raised a hand in acknowledgement and headed their way. His steps faltered when he spotted her, then sped up. Jenny remained seated. He knew her. She didn't think she could stand even if that had been necessary.

Lee sat down without making physical contact. Both Belmarsh old hands knew the rules.

'Jonah Brigson, you're quite the legend in here,' he said affably, but his gaze kept slipping to Jenny.

'Nice to hear that,' said Jonah. 'I mean it's always been about the fucking fame and the fortune for me so at least I've hit one target.'

'You said you were playing a role that I could help you with?' Lee was staring at her breasts. Her skin crawled.

'I lied.' Jonah's tone was cheerful. 'I said what the fuck was necessary to get in. You can get up and leave now if you like, or stay to find why we came.'

'I'll stay. Not much else to do in here but ...' Lee licked his lips, 'remember.'

'Yeah, your reputation proceeds you, you sick dick. Eyes on me or I'll kick you in the balls.'

Lee's eye lit up with hatred but then it fizzled out as quickly as it came. Jonah had got out a packet of cigarettes and now revolved them in his fingers.

'You'll get these if you answer a few questions.'

He shifted in his visitor chair, hand brushing his groin unnecessarily. 'Sure. My pleasure. Jenny, isn't it? I saw you mentioned in the papers.'

Jenny sat rigid.

'No name, of course, but I knew you. I've followed your career very closely. Got attacked when you were a girl and lost your voice, they say. So sad.'

'Hey, fucker, you talk to me, not her. You don't even breathe in her direction. Tell us how you knew the things you told Matthew Upshaw.'

Lee folded his arms, prepared to enjoy himself. 'Upshaw? Upshaw? Nope, don't know him.'

'Yeah, you do. Vio5. You knew each other online.'

He waved that away. 'That's not knowing someone. We never met. He's dead, isn't he?'

'Yeah. That tends to happen to people who hurt those I care about.'

Lee's gaze sprang back to Jonah with real interest. 'Was that you?'

Jonah held Lee with a cold gaze. He made a very convincing killer, thought Jenny, feeling her panic scratch at her control. 'He wasn't walking out of there alive, I can promise you that. So, tell us how you knew about Harlow.'

'Harlow? Harlow.' Lee's lips curved in a smile of satisfaction. 'Lovely place. Full of budding young girls.'

'Have you ever been there?'

'Lived there.' Lee made to reach for the cigarettes but Jonah tugged them out of his way. 'OK, all right, I lived there for five years.'

'When was this?'

'Eighteen years ago. Had a girlfriend with a flat there.'

'Where exactly?'

'John Clare Road.' His tone turned syrupy again. 'We were neighbours, weren't we, sweetheart? Lived opposite. I used to hear you singing, playing your violin, bouncing up and down the stairs in your school uniform.'

'Eyes on me!' snapped Jonah. 'You talk to me, not her.'

His sly eyes went to Jonah's face. 'So sad what happened to her. Some pervert climbed in her window and had sex with her. He went too far though: almost killed her. That wasn't part of the plan. Just take them to the edge, that's the idea. It makes it better for both.'

'Not sex. Rape,' said Jenny. Her insides were churning, blood pounding in her ears. It was him – it was him.

He shrugged. 'She wanted it really. They always do.'

'You are a sick fuck,' hissed Jonah.

'Did I say it was me? No! I had a cast-iron alibi. I was tucked up in bed with my girlfriend, officer. Didn't hear a thing from the flat across from ours.' Lee ran his finger over his lips. 'I'd've liked to have been the one to do it, I admit that. But you can't prosecute someone for wishing.'

Stomach clenching, Jenny got up before she threw up. She knew enough and couldn't stand being in his presence any longer. 'We're going.'

Jonah threw the cigarette packet at Lee. 'Enjoy them while you can. I hear the Essex police are reopening the case. I wonder if your girlfriend will stick by you now?'

Lee smirked as they walked away. He didn't seem to care either way. 'Thanks for the memories, Jenny!'

That did it. Jonah paused, turned and searched the room for a familiar face. 'Hey, Jerry, bro! How are you?'

A huge man with shaved hair and a squashed nose lumbered to his feet abandoning his conversation with the tiny black woman who was visiting him. 'Jonah, my man! I heard you got out?'

'Yeah, just visiting.' He took out a second packet of cigarettes and handed it over on the nod of the warden. Jenny wished he'd just leave so she could escape, but Jonah insisted on talking to the guy. 'That fucker over there? Clive Lee? I really don't like him. Rapes children.'

Jerry turned to stare hard at Lee. 'He does? Then I don't like him either.'

With a nod, the two men came to some kind of agreement.

Jonah put an arm around her. 'Come on, gorgeous, let's get out of here.'

'What did you do?' she signed.

'Me? Nothing.'

She poked him hard in the ribs.

'Let's just say that Lee might not enjoy his time here now he's in Jerry's bad books. The pervs know to keep away from him. Jerry has a weird code of ethics: he raped and murdered his wife when he caught her with his brother – who he also killed in the same attack – but thinks that perfectly sane and what any red-blooded guy would do. If anyone interferes with a child, though, Jerry goes ballistic. You might never get justice from the courts, but I can guarantee you'll get rough justice from Jerry.'

Jenny glanced over her shoulder.

'It's not on you, Jenny. I knew Jerry was likely to be here; it was my decision. I might've even let it pass if Lee hadn't made that last crack at you.'

Was she OK with this? Jenny found she probably was. Having considered herself a loving and forgiving sort of person, she was discovering an Old Testament eye-for-an-eye streak in herself that was disturbing. She'd achieved her aim. The monster was out from under the bed and this was the only retribution she was likely to get for her suffering.

'Thank you.'

'Seriously? You're thanking me? Jenny, I think you might just be my perfect woman!' With a laugh he tossed her back her bag from the locker. 'Come on: let's go celebrate – or at least drink away the memories.'

If only it were that easy for her.

Epilogue

Bridget, Six Weeks Later

Bridget stood in the kitchen with her manuscripts piled on the table in front of her. Released on bail, that's what the letter had told her. The police had said that as she had pleaded guilty to assault that the CPS had decided to drop all other charges and she could expect a short hearing before a sentencing judge at the Magistrates' Court. It might not even result in a custodial sentence, seeing how she was of previous good character.

Character? She'd destroyed that, hadn't she? This would not do. She was a disgrace to Gallant House and to the Jacks. She was of no use to anyone, having only ever done damage when she'd meant to help. Her tenants all saw her now as the evil spider drawing them into her web, when she'd meant it as a reciprocal exchange.

Who are you fooling, Bridget? It might've started like that, but you went far off course. As soon as you stole from a lodger, you were in the wrong and you should've known it.

She still couldn't see what was wrong with the sex with Jonah. She'd thought they'd both liked it. He'd always said it didn't matter to him what they did, but apparently, according to her

358

psychiatrist, who she was seeing on the advice of her lawyer, that had been an exploitative relationship too, a misuse of power.

And I've always thought of myself as the most powerless person in London.

Still, no more of that, thought Bridget. She wasn't going to leave the house again – not even to attend court. And she had important business to transact. There was only one way to make this good – one more sacrifice that she could make to apologise to the house for what she had done. Gallant House was the only thing that cared about her now and she'd not stopped it from being harmed. Still, for all the abuse, it whispered its comfort to her, sang her lullabies and promised all would be well. The lost children were here with her to keep her company too. Especially that boy from the well who tracked in drips of water wherever he went.

Or were they tears?

She wondered if her lodgers would come. She'd invited them for five o'clock this Tuesday in late autumn but had no real expectation that they'd seize the olive branch. They didn't need her; they were doing well enough on their own from what she heard. But she needed them for afterwards as there was no one else. The house mattered even if she didn't. If they didn't come, her plan would still work. She'd arranged things with her solicitor and left instructions. She'd get her last word as she had always wanted, not quite swinging from the chandelier, but close.

But what to do with these? Her life's work. Useless now. Only the house wanted them.

Bridget's gaze when to the kitchen courtyard, ankle deep in leaves that no one had swept up. She'd rather let the house go since getting out of hospital. It all felt too much. She was sorry for that too.

The well. Yes, that would do perfectly adequately for settling everything. She should have time before Jenny and Jonah arrived.

Taking the papers out in bundles, she lined up the manuscripts on the low wall and heaved up the well cover.

Jonah hadn't been in favour of Jenny coming back to Gallant House. She still had more dark days than light where he found her staring at nothing but, when asked what she was doing, she would only say that she was looking into the void. He knew what that meant. She was too nice. She was burdened with an unreasonable sense of responsibility for what she'd done, not taking his own 'good riddance' approach. Going back to the scene would surely only make matters worse?

'I can go see the old cow on my own,' he argued. 'No need for you to put yourself through that. You could go and see Louis and Kris.' The couple had restored their friendship with Jenny after the full details of Bridget's subterfuge emerged. Kris had apologised for being such a judgmental bastard and Jenny had apologised for being such a desperate bitch; Louis had predictably wept happy tears while Jonah made tactless remarks from the sidelines about sentimental fools that had them all ganging up against him. Happy days.

'She asked to see us both,' Jenny said in her soft husky voice he so loved.

'I don't need you to come – I'd prefer if you didn't.'

'Can't I be worried for you too? It was hardly a good place for you either.'

He whistled for a taxi outside their Vauxhall riverside apartment. 'Nothing like it is for you. I've no complaints. By almost killing me, I got you and I got more publicity than Carol knows what to do with.' He knew just how to get her out of her dark place. 'By the way, she'd sent some dates for your magazine photoshoot. Go on: wear just a tea towel and drape yourself over rocks: I dare you.'

'I'm classy. I don't do that kind of thing,' said Jenny, back to her adorable prim self after her walk on the wild side. It was getting harder to tempt her over but he was giving it his best shot.

'It'll sell more downloads.'

'How about a compromise. I wear a tea towel and drape myself over you – in private?'

He shouted with laughter just as the taxi pulled up. Their smiles had even the taciturn driver grinning.

'Where to, mate?'

'Gallant House, Blackheath.' Jonah listed off the postcode which was now engraved in his memory for all time.

'Righto.'

Half an hour later, Jonah paid the taxi and they got out in front of the house. The roof had been fixed but from the looks of it, the decorating hadn't yet been done. They rang the bell. Nothing.

'I suppose we are a bit early,' said Jonah.

'There's a note.' Jenny bent down to pick up a fold of thick letter paper. *'Come in – the door isn't locked.'*

'God, the mad old bird isn't thinking we'll sit through one of her Tuesday gatherings, is she? If she offers you Pimms, refuse.'

Jenny nodded and tried the door. It opened.

The house smelt different: smoke and dust. It reminded Jonah of a battlefield set he'd filmed on recently for his new role in a Second World War drama.

'Bridget, we're here!' he called.

No Bridget emerged. She wasn't in the kitchen, or the parlour.

'Let's go into the snug and see if we can spot her in the garden.' The snug had always felt more their room than hers.

Opening the door, Jonah had a surge of nostalgia at seeing the warty sofas had survived the fire damage.

'Some things just can't be destroyed,' he said, running his hand along the back. 'If the balloon goes up and we've the ten-minute warning for Armageddon, we get under these and we'll be fine.'

'Like Indiana Jones in the lead-lined fridge?' asked Jenny.

'Yeah, like that. Crap film, wasn't it? Should've stopped at three.'

Jenny went to the window. 'I can't see her.'

Jonah opened the balcony door. The railing he'd knocked down was still hanging on by a single screw. The vine had lost its leaves which lay in a slippery mat on the balcony. He stepped out. The ironwork gave a bigger groan than ever.

'Don't!' Jenny grabbed him, but he had spotted Bridget.

'Hey, Bridget, we're here!' Their former landlady was standing by the open well dropping batches of paper into it. She didn't seem to hear them, locked in her own world.

Jenny came out onto the balcony, holding on the vine for dear life. 'What's she doing?'

'I think it's her book.'

'But why? I like her book.'

'Hey, Bridget, don't do that! Jenny likes your book!'

But Bridget was oblivious, completely unaware of her surroundings. She took the last pile of papers and threw them down the shaft.

And with no warning, she stepped over the low wall and followed the manuscript.

Jenny

Jenny screamed. Bridget had been there – and now she wasn't.

'Shit! Fuck!' said Jonah. He scrambled over the edge of the balcony and dropped down, holding onto the vine to reach the ground. Jenny had to jump back into the snug as the old ironwork finally parted from the house and clanged to the courtyard pavement, becoming a steep gangplank. From his swearing, he'd been hit by some of it. Jenny raced down the stairs, through the kitchen and out into the yard. Jonah was leaning over the well shaft.

'Get a rope!'

'Where am I going to get rope?' But Jenny was already ringing the emergency services while going through the gardener's shed. They had to be wondering just what was wrong with Gallant House.

362

Pretty much everything.

She did find a hank of rope in the gardener's shed and rushed back to Jonah. He made a loop around his chest and tied the other end to the vine. He gave it a couple of strong tugs to test it.

'This is stupid. We should wait for help,' said Jenny.

'We are the help,' said Jonah.

'But you don't know how to do this! You'll kill yourself!'

He looked into the well. 'You're right. I've got an idea. Change of plan.' He took the rope off himself and looped it around her the same way. 'I'm lowering you down.'

'Me?'

'Well, you can't do the same for me, can you? And I can't suddenly become some Special Forces hero who knows how to fucking do these things.'

'Jonah, no!'

'No arguments – we've got seconds to save her if she's still alive. I won't let anything happen to you, I promise. But this way, you can lift her head clear of the water and I can support you both until the professionals arrive.'

Jenny decided this was one of the stupider things she'd ever done with Jonah – and there had been quite a few of them. But not having a better idea, she let him lower her slowly into the well shaft. As she went, twirling in the dark, she couldn't help thinking of the layers of history Bridget had written about: lost boys, foolish maids, hopeless rebels, Vikings, cavemen, dinosaurs. Madness – all of it.

The rope cut into her chest reminding her why she was here.

'Bridget?'

No sound. But Bridget had gone in feet first so there was a chance she had landed in the water and come up to the surface. Jenny had no idea how deep the well was. Finally, her feet touched water.

'I'm at the bottom!' she called.

'Can you find her?'

It was a narrow shaft. If she was here at all she would be right next to Jenny. 'Drop me about half a metre.'

The water rose to her thighs. Jenny used one hand to grope around under the surface. This was awful. Her fingers tangled with some long strands of hair. She hauled it up and Bridget's head broke the surface. In the dim light her face was almost luminous, eyes closed. She looked oddly serene, like that Millais picture of Ophelia, floating downstream on her back. Scraps of manuscript, nothing but pond weed now, draped over Bridget's mouth and curled around her neck.

'Got her!'

'Keep hold – help's arrived. They're just fetching the rescue gear.'

And so Jenny's last moments with Bridget took place at the bottom of the well. Jenny knew she was holding a dead woman but oddly it wasn't frightening. If she had to give it a word, she would've said it felt weirdly sacred, a kind of atonement on her part for all that she'd done wrong. Her anger at her landlady dripped away into the icy black water. What was the point of holding this fury close to her chest like some Cleopatra-style asp to bite at her breast? Bridget was gone, and so Jenny's resentment needed to follow. Matt had gone too. Only she was left, their survivor, and she had her own sins to answer for.

And what did her sins amount too? Chiefly, a moment of madness after a shocking attack – the malign atmosphere of the house finally getting to her. Jonah was always telling her that no jury would convict and there was no justice in putting herself through a trial merely so she could tell the police the truth. Sometimes silence was the best option.

It was the house that did it. Here in the void that dived beneath Gallant House, Jenny finally convinced herself she was not entirely to blame. 'Matt, I'm sorry,' she whispered. 'I'm sorry for what you became – and for what I did to you.'

The black heath water of the well soaked her sins away, a dark baptism. She'd leave her deeds down here and find the strength to move on with her life.

The quiet moment was broken when a fireman rappelled down to take over.

'Here you go, love,' he said gently.

A more comfortable harness was slid over Jenny's head and she was pulled to the surface.

Jonah was waiting anxiously in the courtyard. As soon as he saw her emerge from the shaft, he came forward and wrapped her in a towel. His hands were bleeding from the strain of holding the rope but he didn't seem to notice.

'How is she?'

Jenny just looked at him.

'What?' His sweet ugly face was genuinely puzzled.

'You lowered me down a well.' She'd tell him later about the moment of revelation – that didn't suit a time when they were surrounded by men in neon clothing.

'Yeah.' He shrugged as if to say, 'so?'.

'If ever you say I'm not completely loyal to you, remember today.'

That was their code. Neither spoke of love – that had been too polluted for them – but both spoke freely – and longingly – of loyalty.

'Oh, my beautiful Jenny, I'm loyal to you too.' He hugged her.

An hour later, sitting at the kitchen table, Jenny and Jonah looked across at Inspector Khan and Sergeant Foley.

'Hello again,' said Khan. 'I had sincerely hoped I'd seen the last of you two. So, who's going to tell me what went on here?'

'That would be me,' replied Jonah, reading Jenny's expression correctly. 'This probably doesn't look good.'

'Let us be the judge of that.'

Jonah sighed. 'OK, right.' He gathered his thoughts. 'Look,

Bridget invited us over and we were in the snug upstairs looking for her when we saw her jump in the well. I was standing on the balcony trying to get her attention and she just stepped in. I don't think she even registered that we were there. Fucking weirdest thing I've ever seen and I've seen a lot of strange shit. I didn't know it was coming.'

'Why were you here? I'd've thought you would steer well clear of this place.'

'We'd been asked to come by Bridget. She said she wanted to set things right with us. I suppose we were looking for closure.'

Jenny winced. Jonah had a habit of serving up these lines from dramas he'd been in. They stuck out of his conversation like a harmonious passage in his otherwise raucous chorus of crudities.

'We really had no idea she meant to do this,' Jenny added.

Foley spread out a note on the table. 'We searched the house. She left this note on her bed.'

Jenny looked at it in horror. What on earth did it say? Had Bridget set them up?

Catching Jenny's expression, Foley gave a wry smile. 'Fortunately for you both, it explains what she had decided to do – end her life – tidy herself away, as she put it. She wanted you to find her note and call us to recover her body. She trusted you both.'

'You're lucky there, or we'd be looking at you for this,' said Khan.

'What the hell do you mean by that?' asked Jonah, sounding pissed off. 'We tried to save her!'

'Well, you had plenty of reason to dislike her.' Foley pushed across a name and address. 'She wanted you to have this too.'

'What is it?' asked Jenny, speaking before Jonah could start swearing at the police again. She didn't get the sense they were out to get them this time, though doubtless that was what Jonah's past had led him to expect.

'Name and address of her solicitor. She appointed you her executors. You're to settle her estate and give the proceeds to charity.'

Jenny was speechless. This was the last thing she expected from Bridget. Reading the note though, she realised that Bridget was under the mistaken impression that they would care for the house as much as she did and see it properly handled.

'Her last laugh? We get burdened with the responsibility of Gallant House until we can sell it off?' marvelled Jonah. 'Fuck, I have to admit she was a vengeful old bat.'

'And Admiral's Walk next door, as her neighbour, Norman, left it to her,' added Foley.

'She thought we were up to the job of selling two houses on millionaires' row? You're shitting me?'

'I'm not, Mr Brigson – Jonah. It'll take a while for all this to clear through probate. I imagine it will be quite time consuming.' Foley actually looked amused, as far as her professional demeanour would allow. 'We'll get a driver to take you home.'

'In a black and white? No thanks.'

'We can arrange an unmarked police car,' said Khan.

'Still no.'

The detectives left to speak to the firemen who were just wrapping up their retrieval operation. When Jonah followed them a few minutes later, he wheeled out of the firemen the headlines of their findings. He reported back to Jenny that they'd found mushed up paper, many plastic pill bottles, but no more bodies. He had wondered at one particularly insane point about Gillian, the tenant who Bridget said she had been given the boot. Bridget had a fondness for hiding things down the well but she hadn't been a homicidal maniac after all.

That was just Jenny and him, he said before she slapped her hand over his mouth. The police were still in the house and not something she could talk about, especially not as a joke. Her recovery was too fragile for that.

'I'm still reeling,' Jonah admitted, sipping at the tea she'd made him while he'd pumped the firemen for information. 'Did you have any idea she'd do that?'

Throw herself down the well like some ancient druid sacrifice? It made a weird kind of sense seeing how Bridget had been obsessed with the house and the deaths it had witnessed. Killing herself was her final chapter. 'No, but it fits, doesn't it?'

'Are we going to do it?' He asked. 'Sell the houses for her?'

'Do we have to?' Jenny looked round the kitchen she had once loved. She had to admit that the house was seductive. It had trapped Bridget; begun its magic on Jenny even down that well; if she stayed, she feared the little healing she'd found here would turn poisonous.

'We don't owe Bridget anything – fucking opposite of that. I wouldn't mind so much if we get to choose the charity – the Jonah and Jenny Fund.'

Jenny knew he was only half-joking. 'I don't think we'll be allowed to do that. Maybe we can choose where the money goes though? Get something good out of the place.'

'Yeah, finance the dogs' home for a century. Did you have to fucking burn this house down, Jen?' he said. 'You lowered its value on the market.'

'That was obviously my first consideration.'

'How about you sell this one, I take the one without the fire damage?'

Her answer was two fingers and he chuckled. 'Seriously, what do you want to do with it?' He swept his hand to the cobwebbed ceiling. 'What do you say to a quick sale to some nice normal cutthroat developers? Dump the money on some charity for abuse victims. That way we can wash our hands of Bridget's final revenge and move on.'

'We don't want to get caught up with it – that's what happened to her.'

'Then let's get rid of it as quickly as possible. Break the curse. Move on and move in to our own place, somewhere central? The apartment Carol's lent us in Vauxhall is OK, but it's not really us, is it? Not ours. I should be able to afford a mortgage on our own flat with the work coming my way.'

368

She put her mug down carefully. 'Together? You and me, sharing a place, permanently?'

'What do you think I mean?'

She signed her reply with one of the first insults she'd taught him.

He laughed. 'Yeah I am. Just as well that you're in loyalty with me as absolutely no one else would be mad enough to have me as a flatmate. I smoke like a fucking chimney and swear like a … like me. I'm amazed you've lasted this long.' He got out his phone. 'I'm not accepting any lifts from the fuzz. Want to ring for a taxi?'

Jenny pushed his hand down gently. 'I need to get the smell of this place out of my head. Let's walk through Greenwich Park along the meridian.'

'A final farewell to Bridget and the black-hearted Jacks?' He tucked his phone away. 'Yeah, let's do that. We'll lay their ghosts to rest. This isn't our burden to carry.'

With his arm around her shoulders, Jonah and Jenny walked out of Gallant House, following the imaginary line into brighter skies.

Acknowledgements

This novel takes me into areas that require specialist knowledge. I have (so far) not been charged with a crime, so my thanks go to a real-life detective, Matt Walker, for putting me right about police procedures, particularly my penchant for locking people up for too long. It is proving unexpectedly useful to have a friend who served in a Metropolitan Police murder squad.

Thanks too to Dr Nigel Pearson, who helped me with the details of the medical plot. A courageous man who spends his life devising healthcare systems for the very poorest people in the world, he has also found time to read my novels and on many occasions offered advice on matters ranging from sword injuries to snake bites. This time the medical problem is more First World than Third but as ever Nigel has been full of insight.

As for the experience of being an orchestral musician, I never made it further than recorder player at primary school, so I'm deeply indebted to Jamie Reid, composer, and Simon Lee, conductor and musical supervisor on many stage musicals, who both patiently answered my questions. Also, Richard Blackford, composer and conductor, who kindly read the first draft and helped make this (I hope) a better book with his detailed feedback.

There is one family I'd like to thank but will not name – the friends that own the (real) house on Blackheath that inspired this story. You know who you are so thank you! I assure you your house is only a very happy distant relative of the one featured here but my imagination had to start somewhere!

My agent, Caroline Walsh, David Higham Associates, also gave me very helpful guidance on an early draft – thank you, Caroline! My wonderful daughter, Lucy, also volunteered as a first reader – I really appreciate your time, darling. Last but not least, I'm extremely grateful to Kate Bradley at HarperCollins for her expert editorial attention and enthusiasm. Thank you all so much. Any remaining errors are mine.

KILLER READS

DISCOVER THE BEST
IN CRIME AND THRILLER

Follow us on social media to get to know the team behind the books, enter exclusive giveaways, learn about the latest competitions, hear from our authors, and lots more:

/KillerReads  /KillerReads